Portals

Other books by Michael Kimball

The Girl and The Forest
A House for Molly
Alligator Bay
Timken's Christmas

Portals

Michael Kimball

To "Ellen" because I never had the chance to say goodbye and to "Savannah" whom I never expected to find…

Prologue

It was a beautiful sun drenched day bursting with late summer warmth. A man in his mid-thirties stood before a portable grill the couple had brought with them to Stillman's Lake. It was their sixth anniversary. The aroma of sizzling burgers was working its magic on the salivary glands of a large German Shepherd standing nearby, the animal's keen nose savoring the scent-laden air as a human might an appetizer.

Satisfied with his progress the man raised his head, his searching eyes locking on their target. His wife had grabbed their raft and paddled out onto the lake to sunbathe. She was hard to miss as she sat swathed in the bright yellow inflatable, lazily bobbing in harmony with the gentle swells rippling across the water's surface.

They met when she was a junior and he a graduate student in his final year. She had captivated him instantly with her long brown hair and high-set cheekbones. He loved her smile—especially when tossed in his direction. Her soft brown eyes promised a lifetime of alluring mystery. A promise well kept.

Memories of their early days together rose in his mind. His love for her encompassed all that she was. He laughingly referred to it as pretzel love; an intertwining of physical, mental and spiritual into a single delectable treat. She was his best friend. It didn't matter if they were camping in their beloved Adirondacks or grocery shopping at the local supermarket, she was the woman he wanted to be with.

The sound of sizzling meat jumped up a notch as if competing with his memories for attention. The man turned back to the grill, deftly flipping the burgers. Tiny eruptions, caused by dripping fat striking hot coals, sent up tantalizing, aroma-laden smoke. Just about done he thought. Time to get his wife heading back to shore.

Once again, his eyes sought out the yellow raft. He waved, and the lovely form waved back. He motioned for her to come in. He saw her grin and rub her stomach in anticipation. She reached for the oars, in her haste knocking one of them overboard. He could hear her laughing as she leaned over the side, stretching her lithe body its full length, outstretched fingers straining to grasp the wayward paddle.

Smiling at her antics, her husband watched. With a little lunge she closed the gap and grabbed the paddle. In the next instant, he realized she had miscalculated and couldn't help chuckling as she tumbled clumsily into the water.

He was unconcerned. She was an excellent swimmer, keeping herself in shape with daily workouts in the pool. She had a fierce dedication he envied. Once she set her mind to something she was unstoppable. She was also somewhat of a prankster. And as he waited for her to pop up to the surface he pictured her swimming towards him underwater. Baiting him. Trying to work up enough worry with her delayed appearance to goad him into diving in to save her. He knew her well enough to know that as soon as he did, she'd likely grab him from behind as he swam by and scare the daylights out of him! Still, she'd been under now for over a minute. If she was trying to make him nervous she was succeeding.

    The woman held her breath for what she thought must be coming up on her second minute. It was foolish, really, to have lost her balance. She could well imagine her husband's laughter at her expense. She'd be in for a good teasing, she could be sure of it! That's why she had decided, almost the instant she hit the water, she would lure him into the lake.

    She was weaving her way in between rocks littering the lake bottom, some nearly as big as a car. They were custom made for the ambush she had in mind.

    Her body moved with effortless ease through the sun-diffused water. Given the growing discomfort in her lungs, she knew it was getting time to head for the surface. She'd glide through the opening between those two rocks just ahead and push off the bigger one to propel herself upwards.

    She split the gap between the rocks. The opening was a tighter squeeze than she had supposed and she could feel the hard surfaces pressing against her torso. No matter. One strong kick and she would be shooting her way into the sunlit realm above.

    As her right leg contracted for the final kick she felt a jolt ripple through her body. Startled, she nearly expelled the remaining oxygen in her lungs. Her left leg seemed to be caught on something. She twisted around, fighting a growing sense of alarm. Her ankle had wedged itself in a cranny between the two rocks. Her hands moved down her thigh, following the contour of her leg.

    She struggled to free herself, to escape the vice grip of the granite monster holding her fast. Her lungs ached for air. Her body began writhing in a wild series of panicked contortions while her mind screamed its fear...

1

JESSE COULD HEAR the truck laboring as it neared the crest of the hill. Another few minutes and the behemoth would be upon them, its wide metallic girth commandeering the narrow dirt road, churning up clouds of dust and, worst of all, shattering the peacefulness of his private sanctuary just as the three trucks that had rumbled by before this one had. Not that he could do anything about it. His sense of personal invasion was at odds with the fact it was public land. State owned land he had walked on since boyhood. The growing pressure to find new sources of energy had led to renewed exploration in the area and, as luck would have it, his favorite getaway seemed to be a promising source of natural gas. Some outfit out of Texas had hauled their gear and drilling experience all the way to upstate New York and were in the process of punching holes in the earth's crust to get at the colorless, odorless vapors pooled in scattered reservoirs somewhere beneath his feet.

He looked up, spotting Kai some thirty yards away. As usual, the dog was more interested in exploring the grassy strips of meadow between the road and the woods than any mechanical sounds the light breeze bore in their direction.

"Kai!"

Jesse stepped off the road and dropped to one knee, feeling a strong sense of affection and satisfaction as the dog abandoned his pursuits to return to his master.

"Good boy, Kai," Jesse murmured, draping an arm over the animal's shoulders. He pressed him gently to his side, concerned the dog might get it in his head to take a closer look at the noisy machine rolling past. The driver stuck his bearded face out the window and waved.

"You two are walkin' fools!" he hollered, the lump in his cheek ample proof of a serious infatuation with tobacco. Leaning out the window, he launched a slug of dark brown liquid at nothing in particular. "I bet you two got more miles on this road than I do. And that's sayin' somethin'!"

Jesse returned the wave with a nod of his head. "Try and leave some dirt on the road for us to walk on, Lester!" he shouted, as billows of dust formed in the big rig's wake. He stood, releasing the dog. "Good boy, Kai. Go play!"

The animal bounded off into one of the many meadows that lay between the road and the tree-line of the nearby woods. Jesse caught sight of a blue jay feeding in some sumac. The shrub was everywhere and all sorts of birds feasted on the fuzzy red fruits that grew in abundance within the bluish-green leaves of the dense spreading plant. The jay erupted with a harsh jeering sound as he caught sight of Jesse then winged his way into the woods, his echoing cries growing increasingly faint as he penetrated deeper into its midst. Good riddance, Jesse thought. The jays were pretty to look at but they could be a nuisance and bring a quiet walk to an abrupt end with their raucous clamor.

He and Kai had been going on these walks two or three times a week for over three years. Jesse looked down the sloping landscape to his right. There it was about a half-mile off. He could see sparkling patches of light here and there between the trees as sunlight danced on the lake's surface. Stillman's Lake. *The* lake. The last place he had seen Ellen alive.

Ever since Ellen had drowned in the lake he and Kai had taken long walks here. He was thankful for the dog's company. Kai was the perfect companion. In the days immediately following the tragedy Jesse would sob almost uncontrollably, wondering if there were enough buckets in the world to catch the torrent of tears. Kai would sit beside him, perfectly still but pressing close, as if wanting to give Jesse some of his strength; his love unconditional and unwavering. At length, when Jesse's body began to slow its tortured wracking, Kai would lick away the tracks salty tears had left behind.

He and Ellen had picked out Kai together shortly after marrying. Ellen had doted over Kai as a puppy, even going so far as to paint his toenails the same color as her own until Jesse made such a fuss about it she'd finally relented, and in the end limited herself to painting only the dew claw of a foreleg claiming it was the source of Kai's strength. Like Sampson's hair.

Most of his friends said he shouldn't come here anymore. That the walks only served to keep the wound festering and Ellen would have wanted him to move on, to go on living – even if it meant eventually finding someone else. After all, they reminded him, he wasn't even forty yet. Sure it hurt and they knew he and Ellen had loved each other deeply. But life had to go on and he had too much to give to isolate himself.

After the first year he had taken their advice and given it a try, staying away for an entire summer. He'd even gone to a couple of cookouts the gang had organized, although he suspected they were plotting ways to help him 'heal' as they called it. They were good friends and well intentioned, he knew. But he was quick to recognize that some of the introductions to members of the opposite sex were a not-so-subtle attempt to get his mind thinking in new directions. Directions he wasn't ready for and, frankly, wasn't sure if he ever would be.

About the only dissenter from the prevailing chorus was his brother, James. Not too surprising, Jesse mused as he turned down the trail leading to the lake's eastern shore. Although they were twins, he and James hadn't seen much of each other after Ellen's death.

He whistled, and watched as Kai looked up. It was part of their routine, a signal that Jesse was about to change course. Even without the whistle Kai would likely have made the turn. After all, it was a pattern they never deviated from.

Their approach to the lake differed from that taken by the general public. It was different from the way he and Ellen had come, too. Usually, folks came by way of a turn-off from Highway 8. There was a parking area along the west side of the lake. Or, if you were adventurous and didn't mind the potholes, you could continue past the parking lot, taking the dirt road around the lake to the east shore where you were pretty sure of finding a spot you could have all to yourself.

Jesse thought back to when he and James were boys. They had grown up less than two miles from here, often walking over the hills and down to the lake to spend the day fishing. There were plenty of bass and perch. The two had discovered the route that Jesse and Kai now used for their walks. It was more private and lowered the chances of his running into anyone he knew who might be picnicking in one of the more accessible areas.

A faint smile played across his face. His boyhood memories of the days when he and James were close always made him smile. Unless people knew they were twins they would never have guessed the two were even brothers. Jesse stood nearly four inches taller with brown hair and green eyes whereas James was a blue-eyed blonde. They had been inseparable growing up and the lake had offered them endless enjoyment as they fished, camped, canoed, swam and explored every bit of the surrounding countryside.

He reached the shore and headed north towards the spot where he and Ellen had set up their anniversary picnic. The lake was engulfed by trees; mostly pines, beeches and hemlocks with a smattering of sugar maples. He stepped into a small clearing. There were a few yards of sandy beach with a fire pit and a picnic table worn to a dull, bluish-gray color from years of exposure. He walked over to the table and sat down facing the water, arms stretched out across the rough surface, the fingers of his hands intertwined.

As he looked out over the lake he was struck by the beauty of it all. The rolling surface glistened like a sapphire jewel and a light breeze brought with it the distinct smell of pine resin. A few billowy clouds rose majestically higher and higher in a sky dominated by a brilliant sun. He and Ellen had sat right here at this very picnic table more times than he could count. Side-by-side in their bathing suits with bare shoulders touching they would watch the sun burn an arc into the western sky, fascinating them with the countless transitioning hues of emerging twilight. With the darkness came the symphonic sounds of night creatures and the rhythmic lapping of water. Jesse would light the campfire while Ellen poured wine into metal cups and sliced up an apple and a few chunks of sharp cheese. They'd trade the picnic table for two beach chairs by the fire, drinking wine and munching on cheese with the aroma of wood smoke adding to the flavor. They would talk well into the night, mapping the progress of the moon's reflection on the mirror stillness of the water.

Jesse felt the familiar collision of opposing emotions as sweet memories of their time together crumbled beneath the weight of her absence. It was as if he were looking at a beautiful painting only to find the canvas suddenly igniting in flames. It left him with a bittersweet taste in his soul. It was just this sort of emotional whip-saw that made his friends plead with him to stop coming here. Sometimes he thought maybe they were right. After all, there wasn't anything he could do to change the outcome of that awful day and bring Ellen back to life. But that was just the point. He *couldn't* bring her back and here, right here, was the closest he could get to her. To stop coming was to let her go. He'd tried and found he either wasn't able or wasn't willing. He wasn't sure which. All he knew was this was the last place they had been together and it drew him like a magnet.

He looked out across the lake. It was truly picturesque. But loveliness alone couldn't make a person happy. You could bring to mind all the beautiful scenes you could conjure up and if they didn't include meaningful relationships with living things they could only take you so far. Every happy memory he could think of involved people he loved. Surround a guy with all the boy-toys he could dream of and he would tire of them in short order without someone to share life with. Jesse shut his eyes and exhaled slowly. The lake with Ellen, even on the worst of days, had been a source of joy. Without her it was a beautiful but sterile emptiness.

The years had taken some of the edge off the pain he felt as he thought back to their last day together, although he could still touch the panic that had shot through his whole being when Ellen hadn't surfaced after what he knew was too long. Looking back, he saw himself racing down to the water, plunging in and swimming furiously out to where the raft continued to bob up and down in the gentle swells. Time after time he'd dove into the water, desperate to see more than a few feet in any direction. Reaching. Straining. Willing his groping fingers to find her before it was too late. Screaming her name when he broke the surface for the last time, his lungs beyond their ability to hold air anymore.

But it had been too late.

It had taken the sheriff's department's divers twenty minutes to find her. And with each passing minute he'd felt hope drain out of him until his heart had become as lifeless as a dead branch on a tree. Still attached but useless.

Then there was the funeral. He was a shadow walking among the living, playing a part in some awful dream. Waking up in the morning with only an instant of blissful ignorance before reality kicked in, sending a tidal wave of sorrow crashing down, dashing him senseless.

Their network of friends and family were wonderful with everyone trying to be supportive. But in the end it was Kai who helped him the most. Maybe even saved him. Jesse was Kai's one-man flock and the big Shepherd was determined not to lose him.

Jesse fought back tears, willing himself back to the present. "I miss you Ellen," he murmured softly.

He bent down and picked up a stick. Kai loved it when he threw a stick into the lake. He would plunge right in, strong muscles powering through the water. He would always find the stick and bring it back, shaking water everywhere, eager to repeat the performance until Jesse finally called it quits.

Jesse turned and looked but didn't see Kai anywhere. He called but there was no response. He walked down to the shore and looked as far as he could in both directions, shouting Kai's name. His cries were met with silence, the animal nowhere in sight.

Jesse sat down at the picnic table to collect his thoughts. This had never happened before and he was pretty sure Kai wouldn't just wander off.

Movement in the bushes along the edge of the site caught his eye.

"Kai!"

The dog came to him immediately. Jesse bent down and cupped the large, intelligent head in his hands.

"Where the heck have you been, boy?"

Kai wagged his tail in response and lifted a foreleg, offering to shake. Laughing, Jesse took the paw in his own hand then stopped short, letting his breath out in a long, slow exhale as he stared at the single painted nail.

2

IT TOOK SEVERAL minutes before Jesse's mind could begin to rationally process the visual cue his eyes had sent to his brain. Seeing the painted nail on Kai unleashed an onslaught of emotions running riot through his nervous system. It was overwhelming, and it took a while for his breathing to return to normal.

He looked again. There was no doubt about it. A dew claw had been freshly painted. A color he knew, a color he'd seen a hundred times. Iced Mauve. Ellen's favorite.

He felt as though the outside of his skin was made of some sort of tingly material. He shut his eyes, inhaling slowly, struggling to calm himself. There had to be some rational explanation. Something that made sense. Maybe his mind was playing tricks on him. Perhaps it was just sunlight reflecting off the nail, passing through the prism of his memories and picking up some of Ellen's nail polish on its way to his brain. He'd just settle himself before opening his eyes again. A full return to his senses would undo the trick his subconscious had played on him.

Jesse kept his eyes shut, taking five slow deliberate breaths before opening them. When he did, he found Kai looking at him intently, his face betraying the canine signs of concern Jesse had come to appreciate.

"Shake."

Kai lifted his paw and placed it in Jesse's waiting hand, the rough texture of the pad contrasting with the softness of the surrounding fur.

No, he hadn't been mistaken. His mind had played no tricks on him. The dew claw had been painted Ellen's favorite color. That much was certain.

His mind reached for a plausible explanation. They had been there for maybe an hour. Was it possible there was someone nearby who had painted Kai's nail while Jesse was absorbed in his memories? He didn't think so. It would be quite a feat and require a series of unlikely coincidences. Still, what other explanation could there possibly be?

He looked at Kai. "You meet somebody new around here while you were rambling about?" Kai cocked his head as if to say, *you figure it out.*

Jesse got to his feet. "Come on. Let's take a look around."

He began exploring the area, carefully looking for any sign that someone else may have been around, all the while keeping a watchful eye on Kai and keeping him close. He wasn't going to take any chance of the dog wandering off only to return with some new surprise. He searched by ever expanding circles with the campsite serving as the epicenter. They were about twenty yards out when Jesse sensed he was alone. He'd checked on Kai just moments earlier, spotting the dog sniffing at the base of a large, moss covered boulder in the midst of a stand of hemlocks.

"Kai!" he shouted. "Kai, come!" Nothing. He called again and still there was no response. He turned and took a few steps toward where he'd last spotted him.

It was Jesse's ears that first detected a presence. He stared in the direction of the sound, a soft rustling of something moving. A shape was taking form, only a faint glimmering at first but becoming increasingly more solid, like an artist's sketch being filled in after the outline boundaries were defined. The shape came to life and was walking towards him. A moment later, he felt Kai's warm breath as the dog nuzzled his hand.

He was dumbfounded. *What's going on? The first time Kai disappears he returns with nail polish on him. He vanishes again practically under my nose and suddenly reappears as if he's been transported by aliens!*

Jesse had always chuckled at the UFO tales his friend, Ben, liked to tell. Ben was an Area 51 conspiracy fanatic, convinced the military was concealing both aliens and their advanced gadgetry. Right now, renegade aliens made as much sense as anything else Jesse could come up with.

"Come on, Kai," he muttered, "we're getting out of here. This isn't making any sense."

On the way, Jesse kept trying to find some logical explanation for what had happened. For starters, there was the nail polish. It didn't make sense that some stranger had done it. After all, how many people could there be in the world who made it a habit to carry around Iced Mauve nail polish just so they could paint the dew claw of strange dogs? Not to mention the fact that Kai, although friendly by nature, didn't allow strangers to approach unless he got an approving nod from Jesse. The Shepherd's size was imposing and his dark face conveyed intelligence—along with a clear message to strangers that he wasn't your average house pet and they would be well-advised to proceed with caution. Clearly, even if some nut *were* wandering about with a nail polish obsession, they would never get close enough to Kai to paint him. They would have lost a hand trying.

Then there was the matter of Kai's disappearing and reappearing. On the surface, just as baffling as the painted nail. But he was willing to concede that the nail polish incident might have unnerved him enough to where, given the late afternoon's fading light filtering through a canopy of trees and fueled by his earlier shock, his mind might have been playing tricks on him.

He arranged the facts. First, Kai's nail *had* been painted. And painted with what looked to Jesse like Ellen's favorite color. Second, it couldn't have been a stranger. Not only hadn't he seen anyone around or found any traces of someone else in the area but Kai wouldn't have allowed it. So where did that leave him? The only conclusion he could come to was that someone who wasn't a stranger had done it. But who? Sure, lots of his friends knew he visited the lake. A few even loved a good practical joke. But none of them would have ever thought to cross such a sacred line as fooling with his memories of Ellen and their tragic last day together. He was sure of it. He could write off Kai's disappearing act but the painted dew claw was too stubborn to be so handily dismissed. But for now, he was too mentally fatigued to keep turning over the pieces of this bizarre puzzle. He'd push it to the back of his mind and pull it out after dinner and a cold beer.

He reached the dirt road just in time to see one of Luther's pals toiling along in another dust belching rig. It was a constant cycle with these guys and Jesse wondered how they kept from being bored to death. There seemed to be no end to the drilling rig apparatus and pipe they hauled into the hills. The driver leaned out his window and spat a slug of tobacco juice, prompting Jesse to wonder if maybe tobacco was the antidote to a truck driver's boredom. If it was, he was glad he'd chosen a different occupation. He lived in a digital age and was thankful for it. If you had an entrepreneurial spirit and the right background you could do pretty well for yourself. He'd worked hard to get his MBA from Cornell and his consulting firm, Orange Risings, was doing great with clients scattered around the country.

His mind flashed back to Saturday mornings in Ithaca where he and Ellen, a music major at nearby Ithaca College, had often shared coffee and bagels at the Ithaca Bakery or played with their scrambled eggs and sausage while they surveyed the curious assortment of patrons frequenting the State Street Diner. Good old Ithaca. Ten square miles surrounded by reality. He smiled weakly at the bittersweet memories.

9

His Honda Element was parked at the bottom of the road. He opened the rear hatch and Kai piled in. He had a second car, another Honda, but even though Kai loved to ride in the passenger seat of the flashy S2000, with the top down and wind full in his black face, Jesse preferred the more casual comfort of the Element for outings like today. It was easy to clean and afforded them both plenty of room. They could go anywhere they liked and do whatever they wanted without having to worry about tracking dirt, mud or anything else into the vehicle with them. Kai had been sprayed by a skunk once and, although the odor wasn't a pleasant addition to any vehicle's interior, Jesse had been grateful they had driven the Element and not the sports car. Besides, the S2000 was a classic. He'd bought it for Ellen a couple of years before they stopped making them. She'd been ogling the thing for months. It was Spa Yellow with a black interior and boasted two hundred and thirty-seven horsepower coupled to a six-speed manual transmission. There was nothing tame about Ellen, even in the cars she liked. The thought of selling it after her death hadn't crossed his mind. She'd loved the thing and he kept it in the same immaculate condition she had. He chuckled to himself remembering how she'd zoom by and honk, laughing and waving, if she happened to catch sight of him and Kai somewhere out on the road. She'd referred to his Element as the "Turtle" and Jesse had reminded her that in the classic tale of the tortoise and the hare, it was the slower but steadier turtle who had won the race. She'd responded by pulling him close and kissing him full on the mouth, her warm sensuous lips pressing hard against his own, then whispering in his ear, "I'm not your average hare!"

He turned the key and the Element's engine came to life. He lowered the windows. As long as it wasn't oppressively hot or humid he preferred the natural cooling of rushing wind over air conditioning. Catching a glimpse of Kai's head in a side view mirror as the dog thrust it out his own window, he figured Kai did, too.

It was a short drive home. Although Jesse had grown up in the area near Stillman's Lake, in the third year of their marriage he and Ellen had bought a place in the country about twenty minutes away. It was a big house with plenty of room for family and friends and renovating the place had been a labor of love. Jesse enjoyed working with his hands and was able to perform most of the work himself, only using outside contractors for specialty jobs. He did the basic construction and Ellen the finishing work. It had taken three years to translate their shared vision into reality and they celebrated by putting in a swimming pool—something they both relished during the hot humid months of summer. Ellen's daily workouts were rigorous and kept her firm and trim. Her figure drew plenty of looks and Jesse had been proud of her. They'd planned on having at least three kids but had decided to put off starting a family until after the house was finished. Now it was too late.

On the one hand, Jesse was glad there weren't any children. Not that he was afraid of the challenge of being a single parent. It wasn't that. It was just the idea of a child losing his or her mother at such an early age. He could barely manage the loss himself and couldn't imagine what it would be like for a child. On the other hand, having a little boy or girl of their own would have captured a part of Ellen he'd always have. Especially if it were a girl.

He turned onto the road leading to his house. It was almost seven and he was getting hungry. He'd put a steak on the grill for himself and a big chunk of chopped sirloin for Kai and cook them both medium rare.

The house was nestled in the midst of majestic maples and oaks that had probably been there for more than a hundred years. He and Ellen had built a low stone wall along one side of the driveway. It went up as far as the house which was set back fifty yards from the road. The house had a generous wrap-around porch with a hanging swing. A profusion of wild flowers gave the place an atmosphere of tranquility. In the driveway, Jesse caught sight of a car with South Carolina plates. And there on the porch sat his twin brother, James, waving to him.

3

JESSE PULLED UP next to James' car, wondering what could have brought his brother into town. That James hadn't called to let him know he was coming was typical; his brother lived life with surprising spontaneity. It wasn't that James was inconsiderate, quite the opposite. James loved people and got along with just about everyone. He was the sort of person you found yourself confiding in and was genuine to the core. No matter what your personality or vocation, James embraced you with a warm vitality, making you feel special. He often said that, given everyone was made in the image of God, meeting someone new was like being introduced to a part of God he hadn't previously encountered.

That was the problem.

James, for all his positive attributes, couldn't seem to keep his faith to himself—at least that's how Jesse saw it. True, when Ellen died, James hadn't piled a bunch of religious platitudes on him. Like Kai, James had shown how much he cared by the comfort of his presence and the things he didn't say. It was as if he had known there weren't any words that could have possibly helped. But they had gotten into an argument anyway. Or, at least, Jesse had. He'd thought about it afterwards and had to admit he was the only one who had gotten angry.

If there was a God, he'd declared to James, He had some explaining to do! Ellen was a good woman—too good to die at so young an age and too loving to have had the life drained out of her by lake water when her lungs ached for air. He cringed thinking of her thrashing about, desperate to breathe and, no doubt, full of fear. Jesse had spent all the prayers he had in him on that awful day as he searched for her in vain and not one of them had been answered. If there were a God, He was either cruel, uncaring, powerless or all three. Jesse's anger at James had been kindled by his brother's refusal to come to the same conclusion.

James had admitted that he didn't understand why God had allowed Ellen to die but he'd stood firm in his belief that Ellen's dying didn't translate into making God the cosmic villain. Well, if Jesse were God, things would have turned out differently, that's for sure! He would have saved Ellen and let someone else drown. Some child molesting kidnapper or rapist. Someone who deserved it.

12

It wasn't the first time God had let them down, either. As he'd pointed out to James, there was the matter of their parents' death a decade earlier. An icy road on a snowy evening had turned into a night of horror. His dad had lost control and slammed his Buick head-on into a bridge abutment. A week earlier, the car had been taken in to the garage for servicing and, through some oversight, a technician failed to properly reconnect part of the active restraint system. As a result, the air bags had never deployed. Their father and mother were killed instantly.

Jesse had wanted to sue the pants off the dealer and hold the technician liable for involuntary manslaughter but James felt differently. James had talked with the guy who was beside himself with grief, going so far as to encourage the young man to return to work, telling him Jesus could help put his life back together and that he was sure he'd become the most conscientious and trusted technician in the dealership. In Jesse's opinion, if Jesus couldn't keep a car in a straight line when there was a little ice on the road He could hardly be trusted to clean up the mess afterward! James had also gone so far as to tell the man that he forgave him, something that hadn't sat so well with Jesse.

Jesse gave God a reluctant bye on his parents passing, but Ellen's death had depleted all the goodwill towards the Almighty he had left. And now, getting out of the car and finding himself wrapped in his brother's embrace, Jesse felt an awkward mix of resentment and love.

"Hey little brother," he managed to say, collecting himself as he disengaged then took a step back. "What brings you here?"

"Watch how you speak to your elders, Junior," James replied, his welcoming grin widening even more. "You may be taller but remember, I'm older."

"Yeah, by what? A minute?"

"One minute and twenty-two seconds, if you please. Darn near a lifetime to a good quarterback down by only three points in the fourth quarter of a game." He slapped his brother on the back. "That is, unless you're a New York Giants fan."

Jesse rolled his eyes. "Don't start with me, James. Your Rams don't get high draft picks each year because they're such a powerhouse you know."

"But as for why I'm here," James continued, oblivious to the inference, "I confess it is for no other reason than to spend time with my favorite brother."

"I'm your *only* brother," Jesse said dryly.

"Yeah well, you could have fooled me. It was so darn crowded there in the womb I figured we were at least triplets, if not quads! Anyway," he added, "things have slowed in the real estate business so I thought I might as well take advantage of the situation and come up and see how you're doing." He paused, his expression growing serious, his eyes searching Jesse's for clues of what his brother might be feeling. "Maybe I should have called first but I didn't want to take a chance on you saying no. We haven't seen each other in a while, Jesse. I've missed you."

Jesse's eyes dropped. James was right. If he'd called first, Jesse would have come up with five reasons why it wouldn't be a good time to visit. None of them would have held water. But now that James was here he was surprised to find himself more glad he had come than irritated he hadn't called first.

"No problem, James. Heck, if you'd called ahead it would have been so out of character I'd have wondered who was impersonating you. Come on, let's grab your gear and get dinner going. I don't know about you but Kai and I are starving!"

They went inside, Kai trailing happily behind. The dog was glad to see James, too. Somewhere in his canine brain he understood James was family and treated him accordingly. Jesse led the way to the guest room, leaving James to unpack and shower before dinner while he headed to his own room.

Jesse leaned forward, both hands against the front wall of the shower, palms flat against the textured ceramic tiles, his head directly under the powerful stream. It felt wonderful, like being in your own private world. He watched the water falling from around the contours of his head to the fiberglass floor and down the drain. The combination of sound and water evoked a welcome sense of peacefulness. It had been quite a day and James' sudden appearance had afforded him a temporary respite from the afternoon's events. Now, as he began to relax, the realization of what he had experienced began drifting back towards center stage.

14

He had mixed feelings about saying anything to James about it. True, his brother had a good mind and could be absolutely counted on to keep anything Jesse shared between just the two of them. But he also had the frustrating tendency to inject God into every aspect of life. The way Jesse figured it, if there were a God, He had better things to do than go around painting dogs with nail polish. Even aliens sounded more plausible!

Jesse decided to play it by ear. He didn't even know how long James was staying. Given his track record, he could wake up tomorrow and find a note saying his brother was already on the road and thanking him for the evening. James was like that, sometimes just floating in and out. Once, when Jesse had asked him about it, he'd only shrugged and smiled, saying that his mind had a mind of its own and had a kind of restlessness to it. It was an oddity, he admitted, but he hoped there were enough offsetting positive attributes to balance things out.

Jesse toweled off, dressed, and headed to the kitchen. He grabbed a couple of steaks out of the refrigerator together with some mushrooms, an onion, and the makings for a Caesar salad. He tossed the onion to James as he rounded the corner.

"Chop that up little brother." He pointed. "There's a cutting board and you can take your pick of weaponry from the butcher block."

James caught the onion in one hand. "You really know how to make your guests feel welcome, bro."

Jesse grinned. "If you were a stranger, I'd pour you a glass of wine and let you sit and watch. Blood relatives get their hands dirty."

"Speaking of wine," James said, "Do I get to pick? That's one of the nice things about visiting New York. You guys have high taxes but you also have a lot of good wine."

"It eases the pain of taxation," Jesse explained. "Not completely though, there's not enough wine in the whole state to do that. But it helps." He cut two thick slices from a loaf of French peasant bread then started sautéing the mushrooms. "I'll head out to the grill and get the steaks going. Toss the onions in with the mushrooms. You're better at Caesar salads than I am so you get that privilege, too. But just to take the sting out of it, go ahead and pick the wine."

15

The two of them went to work, Kai wandering from one to the other but eventually planting himself near the grill where Jesse had added a generous portion of chopped sirloin to the two steaks already sending up their mouth-watering aroma.

Jesse looked affectionately at Kai. "I'd like to think you're here because of my great company, fellah, but I've the sneaking suspicion it has more to do with gluttony."

He closed the lid of the grill and went back into the house where he found James emptying the mushrooms and onions into a serving bowl. Jesse grabbed the salad and bread. He'd set the table out on the deck when he put the steaks on. "All we need now is the wine, little brother," he called over his shoulder as he headed back outside. "Like I said, your pick!"

Jesse set things down on the table and grabbed the steaks off the grill, but not before tossing Kai his own share of the feast. The dog caught it mid-air and gulped it down before Jesse finished pouring the water and taking his seat. "Glad you took your time and savored every bite, big guy."

James appeared, holding a bottle of Bully Hill's, 'Love My Goat'.

Jesse raised an eyebrow. "Good stuff, but you didn't break the bank with that pick."

"Give me time," James said, laughing. "I figured I'd ease into it and hit the heart of your treasure trove just about the time we've had enough of each other. Like the taxes, it'll help ease the pain."

The brothers spent the next hour and a half enjoying the meal and catching up on each other's business ventures and life in general. The table was on a tier of the deck overlooking the pool. The sun had gone down and Jesse had lit a number of Tiki torches, the citronella serving to keep the mosquitoes at bay. A slight breeze brought with it a hint of the honeysuckle growing in profusion along one length of the deck. Ever present wildflowers —phlox, lavender, lilies and roses—offered up their muted colors in the flickering light of the torches, their perfume a gracious complement to the aromas of the night. Fireflies, their miniature lanterns twinkling in random patterns, could be seen scattered throughout the distance. Every so often, the deep bass of a bullfrog rang out from a nearby pond. Jesse had just poured the last of the wine when James touched on the subject they had both been avoiding.

16

"How are you really doing, Jesse?" he asked gently. "We haven't talked much since Ellen's funeral and that was three years ago. You were pretty angry at God then and I guess that made me guilty by association. I've reached out a few times since but it always seemed as though you preferred to keep some space between us." He hesitated. "That's why I didn't call. I thought it was time, whatever your reaction, to talk face to face so I figured I'd chance it and just show up." He looked at Jesse with mock fear. "I'm glad you fed me a steak instead of my wearing it to nurse a black eye!"

Jesse had to concede the wisdom of his twin's approach. James had taken a calculated risk and, so far, it had paid off. The ice was already thawing. Not that he'd come around to James' way of thinking. Not by a long shot. But James was a good brother and a good friend, however misled in his thinking, and he knew his twin cared deeply about him. He suddenly realized he felt the same way.

"I'm better," Jesse answered softly. "Although I think it's a lie that time heals all wounds. It doesn't—at least not in three years. And I'm not convinced that even thirty more would do the trick. Time blunts the blade so the pain isn't as sharp as it was at first but I don't hold out much hope for total recovery. I guess it's something you get used to—if you can get used to paralysis of the heart," he added with a tinge of bitterness. "As for God, my opinion of Him hasn't changed so you might want to keep clear of the subject of religion. Nothing mandatory, mind you. Just a suggestion. I'm not above using physical violence to underscore my point of view!" Jesse flexed his biceps, his face softening. "The ammo in these guns ought to be able to silence the opposition, don't you think, little man?"

James laughed. "Better save those pea shooters as a weapon of last resort, Junior. We're talking brains against brawn and you know how that will end!"

"Yeah, that's why you're in the real estate business in the middle of a global economic meltdown fueled by a housing collapse and I've got clients beating a path to my door from the four corners of the globe," Jesse retorted. "Might want to trade your brains in for version 2.0."

James winced. "Ouch! But I guess if the four corners of the globe are limited to the lower forty-eight, you've made your point!" He turned to Kai who was gnawing on a steak bone they'd donated from dinner. "I wouldn't be surprised to find, Kai, that you are the *real* mastermind behind my brother's good fortune."

At the sound of his name, Kai dropped the bone and trotted over to the table. He sat in front of James and lifted a paw in the familiar greeting. James chuckled and took the paw in his hand, his eye catching a glimpse of the painted dew claw as he gave Kai a playful shake.

"What's this?"

Jesse's brow wrinkled into furrows. "*That*, little brother, is a mystery." He stood and began gathering up the plates. "Help me clean up. We'll take a swim in the pool and then I'll tell you all about it over beers in the hot tub."

It didn't take long before the two of them had the kitchen back in order. Living alone, Jesse preferred to wash the dishes by hand after each meal rather than store them in the dishwasher until it was full enough to run. But if he had guests he opted to make use of the thing.

It still felt strange to be in the kitchen without Ellen. Whereas many of the couples he knew either took turns with the cooking or deferred to the person with the most culinary talent as head chef, Jesse and Ellen had, for the most part, cooked as a team. Jesse had handled the meat and fish, Ellen the pasta. They'd split the assorted sides. Ellen had done the salads because Jesse wasn't fond of carrots and always left them out. No one told the other what to do or how to do it and they'd moved about the kitchen genuinely relishing each other's company. Once a week they would take turns picking out a new recipe. Only on those occasions had the picker taken a lead role in the preparations. Now, as he flicked off the kitchen lights, he felt the familiar heartache of his wife's absence.

"Three years, Ellen," he muttered to himself, "and yet it feels like only a moment ago."

He followed James up the stairs where the two changed into swimming trunks, Jesse having tossed his brother one of his, a gaudy design a client had sent him as a joke. They met outside at the pool.

"I know you're trying to goad me into being embarrassed by this stunning swimwear of yours," James said, contorting his body into various poses, "but where I come from, the man makes the clothes. Dress me as you will but you just can't keep the handsome down."

"Let's just see if the handsome is waterproof," Jesse replied with a laugh, giving James a hard shove, sending him careening into the water.

With reflexes born of years of brotherly practical jokes, James managed to grab his brother's hair and yank him into the water with him. Jesse came to the surface howling. "What kind of sissy move is that you filthy water rat? You darn near scalped me!"

"Just reminding you to weigh the cost of every devious ploy that floats through your degenerate mind, Junior!"

The two swam, playing a game with a golf ball they'd invented when they were kids. Played in the deep end, the golf ball is sent down to the bottom of the pool. The objective is to grasp the ball using your only your feet, usually by squishing the ball between the toes of one foot then raising it above the water where it can be seen by your opponent to score a 'goal'. Both players vie for the ball at the same time and can use any means at their disposal to knock the ball out of their opponent's grasp, just as long as they don't use their hands. The first to score three goals is declared the winner. It is a game stretching one's lung capacity to the limit.

James scored first. He'd waited for Jesse to take the plunge to the bottom and locate the ball. Then, while he was making his way back up, he'd shot down and grabbed his brother around the waist in a leg lock, proceeding to hold him under until he ran out of breath and dropped the ball. While Jesse was heading back to the surface, James recovered the ball and pushed off the bottom at an angle, keeping as much distance between himself and Jesse as possible. Triumphant, he lifted a foot, displaying a gleaming white golf ball wedged between his toes.

"Score one for the Rams!" he cried triumphantly.

"Your first and last," Jesse shot back, a determined look on his face, body poised for action. "Toss that little rock back in and we'll see who ends up winning the game!"

They battled it out for twenty minutes before Jesse made the next score, both men sucking in great gulps of air, lungs nearly spent. With the score tied, it was anyone's game. James feigned lethargy, drawing in deep, slow breaths, giving no sign he was about to dive, hoping to catch Jesse off guard. Jesse, knowing he had a slight edge physically, was counting on his brother playing head games. He pretended to use the lull in the action to recover, too. So, when James silently slipped under the water, Jesse was ready for him. They reached the bottom at the same time, their feet banging away as each, in turn, fought to keep a grip on the golf ball. In the end, it was

James who headed up first. As he broke the surface he sucked in a quick breath of air and was ready to go back down when he heard Jesse laughing. He turned and saw him treading water, leg outstretched, a foot revealing the white prize squished between his toes.

"And the New York Giants come from behind to knock off the Rams!" he crowed. "Not much of a victory as wins go, but accomplished in typical Giants come-from-behind fashion!"

"Okay, I guess I have to give you this one," James conceded. "Home turf advantage and all. We'll see if you can keep your string alive tomorrow night."

Jesse was quick to grasp the implication. "So I have the honor of your company for at least another day?"

"If you're not afraid of losing in a rematch, you do."

They climbed out of the pool and walked over to the hot tub. Jesse removed the cover and the two sank into the steaming water, a small portable refrigerator within arms reach.

"Beer?" Jesse asked.

"No thanks. But I'll take a water if you've got one in there."

"I'd have thought you swallowed enough water in the pool."

"I did. But I think I'd like to try the un-chlorinated variety," James replied. "Just for a change of pace."

Jesse tossed him a bottled water, twisting the top off a bottle of Black & Tan for himself. He hit the switch and the tub came to life, jets spitting out a mixture of hot water and air. Bubbles appeared amidst the rising steam and for several minutes the two sat quietly, enjoying the effect of the liquid massage, the hot water relaxing their muscles. It was Jesse who broke the silence.

"The nail polish you saw on Kai's dew claw," he began, "did it remind you of anything?"

"Sure," James answered slowly. "I remember when Ellen used to paint Kai's nail like that. I'm not sure of the color but I know she used to do it."

"That's right. She did. And as for the color, it's Iced Mauve, her favorite." Jesse sipped his beer before continuing. "Tell me the truth, James. What did you think when you saw it?" He watched his brother closely.

James looked away. "I thought maybe you'd done it to keep Ellen's memory close," he said softly.

"And what would you say if I told you I hadn't?"

"I'd say Kai is more talented than I gave him credit for."

"I never thought of that option," Jesse chuckled. "I guess I was stuck on aliens."

James raised an eyebrow. "Aliens?"

Jesse spent the next several minutes filling James in on the afternoon's events.

"So what do you think, now?" he asked when he'd finished. "One smart dog or aliens?"

James let out a low whistle.

"That's quite a story, Jesse. But I think we need another option." He hesitated. "I agree that it seems unlikely anyone did it. After all, you didn't see any signs of someone else while you were there and, like you, I can't imagine any of your friends even thinking of pulling a stunt like that. So if you didn't do it, a stranger didn't do it, nor a friend, aliens or Kai himself…" He grew quiet.

"Okay, Stephen King, you've set the hook," Jesse confessed. "Out with it!"

"Well, the way I see it, there are really two mysteries. Or if you look at it another way, two phenomenon. One is the painted nail and the other Kai's disappearance and reappearance."

"But I told you," Jesse reminded him, "Kai's vanishing act might just have been the result of my eyes playing tricks on me. Not so far fetched given the shock of seeing the Iced Mauve and all."

"That could be," James agreed, "but it would get us nowhere. So bear with me." He took a drink of water before going on. "Let's just assume, for argument's sake, that Kai really did disappear. Maybe not just once, but twice."

"What do you mean, twice?"

"I mean you actually spent time looking for him twice, Jesse. The first time you looked for him he eventually showed up with the painted nail. But you went looking for him a second time. The time where you said you'd been keeping pretty close tabs on him when he seemed to vanish into thin air. In the case of both incidents," he pointed out, "Kai is the common denominator."

"I still don't see where you're going," Jesse said.

"I'm saying that besides the options you've looked at already, and we both agree get you nowhere, there's another option. A *supernatural* one."

Jesse stared at his brother with a look of disbelief.

"You're kidding, right? What are you trying to say, James? That there is the God option, here? He brought his bottle to his lips, finishing the beer off in two gulps, then shook his head in wonder.

"Look James. I'm glad you're here. You were right, it's been too long since we've connected. But if you're going to take what happened today and overlay God onto it you're in the wrong camp." He punched the controls and the hot tub went silent.

4

AT BREAKFAST THE next morning the two brothers kept the conversation away from the previous night's hot topic. They woke up with a good appetite and dug into blueberry pancakes and bacon.

"Sleep okay?" Jesse asked between mouthfuls.

"Yeah, except for some crazy dream I had about you winning a game of swimming pool golf." James poured more syrup on his pancakes.

"Welcome to reality. If I remember rightly, you asked for a rematch. Having second thoughts?"

James wore his best poker face. "Nope. I practiced holding my breath before breakfast and I'm up to over three minutes. I figure that ought to be enough to ensure a victory in tonight's game."

Jesse rolled his eyes. "A bit early in the day for you to start hallucinating. What's the matter, forget to take your meds?" He finished off his orange juice, sitting quietly for a few minutes before speaking again.

"I was thinking about last night. Our conversation in the hot tub." He looked across the table at James. "I know you mean well. You always do. I guess when it comes to God we find ourselves on opposite sides of the fence. But in this case, I guess the supernatural has as good a claim on what happened as aliens. So I suggest we put it to a test."

"What do you have in mind?" James was intrigued.

"Nothing too sophisticated, just a simple experiment. I figure if God had something to do with painting Kai's nail then He did it for a reason, right? I mean, it wouldn't be something He did on a whim."

"I never said that *God* painted the nail," James reminded him. "I only said the supernatural may be an explanation worth considering."

"Okay," Jesse agreed, thinking back to their earlier conversation, "but didn't you mean to imply God had something to do with it? After all, when you say the word, 'supernatural', aren't you talking about God?"

James stood up and began clearing the table, raising a hand when his brother started to push his own chair back. "You made the breakfast, bro. I'll handle the dishes." He continued the conversation as he loaded the dishwasher.

"You're right in the sense that when I refer to the supernatural, I mean those things that are not part of the physical world we live in." He paused, wondering how Jesse would take what he was about to say next. "But the supernatural has more to it than God. Like this world," he waved a hand in the air, "the supernatural contains things God has created, both creatures as well as objects."

"What do you mean?"

"Well, take heaven for example. The Bible speaks of it as a literal place with objects—like walls, gates and thrones." He looked at Jesse. So far, he seemed to be taking the conversation in stride.

"Okay. I've read the Book, too. I suppose what you mean by 'creatures' are beings such as angels and demons and the devil?"

"Exactly."

"Are you saying, then, that our list of possible causes under the heading of supernatural needs to include not only God but angels, demons and devils?" Jesse's eyebrows were starting to meet in the middle.

James held up a hand. "All I'm saying is that if the cause is something supernatural—and it's a big if!—then the cause could either be from God Himself or forces either aligned with, or opposed to Him."

Jesse rubbed his face. "James, you're getting weirder by the minute."

"I'll take that as a compliment," his brother said, chuckling. "In any event, no matter if it were from supernatural friend or foe, like things here on earth, nothing happens that God doesn't allow." He stopped short, realizing he'd just served up the core of his brother's contention. He watched as Jesse scowled.

"Sorry, Jesse," he apologized, "I didn't mean to revisit a sore spot. I try to choose my words carefully, and I've no desire to hurt you or make you angry but I can't always avoid it. If I leave out all the words that rattle you I'll be tongue tied and what I believe to be true won't see the light of day." He

24

finished loading the dishwasher, giving his brother time to sort through his feelings.

Jesse pushed back his chair, walking over to an open window, breathing deeply so his lungs could soak in the early morning's fragrant bouquet. He looked at the sky. All the signs were there. Today was shaping up to be just as beautiful a summer's day as yesterday.

For several minutes he had struggled to keep himself composed. James really knew how to open wounds! To Jesse's way of thinking, if God could sit back and allow Ellen to drown, God could twiddle his thumbs while devils painted Kai's dew claw. At least God would be consistent.

"I think this argument of ours is entering a new phase, little brother," Jesse said with a sigh. "It can't be helped given our respective opinions of the Almighty. But maybe my experiment will shed some light on things, one way or another." He opened a cupboard revealing a large bin full of dry dog food. A metal scoop sat atop the mound of kibble. He grabbed it and filled Kai's feeding bowl, setting it down in front of the animal. Kai didn't move.

"Okay."

Jesse had trained Kai from a puppy to wait patiently until he was given the release command. The dog instantly transformed from immovable statue into an eating machine and, seconds later, the dish was empty with Kai looking up, hoping for more. Jesse tossed him a biscuit. Extra-large.

James was relieved to see they had avoided a meltdown.

"What do you have in mind?" James repeated his earlier question. He had to wait several moments for an answer as Jesse was getting his face licked by Kai as a thank-you for the morning's sustenance.

"Like I said, nothing complicated." Jesse reached into a pocket of his shorts and pulled out a small bottle, passing it to James.

"Nail polish remover?"

"Yep. We're going to clean Kai up of all traces of nail polish, load him into the Element, head back to the lake, and pay a visit to the supernaturals whoever they may be. Friend or foe, if it was supernaturally authored, whoever did it, did it for a reason. Maybe to get my attention." He opened the bottle and busied himself removing polish from Kai's nail. "Well, they got my attention, all right—that is, if they really exist and are the responsible party. Something I highly doubt. But if they do and they are, I figure they'll issue a repeat performance to get their point across."

"And if nothing happens?" James asked, suspicious of Jesse's motives.

"Then maybe you'll come to your senses," his brother smirked. "I doubt it, but it doesn't hurt to try. Besides," he mused, "I need to know."

5

SAVANNAH WAS RUNNING behind, not the sort of start she had intended. This was her first day as the new director of the Stillman's Lake recreational complex. It wouldn't look too good if the staff found their new boss pulling in late.

She had come east from Kansas. Living in a big city like Topeka had its social and cultural perks but, in her mind, it couldn't compete with the magnificent splendor of the Adirondacks. She'd visited the area a few years back and fallen in love with the countless lakes strewn across the Adirondack Park, their crystal clear water allowing the brown bellies of the lakes to be mirrored on the surface. She'd been amazed to learn just how big an area the Park covered—over six million acres. Half the land was publicly held and constitutionally protected so as to remain a "forever wild" forest preserve. The other half was private land with farms, businesses, homes and camps. Created in 1892, the Park formed the largest publicly protected area in the contiguous United States. This made it greater in size than Yellowstone, Everglades, Glacier, and Grand Canyon National Parks combined! The boundaries of the Park included whole towns—places like Lake George and Lake Placid, home of the 1980 Winter Olympics.

A graduate of Northern Arizona University with a degree in Parks and Recreation Management, Savannah had lived in Flagstaff for a couple of years before returning to her native Kansas then gradually migrating east until finally landing at Stillman's Lake. The position of director was a dream come true, the payoff of several years hard work. Over and over along the way, she had had to prove herself the equal of male counterparts. To be honest, she was better than most of the guys and it had nothing to do with gender. She had studied hard at school, in the field, and on the job, holding fast to the belief there wasn't anyone, regardless of position, she couldn't learn something from. It was this kind of attitude that had earned her the grudging admiration of even her most reluctant co-workers.

She finished brushing her teeth, swirling Listerine around inside her mouth before spitting it out. "Let's go, Jenny. If we push it a little, we should still get there before the others."

She opened the hatch of her Subaru and the Golden Retriever jumped in. Savannah climbed into the driver's seat, reaching up to stab a button on the remote to open the garage door. She backed out, hit the button again, and took off. She was a half-block away before the garage door fully closed.

She kept the back seats of the Subaru flipped down to give Jenny more room. The Golden was only nine months old but had proved herself a quick learner and a loyal and loving companion. As they headed north to Highway 8, Savannah could sense Jenny's closeness. She smiled, reaching up to stroke the young dog's neck. Jenny liked to be close but didn't crowd. In fact, there weren't many downsides to Jenny—with one notable exception: she was a constant source of yellow hair. The shedding was worse at predictable times of the year but it never totally disappeared. Savannah brushed her twice a day, which helped. Still, she was glad she was wearing khaki shorts and a light colored shirt. Savannah shuddered to think what she might look like if she emerged from the vehicle wearing something black! She made a mental note to give the Subaru a thorough cleaning, inside and out, come the weekend. She couldn't remember the last time she'd done it.

Savannah wished they made cars with some kind of system where you could just throw a switch, sending an electrical charge blasting through the inside of your car, causing every last dog hair to lose its grip on whatever surface it had staked out for itself. Flip another switch and a super-sucking vacuum would come alive with enough power to round up the now helpless hairs. She wondered why no one had come up with one. It sounded good to her. They could add an extra hundred bucks on the sticker price and she would hand the cash over with a smile.

She merged easily onto Highway 8. One of the added benefits of living in a small place like Stillman's Lake was there was no such thing as morning traffic jams. The few extra cars added to the roadways at the beginning and end of every workday did little to tax the highway's capacity to move folks along to their destinations on time. Savannah figured if someone developed road rage here they were probably a mental case to begin with.

A few minutes more and Savannah found herself entering the parking area behind a log building serving as the welcome center for the complex, as well as being where the director's office was located. She shared the office with her assistant but that was fine by her. She'd met Bev two months earlier when Savannah had first interviewed for the position and concluded the woman was the glue holding the place together. Bev was a handsome, gray-haired, outdoors type woman in her sixties, still very much active. Bev had been working at the complex for the better part of thirty

28

years. She was proud of the fact she was the first official employee, back when the recreational complex wasn't much more than the lake itself with a handful of horseshoe pits and a couple pavilions. Given her history, Savannah wasn't surprised to find Bev's Camry already in the lot.

Savannah parked beside the Camry and got out, popping the Subaru's hatch. Jenny jumped to the ground, following her master inside where the wonderful aroma of freshly brewed coffee filled the air. Bev smiled in greeting and handed her a cup.

"Here, Savannah. Get your coffee while you can before the others get here. Once the men walk through the door they make a beeline for the pot claiming they can't get going without their morning cup of Joe." She bent over, cupping Jenny's golden head gently in her hands. "And how are you this morning, Jenny? Nervous, today being your first day and all?"

Jenny looked up at the kind, gentle face of the older woman before lightly licking her hand.

"Well, aren't you the well-bred young lady! You just come with me and I'll show you something I made you as a welcome gift."

Savannah nodded her consent. "Go ahead, Jenny."

Bev led Jenny over to the stone fireplace. On the side closest to Savannah's office was a wooden box, its rear wall about eighteen inches high. The two sides started flush with the back but gracefully diminished in height as they curved towards the front which was only a few inches in height. The box was made of cherry that had been stained a deep auburn, the cushion laying inside the box the color of milk chocolate. A small brass oval engraved with the word, *Jenny*, was fastened to the front.

"This is your bed, Jenny." Bev's voice was soothing. She knelt, stroking the Golden with one hand while patting the cushion with her other. "Come on, girl. Try it out. I made it myself." She beamed triumphantly as Jenny, tail wagging, stepped lightly onto the bed, moving in a tight circular motion before plopping down, a picture of contentment.

Savannah looked on, sipping coffee and basking in the rustic warmth of the spacious room. The building was of post and beam construction, affording those within its walls generous helpings of open space. She gave Bev a warm hug. "The bed is beautiful! Jenny loves it. How thoughtful!" If the rest of the staff were half as friendly as Bev, Savannah had no doubt she would feel like she'd landed in paradise.

She glanced at the clock, a vintage grocery store model from back in the day when grocers would be awarded clocks by suppliers when sales of sponsored products were good. The others would be arriving any moment.

As if on cue, the door swung open and four men spilled into the room, their laughter and conversation trailing off as they caught sight of Savannah who decided to take the initiative.

"Good morning! I'm Savannah. Savannah Garret. As I'm sure you already know, I'm the new director." She lifted her mug, smiling. "I've already got a head start, so why don't you grab some coffee and we'll spend a few minutes getting acquainted before starting in on the day's work."

A man who appeared to be the oldest of the bunch beamed. "Well, you sure don't have to beg me to grab a cup of Bev's coffee!" He slapped one of his companions on the back. "We let Kenny here try his hand at brewing us up a pot once when Bev was out sick and the sludge nearly killed us!"

Bev looked indignant. "You know darn well, Stanley, I wasn't sick! I had to take care of my brother. He's ten years younger but as helpless as a new-born calf. That's what happens if you retire and go to seed. First your muscles decompose then your mind. But in your case," she joked, "the process might just be reversed!"

They all got a kick out of the good-natured ribbing and the next few minutes saw everyone filling their mugs with steaming coffee. Stanley wandered over to Jenny and Savannah noticed the dog taking to him right off. He was speaking softly, his hand caressing the lush fur of her chest. Savannah was pleased. When she'd interviewed for the position with the board of directors she had let them know of her hope that they would let Jenny accompany her to work. She had assured them she would arrange to erect a kennel where she could put the dog during times when it was necessary for Jenny to be out of the way. The Golden was well-behaved and of gentle temperament. Savannah had taken the risk of bringing Jenny with her to the interview, gambling on Jenny's ability to charm pretty much everyone she met. Savannah had been delighted to find the board sympathetic. She wasn't sure she would have taken the job if she'd had to leave the dog home alone. It would have been hard on both of them. Her next concern had been how Jenny would be received by the staff, the board making it clear that having a dog at the complex was a privilege they couldn't extend to everyone. It was a negotiated perk and Savannah hoped it wouldn't become a bone of contention.

The six of them spent the next forty-five minutes getting to know each other. As Savannah did more listening than talking, you could see the men starting to relax. They had worried she might have been the type who carried a chip on her shoulder towards the opposite sex, charging them with the collective abuse of women throughout the ages by the mere fact of their gender and looking to get even. But there was nothing about Savannah to suggest any kind of bias. Not in gender or anything else. They liked her and she took an immediate liking to them, filling everyone in on Jenny's status and apologizing that she couldn't extend the privilege to everyone. They seemed to appreciate her candor and let her know it was okay—that is, as long as she shared Jenny with them! Savannah smiled, saying she was sure Jenny would enjoy being the center of so much attention. When they finished going over the day's schedule, the men headed out to their assignments.

"Looks to me like you've made a good impression on them." Bev headed towards her desk. "I figured as much." She turned on her computer. "Those guys are hard workers with a deep affection for this place. To them, and to me, it's more than just a job. We love the lake and take pride in helping others to appreciate the beauty here. The more you appreciate nature, the more insight you have into the God who created everything."

Savannah kept quiet. She'd have to think on that one.

The next hour was spent settling into her office. It was a beautiful summer morning with warm, bright sunlight. The welcome center opened to the public at ten although there were plenty of folks who came earlier to walk the trails or fish. The facility wasn't set up for overnight camping so they didn't have to staff the place around the clock. The welcome center closed at four but anyone who wanted could stay as long as they liked, up until midnight.

They had an arrangement with the county sheriff's department to patrol the complex twice a night, sometime between midnight and one in the morning and then again between two and four. The exact timing of the patrols varied so folks who were the sort to cause problems couldn't predict when the police might come around. The arrangement worked pretty well.

Occasionally, a deputy would come across trespassers—usually high school or college kids trying to use the place as a lover's lane or rendezvous for a drinking party. Unless vandalism was involved, the police would chase the offenders out with a warning. Of course, that was after the cops lit up the place with the blue and red light bars atop their cruisers and freeze panicked kids with commands barked out through a loudspeaker. Licenses and registrations were checked and those smelling of alcohol were put through varied antics they were sure to fail. If anyone was too drunk to safely drive, a sober person became a designated driver. If everyone failed the sobriety tests, well then, that was when things got interesting. It was pretty tough explaining to your parents why the sheriff's department was giving you a ride home.

Bev had given her the low-down on the complex when she'd interviewed. In return, Savannah had made it a point to take Bev out for a leisurely lunch and pump her for the straight scoop on how the facility operated, knowing it would help her make a more informed decision about coming on board. Bev had avoided even the hint of gossip, sticking to sharing with Savannah what life at Stillman's Lake and the surrounding area was generally like. She had spoken with clearly evident affection for the place and her what-you-see-is-what-you-get manner was no small part of what had attracted Savannah. Now, as Savannah got ready to head out for a tour of the complex, she realized how fortunate she was she could do it with total peace of mind, knowing the welcome center was in Bev's capable hands. She grabbed one of the two-way radios and headed for the door.

"Jenny and I are going out to make morning rounds, Bev. Give me a shout if you need me." She waved the radio.

Savannah backed one of the ATV's out of the garage. She patted the seat next to her and Jenny scrambled in. The lake was large. It would take several hours to go around the whole lake in an ATV, certainly more time than she could afford to spend on a daily basis. As the maintained sites were limited to the southern half of the lake she decided that, as a general rule she'd alternate, taking one side of the lake one day and the opposite the next. She'd already seen the west side during the time she'd spent looking around when interviewing, so she took the dirt road leading to the more secluded east side.

She and Jenny spent the next hour stopping at various sites, taking notes of the characteristics of each, thinking it would not only help with scheduling any needed maintenance but would serve to build her knowledge of each site's unique characteristics. Savannah wanted to be able to publish a directory so visitors could get a feel for the sites ahead of time and find a match for their own interests and needs.

She was pleased to find the sites well cared for, with only minor maintenance needing to be done on just a handful. Her biggest concern was with the dirt road. She had to pay close attention to where she was going and keep her speed down or one of the many potholes rewarded her with an unexpected jolt. Savannah had already rattled her teeth more than once, nearly spilling poor Jenny out of the passenger seat.

She pulled into the next site, killing the ATV's motor then hopping off, Jenny joining her as she walked down to the water's edge.

The lake was calm as the wind usually didn't pick up much until later in the morning. A quick scan revealed only two boats out on the water. One of the boats was a bass boat with a huge motor that gobbled gas but got you from here to there faster than your buddy could bait his hook. The other looked to her like a restored Hackercraft. A true classic.

She turned, walking around and scribbling notes. She liked this site. It felt more private than the others but had a great view of the lake and offered an attractive patch of sandy beach. The picnic table had character, too, its wood grayish-blue with age. But it was solid and in good shape.

She spied something on one of the benches. It was a bottle. A small one. Savannah picked it up. It turned out to be a bottle of nail polish. She looked it over, trying the cap which offered little resistance. The bottle had been opened but, judging from the contents, not much had been used.

Must be someone accidentally left this behind. She'd take it back with her and put it in the welcome center's lost and found.

"Come on, Jenny. We've toured enough for one morning." She moved toward the ATV, shoving the bottle into a pocket of her shorts. Before she had taken three steps she realized she was alone.

"Jenny?" She turned, looking in all directions. "Jenny! Here, girl!"

She stood still, listening. In all the glory of the summer morning, nothing came to her ears save the chirping of birds and the rhythmic sound of gently sloshing water as the lake greeted the shoreline.

6

JESSE AND JAMES made their way to the lake, taking the same route Jesse had the day earlier. They even waved to Lester as he drove past, his head poking out the truck's window, his cheek looking as though he'd just popped a marshmallow into his mouth.

James was amused. "Friend of yours, Jesse?"

"Yeah, we share joint ownership of the road together with all the mineral rights for miles around. Lester spends all his royalties on chewing tobacco so he has to keep driving to feed his habit."

"And what do you do with your profits?"

"My millions are safely stashed away in a number of offshore accounts. I plan on retiring any day now. But don't get any ideas, if anything happens to me, Kai gets it all."

James laughed. "That figures."

They worked their way down to the lake. Every now and then, the brothers would be reminded of some boyhood adventures they'd had that were somehow connected to where they were walking. They swapped stories, each tale bringing back fond memories and reminding them of how close they'd been. Being twins, they were ready-made best friends and could hardly remember times growing up when they hadn't been together.

One of their favorite stories involved a friend who had joined them for some winter sledding. They'd spent hours with snow shovels building banked curves for running a plastic sled down the very trail they were now on. The twins had developed a technique they called a 'double' where one of them would lie on his back with his feet towards the front of the sled. The other would lie belly down, on top of him, head to the front. The top boy steered and held the bottom boy's life in his hands as the kid on the bottom was helpless and could only watch as the world whizzed crazily by at breakneck speed. Jesse and James had made the first run together, with Jesse on the bottom while their friend, Zak, watched. When Jesse had gone up to take a run with Zak as the helpless passenger, James had decided to make their run more exciting. He'd grabbed a shovel and started making a ramp. Two hunters happened to be walking by and, as they couldn't see Jesse and

Zak making their way up the hill because of the turns and the trees, they saw what looked to them like some nutty kid shoveling snow on a trail in the middle of nowhere. They'd stopped to ask James what he was doing. James had obliged, filling them in on his plan, and the hunters, anticipating too good a show to miss, had made themselves a couple of front row seats in the snow. A few short minutes later, Jesse hollered down they were ready to launch. James, barely able to contain himself, shouted back that everything was set at his end and they were cleared for takeoff.

Jesse and Zak had come racing down the course at breakneck speed, Zak screaming bloody murder and Jesse grinning from ear to ear. At the last second, Jesse had caught sight of James' remodeling job and tried jamming the tips of his boots into the snow to stop the sled. But it was too little too late. The sled hit the ramp and went airborne. Jesse was lucky, in that being the one on top, coming down the trail head first, he'd flown through the air in a standing up position. Zak wasn't so fortunate. He'd gone vertical, too. Only upside down. When it was all over, he'd looked like someone had planted him headfirst. James was laughing so hard he thought he'd pee his pants and the two hunters declared it to be one of the craziest things they'd ever seen.

"I don't think I ever enjoyed sledding more than on that day," James declared. It was pretty crazy being the helpless one on the bottom of a double, watching trees flying by and hoping the guy on top didn't crash into anything."

"I'm not sure Zak would agree," Jesse countered. "At least not so far as the ending was concerned. I think the poor guy was in shock. And if you recall, he never went sledding with us again."

"Yeah, you've got a point. But I bet those hunters have told the story a hundred times!"

Their reminiscing was interrupted by a change in Kai's demeanor. They had worked their way to the lake and were getting close to the site where Kai had turned up with his nail painted. Jesse could tell from the Shepherd's body language there was something nearby. He signaled Kai to stay put while he and James held their ground.

They heard a female voice calling out for someone named Jenny. A few moments later, they caught sight of a Golden Retriever. Jesse nodded to Kai who went up to the newcomer without hesitation. They touched noses, tails wagging. The brothers moved forward and Jesse knelt, running his hand along the Golden's back.

"It's a female, James, and a real beauty. Young, too, from the looks of her. I wonder if this is Jenny." He continued stroking the animal while looking for an ID tag. All he found around the dog's neck was a collar. No tag.

"There you are!"

Jesse looked up. A woman was walking towards them. Her khaki shorts gave way to legs showing muscle outlines consistent with someone who kept in shape. Her stylish blonde hair was cut short and she had the sort of natural tan that comes from spending time outdoors. He put her somewhere in her early to mid thirties.

"I take it this is your dog?" He rose.

"I'm Jesse and this is my brother, James." He motioned towards Kai who was standing quietly next to Jenny. "And that's Kai."

Savannah broke into an amused grin. She pointed at his chest. "So you're Jesse and...," she swiveled, her finger now pointing at James. "You're James." She paused before raising an eyebrow. "So where's the rest of your gang?"

Jesse laughed. "Our dad had a strange sense of humor."

"Your mom, too?"

James spoke up. "Our parents made a deal when they got married. Dad got to name any boys who came along and mom the girls. Jesse and I are twins. Dad liked names that start with the letter J. Mix that together with his off-beat humor and you get Jesse James split between the two of us."

Savannah laughed. "Let me guess. You have twin sisters as well. Not one to be outdone by your father, your mother named them Annie and Oakley. Am I right?"

"It might have happened that way, knowing Mom," Jesse conceded, grinning. "But as fate would have it, no girls came along. Not even any more boys. Kind of a shame," he added. "We would have loved having a sister."

Savannah extended a hand. "My name is Savannah." She shook Jesse's hand and then James' before kneeling beside the Golden. "This is Jenny."

"We thought so," James said. "We heard you calling for her as we came down the road."

"You don't see too many people out on this side of the lake. Especially during the week." Jesse paused, looking at her closely. "I've been coming here for a long time. Years. I don't recall ever seeing you. New to the area?"

"Yes, I moved here two weeks ago to take a position here at the complex. Today is my first day. I was touring the sites on the east side of the lake with Jenny and was just about to head back to the welcome center when she disappeared." She took the Golden's head in her hands, looking into the animal's eyes as if searching for clues. "I don't know what got into her. She's young but well behaved. She's never done anything like this before." She glanced at Kai. "But I suppose if she suspected such a handsome fella was coming her way she might not be able to resist the temptation." She reached over, giving Kai a playful pat on the head. "He's beautiful. And about the biggest German Shepherd I've ever seen!"

Jesse couldn't help feeling proud of Kai. The dog was special and he was pleased Savannah took notice. She looked so at ease, Jenny on one side and Kai on the other, an arm resting on each of their backs.

"What job did you take here at the lake?" James asked.

"I'm the new director." Her tone was matter-of-fact. "I'm from Topeka but got hooked on the beauty of the Adirondacks during a visit a few years ago. I'd always hoped to find a job that would allow me to live here doing something I loved." She gave the two dogs a group hug then stood. "Like I said, it's only my first day, but so far I love it here." She giggled. "I may have to pinch myself to be sure I'm not dreaming!" She looked at Jesse. "Did you say you've been coming here for years?"

"Pretty much my whole life. James and I grew up near the lake. When I got married, my wife and I wanted to stay close so we bought a place just a few miles away. We loved coming here. It was one of our favorite places."

Savannah watched as Jesse's face took on a faraway expression, as if he were looking at something in his mind's eye.

"You make it sound like the two of you don't come here anymore." She saw pain shoot across his face and instantly regretted her words.

Jesse spoke slowly. "No. We don't come here together anymore." He took a deep breath. "My wife died three years ago."

"I'm so sorry," Savannah said gently. "I didn't mean to pry."

Jesse found her green eyes holding him in a warm, steady gaze full of compassion. Normally, talking about Ellen to a stranger made him uncomfortable and he would find a quick way to end the conversation and walk away. But there was something different about Savannah, something safe.

"It's okay," he said quietly. He smiled, a warm, genuine smile that let Savannah know it really was okay. "I like coming here. I usually come at least once a week, sometimes more."

Savannah was relieved. She was glad he wasn't angry. Something about Jesse attracted her. Something beyond the surface. An idea came into her mind.

"You know, Jesse, you could really be of help to me."

"How's that?"

"I want to get a good feel for not only the recreational complex but the surrounding area, the context in which Stillman's Lake exists. I'm planning on talking with my co-workers, and of course I'm getting acquainted with the lake and the neighboring area myself, but it would really help to have the input of someone who isn't on staff. I need someone who knows both Stillman's Lake and the land around it and is willing to share their experience. I need everyone's input to develop the kind of plans for the future that will keep the lake an important part of the lives of those who live here, as well as tourists who come to visit." Savannah's eyes sparkled with enthusiasm. "I'd be grateful if you'd consider giving me some of your time."

James had been silently taking in the exchange between the two with keen interest. He couldn't help thinking he was watching the birth of some kind of connection between them. Granted, Jesse was a good-looking guy and Savannah a head turner, but that was surface stuff. It was his guess something deeper was happening that didn't have anything to do with romance. Something God was behind. Okay, God was behind everything, you just didn't always recognize it. God was always at work and once in a

38

while He gave you a ringside seat to something special, something like what was unfolding right in front of him.

He decided his brother could use his help. Jesse would either thank him when they got back to the house or clobber him, but James figured it was worth it either way. What were brothers for? Let the big guy squirm a little.

"That's a great idea, Savannah!" James offered. "I'm up visiting Jesse from where I live in South Carolina." He seized the opportunity. "The two of us have had an ongoing debate over who makes the best barbecue. Jesse does chicken and I do pork. How would you like to come over for dinner tonight? We can tell you what it was like growing up around here. The lake was a big part of our lives. My brother and I will cook some of our specialty barbecue and you can cast the deciding vote on which is best." James was on a roll. "How about it, will you do us the honor?"

Savannah stole a glance at Jesse. He was looking at James, amused. She wondered what he thought of his brother's inviting her to *his* house without bothering to ask him first.

"Sounds like an invitation to a family feud," she ventured. She was glad when Jesse spoke up.

"Not really. James here knows that his pork, although admittedly tasty, is still only second place fare." He winked at her. "But if you're willing to put up with his boasting as an appetizer, we'd love to have you join us. Besides," he went on, nodding towards the two dogs who were playing with each other a few steps away, "it looks like those two have hit it off and it'll give them a chance to get to know each other better." He called Kai to his side.

"We'll eat at seven. If you're comfortable, you're welcome to bring your bathing suit and go for a swim in the pool. Come anytime after six."

He looked sincere, Savannah thought. It didn't take her long to make up her mind.

"Thanks, I'd love to!"

7

ALTHOUGH THE TWO brothers proceeded with Jesse's experiment after Savannah's departure, the chance encounter had radically altered their mood. James kept his thoughts to himself, feeling like their meeting had accomplished much of whatever was intended by their coming. As he studied his brother, he could tell Jesse was more preoccupied with the world inside his head than the one before his eyes.

Eventually, they allowed themselves to relax and enjoy the glory of the summer morning. The sun was climbing in a sea of blue sky with only a few wisps of clouds here and there. The air smelled of damp earth, drying out from the morning dew. The distant cry of a red-tailed hawk mingled with the familiar chirping of nearby chickadees and robins. Now and then there was a rustling in the ground cover as a curious chipmunk made his presence known, scampering from one position of perceived safety to another, anxiously looking about when a red squirrel sounded a scolding alarm from her perch above their heads.

James had to admit he preferred the northern summer mornings over those in South Carolina where he lived inland where no ocean breezes softened the sun's sweltering blows. During the summer, he kept his windows closed and the air conditioning going. He was a runner and, back home, would be out doing his daily miles early enough to greet the rising sun. Here in the north, he could grab an additional hour's sleep without paying for it with heat stroke.

Since encountering Savannah, he and Jesse had been at the site of Ellen's drowning for over an hour and nothing unusual had happened. Kai hadn't disappeared and, when last they'd checked, there had been no reappearance of Iced Mauve on any of his nails.

James had wondered about how things would go when they got to the site. Would his brother want to talk? Maybe vent his anger? Or would he clam up, ball his hands into tight fists and stare at the lake with sullen eyes.

Jesse hadn't done any of these. In fact, he'd acted quite normal, throwing a stick into the lake for Kai to fetch and asking James about his work and life in the south. Sure, once in a while he'd zombie out for a few minutes, a sojourner in a private world of his own, but for the most part, he'd been fine. Even light-hearted. James guessed meeting Savannah had had a positive impact on him, serving as a safety brake for thoughts and emotions which might normally, given the setting, have weighed his twin down.

Around eleven, Jesse suggested they head back, grab something to eat for lunch somewhere, then stop at the grocery store to pick up a few things for dinner. He had some chicken in the freezer but preferred to use fresh poultry for his entry in the barbecue contest. He had some pork somewhere in the freezer, too, he assured James. He hinted it might be coming up on its six month anniversary in the deep freeze but said he didn't think anyone would notice given all the jazzed up spices James used in his rub. James shot him a look that plainly let Jesse know he planned on buying fresh pork at the grocer's, thank you very much.

Their lunch consisted of hot dogs and fries at Arman's, a local haunt known for its Texas hots, and washed them down with extra-thick shakes; pineapple for Jesse and chocolate with coconut for James. Kai settled for a double cheeseburger and a bowl of water. When they finished, they climbed back into the Element and headed to the store where each went his separate way, collecting the meat and accoutrements he felt confident would capture Savannah's winning vote and show the other for the second place barbecue wanna-be that he was.

Their afternoon was spent in a comedy of clandestine preparations, including a confrontation over what wood chips were to be used in the smoker. James preferred a blend of Red Oak, Hickory, and a touch of Pecan while Jesse's mix consisted of Wild Cherry and Apple.

"James," Jesse drawled, "unless you hauled some pecan chips up with you from South Carolina, I'd say you're out of luck. Last time I looked, we were a bit thin on pecan trees here in the Adirondacks."

"You'd be surprised if I had, wouldn't you?"

"Actually, nothing you said or did today would surprise me after this morning."

James grinned. He was wondering when Jesse was going to say something about his impromptu invitation to Savannah. "I guess, living in the south and being the gentleman that I am, together with meeting a woman with a delightful southern name and it being her first day on the job and all, it struck me that *someone* ought to show some hospitality!"

41

"Yeah, well don't think for a minute that I'm so naïve I don't know what's going on. I've had a couple years now of friends' well-intentioned but devious maneuverings, trying to get me hooked back into the social scene." He placed his own woodchip blend into the Horizon Ranger's firebox. "But I have to admit, there's something about Savannah that's different from most women I've come across."

"How so?"

"There's a genuineness. Nothing about her seems put on." A smile crept across Jesse's face. "Did you notice, no store-bought tan?"

James feigned a look of shock. "Heck no, Jesse! I didn't notice a thing about her by way of physical attributes. I was too caught up in the cerebral conversation the two of you were having." He broke into a grin. "Did I notice? You bet I did! She's a beautiful woman. That's one of the reasons I asked her to dinner. You're not the only eligible male in the neighborhood, my beloved brother." He finished making his rub and began gently massaging the mixture into the mound of pork in front of him. "The South shall rise again!" he shouted gleefully.

Savannah pulled the ATV up to the refueling station. Danny, one of the staff she'd met at the morning's meeting, was just finishing gassing up one of the two commercial riding mowers the center used in keeping the nearly forty acres of lawn looking their inviting best. The vast areas of grass were a favorite with the younger crowd who played endless games of ultimate Frisbee and spread out blankets for reading and sunbathing. Most were well-behaved, keeping their music at a volume where you had to be within twenty yards or so to hear it. It was a concession to the varied musical tastes abounding within their generation.

"How'd the morning tour go, Savannah? The place looks good, doesn't it?"

Danny was of Italian descent, his smile legendary with the young girls. At least according to Bev. She hadn't passed it along by way of gossip, just as an encouragement to Savannah to keep an eye on the young man. He was only in his mid-twenties and Bev feared his hormones got the better of his good judgment on occasion. Nothing serious, but Bev had insisted that Stanley talk to him when, earlier in the summer, Danny had gotten into the habit of mowing dressed only in shorts, shedding his shirt and footwear in favor of showing off his tanned and toned physique. Even after the talk, Danny still managed to take his breaks near the vending area, timing them so as to conveniently coincide with the arrival at the Coke machine of whatever young lady he happened to have his eye on that day.

"Hi, Danny." Savannah offered him a friendly but guarded smile. "Yes, the complex looks pretty good, at least the east side of the lake where I spent the morning. Except for the potholes in the road," she said, frowning.

Danny turned on the charm, flashing her a dazzling smile displaying a perfect set of bleached-white teeth. When he'd first heard the new director was a woman, he'd had his doubts. He still didn't know if Savannah knew her stuff. But she certainly set a high standard for feminine good looks and, even though she was ten years his senior, Danny figured he shouldn't hold that against her. Heck, being new to the area, she was probably lonely. Wouldn't hurt to be friendly and show her around. Might even advance his career.

"The potholes are Stan's idea," he confided. "Stan says if we make the roads in the outlying areas smooth, people end up driving too fast. The speed limit is posted at fifteen but a nice road is an invitation to go faster. So Stan has us create potholes to keep everybody paying attention and driving slowly. There's actually a pattern to them. If you know the pattern, you can drive pretty fast. The police know the pattern so they can always catch up with someone if they have to.

"There's been some interesting chases over the years from what a friend of mine on the force tells me," he went on. "Not many, just a handful. Drug related stuff. Hard for the bad guys to figure how the cops caught up with their decked out four-by-fours when they were bouncing hard enough to hit their heads on the roof!" He laughed. "I've heard they even have a video of one of the chases down at the Sheriff's office. Shot it from the dash-mounted onboard camera. They ought to post the thing on YouTube!" he chortled.

Savannah couldn't imagine a worse thing to do. Post something like that online and you'd attract a hundred wackos looking to make a name for themselves as the ones who successfully outran the Stillman's Lake cops and lived to tell about it. Or gloat about it.

She took Danny up on his offer to refuel her ATV and headed into the welcome center where a handful of visitors were milling about studying maps of the complex, looking at exhibits, or asking Bev questions ranging from where the best fishing was on the lake to if the johns were the composting kind. No matter what they asked, Bev had an answer. She gave Savannah a reassuring look that said, *Don't worry, I'll handle the folks out here. You go ahead and do what you have to do.* Bev was the glue holding the place together all right.

Savannah went into the office and sat down at her desk, Jenny preferring to stay out where the people were. The Golden loved people, especially kids. Jenny meandered about the large room, mingling with guests and enjoying their attention as if she'd been there for years.

Savannah reflected on the morning's events, amazed at herself for accepting an invitation for dinner with two men she'd just met in a town that she had just moved to. They seemed nice enough. But these days, one needed to be careful all the same. Had she acted rashly?

The thought came to her that if they were regulars here at the lake, Bev probably knew them. She had thought about mentioning the two brothers to Danny when she'd pulled up at the pump but had changed her mind. The last thing she needed was to be the center of a juicy chunk of gossip! Bev would keep it to herself without reading anything into it and making it more than what it really was.

What then was it really? she asked herself.

She'd been totally sincere when she had talked about wanting to get an outsider's take on the complex and building up her knowledge of the general area. If Jesse had lived here all his life and came to the lake as often as he claimed he'd be a great candidate. James didn't live here anymore but had grown up here. He could identify the changes that had taken place since he left and give his opinion as to whether the complex was heading in what he thought was a good direction. Especially for folks visiting from out of town. The two struck Savannah as tailor-made for the sort of research she had in mind. She assured herself that was all there was to it.

For the rest of the morning, Savannah attacked her to-do list. When lunchtime arrived, she insisted on covering the front reception area while Bev ate first, telling the hard-working woman that, after what Savannah had observed, she deserved a break.

Twenty minutes later, Bev walked out of the office and over to where Jenny lay sound asleep in her new bed.

"Looks like golden girl has tuckered out after a busy morning." She took in the peaceful sight with satisfaction. "I'm glad she likes her bed. She looks comfy in there." Bev thought a moment. "Maybe I ought to make another one of those for Stanley. It would make a dandy Christmas gift, don't you think, Savannah? I could put it over there on the other side of the hearth and tell him it's being reserved for his retirement. That'll get him going!" She giggled at the thought.

Savannah rolled her eyes. "I can see where the two of you keep things lively around here! Just don't be giving anyone any ideas about retirement. At least not during my watch. I don't know what I'd do without either of you!

"By the way," she added, switching subjects, "I met a couple of guys out on the east side of the lake while I was out. Brothers. Twins, actually. Said they'd grown up around here."

She noted Bev's instant recognition.

"That would be Jesse and James Whitestone. Their father was a real character. Great guy but a strange sense of humor. Their mother was a good friend of mine."

"Was?"

"She died, together with her husband, in a freak car accident some time ago." Bev waited a few moments before going on, her voice soft and thoughtful. "Jesse's wife died, too. Not in the same accident, mind you, in a different one." She hesitated to say anything more about Ellen's drowning. After all, it was Savannah's first day. Airing such a painful part of the lake's history could wait.

"How sad!" Savannah's face registered genuine concern. "Jesse said that his wife had passed away but didn't say anything about the circumstances."

Bev remained silent. If Savannah didn't press her, she wasn't about to say anything more.

"Anyway, we talked for a while and I shared with them how I wanted to get some outside opinions on our complex; what folks appreciate about it and what they'd like to see in the future. I asked Jesse if he'd consider sharing some of his thoughts and, before I knew it, James asked me to join them for dinner saying it would provide the perfect setting for an interview."

45

"Did he say anything about having barbecue?" Bev probed, already guessing the answer.

"Yes, he did. In fact, he said the two of them would each be cooking their own specialty and they want me to judge which is better. How did you know?"

"Good gracious," Bev blurted. "Do boys ever grow up? Those two have had a running feud about which one makes the best barbecue ever since they were old enough to put a match to a smoker! Here you've been on the job only a couple of hours and somehow manage to get yourself caught up in the debate!" She eyed Savannah, lowering her voice. "To tell you the truth, those two make some of the best barbecue chicken and pork you'll ever put inside your mouth. If you're smart, you'll stall for time and force them to invite you back again!"

"I take it you think it's safe for me to go?" Savannah found the whole thing amusing.

"Couldn't be safer. Those two are the cream of the local crop. Of course, James doesn't live here anymore and must be up visiting. Jesse is a hard-core permanent resident." Bev grew thoughtful, wondering if she should say anything more to Savannah about the circumstances surrounding Ellen's death. She hated the thought of her boss getting blindsided but figured it was unlikely the subject would even come up. After all, it wasn't the sort of dinner conversation you just tossed out into the air. Jesse sure wouldn't say anything and James was as savvy as they came. No chance of him sticking his foot in his mouth. Bev decided to stick with her earlier intuition that now wasn't the time to fill Savannah in on the incident.

"Don't you worry about a thing, Savannah. Go and enjoy yourself! The Lord has done a good thing for you today in arranging for the three of you to meet. I'm sure of it. Just don't come dragging in here tomorrow morning looking like you've only had a few hours sleep! Those two can keep a body up all night with their stories. And they've got some good ones!"

Not sure God had anything to do with it but satisfied she hadn't foolishly entered into a dinner engagement she should have avoided, Savannah went back into her office, grabbing her lunch out of the portable fridge the two of them shared. She was hungry and glad she hadn't skimped on the chef salad she'd made for herself.

The remainder of the afternoon went by quickly. Bev and the rest of the crew headed out at four-thirty. Savannah had a few more emails to deal with so didn't lock up until after five. She figured she had plenty of time to get herself ready for dinner. She and Jenny would be home by five-thirty. Jesse had said it was a twenty minute drive from the complex to his place. She hadn't told him where she lived but after looking up the address he'd given her online, she'd noted he lived in the same direction relative to the complex as she did. Just farther out. That meant she would have plenty of time to get ready. Not having much to do over the weekend, she'd made some Crème Brulee. It was her first time but the popular dessert had turned out well, she thought. She had only taken a small sampling so there was plenty left.

She loaded Jenny into the Subaru and headed home, a pleasant sense of anticipation taking form somewhere inside.

"How about it, girl?" she asked, reaching back. "You up for a date with that good looking Shepherd?" Jenny looked at her without a hint of change to her demeanor. *Must be nice to be a dog. A few sniffs and some tail wagging and you're pals.* Savannah hoped the evening would go well for the humans, too. Minus the sniffs and tail wagging.

She pulled into her driveway, hitting the button on the garage door opener, timing it so she didn't have to come to a complete stop. She let Jenny out into the fenced-in back yard then headed inside to get ready for the evening.

Savannah thought about Jesse's swimming invitation. She'd have to play that one by ear. She'd figure out what to wear while showering.

Tossing her shorts into the hamper, she felt something in one of the pockets. It was then she remembered the nail polish she'd found at one of the sites. She had meant to put it in the lost and found but forgotten about it. She took a closer look. The bottle's shape was familiar and the distinctive black cap with gold band lettering confirmed it was a Revlon product. A label affixed to the bottle's bottom bore the code 1271-78 but she couldn't find anything else. She painted one of her toenails, examining the results. It was sparkly but not overdone and produced a nice, mauve-like color.

8

SAVANNAH PULLED INTO Jesse's driveway. She'd grabbed one of her bathing suits just before leaving the house, not at all sure she would take Jesse up on his offer of a swim. But it wouldn't hurt to have it with her just in case. A swim in the pool would be a welcome relief after the heat of the long summer day.

She parked next to a celery green Prius with South Carolina plates she assumed belonged to James. She got out and headed towards the house, Jenny walking sedately at her side. The house was a pale yellow color and set back from the road. A large, wrap-around porch greeted her, a chair swing dangling from its ceiling tempting any passers-by to sit and take it easy for a while. The early evening breeze carried in it the smell of flowers—no surprise given the profusion of wildflowers all about the place. The breeze carried another aroma as well: barbecue. Savannah felt suddenly famished. The aroma was mouth-watering and she noticed Jenny's twitching nose sampling the air, her canine eyes wide with anticipation.

"Mind your manners, young lady!" Savannah admonished. "I don't know if they cooked any for you or not. But if they didn't, maybe I can sneak you some of mine." She heard a soft chuckle and turned to find a smiling Jesse coming towards her.

"Around here we take care of all our guests, two or four-legged!" he reassured her, smiling warmly in response to her blush and setting her at ease. "I'm glad you're here." He knelt, gently massaging Jenny behind her ears. "And it's good to see you, too, Jenny. Kai's been looking for you." As if on cue, the Shepherd appeared from around the corner, tail wagging.

Savannah smiled sheepishly then sniffed the air. "Smells wonderful!"

Jesse motioned towards the direction he'd come. "For the full effect, just follow the yellow brick road."

To Savannah's surprise, a sidewalk, inlaid with yellow bricks, met her steps as she rounded the corner of the house. It began underneath a white trellis adorned with a profusion of flowers, their delicate size and vibrant, deep pink color serving as an enchanting entrance to the world behind the house. For a moment, Savannah stood still, charmed by what she saw. "Rosa Moyesii Geraniums," she breathed. "How lovely."

Jesse was surprised. "How did you know?"

"Their drooping hips are so unique. They're a favorite of European chateaus."

"I'm impressed. You know your roses."

Savannah smiled. "At least some of the wild ones I do. It's a part of my job I love." She looked at him, wondering. "Did you do all this, Jesse?" Her voice was soft and he found himself caught up in the warmth of her eyes.

"Yes—together with Ellen. We both loved *The Wizard of Oz*, at least the classic version with Judy Garland. We thought it would be fun, and sort of romantic, to have our own yellow brick road. The back yard was our land of Oz. We spent a lot of time together out here."

Savannah could detect only the slightest hint of sadness in his voice. She tried to imagine what sort of man would work together with his wife to create something so endearing. She searched his face for clues to the man inside. "I'm impressed."

Jesse smiled. "Let's just hope my chicken barbecue impresses you as much."

The yellow brick road led around back, emptying into a world that was as naturally charming as the large, rambling house. With each step, the tantalizing aroma of barbecue increased in intensity.

James waved from the balcony of an expansive deck overlooking a swimming pool much larger than most private pools she'd encountered. "Did you bring your suit, Savannah?" he called out. "The barbecue is ready but it can keep for a while if you'd like to take a swim first."

"To tell you the truth, James," she replied, "I don't think I could wait any longer. The aroma is driving me crazy!" It was the truth, too. As inviting as the water looked, she couldn't wait to sample what the brothers had prepared.

James beamed. "Fair enough. I guess the sooner we eat the sooner the truth will emerge as to who the real king of barbecue is around here!"

Savannah was shown to her place at a table already set for the occasion. The brothers insisted she relax for the few minutes it would take to bring out the food. They soon reappeared with James carrying two serving bowls; one filled with rice pilaf and the other salt potatoes. Jesse had mixed vegetables in one hand and summer slaw in the other. Two bottles of wine and some flatbread were already on the table.

"This occasion deserves a special prayer of thanks," James insisted. "Don't you agree?"

He didn't wait for an answer, extending a hand to each of them and bowing his head. Savannah caught what looked like the trace of a scowl cross Jesse's face. Shyly, she reached out, taking their hands in hers. Apart from their introductory handshake earlier that morning, it was their first physical contact and her emotions reacted to it with a slight increase in her pulse.

"Father, I thank you for the food you provide to nourish our bodies. Even more, I thank you for your Holy Spirit who nourishes our souls with the comfort of your presence. We're glad to have made a new friend today in Savannah and are grateful you are watching over her, together with all your children, for good. Help us to recognize that good in all its surprising forms. Amen." James gave her hand a light squeeze before he let go.

"Two wine glasses?" Savannah asked, noting the two glasses before her.

"You bet," Jesse replied. "We've got both pork and chicken. That calls for choices in wine as well." He poured a small amount of Shiraz into the glass having the larger bowl and a Riesling from a vineyard in the nearby Finger Lakes into the other. "You get to pick which you prefer."

"I'm afraid I have to warn you, I'm not a connoisseur. Not by a long shot. I know there are red, white, and blush wines and some are dry and others sweet. But that's about the extent of my knowledge."

"You don't have to be a wine expert to know which you enjoy and which you don't," Jesse assured her. "Just ask James." He shot James a look that seemed to say, *There, we're even. And don't go blindsiding me again with your religious stuff!*

"Take this Shiraz," he held up a bottle. "If the grapes that produced this Australian wine were to be harvested in France, Argentina, Chile or here in the States, the wine produced would be called Syrah. In South Africa, the

50

name goes back to Shiraz. Same grapes, different name. Go figure." He thought for a moment. "Admittedly, there is a difference in taste. You drink the Australian stuff when it's young, within five years of bottling and it has a big bold taste to it. It's the most popular of Australian wines in terms of production."

Savannah opted for the Finger Lakes Riesling, preferring it's dry, fruity taste to the more robust Shiraz.

By way of previous agreement between the brothers, who had flipped a coin for the honor, James served up some of his barbecue pork. They passed around the sides, filling their plates with what seemed to Savannah food that both looked and smelled delicious. She couldn't wait to dig in. Under watchful stares, she lifted a forkful of pork to her mouth, closing her eyes and savoring the taste. "Oh, my," she murmured. "Oh, my." She kept her eyes closed for a few moments longer before opening them again. She turned to James. "This is incredible!"

James' face lit up. "Glad you like it."

"Like it? James, I love it! It absolutely melts in your mouth. This has got to be the best pork I've ever had!"

James turned to his twin. "I knew it!" he cried, triumphantly. "Ah, Junior, we might never get past the pork. We may even have to save your chicken for Kai and Jenny. I'm sure *they* won't mind." He looked over at the two dogs lying side-by-side nearby, their faces full of expectation.

"Junior?" Savannah tossed Jesse a playful look.

Jesse grunted. "Yeah, little man here was born first and it went to his head. I never had the heart to tell him I had to stay behind and push from the rear because he didn't have the muscle to get out on his own."

He turned to his twin. "Enjoy your brief moment of glory, James. I admit, your barbecue tastes pretty good—that is, until something superior comes along." He slid a portion of chicken onto Savannah's plate, adding, "And this, Ms. Director, is just such fare."

The two men watched as Savannah sampled the chicken. Jesse had encouraged her to take some water first, to rid her mouth of any toxic waste the pork may have left behind, he said. As with the pork, the flavorful chicken melted in her mouth, sending her taste buds into ecstasy and eliciting

51

a stream of praise from her lips. Jesse sat back in his chair, certain of a first-place victory.

The rest of the meal passed with the brothers trading barbs and encouraging Savannah to have one helping after another of their particular barbecue. She obliged them both until she felt that if she ate another bite, she'd explode. Together with the salad, vegetables and bread she felt stuffed to the hilt.

She tapped her water glass with a spoon, signaling for attention. "I am now ready to render my judgment as to which barbecue I prefer," she announced. "But before I do, I wish to offer a toast to both chefs." She raised her wineglass. "To the Whitestone twins, true and remarkable gentlemen each. Not only for your culinary prowess but for your warm hospitality in helping to make my first day on the job such a memorable occasion."

They touched glasses to a chorus of, "Here, here!"

"And now," she went on, "without further ado, I'd like to announce the winner." She could read in their faces that, although there was a good-natured rivalry between them in the matter, the affair also bore all the marks of genuine competition. *These two take their barbecue seriously!* She paused, deliberately allowing the suspense to build until the air was saturated with anticipation.

"And the winner is…." She let her words hang before quickly sitting down while blurting out, "It's a tie!"

Both men groaned.

"You've got to be kidding!" James protested.

"I'll say!" Jesse agreed. "Shall we make her walk the plank or just toss her over the balcony into the pool?"

Savannah laughed. "Come on, guys! You didn't really expect me to choose sides now, did you? The truth of it is that I need more time. Maybe a second or third round would help me decide." She held up her hands, palms out, as both Jesse and James hastily grabbed more barbecue.

"I don't mean *now*," she chided. "This isn't the sort of thing you can decide by sheer volume. This is delicate stuff. It's going to take time to sort it out. At least two, maybe even three more dinners."

"Oh, I get it," Jesse snorted. "I bet you just happened to say something about coming here to Bev and she encouraged you to milk it for all it was worth and see if you couldn't wrangle a few more barbecues out of us." He nodded to James. "We've been down that road a few times."

"You bet we have," James chimed. "Bev has proven our most stubborn judge. We've tried pinning her down but she's side-stepped us for years."

"Confess!" Jesse challenged, his face wearing a mock look of anger. "Fess up or we'll make you clean the smoker!"

"Looks like you've caught me red-handed," Savannah confessed. "I guess I have to plead guilty and throw myself on the mercy of the court!"

All three laughed and Savannah couldn't help thinking maybe she really should pinch herself. The day had turned out to be so much more than she had expected. If this was any example of what life was like in Stillman's Lake, the folks around here should bottle it!

She suddenly remembered the Crème Brulee. "Oh! I brought dessert! Crème Brulee."

"Crème Brulee?" James echoed, eyes widening. "I love the stuff!" He turned to Jesse. "Sounds like fair payment in return for the barbecue, wouldn't you say?"

"I would, indeed. Sounds great." He gave a satisfied sigh. "What do the two of you say to a swim first, then coffee and the Crème Brulee in the hot tub afterwards?"

His suggestion met with hearty approval. They were all pleasantly full and the thought of deferring dessert for a while sounded perfect. They decided to clear the table and feed the dogs before taking a swim.

"So, which of us is going to take care of the smoker?" Jesse challenged, looking his brother in the eye.

James reached into a pocket of his shorts and fished out a coin. "I tell you what, let's flip for it. Heads you win and I take care of the smoker and clean up all the really messy stuff while you two clear the table and feed the dogs. Tails and you get the dirty work."

He tossed the coin into the air, catching it before expertly flipping it over. He slowly lifted his hand to reveal the coin.

"Looks like heads to me," Jesse smirked.

"Ah, well," James sighed, placing a hand on his brother's shoulder. "I guess the toughest guys get sent to do the toughest jobs." He watched with satisfaction as Jesse and Savannah gathered up as much from the table as they could carry and headed towards the kitchen. A smile played over his face as he watched them go. He was turning the coin over in his hand, chuckling to himself as both sides of the quarter displayed the same bust of George Washington. *You sure come in handy when somebody needs a push in the right direction.*

9

SAVANNAH FOLLOWED JESSE into the house. They entered through a set of French doors, passing through a large airy dining room. The kitchen had an inviting atmosphere and struck her as the sort of place anyone who enjoyed cooking would thrive in.

Jesse pointed. "You can set stuff down anywhere on the counter. I'll put the leftovers in the fridge and stick the dishes in the dishwasher. If you like, you're welcome to relax out on the deck while I clean up."

"Do you mind if I stay and help?" Savannah was looking at him. Was he imagining things or was there more than a simple desire to be helpful in her voice.

"Sure, glad to have your company."

He was, too. Jesse found her presence a mixture of comfort and intrigue. He reminded himself they had only met that morning. It was way too early to be having romantic imaginings. But there wasn't any doubt he was attracted to her. He couldn't kid himself about that. Sure, James had talked his own interest up but Jesse knew better. His twin was simply coating the medicine he thought Jesse needed with manly competition so he'd open wide and swallow like a good boy. Well, nobody needed to coat Savannah with anything.

In a way, he felt guilty. What would Ellen think of this cocktail of emotions coursing through him? They had talked about remarrying a few times during their marriage, believing it a topic every couple touched on at some point. The notion one or the other would die first was a given. Unless, of course, there was some tragic accident involved taking them both at the same time. Like the one that took his parents. Their going together was the only good he could glean out of that awful tragedy. Both he and Ellen had told each other to follow their hearts, that regardless of age, if just one of them should die they wanted the other to know that his or her happiness was important to them. They were secure in the knowledge they deeply loved each other and always would. Something death was powerless to change.

The unselfish desire to release their mate to the freedom of attaching themselves to someone else arose out of a wellspring of love. Love was inclusive, not exclusive, Ellen had said, jabbing him in the ribs and telling him not to get carried away when he'd raised an eyebrow in taunting jest. She'd laughingly clarified that as long as they were both alive their romantic love was as exclusive as could be!

Now, as he handed Savannah some storage containers, watching her working alongside him in the same kitchen in which he'd spent countless hours with Ellen, he could feel the friction of colliding emotions, like tectonic plates brushing up against each other, sending shockwaves to the surface. He hoped his emotional foundations were strong enough to withstand the tremors.

Jesse loaded the dishwasher while Savannah put away the leftovers. She noted the contents of the refrigerator were, if somewhat sparse, well organized. From what she could see, this was a trademark characteristic of his. Everywhere she looked she found marks of thoughtful attention. She wondered how Jesse would react to something out of left field. Something spontaneous. Then again, wasn't their being here together spontaneous enough? Maybe, she allowed. But James had been the one who had come up with the idea.

The kitchen chores done, Jesse and Savannah headed back outside where James was finishing up with the smoker. Jesse had set aside a generous portion of barbecue, vegetables, and rice for the dogs before turning the rest over to Savannah bound for the fridge. Although Savannah told him she rarely gave Jenny table scraps it was more a matter there weren't that many scraps to share, given her dietary habits, than an objection to Jenny having people food.

Jesse handed the Golden's share to Savannah. "Why don't you feed Jenny while I take care of Kai? He's a good natured fellow until it comes to barbecue." He winked and nodded towards James. "When it comes to barbecue, he gets as carried away as my brother and has a tendency to eat not only his own portion but his guest's as well."

By the time they finished feeding the dogs, James joined them. "Whew!" he exclaimed, wiping his forehead with the back of his hand, "I'm glad that's done!" He looked longingly at the pool. "I don't know about you two but I could really use a swim."

Jesse showed Savannah the deck-level dressing room then headed upstairs to change while Savannah went out to her car to get her bathing suit and the Crème Brulee. She hit a button on her key fob, the Subaru responding with a familiar click as the locking mechanism obeyed the electronic command to release its grasp. She lifted the hatch, taking out a canvas tote bag containing her bathing suit and a small cooler holding the Crème Brulee. As she swung the hatch closed she caught sight of something on the outside of the window. It appeared to be words scrawled in the light film of dust laying on the surface of the glass. The letters were clear enough, even with the oncoming twilight, for her to make out the three word message: FOLLOW THE DOG.

Follow the dog?

What the heck did that mean? And what dog? Jenny? Kai? She looked around, half expecting to see Jenny and Kai coming around the corner, partners in some new surprise Jesse and James had up their sleeves. Not seeing anything unusual she walked back around the house, turning the discovery over in her mind. Now that she thought about it, she had no idea when the message might have been written. Or for that matter, where. For all she knew, a visitor to the complex could have done it earlier in the day. Some kid, inspired by the sight of Jenny, with nothing to do.

She reasoned the only time the brothers could have done it was when they had gone into the house to bring out the food earlier in the evening. But they hadn't been gone very long. Not nearly long enough to come out and write on her window. James, on the other hand, would have had plenty of time when she was inside cleaning up with Jesse.

Savannah shrugged. She'd just play dumb and act like she hadn't seen anything. If either of the brothers were responsible for the message it would drive them nuts and she doubted they could hide it from her for long. If they didn't say anything or act suspicious she'd chalk it up to some bored adolescent.

Inside the changing room, Savannah hung her clothes on the wall hooks. She'd brought both her bikini and one-piece, undecided as to which she preferred. She chose the mint green one-piece. She could hear Jesse and James talking by the pool. From the sounds, they were busy lighting torches she'd seen around the deck. She put on a cover-up and slipped on a pair of flip-flops. Spying a pile of fresh towels on a shelf near the door, she grabbed one on the way out.

For a moment, the three of them froze, staring at one other. It was as if they were kids back in high school, checking each other out although desperately trying to hide it. Jesse had counted on the sight of Savannah in a bathing suit taking his breath away and had steeled himself, commanding his jaw to keep his mouth closed. James wasn't as fortunate and found himself gawking before Jesse dealt him a blow between the shoulder blades. "What's the matter, little man?" he drawled. "Don't they have any beautiful blondes down South where you come from?"

Savannah felt blood rushing to her cheeks but was pleased Jesse found her attractive. "I can see this is going to take some courage," she intoned. "I'm already self-conscious enough being the only female." She took off her footwear, dragging her toes through the water to get a feel for the temperature. "I guess the best thing for me to do is to get in the water as quickly as possible!" She tossed her cover-up aside and dove into the pool, giving the two men only the briefest impression of the outline of her figure before disappearing, a shimmering green streak gliding below the surface.

The three of them spent the next half-hour enjoying the refreshing coolness of the water, talking all the time. The brothers wanted to know about her life in Topeka, her family, and what her childhood had been like. She shared with them that she was an only child, blessed with kind and loving parents who were still in good health back in Kansas. They, in turn, recounted some of their childhood adventures, including the famous sledding story. Savannah thought it was hilarious and tried to picture a young Jesse flying through the air. She felt sorry for Zak and suspected there were plenty more examples of collateral damage from hanging out with the twins during their formative years!

"You two ready for the Crème Brulee?" Savannah was eager to contribute something of her own to the evening. She'd been having a wonderful time and appreciated the relaxed but respectful atmosphere her hosts extended to her. She felt both safe and appreciated.

For their part, Jesse and James found it natural to offer Savannah the honor of treating her like the precious woman she was. They appreciated her femininity but were no less impressed with her obvious intelligence and fine sense of humor. For his part, James was already working on the next phase of his plan to help nurture the relationship along between his brother and this lovely woman who had so suddenly popped into Jesse's life.

Not that James imagined he knew what God's plans were for the two of them. He didn't. All he had was a sense their lives were connected in some way. A way that was good for both of them. He intended to be praying for them, trying to discern what, if anything, God may ask him to do. The prayer part was certain. Anything else he was to do would come from the foundation of that prayer.

Jesse volunteered to make coffee and serve up dessert. "You two might as well relax in the hot tub," he offered, flipping off the tub's cover on his way to the house. Kai and Jenny had worn each other out and were lying contentedly nearby, barely visible in the gathering darkness. "Keep an eye on James for me, Kai. You've got my permission to dismember him if he steps out of line."

Savannah and James lowered themselves into the tub, their bodies reacting to the hot water, every muscle relaxing to its fullest. Seeing as they were going to take the final course of their meal in the lap of water-borne luxury, it made sense to James to keep the jets off and the water still.

"I take it you and Jesse are in perpetual competition," Savannah remarked, amazed how the two of them could keep it up.

James grinned. "Is it that obvious?"

Savannah smiled but said nothing. She leaned back, treating herself to a view of the heavens. The night sky was salted with stars, their lights varying in intensity depending, she supposed, on their size, composition, and distance from the earth. James joined her in admiring the bliss of the night-time sky. "It's really something isn't it?" he said with wonder.

"It's beautiful. And awesome. I think I could stare at it for hours."

"God made two great lights—the greater light to govern the day and the lesser light to govern the night. He also made the stars," James quoted softly. "It's a verse from the first chapter of Genesis," he explained, noting the look of surprise on Savannah's face. "Everything we see around us, both on earth and in the heavens, is the work of His hands. It's one of the ways He reveals himself to us." James paused, turning to look at Savannah until her eyes met his own. "Even you and Jesse are examples of God's handiwork." The words were gently spoken.

Savannah could tell James was sincere. The way he looked and spoke made it clear he wasn't just making idle talk to pass the time until Jesse returned. The man was serious.

She marveled how the two brothers were a walking paradox in that they were full of so many dissimilar similarities. Although twins, they were very different physically—though bearing sufficient family resemblance to certify their kinship. James was nearly a head shorter and a blue-eyed blonde whereas Jesse had brown hair and green eyes that differed from her own only in terms of hue. Hers were a bright, sort of emerald color whereas Jesse's seemed to have been infused with the dark greens of the Adirondacks, as if nature had imparted part of herself into him as a gift. Jesse was more laid back, too, while James seemed to hum with life, as if powered by nuclear energy. Yet, although the two were different in so many ways, they both exuded a shared sense of calmness and an appreciation for nature and the world around them.

From James' suggesting prayer before they ate and his quoting of the Bible, Savannah took it he was the religious type. That was okay with her as long as he didn't go overboard. She hadn't given God much thought over the years and seemed to get along well enough without Him. As for God having made her, had He been there when her parents had conceived her? She chuckled. Her mother would have been mortified!

Her thoughts were interrupted by Jesse's return. He carried a tray bearing three helpings of Crème Brulee and an old-fashioned clear glass coffee pot. She hadn't seen one of those in ages! He handed the desserts to Savannah and James then joined them in the tub, lowering himself slowly into the steaming water.

James was the first to sample the Crème Brulee. "Savannah! This is scrumptious!" he declared, shoveling in another mouthful.

Jesse took a bite, nodding his assent. "It sure is." He ate slowly, savoring the delectable vanilla custard. "One of your many specialties?"

Savannah shook her head. "I enjoy cooking but I don't claim expert status, that's for sure! Actually, this was my first attempt at Crème Brulee. I've eaten it several times in restaurants. I didn't have much to do over the weekend so I thought I'd give it a shot."

"Well, anytime you want to experiment and try out a new recipe you're welcome to use my kitchen as your laboratory. Of course," Jesse added, "that means I'd have a fifty percent stake in the results."

They finished the dessert, relaxing quietly and sipping coffee, content to leave the hot tub's jets turned off and allowing the conversation to go wherever it wanted. As the topic touched for a moment on sports, James suddenly remembered his loss to Jesse in the previous night's contest. This led to explaining the game of swimming pool golf to Savannah, who was highly amused. "You mean to tell me your feet are big enough to grasp a golf ball with your toes?" She tried to picture it in her mind.

"Sure!" James said. "I'll show you." He hopped out of the tub, returning momentarily with a golf ball he tossed into the water. "Show her how it's done, Big Foot."

Jesse obliged. In a matter of seconds, Savannah was staring at a tanned foot poking above the water, vapors of steam swirling around toes firmly grasping an optic yellow golf ball. She saw the toes relax their grip and, with a plunk, the ball disappeared back into the water.

"Your turn." Jesse grinned.

"My feet are half the size of yours," Savannah pointed out. "I could never get a grip."

"It's easier than it looks," James offered. "It has more to do with technique than foot size."

Savannah felt around the bottom of the tub with her foot until she located the ball then pressed down, allowing the small sphere to nest itself naturally in the area around her big toe and the ball of her foot. The grip felt tenuous and the ball slid out as she began to lift.

"I'm not sure this is going to work."

The brothers began to chant in unison, goading her on, their voices rising in a slow crescendo. "Go!, Go!, Go!, Go!, Go!"

"All right, all right," she said, her face taking on a look of determination. "One more try. Anything to quiet the crowd."

Her foot found the ball again and, this time, she pressed down harder and felt the golf ball spreading her big and second toes, lodging itself more

61

securely between them. A moment later she held the orb aloft, a triumphant, "Yes!" bursting from her lips.

Jesse only caught a momentary glimpse by the flickering light of a nearby torch but the image of what he thought he'd seen made him catch his breath. "This might sound strange, Savannah, but would you mind if I looked at your foot?"

The question took her by surprise. "My foot? Why? Did I break one of the rules? An illegal touch or something?" she joked. Seeing the serious look on Jesse's face drained the elation from her own. "What is it, Jesse? What's the matter?"

James was bewildered as well. "What's up, bro? You look like you've seen a ghost?"

"Maybe I have," Jesse muttered. "Please, Savannah. I know it sounds goofy but it's important." He looked at her imploringly. "Trust me. Please."

Savannah took a deep breath. She had no idea what this was about. But, whatever it was, it was important to Jesse. That much was clear.

The golf ball was still in the grasp of her foot. "With or without the golf ball?" she asked innocently.

"You can drop the ball. All I need is the foot." Jesse offered her a faint smile, his face relaxing a bit. He reached out. "Just set your foot in my hand, Cinderella," he said, a light smile crossing his face.

Obediently, Savannah lifted her foot, allowing it to rest in Jesse's waiting hand, balancing herself by placing both hands, palms down, on either side of her. James slid over next to his brother, both men staring intently at her foot. Jesse looked at her. "I need to turn your foot towards the light so I can see better." He gently rotated her foot. Still not satisfied, he opened the portable fridge and fished out a flashlight.

"Interesting place for a flashlight." Savannah wiggled her toes. "What's going on? Do I have some sort of deadly toe fungus?" The absence of a reply unnerved her. "Come on, guys? Out with it! What's going on?"

Jesse switched off the flashlight.

"You have a painted toenail. Only one. Why just one?"

"You're kidding, right?" Savannah was incredulous. Was all this about nail polish? She hoped there was more to it. "Okay, I'll bite. But it has to be a fair trade. First you tell me why you keep a flashlight in your refrigerator, Jesse, and then I'll tell you why only one of my toenails is painted." Her words had the desired effect as all three felt a drop in the tension that had been building.

"It's simple," Jesse began. "A flashlight comes in handy out here. But if I leave one out in the open, sooner or later Kai runs off with it and buries it somewhere in the yard. I guess he considers it a bone. So I got into the habit of keeping the flashlight in the refrigerator."

"Makes sense to me," Savannah admitted.

"Now your story," Jesse prodded.

Savannah filled the brothers in on her tour of the east side of the lake earlier that day and how she had found a bottle of polish at one of the sites shortly before the three of them met. She explained how she had intended to put the polish in the welcome center's lost and found but had forgotten about it in the course of the day until she got home. She told about trying out the color to see what it was like by painting one of her nails.

"End of story. Satisfied?" She looked at the two of them. They seemed awfully interested in a story about nail polish.

James spoke up. "You need to do your best to trust us, Savannah. There's more to all this than meets the eye." He looked at Jesse. "I suggest you fill her in. After all, trust runs in both directions."

Jesse shook his head. "You're right," he agreed. "But I'd like to ask Savannah a few more questions first." His eyes engaged hers in a silent exchange that went beyond words. "I promise when I'm finished I'll explain why I'm so interested."

Savannah took a deep breath, nodding her consent. "Okay, Jesse. What do you want to know?"

It didn't take long for Jesse to learn the details. When she finished answering his questions he realized Savannah's experience was somewhat akin to his own. They had both come upon nail polish that looked to him like Iced Mauve and both had lost sight of their dogs for an unexplained period of time. And at the center of it all was Stillman's Lake. In particular, the east shore and the site of Ellen's drowning.

Jesse was quiet for a time, trying to decide how much of his own story to share. He decided to go slowly. Telling Savannah about Kai's painted dew claw was one thing. Delving into the details surrounding Ellen's death was something else. He suspected Savannah didn't even know about the incident. Most likely, although most of the staff at the complex were well aware of what had happened, they hadn't mentioned anything about it to her yet. After all, it was human nature to put your best foot forward. They would have wanted her to feel comfortable.

"It seems we have something in common," Jesse began, "and as strange as it sounds, it has something to do with nail polish and dogs." As if somehow aware of their part in the story, Kai and Jenny lifted their heads, looking towards the hot tub from where they lie resting in the lush grass of the nearby lawn.

As Jesse had promised, he shared with Savannah the details concerning his own experience at the lake the day before, leaving out any mention of Ellen or the accident. He wondered if James would muddy the water by bringing up Ellen and adding that whole can of worms into the mix. He hoped not. He wasn't ready to go there with Savannah. Not yet, anyway. He was relieved when his brother kept silent.

Savannah listened carefully. She agreed there were curious coincidences in the two tales. She had the sense that Jesse was holding something back. The seriousness in his voice and the look in his eyes had more gravity than was warranted on the surface of things. She'd be patient. After all, Jesse had shown her nothing but kindness and warm hospitality. Sure, there was something unsettling about the whole thing. Rather mysterious… An image of her car's rear window with its message written in dust popped into her mind.

"There's more," she said slowly. "I need to show you a window."

10

TWO DAYS HAD passed since Savannah had shown he and James the writing in dust on the rear window of her Subaru. Jesse didn't know what to think. As Savannah said, she had no idea when or where the message had been written. Could it be a coincidence? Something etched in the dust by the sheer whimsy of a passer-by?

As he sat on the deck surveying the early morning sunrise, Jesse doubted it. It wasn't like the usual WASH ME! most pranksters liked to write, as if they were self-appointed advocates of neglected vehicles. D-O-G was one of the three words the anonymous author had scrawled. As in Kai or Jenny? He shook his head and wondered.

The three of them had spent nearly an hour standing around in the driveway, speculating on what the message might mean, before Savannah had reluctantly said good-night and left for home. Work was waiting for her in the morning she'd reminded them. She needed her rest and would have trouble enough falling asleep after the events of the day.

Jesse and Savannah had agreed to reconnect at the lake in two days. Savannah had needed the time to attend to other matters at the complex requiring her attention. Today was Thursday and Jesse was supposed to meet her at the welcome center after lunch.

As for his brother, James had gotten a phone call early the next morning from his office. Something about a hot piece of commercial real estate one of his best clients was putting on the market, insisting James handle every detail of the listing personally. Jesse's twin had left for points south after breakfast, assuring him everything was in God's capable hands and that James would be praying for him and would stay in touch. With smartphones and computers it would be easy enough. Jesse had offered his hand. James had shaken it but used the grip to pull his brother into a warm, heartfelt embrace.

James could pray for him all he liked, Jesse figured, but he doubted it would accomplish anything more than burning off a few cerebral calories. Might as well try dialing God on his cell phone! But at least they'd managed to mend some fences between them. James hadn't behaved perfectly but at least he hadn't been obnoxious. And until the mystery was cleared up, Jesse appreciated his brother's insights, even if they included the supernatural. Might as well have an open mind, right? Then, after the mystery was solved and it turned out to be of natural origin—of which Jesse had no doubt—the tables would be turned and maybe James would come to his senses. One could always hope.

Jesse had used the last forty-eight hours to stay on top of things with his consulting firm. Orange Risings was made up of an elite group of people with diverse talents. They were idea generators. And not just little ideas, either. Their clients usually brought them in when they were either falling behind their competition and needed a good kick in the innovative seat of their corporate pants or when they had what they believed was the next billion dollar widget and needed help developing a strategy that would take it from concept to reality without leaving a blood trail from the corporate coffers. It was a fast-paced world and truly good ideas were worth their weight in Google stock. Especially if you had a track record of not only coming up with them but bringing them to life.

From the start, Jesse had structured Orange Risings with maximum flexibility for those who worked there. Especially himself. He could disappear for days at a time if he needed to.

Then there was Savannah. He was surprised by how much he had thought about her over the last two days. In thinking about her, Jesse had begun to think more about life in general. He'd been alive for the past three years but had he been *living?* He wondered. The one thing he knew he had been doing these past three years was grieving. Wasn't grieving part of life? After all, who was there on planet Earth of any significant age that hadn't tasted sorrow? Heck, you came into the world crying, not laughing. Must be a clue in there somewhere. Savannah had brought more than a superficial smile to his face. It was as if his heart smiled first, then released the smile so it could work its way through his chest on up to his head where it spread across his face.

Kai walked over to where Jesse sat, settling himself beside his master, the two of them looking out at the sunrise as if sharing the same thoughts. Jesse draped an arm across the Shepherd's back and watched as the great yellow circle finally broke free of the earth.

"What would I have done without you, big guy?"

Savannah headed into her office to clean up some paperwork. The usual morning meeting had gone well enough. With one exception. For some reason, Danny kept shooting her goofy grins when he thought no one else was looking. He didn't even seem to mind if she noticed. In fact, it was her guess that was his intent. She thought it best to let it go for now. But she would talk with him about it later, before the day was over. She sure didn't want it to become a standard part of their morning routine!

The past two days had been uneventful with business as usual. At least as usual as she could expect for it being her first week on the job. Jenny hadn't unexpectedly disappeared again and no more messages had popped up on her car windows. Maybe she shouldn't have washed the Subaru the next day. Maybe if she'd left some dust on it... She chuckled. Too bad! Her car wasn't built to be someone else's memo pad!

"You look lost in thought." Bev was standing in the doorway, looking at her, a bemused expression on her aging face. "If you heard a good joke, now is the time to share it! My water pump is on the fritz and my plumber says he won't have the parts to get it going again until tomorrow afternoon."

Savannah had learned from Bev when she'd interviewed that the sexagenarian was a widow and lived alone. Savannah was no plumber but she knew enough to realize that a broken water pump meant no water. No water for cooking, bathing, drinking, or even toilets. For anyone—man or woman—that was uncomfortable! Of course, Bev could weather it and would do so with a smile. But Bev was not only a co-worker and valuable member of the staff, Savannah considered the older woman a friend.

"I have something better than a joke for you." Savannah put on her best no-nonsense face. "I'd like you to be my guest for both dinner and breakfast. I've got two extra bedrooms and some stir-fry I've been dying to make but need someone to share it with."

Bev couldn't help but be touched by the younger woman's sincerity. Sure, she could manage without fresh water for twenty-four hours. She'd done so and more on occasion over the course of her sixty-five years. But she sensed she should accept. Not so much for her own sake but for Savannah's. Bev appreciated what she considered God's way of making her sensitive to special opportunities He wanted her to be a part of. At least that was her interpretation of the nudging she was feeling. Besides, stir-fry wasn't something she was inclined to whip up herself. She'd had it a few times and liked it. Here was an opportunity to enjoy both a good meal and the company of a wonderful new friend.

"I'd love to, Savannah. How thoughtful of you to ask! I haven't had stir-fry in quite some time."

"That settles it then," Savannah agreed. She wrote down her address then handed it to Bev. "Here. You gather up the things you need from your place after work and come right over."

They heard the sound of the electronic chime announcing visitors to the welcome center. Bev hurried out to greet them, thanking Savannah as she left and promising not to be long in coming once their workday ended.

Danny was doing routine maintenance on some of the equipment in the complex's main garage when he saw a yellow Honda S2000 pull up to the welcome center, discharging a single passenger while a huge German Shepherd remained in the car. The dog sat in the passenger seat as if he were a human.

Pretty fancy car for hauling a dog around. I wonder what brings him here?

Danny had seen the two before, but only when he was given a job to do somewhere along the east shore of the lake. He'd tried striking up a conversation with the guy once. Seemed friendly enough but distracted, as if his mind were somewhere else. Danny had thrown a stick into the water for the dog, too. The animal hadn't moved a muscle. Just stood there looking at Danny as if he were a trespasser on their private property. He'd mentioned seeing the man to Stanley, demanding to know if the guy had all his marbles. Danny didn't want to be out there working by himself on a remote site and get whacked off by some nut with a killer dog.

Stanley had drilled a look right through him, telling him Jesse Whitestone had more right to wander around the east side of the lake than any of them. He'd let Danny know in no uncertain terms if there were ever a conflict between Danny's work and Jesse's wanderings, Jesse was the clear winner. No questions asked. Did Danny understand?

Yeah, he understood. He understood that Stanley didn't treat him with the respect he deserved. The guy had gotten on his case about mowing in just his shorts, too. Of course, Bev had probably put him up to it. Danny was no dummy. He wasn't anyone's flunky, either. Those two might have seniority but they were ready for the slaughterhouse. One foot from the grave. The way Danny had it figured, it wouldn't take their new boss long to discover the two of them were over the hill and it was time to put fresh blood in charge. He caught a glimpse of himself in the side mirror of one of the pickups. He flashed a wide smile. Yeah, that was it. His calling card. More dazzle than a woman could handle! It might take a couple of weeks but he'd have Savannah eating out of his hand.

He was a pretty good mechanic. Even Stanley said so. If it weren't for the fact the maintenance stuff kept him away from the babes Danny would be happy to spend the greater part of his time in the garage. His tan could hold its own for twenty bucks a month with or without the sun.

He wiped his oily hands on a rag, stealing another look at the yellow Honda. Old Marmaduke was a patient boy, he'd give him that much. The dog had been sitting out there for a while now. As Danny watched, the Shepherd's ears perked up, his head turning in the direction of the welcome center's sprawling porch. Danny followed the animal's gaze. Jesse was coming out the front door, Savannah with him. The two stood on the porch talking for a few minutes before Jesse turned and headed towards his car, a smiling Savannah waving good-bye.

Danny frowned. What was the guy up to? It sure didn't take him long to go from mister-owns-the-east-shore to chumming it up with his new boss! This was something he hadn't counted on.

No problem. He'd just adjust his timetable and accelerate things a bit to compensate.

11

JESSE SLID INTO the driver's seat of the Honda, pulling out his cell phone to check for messages. He'd felt the gentle vibrations of the device contending for his attention while talking with Savannah. He often changed the setting making the smartphone totally mute. That was good enough as he routinely checked his communications. He wasn't about to wear a cyber collar around his neck. He quickly located the guilty email. One of the associates in his consulting firm wanted his input on a proposal for a major defense contractor. Orange Risings had worked with some of their people in Orlando before. It was a great fit if it happened to be a winter project. Not much fun if it was summer, though. Jesse tapped out a brief reply on the on-screen keyboard, noted the time, and stuffed the phone back into the pocket of his jeans.

He looked over at Kai sitting patiently in the passenger seat, looking as pleased as Jesse would have been if he had season tickets on the fifty-yard line to the Giants home games. The dog was a great source of companionship and Jesse continually marveled at the animal's intelligence. He'd read somewhere that German Shepherds were ranked as having the smarts of an average sixteen year old human. Jesse wasn't sure, given the mix of what he saw in the town's population of sixteen year olds, if that was a compliment or not. It could look pretty iffy at times.

"What do you think, Kai? There's still some afternoon left. Shall we head over to the east side of the lake while we're here?"

The Shepherd gave him a look that showed Jesse the dog clearly understood the underlying message: *What do you think, Kai? Shall we go visit Ellen?* Kai barked his consent in his deep canine baritone. He was always ready for whatever Jesse asked of him.

Jesse pulled out of the parking area, following the dirt road leading to the lake's eastern shore. He was intimately familiar with the route and had memorized the pothole pattern. He didn't use the knowledge to take liberties with his speed, only to protect the car's suspension and his dental work. If you let your mind drift you were apt to be brought back to the present with a fierce jolt. No sense in falling into one of the man-made craters if he didn't have to. He planned on parking at the first empty site they came across. He and Kai would walk from there as he preferred to approach the past on foot.

70

The fact he so revered Ellen's memory he was repulsed by the very thought of breaking in on the site of the accident in a motorized vehicle was something Jesse wondered about. Had her memory become his idol? If he understood Christianity right, an idol was anything you worshipped, a false god enjoying a higher place in your affections than God himself. If that were the criteria, Jesse mused, then he had a whole lot of idols in his life. Just about everything carried more weight with him than God. If God wanted top billing in Jesse Whitestone's life He should have done a better job of watching over Mrs. Whitestone.

Jesse could feel the muscles in his hands contracting, his grip on the steering wheel as tight as his pain was deep. He would gladly rip the steering wheel right off if it weren't for the fact that it was a part of... *her* car. And Ellen had loved this little yellow car. "Zoom, zoom!" she'd purr, whenever she slid her lithe body into the driver's seat, motioning him around to the other side. Jesse reminded her once that the phrase was used by a competitor, not Honda, in their commercials. Ellen had shot him one of her patented looks. Could she help it if someone had deliberately bugged their garage, stolen her trademark phrase and stuffed it into some mystical little boy who whispered the words as one of their slow-as-a-turtle cars flashed by on the television screen? Don't get me going, she'd warned him, or she'd go after them for identity theft.

That was always the way it was when he came to the lake and got close to the site where they had spent their last moments together. The memories lined up and went on parade and he couldn't for the life of him figure out if they did it to comfort or torment him.

The very first site was occupied by some folks from out of town. There were Maine tags on their minivan, anyway. They looked like a couple in their late twenties or early thirties with a toddler and one even younger. The father was getting ready to fire up a portable grill, the mother splashing around in the shallows with the toddler, the infant cradled in her arms. Jesse throttled an urge to yell at the guy and tell him to be sure to keep his wife and kids out of the water.

He parked two sites beyond the Maine family. He didn't want them to get spooked by some guy parking his car right next to them then hoofing it further up the lake with his dog.

At this time of the year, unless it was raining, the days all seemed pretty much alike. Some days you could have a blazing sun without a cloud in the sky. But those days were rare. After all, the Adirondacks wasn't Arizona. Most of the time the sky presented you with an assortment of cloud types and patterns, keeping you guessing. But the smell of the North Country never changed. Earth and pine were the core ingredients with varied flavorings contributed by the bushes and wildflowers according to their season. Jesse drew in a deep breath and held it, allowing the pores of his soul to soak in the familiar odors. He couldn't imagine anything his spirit appreciated more than long draughts of Adirondack air.

Jesse headed up the road, Kai walking dutifully by his side. It didn't take long before they arrived at the site.

After spending a few minutes at the water's edge, looking out across the wide expanse of the lake, he turned, walked to the picnic table and sat down, all the while keeping one eye on Kai. The dog was sensitive to Jesse's moods and, staying close while not being underfoot, settled himself a couple yards away, panting lightly in the afternoon heat.

As Jesse sat, he found thoughts of Savannah floating into his field of consciousness. It surprised him, but only a little. Savannah was gaining prominence in his mental life. Seeing her again that afternoon had only reinforced his opinion there was something special about her. Strange he thought, as he sat watching a chipmunk gathering up the crumbs of some visitor's wayward hot dog bun, how Stillman's Lake was the common ground between Ellen and Savannah. It was as if the lake were trying to make amends for taking Ellen by offering Savannah.

Jesse shook his head. That was nonsense! The lake was full of water. H_2O. There were no brain cells in that molecular structure. No nerve endings that cared one way or another how he felt. Life had as many odd coincidences about it as it did things that made no sense at all. Savannah's being here was pure luck of the draw.

He looked at Kai, wondering what it would be like to live such an uncomplicated life. Might not be too bad if you had the right owner. Eat. Sleep. Play. Not a lot of variation but, then again, the simpler the life the less chance of a glitch in the works. If you were a dog, your quality of life hung on the one who shelled out the cash for you when you were a puppy. If it happened to be someone who knew what they were doing and had done their homework, chances were it would work out well for both parties. If it were a spur of the moment emotional whim you'd better watch out! Lose your adorable puppy looks and you might find yourself knowing a lot more about the inside workings of the local animal shelter than you ever wanted to know! After thinking about it, Jesse was glad he was the human and Kai the dog. For them, it worked out fine.

He got to his feet. "Come on, Kai. Let's get back to the car and head home. I think we might have some leftover barbecue we can heat up for supper."

Kai sat looking at him.

"What's up, big guy? Let's go!"

The dog didn't move.

Jesse frowned. This wasn't normal. Kai was always eager to please and if the Shepherd wasn't moving he likely had a good reason. The message on Savannah's car window flashed through his mind. *Follow the dog.* At the moment, Kai didn't look to be going anywhere. He was just sitting. In fact, it almost looked like he was staring at something, his dark face a picture of canine concentration.

Jesse tried to adjust his own line of sight to match Kai's by kneeling beside him, placing his head next to Kai's. His breathing slowed as he strained to detect what it was that so arrested Kai's attention. He could feel the dog's rib cage slowly expanding and contracting against his side. The summer air was still, the humidity on the rise. He could feel beads of perspiration forming on his forehead. In the stillness, the rhythmic lapping of lake water became amplified as it made contact with the shoreline.

And then he saw it.

He was sure both he and Kai were concentrating their attention on the same object. It was about twenty yards out and covered with moss on its northern flank. A boulder. The same massive rock whose base he remembered seeing Kai sniffing around just before he'd lost track of him the day his dew claw had been painted.

Okay, now what?

As if reading his mind, Kai began moving forward in the direction of the boulder.

Follow the dog...

Okay, he'd bite.

He followed Kai. His guess was right on the money. The Shepherd led him up to the boulder before changing direction and moving slowly to the right, working his way around the monolith, his keen nose held aloft as if feeling his way by scent alone. Jesse stayed close, his left hand in contact with the boulder. The rough surface was warm to the touch even though the area was well shaded by surrounding hemlocks. Jesse was puzzled by the contradiction.

They had traveled nearly half-way around the boulder when Jesse's hand felt the beginning of a fissure his eyes detected at the same time. The fissure started about four feet up from the base and sloped down, looking like an inverted V. It was apparently deep, too. Too deep for either his eyes or hand to probe its depth. Jesse felt Kai brush against his leg. "Stay!" He hissed the command but knew it would be useless. Ducking his head, he squeezed through the narrow opening and followed.

12

SAVANNAH LOOKED UP to find Danny standing in her office doorway, his familiar smile replaced by a look of mild concern. She put down the report she was reading.

"What's the matter, Danny?"

"It's your car, Savannah. There's a problem."

"There's a problem with my car? What kind of problem?" There was a hint of apprehension in her voice.

Seeing her pushing back her chair, Danny raised a calming hand. "You don't need to worry. It's just a flat tire. We've got everything we need to fix it right in the garage. We get flats around here all the time." His look of concern changed into a reassuring smile.

As if anticipating her objection, he quickly added, "And if you're thinking it isn't right to use the complex's resources to fix a tire on your personal car, don't worry. Like I said, flats happen a lot here because of the nature of the place. Folks get careless and all sorts of things get left on our roads, some of them sharp enough to put a hole in something. Most of the time it's a tire on one of our own pieces of equipment. Sometimes, though, a visitor gets a flat. As a courtesy, we repair it for them whenever we can. It actually ends up being safer than having them mount their spare. It's great for goodwill, too. But, if it will make you feel any better, we accept contributions. A lot of the guests insist on giving us something for our trouble. Usually five or ten bucks. Bev puts it in the petty cash fund."

Danny turned up the wattage to his smile. "All I need is your car keys so I can get to your jack and lug wrench." He glanced at the wall clock. "It's quarter of four. I can't guarantee I'll have it done by the time we close up but, if not, it won't be much longer."

Savannah was caught off guard. Engrossed in her work and distracted by Jesse's visit, she'd forgotten all about her plan to talk with Danny about his behavior in the morning's meeting. Now, here he was standing right in front of her offering to fix her flat tire. Her instincts told her she should thank him but decline his help and go out and put on the spare herself. The problem was, with her commitment to Bev for dinner and

75

overnight lodging, she really needed to get home as quickly as possible. Against her better judgment, she found herself grabbing her purse and tossing Danny the keys.

"Thanks, Danny. I appreciate your help. Bev has plumbing problems at her house that won't get fixed until tomorrow so she's staying with me for the night. I need to be able to get home and get things ready for her."

Danny caught the keys in one hand and gave her a wink. "Like I said, it won't take long."

Walking to Savannah's car, Danny pressed the button on the key fob, unlocking the hatch. Retrieving the lug wrench and jack, he went to work and had the front passenger tire off and into the garage in no time.

The tire was, indeed, flat. That had been easy enough for him to engineer. No need to put a hole in a perfectly good tire. He'd simply unscrewed the valve stem cap and removed the guts of the valve with the small tool he carried. It came in handy if one of the babes he had his eye on was playing hard to get. He found they most always accepted his help when their car was disabled.

Catching women off guard was part of his strategy. They had to make a split-second decision. If they said no, they would feel like they had offended someone who simply wanted to be a good Samaritan and lend them a hand.

In the case of single women, he made sure they stuck around while he did the repairs—or what he made look like a repair. When he needed to, he would turn his back towards them, blocking them from seeing what he was really doing. Worked every time. If they were naïve enough to ask him what they could do to thank him, he suggested an early dinner or some ice cream at a drive-in down the road. The way Danny saw it, there wasn't a member of the opposite sex alive that could resist his brand of mojo if he had an hour with her alone. It was just one of the laws of nature. Like gravity.

In Savannah's case, what he was really after was her keys. Two in particular: the key to the welcome center and her house key.

There were only four keys on the ring. The one for the Subaru was easy. There was another key stamped U.S.P.S. That was easy, too. It was either the key to the post office box the complex had down at the Post Office or to

Savannah's own box. That left only two keys. Chances were good that at least one, if not both, were what he was looking for.

He glanced at his cell phone. Four-twelve. The welcome center closed at four with the staff leaving at four-thirty. He didn't have a lot of time.

Danny walked over to a machine mounted on the bench. The complex had locks all over the place and had found it helpful to be able to make their own replacement keys. They'd bought the duplicating machine years ago and, although it was Stanley who made any spare keys, Danny had taught himself how to work the thing. It was actually pretty simple. Almost foolproof. Put the original in the holder on one side and the proper blank into the one opposite. Then it was pretty much a case of tracing the notches of the original with a guide, letting a cutting wheel etch an exact match in the blank.

He found the blanks he needed and went to work, the grinding noise from the machine unwelcome but unavoidable. He finished one key and began working on the other. Another minute and he'd be…

"What's going on, Danny?" It was more of a challenge than a question. Danny didn't have to turn around to know the voice belonged to Stanley. *Great! Will this guy ever learn to keep his nose out of my business?* He kept his head down, continuing the cut.

"Just finishing up here, Stanley. I broke a key off in the door of the old Dodge. I know! You warned me not to lock the pickup's door because we'd likely break a key just trying to get back in."

There, he was finished. Now if the old geezer would only swallow the bluff. Danny turned to face the older man.

"I'm sorry, Stanley. I was embarrassed. I should have listened to you and I didn't. I thought I could make a duplicate key before you knew about it and chewed me out." He noticed Stanley's eyes shoot to the machine and anticipated the next question.

"I've watched you make keys lots of times. It didn't look like there was much to it. You said so yourself. You said as long as you got the right blank and took the time to set things up properly it was a no-brainer." Danny shot him a grin. "You were right. See!" He held up a shiny new key.

Danny held his breath. This was the tricky part. From across the garage, Stanley wouldn't be able to tell if the key was to the Dodge or any one of the other gazillion locks in the world.

It sounded plausible but Stanley was still suspicious. He'd seen enough of how Danny operated in the two years the younger man had worked there to make him regret hiring him in the first place. Stanley had been on his way into the welcome center to catch Savannah before she headed home. He needed to talk to her. The sound of the cutting wheel had caught his attention as he walked by the garage and he had thought it best to take a look. But if he didn't get to the office quickly, he might miss her. He gave a parting grunt and left.

Danny felt a thrill shoot through his entire body. He was glad Stanley had shown up. Confrontation was exciting and produced an exhilarating rush. He was looking forward to the challenges he knew lie ahead.

Savannah shut off her computer and gathered up her things. Bev had left about twenty minutes ago, telling her it would take her about an hour to go home, pack the few things she needed, and get to Savannah's. She didn't know if chocolate chip cookies went with stir-fry but she had made a batch yesterday for the neighborhood kids and would bring what was left with her. Savannah assured her that, in her book of menu planning etiquette, chocolate chip cookies went with everything.

Stanley had stopped in for a few minutes, too, to let her know he'd talked with a young family from Maine that had been picnicking out on the east shore. They'd assured him they had had a wonderful time but were concerned about the amount of litter they encountered at their site. It was such a nice one they considered the ten minutes it had taken them to tidy up a good investment. As a lot of the trash consisted of beer cans of a brand noted for its low price, they wondered if it might have come from a previous night's outing by thoughtless party-goers. They didn't want to get anyone in trouble but they thought it best to let the staff know. Stanley had thanked them and apologized, assuring them that it wasn't the norm and he would be looking into it. He had suggested to Savannah they call the Sheriff's department so they would be sure to include the east side of the lake in tonight's patrol. Just to be on the safe side.

Stanley had left at the same time as Bev, leaving Savannah to lock up. They were used to her being the last one out. The two of them were so engrossed in conversation about plumbing, and water pumps in particular, that neither noticed Danny. He had finished putting air into Savannah's tire after restoring the valve stem to working condition and was tightening the last of the lug nuts when the two came out of the welcome center. He ducked low as they walked to their cars. They never saw him.

Savannah exited a few minutes later. Reaching for her keys to lock the door she remembered she'd given them to Danny who, she hoped, was close to being done with her car. She looked across the pavement to where she'd parked, relieved to see the young man stowing the jack back inside the Subaru. She walked over, anxious to be on her way.

"Everything go all right?"

Danny shut the hatch. "Fine. It was a really small hole." He held up a tiny finishing nail he'd grabbed from the carpenter shop. "I can say with complete confidence your tire is as good as it was yesterday." He couldn't resist the irony.

"Here's your keys." He held her keys close to his chest, holding the ring by the electronic fob so the keys dangled straight down. He was all smiles.

Savannah regretted taking Danny up on his offer. He was manipulating her. Forcing her to come the distance between them to get her keys. She went no further than she had to, closing the gap by reaching the full length of her arm, plucking the keys from his hand, her eyes meeting his with intentional coolness. She would definitely be making a conversation with Danny one of tomorrow morning's top priorities. For now, all she wanted to do was leave as quickly as she could.

She chose her words carefully, aiming for neutrality. "Thanks, Danny. I'm glad to have the tire fixed."

"Here, let me get the door for you, Savannah." Before she could react, Danny had his hand on the handle, opening her door, still flashing his megawatt smile.

Savannah hesitated for a moment, their eyes briefly connecting. And in that momentary connection she thought she saw a flash of taunting laughter leering at her from somewhere inside his brown eyes, sending a chill down her spine.

Danny stood in the empty parking lot watching Savannah drive away, a smirk pasted across his face. Reaching in his pocket he took out an empty key ring, patiently loading it with two shiny new keys. When he was done he held the ring between his thumb and forefinger, raising it to the height of his eye, gently rocking the keys back and forth across the fading image of the Subaru carrying what he considered one of the hottest babes he'd ever seen.

13

BEV ARRIVED AT Savannah's and the two were soon sharing stories about their families and life outside of work. Bev had never traveled west of the Mississippi and enjoyed hearing about the younger woman's growing up as an only child. With a whopping eight brothers and sisters, Bev couldn't imagine what it would have been like. "Weren't you lonely?" she wondered.

Savannah shook her head. "No, not really. I guess if you never had any siblings to begin with it's hard to miss them. My parents spent a lot of time with me. We were always doing things together. My father was a lawyer, the public defender variety. My mom looked after me and the house. I was lucky to have her all to myself."

"Will you do the same when you have children of your own?" Bev asked. "It seems to me there's a lot of pressure placed on women today to stay on the job, children or not."

"I think you're right," Savannah answered, adding teriyaki sauce to the stir-fry. "As a professional woman, I'm attracted to a career. Yet I'm glad my mom chose to stay home even after I started school. It was comforting knowing she was there. In today's world, I think the pressure has as much to do with the economics of supporting a family as anything else." She finished the stir-fry, dividing the contents of the wok onto two plates. "Thankfully, it's not a question I have to face right away—although I admit I've thought about it.

"I think I'd be torn. On the one hand, I love my work and like being around other people who are working as a team in pursuit of solid objectives that can be defined and measured. On the other hand, I realize how special it made me feel to have my mom around. I can't imagine how differently I might have turned out apart from that wonderfully nurturing and supportive environment that was so full of love." She shrugged as she took a seat at a small bistro-style table across from Bev. "I guess I'll just have to work it out together with my husband if and when that day arrives."

Bev asked if Savannah minded her praying aloud before they ate. After gaining her consent, Bev asked the Lord to bless the food and their evening together.

81

Taking a bite of stir-fry, Bev pronounced it to be a refreshing change from her usual fare, saying she guessed a person could get into a cooking rut of sorts if they lived alone long enough.

The two friends continued talking along the lines of their earlier theme, with Savannah fascinated at Bev's tales of her early years at Stillman's Lake. The older woman had given her an overview of the history of the complex when she'd first interviewed but now they had the leisure to explore in greater depth, with the meaning of each story enriched by Savannah's own growing familiarity with the complex. As Bev shared, Savannah could picture it in her mind, tying the story to its particular geographic setting. Through Bev's reminisces, Stillman's Lake took on the personality of a maturing child; noisy and undisciplined at birth but growing in beauty and composure as the years passed with an increasing ability to give back in return for the care shown it.

"It sounds to me like Stillman's Lake has an enviable history," Savannah summarized. "It's exciting to be a part of its future!"

Bev's silence betrayed the struggle in her mind. Was now the time to tell Savannah about the drowning? Savannah had related to her how much she had enjoyed the outing at Jesse's place. Savannah had even told her the twins were wise to Bev's having put her up to trying to con them out of future barbecue invitations. From the subtle signals Savannah's body language gave off it was Bev's guess she'd had more than just an average good time. Her suspicions were further heightened by the sparkle in Savannah's green eyes when Jesse had shown up at the complex earlier in the day. It was plain to Bev her boss was nursing a growing attraction for the elusive widower. It was about time, too, that Jesse Whitestone took a few steps towards the future instead of having one foot planted in the past. At least, this was Bev's opinion.

"What's the matter, Bev? You've gotten awfully quiet. I hope it isn't the stir-fry!" Savannah joked.

"No, honey, it's not the stir-fry. That was delicious." Bev passed the plate of chocolate chip cookies she'd brought. "It's just that there is a piece of history I need to tell you about. A relatively recent event in the scheme of things but an important one—especially now you've met Jesse."

"How does Jesse fit into it?"

Noting the look of concern appearing on the younger woman's face, Bev hastened on. "Now don't get alarmed, Savannah. Jesse Whitestone is as good as they come! I told you so back when you asked me if I thought it was okay for you to have dinner with him and James." She paused, gathering her thoughts. "It has to do with Jesse and his wife, Ellen." She handed Savannah another cookie. "You munch on this while I tell you about it."

It took Savannah two more cookies before Bev finished the story of Ellen's drowning. Normally, Savannah was careful about her intake of sweets. But this warranted an extra dose of comfort food.

Jesse's frequent visits to the complex, and the eastern shore in particular, were now cast in their rightful context. One that flooded Savannah's sympathetic heart with compassion. How awful! She couldn't imagine how she would cope with such grief. Bev had done a good job of filling her in on Jesse and Ellen's relationship and how easy it had been for everyone to see how deeply in love the two were.

"I wouldn't want you to get the idea their marriage was perfect," Bev warned. "It wasn't. No one's is and no marriage ever will be. They had their differences and occasional spats. But there was still something special about the two of them, that's for sure. Maybe that's why Jesse's grief runs so deep. He's an incurable romantic! I suppose, as he reflects on the past, he filters out everything except the good stuff. A little out of balance but understandable. He's not sure if people get more than one shot in life at something so special. I think it's one of the reasons he rarely dates. In real life, Ellen was tough competition. In the idyllic version he keeps in his heart's pocket, I didn't think anyone stood a chance. That is," she added, reaching out to take Savannah's hand, "until you came along.

"And don't act so surprised," she admonished, seeing Savannah's face flush. "I'm still woman enough to know when sparks are starting to fly!"

Her expression changed to one more serious. "I've known Jesse since he cast his first fishing line into Stillman's Lake and I count him as one of my dearest friends. There's nothing in the world I wouldn't do for that boy. And you, Savannah," she gave her hand a squeeze, "our friendship is still young and has the interesting twist of you being my boss and all," her faded blue eyes twinkled. "But honey, that's small stuff. I haven't a doubt in the world you're going to become one of my dear ones, too."

Savannah was deeply touched. Bev was special, already endearing herself to Savannah as wise and trustworthy. It was as if she were a surrogate for her mother, so far away in Kansas.

The two of them gathered up the dishes, making short work of the kitchen chores before heading out into the cooler evening comfort of Savannah's screened-in porch. They entered the porch through a doorway off the kitchen. Overhead hung a sign reading, *Welcome to the porch!*

The charm of the room had delivered the impact the realtor hoped for, chasing away out of Savannah's mind any residual hesitation about buying the house. She could picture herself spending countless hours within its generous proportions, reading and entertaining family and friends. Jenny enjoyed it, too, alternating between spending time on the porch near Savannah and exploring the fenced-in backyard of over an acre. She and Bev would have eaten their dinner on the porch but Savannah hadn't yet purchased the casual dining set she had in mind.

The two women alternated between talking and simply relaxing, with Savannah browsing through a trade magazine and Bev excusing herself before returning with a large, much-used Bible in her hand. She settled herself in a comfortable lounge chair and, minutes later when Savannah looked, appeared to be engrossed in whatever it was she was reading, a faint smile playing across the lips of the elderly woman. Savannah noted how tenderly Bev handled the worn tome. Savannah chalked it up to the era in which Bev had been born, thinking she was probably raised at a time when going to church every Sunday was the norm. She suddenly realized that she herself had been brought up in a family that went to church every Sunday, each time sitting in the same seats in the same pew.

Savannah found the whole church thing rather boring and couldn't see where it connected with life in today's world. Looking back, it struck her more as a social club, a place where people connected and spent time together like the V.F.W. or Moose Lodge. With all the technology people had at their fingertips now, you could accomplish the same thing through the many social media sites. Except for the food. She could still remember the smell of potluck dinners with folks bringing enough food to feed an army! She supposed sharing the leftovers with their neighbors had been part of the attraction. She wondered how this gentle, gray-haired woman beside her reconciled the tragedy of Ellen's drowning with a supposedly loving God.

She decided to ask. "Bev, I'm sorry to interrupt your reading but I have a question." She hesitated. "About God. Do you mind?"

Bev looked up and smiled. "Of course not."

"Jesse Whitestone is a friend of yours, right?"

Bev peered at her over the top of her reading glasses. "I thought your question was about God."

"It is, but it concerns Jesse. Ellen, too."

"Like I said earlier, Savannah, I consider Jesse one of my dearest friends."

"Did you consider his wife a friend, too?"

"I sure did." Bev's countenance took on the expression of someone leafing through pages of fond memories. "They used to invite me over for dinner once or twice a month. I imagine, having been to Jesse's, you've seen the yellow brick road?"

Savannah nodded. "I have. So then, did you consider Ellen to be a good person?"

"It depends on what you mean by good." Bev's eyes sparkled with intrigue. "If you're asking me how Ellen stacked up against what folks usually think of as good, then yes, I'd say she was a good person."

"Isn't that what it means to be a good person?" Savannah had the suspicion there was more. "That you're someone who is kind and considerate to others, treating them fairly and being concerned with their welfare?"

"That's a start."

"What else is there?"

Bev thought for a moment. "I doubt we've touched on the question you first wanted to ask me about God. I have a guess as to what it is. But even though we may be taking a detour, I think it's a helpful one.

"There are different ways of measuring things, Savannah. If we use purely human standards for determining what makes something good we can run into trouble. Society's standards can be fickle. Take entertainment," she went on. "What passes for good entertainment today would have shocked

85

most folks fifty years ago." She winced. "The same could be said for music. The point I'm getting at is that God took the time to tell us what *He* means by good." She tapped the open book in her lap. "It's a standard that doesn't move around with the shifting winds of changing times. It's like the North Star. It serves as a fixed point and can be counted on for safely navigating through the rockiest waters life can throw at you."

Savannah pressed on. "So, if you measure Ellen by God's standard, was she a good person?"

Bev met her gaze. She appreciated the younger woman's sincerity. "I don't know. God does, though."

She could tell by Savannah's expression her answer left the younger woman dissatisfied.

"Savannah, honey, it isn't my job to go around judging others. Sure, I can make judgments about their behavior and if what they're doing is good or bad. But when it comes to the person and the motives behind the behavior, that's another story. That's God's business, not mine. He's the only one who can look under the covers and see what's in their heart."

Bev's eyes softened. "In the Bible, there's an interesting story about a rich young ruler who came to Jesus asking Him how he could have eternal life. I think it was his way of asking Jesus if he was a good man."

"And what did Jesus say?"

"Jesus pointed to some of the ten commandments."

"And?"

"Well, the young man claimed he'd kept those commandments."

"What happened next?" Savannah was curious.

"Jesus told him to sell everything he had, give it to the poor, and then follow Him."

"That must have been a shock. Sounds pretty extreme! Did he do it?"

"No, he didn't. He was wealthy and maybe he thought his riches would keep him safer in the world than God could.

86

"You see, Jesus could peer into the young man's heart—as only the God who created us can. The young man thought he was good enough to earn his way into heaven. Jesus loved him enough to help him see that God has a different standard for goodness. In fact, Jesus told him, 'No one is good except God alone'.

"My point, Savannah, is that Ellen, Jesse, you, me—we're all in the same boat as this young man in the Bible story. We may do some good things as measured by society's standard, but if only God is truly good, we're not. Not by ourselves, anyway."

She noted Savannah's bewilderment and chuckled. "Don't you worry. I know it's a lot to take in and it leads to a bunch more questions. And we haven't even gotten to your original question yet! The one you were going to ask before we developed a case of cerebral popcorn and headed down the rabbit trail we've just been on!"

Savannah giggled. "Cerebral popcorn? I never heard that expression before!" She tossed her magazine aside and got up to open the screen door to let Jenny in. Her head was swimming. She needed time to sort through what Bev had already said before taking the conversation farther. She decided to change the subject.

"Speaking of popcorn, why don't we make a batch and watch a movie. I'm a big fan of the classics and I'm sure we can find something we'd both enjoy."

"I'd like that," Bev replied. She would have liked it even more if they had continued talking about God but she'd long recognized the value of patience when dealing with such an important topic.

At Savannah's invitation, Bev looked through her collection of DVDs while Savannah made popcorn in a big pot with a lid and crank especially made for popping corn. Savannah had bought it at a restaurant offering a vintage theme and loved it. In her opinion, it made better tasting popcorn that was less expensive to boot.

They settled on *The Philadelphia Story*, a 1940 film adaptation of a play by Philip Barry. The film starred Cary Grant, Katherine Hepburn, and Jimmy Stewart—favorites of both women. They spent the next two hours munching on popcorn, enjoying the film's witty comedy.

When the movie was over, Savannah led the way to the guest room. It was attractively appointed with a bathroom of its own. Bev thanked her, telling her again how much she had enjoyed the evening. Savannah gave her a warm hug before heading off to her own room, Jenny padding silently behind.

Savannah was startled into wakefulness by the insistent ringing of the telephone on the stand beside her bed, the caller ID showing it coming from the county sheriff. The amber glow of the nearby clock read 1:47 AM. She groped for the receiver. "Yes?" Savannah struggled to shake the sleep from her head.

A woman's voice floated into her ear. "This is Sergeant Wilson. I'm the duty officer here at the county sheriff's. We have this phone number as the one to call in the event of an off-hours emergency at the Stillman's Lake recreational complex."

"Yes, that's right. I'm Savannah Garret, the director. Is there a problem?"

"We're not sure. Our patrol reported finding a vehicle seemingly abandoned inside the complex."

"What do you mean, abandoned? What kind of vehicle? Where?" Savannah was now wide awake.

"The officer spotted the vehicle at a site on the east side of the lake. He's searched both the immediate and surrounding area and can't find anyone. We've checked the registration to determine the owner. It's a convertible. A yellow Honda registered to a Jesse Whitestone."

14

IT TOOK A while for his eyes to adjust to the darkness and, in the meantime, Jesse thought it best to take as much non-visual stock of his surroundings as he could. Instinctively, on entering the fissure, he had extended his right arm in front of him, pushing it into the darkness as a substitute for his loss of sight while keeping his left hand in contact with what rock served for interior wall.

"Kai, you in here, boy?" His voice sounded dead, as if the walls had sucked the moving molecules of sound from the air.

There was no response. He neither heard Kai nor felt him as he knelt, still groping, in the darkness. He stayed absolutely still, focusing his attention on what his ears might bring him.

Silence. Complete and utter *silence*. The total absence of sound. He doubted Kai was here.

He felt the floor, surprised to find it wasn't dirt. It felt like stone, similar to the surface of the wall yet different. He'd assumed it would be earthen. He thought it strange, too, his eyes didn't seem to be getting accustomed to the darkness. Sure, he'd expected it to be darker inside, but certainly the entrance to the fissure would let more light in than this.

Turning around, Jesse kept his right hand in contact with the wall instead of his left. He wasn't about to lose all sense of orientation if he could help it. Although he was certain he hadn't taken any more than a few steps since entering, he could see no opening through which he might have come. Blackness was everywhere. He raised a hand above his head, rising slowly, reaching up in an effort to make contact with whatever amounted to the ceiling. Nothing. He stretched as high overhead as he could but his searching fingers found nothing but air.

He thought about jumping. Could be risky, he supposed. Unless he jumped in small increments of increasing height. The last thing he wanted was to knock himself out banging his head on a rocky ceiling!

It was more awkward than he supposed. Absent of any reference points because of the darkness and with every noise swallowed up the moment it was born, he imagined the exercise would make for great comedy if posted online. He was relieved, though, at having the thought. It helped slow the mounting tension.

After six or so attempts without success he threw caution to the wind and jumped for all he was worth. He was six-two. He figured if he added an additional three to four feet for his combined jumping and reach, he had been somewhere in the ten foot range without coming into contact with anything.

Jesse tried to conjure up an image of the boulder from the outside and guessed it was possible it was more than ten feet in height. But it couldn't be too much more than that. He thought he remembered, as he'd approached the monolith with Kai, that he could see over the top. But maybe he was wrong or it was an illusion created by the differing height of the surface he was standing on at the time. The idea came to him to start at the wall and trace upwards. He'd at least be able to tell how far up the wall went before it began slanting towards the horizontal.

The results of this experiment was surprising, too. No matter where on the wall he chose, or how high up he followed it, he couldn't detect the slightest variation from vertical.

He didn't know how long he'd been inside whatever it was he was inside of but he figured it couldn't have been more than ten or fifteen minutes. And at this rate, ten or fifteen minutes was long enough. True, he couldn't see where he'd come in and that nagged at him, but maybe there was a rational explanation. Anyway, the boulder was relatively round and of a finite size. As long as he kept contact with the outside wall, common sense told him he could travel around the perimeter and, in so doing, would inevitably find the fissure and his way back out.

Things had proven crazy enough, though, to convince him to take precautions. Like placing something on the floor to serve as a marker for his starting point in case he couldn't find the way out. He wouldn't want to either think he'd gone all the way around and hadn't nor continue to go round and round wondering if he'd gone far enough. One complete circle would suffice. All right, he told himself, two if he had to. Just to be sure.

He'd done some search and rescue training with Kai. Although never called out, it was something they both enjoyed. They had trained with others in environments simulating conditions commonly encountered in search and rescue. He was glad they had, as he told himself to think of his present situation as just another training exercise. It helped, but it would have helped a lot more if Kai were with him.

He thought about using one of his sandals for a marker but decided against it. If he found the exit, he didn't want to have to spend time retrieving footwear. He'd had enough of the place. The biblical story of Jonah in the belly of the big fish came to mind and made him chuckle. It was another good stress reliever. He could relate. Now if he could just get the boulder to cough him up he'd be fine. He recalled how, in Jonah's story, the fish vomited Jonah out. Jesse preferred a more sanitary exit.

Searching his pockets, all he could come up with was some change and his wallet. Usually, he carried his phone with him but he'd taken it out of his jeans, stashing it in the console of the Honda before getting out of the car. It was habit. He'd drowned two smartphones by fooling around with Kai near water. Besides, using either the phone or the wallet as a marker was worse than a sandal. In the end, he opted for his shirt. He carried another in the car so it wouldn't be a big deal to leave it behind. Maybe a thousand years from now someone else would stumble into the place and find it. He hoped they were smart enough to bring a flashlight.

Taking off his shirt and placing it on the floor, Jesse was careful to position the shirt where the floor met the wall, stretching the fabric out as far as it would go towards what he hoped was the center of the cavern. Then he began, dropping and going forward on all fours so he would be sure not to miss either the way out or his marker. If things went the way he hoped, his shirt was a goner.

The time it took for a single pass felt like an eternity but couldn't have been more than a few minutes before Jesse's hand came into unwelcome contact with his shirt. He assumed he had been going in a circle. But in the pitch dark he couldn't be sure. He couldn't tell if he was going in a circle, a straight line, or zigzagging around like a lunatic. It gave him a real appreciation for reference points: sights, smells, sounds—anything he could use his senses to get a fix on. All Jesse had was touch. It was better than nothing but wasn't much by way of a reference.

He circled again. Slower but with the same result. And this time, he thought he heard something. Unfortunately, it was only the near-audible pounding of his heart as whatever state a person experienced prior to panic began kicking in.

The whole experience was so unreal he wondered for a moment if he were dreaming. He'd heard the old adage of pinching yourself to make sure. He felt foolish, but gave himself a hard pinch on the arm anyway. If pain was a reliable indicator he could rule out dreaming. It would have been more a nightmare, anyway. He slumped to the floor, back to the wall.

The last thing Jesse could think to try was a trip away from the sides, attempting to go directly across the floor to the opposite side. He'd been reluctant to lose contact with the wall as it gave him a sense of security. But having yielded no clue as to how to get out, it seemed worth the risk to see if there was anything else in the darkness he might use to get his bearings or, better yet, make his escape. The word *tomb* kept creeping into his mind and, if nothing else, another experiment might help combat his growing alarm.

Without reference points, he wouldn't be surprised if his aim was less than perfect. Either way, he couldn't imagine it taking him more than a few seconds to walk across to the opposite wall.

He took several slow breaths to settle himself then took off, stopping after the first step, reaching behind to assure himself the wall was still there. It was. He moved forward, walking with his arms outstretched in front of him, his stride uncertain. The hindering impact of total darkness on locomotion was amazing!

Even with his wobbling gait, it took less than a dozen strides before his hands connected with what he supposed was the opposite wall. This at least confirmed he hadn't lost his mind, as it was roughly what he would expect—that is, if the whole inside of the boulder were hollow. That it might be possible that the boulder was a large, hollow sphere seemed far-fetched. But how else could he account for the relative spaciousness of the midnight interior around him?

He decided to make another trip across the floor, this time down on his hands and knees so he might be sensitive to any discovery he might make use of by way of touch. Besides, walking without the benefit of at least touching the wall proved a challenge to his sense of balance. Better to become a human ant for a time.

He began creeping slowly forward, concentrating his attention on every morsel of sensory data generated by his fingertips. The floor struck him as being perfectly level, a textured, unbroken expanse of rock-like flooring. It was unnerving.

What's this?

His hand detected a change. A round object the size of a Frisbee in the floor. The sphere was inlaid, rising above the floor's surface by what he guessed to be no more than a quarter inch. Enough to where he could detect its presence by touch but not enough to have caused him to trip if he had walked into or, rather, on it.

As his fingers tried to interpret what the sphere might be or its purpose, he found what appeared to him a circular pattern radiating out from the object, narrow at first then widening as it went along. He decided the sphere made, if nothing else, a useful reference and might even serve as the center of the cavity holding him prisoner.

The thought he might be trapped was one he had held at bay until now. But having examined so much of what he had initially supposed to be a shallow fissure, only to find himself in the blackest of hemispheres with no apparent way out, demanded recognition. By this time, he might have been inside for an hour. Maybe more. It was hard to orient oneself spatially and even chronologically. Without fixed points and some sort of visible movement of *something*, he might as well be frozen in a block of ice.

Jesse decided to stand. Or at least make the attempt. On the perimeter, he'd used the wall to steady himself. Out here in no-man's-land, something so simple took on different challenges. He straightened but lost his balance momentarily, taking a step to keep himself from falling.

He was instantly bathed in an atmosphere of soft light. It was nearly blinding at first, given the amount of time he'd spent in total darkness, and it took his eyes several moments before he was able to gain anything recognizable from their use.

Once he could see, he let out a gasp. It made about as much sense as the most outlandish fantasy movie he'd ever seen. Fear growled inside of him like a living beast. But the fear had nothing to do with the objects themselves. It was simply that they had no business being in his vision at all. Not here inside a rock.

A swirl of bright yellow caught his attention. He looked down. To his utter amazement, he found himself looking at what appeared to him to be a replica of the yellow brick road from the *Wizard of Oz*. There it was, a bright yellow swirl issuing out from the gray orb he'd discovered with his hands at its center, the gray border continuing to follow along the sides of the ever-

93

widening curve of yellow, with red brick being the complementary color in the gaps between the swirls. Of course! It was the circular pattern his fingers had traced earlier. What in the world was something like this doing here?

He could sense the light steadily increasing in intensity then holding at a comfortable level. His gaze returned to the objects that had originally captured his attention.

Just off the center of the floor, at about the point where the curve of the yellow brick began to curl back on itself, there was what appeared to be either an exact replica of his favorite overstuffed chair from the library of his home or its identical twin. Next to it was a round pedestal stand. And on the stand, what looked like a black, leather bound book.

Jesse stayed where he was, doing his best to get his heartbeat lowered back to something less than a hundred. This was the stuff of fantasy novels!

He looked up, expecting to see some kind of overhead lighting system. All that greeted his anxious eyes was a dark expanse whose height was wholly indiscernible. Try as he might, he could not identify the source of the light.

A thought came to him. He pressed down on the gray disc at the center of the yellow brick road. The light began to fade. He quickly pressed again. He'd had enough of the darkness. The light reversed itself, returning to its previous level.

This is crazy! Did I hit my head on the way in and all of this is some weird hallucination? Some figment of my concussed imagination?

The chair looked inviting and he needed to sit down. He might as well. He'd already looked around for a door or exit of any kind. There was nothing but unbroken stone wall surrounding him on every side.

Jesse walked over to the chair and sat down. His body fit into contours matching those of his chair at home. He glanced at the book. It was a small book with black leather covers. And on the front cover was a single word: *Portals*. Holding the book in his hand he tried to figure out what color or material comprised the lettering of the one word title. It was almost as if the letters were the color of fire. Not some stagnant image of fire but something in motion, almost living. It was beautiful.

He opened the book.

94

The first page was blank, but the next bore what appeared to be a handwritten inscription: To Jesse from Tsor. An opportunity to change the past...

It was all Jesse could do to keep some semblance of composure. Who was Tsor? Or, for that matter, *what* was Tsor? It was a pretty weird name. Maybe his friend, Ben, was right and Area 51 was alive and well. Or worse yet, James was right and something supernatural was going on. If it were up to Jesse, he was rooting for aliens.

He turned the page. The content was typeset, like any other book. There was nothing to be done but read. Maybe the book would tell him how to get out of the rock which had swallowed him alive.

> First of all Jesse, I want you to relax. You're not a prisoner and you're not going crazy. You are here because I want to give you a gift. A fantastic gift. Something you've only dreamed of: the power to change the past.

> This power isn't something I can simply hand you. Without proper preparation it would do more harm than good.

> Once you've taken a closer look at this book you'll find that all the pages following this one are blank. This is because you and I will be filling them in as we go along.

Abruptly, Jesse turned to the next page, sure that when he had first flipped through the book, he'd seen page after written page. But now, all those pages were blank.

> He returned to where he'd left off.

> As I was saying, Jesse, before you turned the page to check and see if my words were true...

Jesse's heart began beating like an out of control jack hammer.

> ...we will be filling in the pages of the book together. I'll be providing you with knowledge and instructions and you will be writing down any questions you have.

> That's enough for now, my friend. Just turn the page and you'll find directions for getting out.

Jesse turned the page again. Slowly. The page, which only a moment before had been blank, now contained words.

You get out by following the yellow brick road. Just a small bit of light humor. I thought the road and the chair might make you feel more at ease.

P.S. Time is a funny thing. When you're here with me, time is meaningless. You may find when you leave that, although you feel as though we spent hours together, only a few minutes have passed outside. Or we may be together for only a short time and hours have gone by in the world beyond this room. As Einstein said, "Reality is merely an illusion, albeit a very persistent one..."

15

TSOR WAS AS good as his word and, within moments, Jesse found himself back in familiar settings outside the rock. He'd felt rather foolish imitating Dorothy as he followed the yellow brick road, but it had led to the fissure and the way out. At first, he had looked to see where the yellow brick had met the wall and walked over. As it hadn't gained him anything, he'd swallowed his pride and gone along with the instructions verbatim. And sure enough, the reward for his obedience had been the reappearance of the fissure.

Moonlight and twinkling stars greeted him outside. He had no idea what time it was. Or for that matter, what day. Tsor had made it clear time inside the rock might not be the same outside. Nor could he count on the difference being consistent, as if inside the boulder was just another time zone and all he needed to do was add or subtract a certain number of hours. What time or what day was up for grabs. Hopefully, it was either Wednesday night or early Thursday morning.

His next thought was for Kai. He tried calling for him but to no avail. He had followed Kai through the fissure but couldn't say for sure if the dog had been inside with him or had turned around and gone back out before the fissure closed. One thing was certain, this Tsor character had better not have taken Kai hostage. Jesse's jaw tightened. Supernatural or alien, Tsor would have bitten off more than he could chew if he had!

Jesse supposed Kai could be hanging around the car, waiting for him to return. It wasn't likely, though. The Shepherd knew he'd entered the boulder. Once separated, if at all possible, Kai would spend the rest of his life at their point of last contact waiting for Jesse to return. Given the lack of options, Jesse headed back towards where he'd parked the Honda.

It was only a matter of minutes before he saw lights from at least two vehicles in the general vicinity of where he remembered parking. As he drew closer, he recognized one of the vehicles as a cruiser belonging to the county sheriff's department. The other was Savannah's Subaru. His Honda was where he'd left it, its sleek yellow body bathed in the cruiser's headlights. A deputy sheriff talking with a visibly concerned Savannah rounded out the scene. They were peering into Jesse's car, the officer using a flashlight to comb the vehicle's cabin in search of any clues as to its missing owner, the contents of the console storage compartment scattered on the deck behind the driver's seat.

"I hope you're not going to tear my car apart looking for me."

The officer spun around, painting Jesse squarely in the face with his flashlight. Jesse raised his hand in an attempt to fend off the glare.

"Who are you?" The question shot out of the deputy's mouth with practiced precision coupled with a carefully manicured tone of authority.

Savannah was quick to react. "It's all right, officer. That's Jesse... uh, Mr. Whitestone, the owner of the car."

It took Jesse the better part of a half-hour to convince mister flashlight he wasn't some sort of middle-aged peeping tom on the lookout for any teenagers that might be using the place for late night rendezvous of the drugs, sex, or alcohol variety. Not that these were common occurrences at the complex, but all three happened on occasion. Jesse was pretty sure that, without Savannah's speaking up for him and assuring the officer no charges would be filed against Jesse for trespassing, he might have had to spend the night answering more questions at whatever place they took you when they thought your story sounded fishy.

Admittedly, his story *did* sound pretty lame. Jesse claimed he had lost track of his dog and been searching for him for hours. The deputy pointed out he'd been in the area himself for nearly two hours, calling out and looking for the car's owner, and hadn't heard or seen anyone. All Jesse could say was that his hearing wasn't so good and he supposed he'd ranged quite a distance in his search for Kai. He could tell the deputy wasn't buying it but couldn't do anything given Savannah's clear indication no charges would be pressed by the complex. It wasn't in the guy's nature to drop things but he didn't have a choice.

"Okay, Mr. Whitestone, I guess you're free to go home and get some sleep like other *normal* people. I suggest when you do find your dog, you keep him on a leash next time you're out here." The officer snapped off the flashlight, shoving it back into the arsenal of gadgets on his belt before climbing into his cruiser and off to what Jesse supposed was the next major crime scene.

Savannah grabbed Jesse's arm. "Where have you been?"

He could tell by the troubled look in her eyes she hadn't bought for a minute the story he'd laid on the deputy. He took a deep breath. "I'm not sure you're going to believe me when I tell you." Jesse put his hands on her shoulders. "This isn't something I can explain in ten minutes. It's going to take a while. We need to go somewhere and talk."

"It's almost three in the morning, Jesse! Today will be only my fifth day on the job." She shook her head. "As much as I'm dying to know where you've been, I have to go home, get some sleep and be back here in time for the morning meeting.

"Remember me telling you about Bev's plumbing problems and that I had invited her to spend the night at my place? Well, she's there now. She volunteered to stay with Jenny while I came here. The sheriff's department called about an hour ago reporting what looked like an abandoned vehicle. When they told me the make of the car and who it was registered to, I had to come."

Jesse thought he saw a mixture of concern and relief on Savannah's pretty face. He understood if it had been any other vehicle than his, she would have left the matter in the hands of the police and gone back to bed. Yet, because of him, even though their relationship was only days old, she'd come.

He looked at her. She hadn't bothered to put on makeup or fuss with her hair. She had just come. To Jesse, she couldn't look lovelier. Savannah had a natural beauty that didn't need cosmetic embellishment. Her blonde hair, even in disarray, looked great with its short sweeping cut across her forehead before being tucked behind an ear. She had a delicate nose and generous, inviting lips, the green of her eyes visible even in the moonlit night. Reluctantly, Jesse released her shoulders from his grip, savoring the memory of the warm softness of her skin.

Although his first impulse was to talk about what he had experienced *now*, maybe it would be best if he had time to himself to sort through it. As the adrenalin rush subsided, he could feel fatigue's fingers reaching out, dragging him towards sleep.

"Okay, Savannah. I guess it can wait. For a while, anyway."

He had an idea. "Do you think we could meet back here later this afternoon. Say, around 3?" He could see her struggling, torn between

99

wanting to hear him out and her desire to be faithful to her job. Under the circumstances, he decided a nudge in the right direction was called for.

"Look Savannah, what just happened to me took place here at the complex and has a potential bearing on both the staff and the visitors who come here." It was the truth, too. Alien or supernatural creature, this Tsor had power. So far, he hadn't seemed threatening. Quite the opposite. Tsor had taken obvious pains to make Jesse feel as comfortable as possible given the fantastic circumstances. The only nagging concern Jesse had was –

"Kai!"

The big dog was walking towards them from out of the shadows, tail wagging. The Shepherd walked up to Jesse then sat looking up at his master, his intelligent face seeming to convey more knowledge than their common vocabulary would allow. The moment Jesse knelt the animal lifted a paw, resting it on Jesse's thigh.

Jesse and Savannah saw the painted dew claw at the same time.

Savannah's lips parted as she allowed the air in her lungs to escape in a slow stream of silent amazement. Her eyes locked on the now familiar color of Iced Mauve, Savannah uttered her agreement. "You bet. Here at three will be fine."

16

JESSE HEADED FOR home, his body weary but his mind churning. He was trying to sift through his experience and arrange the facts—as fantastic as they were!—in logical order so when he met with Savannah he wouldn't leave anything out.

Now that he was in the car, Kai by his side and the two of them driving along on familiar roads, the entire episode seemed ludicrous. The sort of babble coming out of the mouths of people who were either on drugs or mentally deranged. That it had all taken place, Jesse was certain. Kai's painted nail alone was visible proof strange things were in the air.

If he dismissed all emotion and looked at it logically, Jesse kept coming back to the same conclusion: there were only two possibilities. All joking aside, it had to be either extra-terrestrial beings possessing both intelligence and significant other capabilities or James was right and the supernatural did exist. In either case, the offer on the table was one supposedly giving him the power to change the past.

As to what past, Jesse gathered, given the repeated painting of Kai's nail and the location of the boulder, it had to do with Ellen. Could it possibly mean he could actually change the outcome of that awful day? That if he learned from Tsor and followed his instructions he could, from his relative position here in the future, save his own wife in the past? If it turned out this was truly the offer, Tsor could count him in! There wasn't anything Jesse wouldn't do to erase that day from the history books.

The emotion connected with the possibility of seeing Ellen alive again was overwhelming. He downshifted, bringing the car to a stop on the side of the road. Tears began streaming down his face, accompanied by deep sobs that wracked his body and burst from his lips as anguished, guttural echoes of pain and sorrow reared in the depths of time.

Savannah gratefully took the mug of fresh-brewed coffee from Bev, drinking it as quickly as the dark liquid's temperature would allow and hoping the caffeine kick would jumpstart her brain. The morning meeting was starting in fifteen minutes and Savannah wanted to be at least semi-coherent.

101

After her first cup she felt more awake. She thought back to the night's events. There really wasn't much to process. All she knew was, for some reason, Jesse must have gone to the east side of the lake after saying goodbye to her here at the welcome center. Why he went out to the lake was anybody's guess. Remembering what Bev had shared with her about the drowning incident, Jesse's frequent visits to the lake took on deeper meaning and Savannah supposed he might have gone out to the site of the accident just to... Just to what? *What does a man think about who has lost the woman he loved, the one he welded himself to as his lifelong mate?*

Savannah didn't have the answers. She had lost both sets of grandparents at different times in her life together with a close friend. So she knew something about the loss of a loved one and the sadness of death. But a spouse... that was deep water. Territory she knew nothing about.

The morning meeting proved routine and neither she nor Bev mentioned anything about the night's events. She'd told Bev upon returning home about finding Jesse, together with the story Jesse had told the police about looking for Kai. That the older woman knew better, Savannah saw in her questioning look. But Bev was also wise enough not to press her with questions.

Danny's behavior in the meeting was absent of the mischief of the previous morning's but Savannah knew she needed to follow through on the commitment she had made to herself not to procrastinate in speaking to him. As the meeting ended and the staff dispersed to go about their business, she asked Danny to come into her office.

"How's your car? I hope you don't need me to fix another flat so soon." Danny was relaxed and feeling good about being invited into Savannah's office, casually leaning against a file cabinet, grinning. Savannah could tell he was clueless and wouldn't see it coming. So she tried to be as gentle as possible while still being clear and firm. It wouldn't do to leave any doubt in Danny's mind as to how she felt about his antics.

"Danny, I appreciate your helping me with the flat tire yesterday, but that isn't what I want to talk to you about." She pointed to a chair across from her desk. "Please, have a seat." She kept her voice cordial, wanting neither to offend him unnecessarily nor give him reason to think the matter was anything other than business.

Savannah thought she saw a flicker of doubt drift over Danny's face before he muttered, "Sure," and sat down.

"Danny," she began, "I want to be clear that I look forward to getting to know each and every person on staff, and that includes you. After all, we're a team here and we ought to know enough about one another so we can work together effectively as a team. Over time, it wouldn't be surprising if friendships develop." She saw his face light up and decided she had better qualify her last remark.

"However, any friendships that may arise need to do so out of a mutual respect for one another, and there are limits as to what behavior is appropriate in the workplace. We're all adults and we need to act in a professional manner at all times when on the job.

"Look, Danny," she said, looking squarely at him, "I don't want to offend you, but I also want to be clear so there's no misunderstanding. Your behavior in yesterday morning's meeting crossed the line." She paused before going on. "I'm encouraged it was better today. But I need you to keep to the same level of respect and professionalism you demonstrated the morning of my very first day. Okay?"

She waited for an answer, visibly noting the darkening of his face. She didn't think he was the type to explode right there in her office but you never knew.

As quickly as it had come the shadow disappeared, replaced by his trademark high-voltage smile. "Sure, Savannah. I understand. I guess I got carried away. Youthful enthusiasm and all. It won't happen again and I apologize." He stuck out his hand.

Savannah wished she could end their conversation without a gesture requiring touch. Danny had a real knack for holding the high ground in the unspoken battle she feared was shaping up between them. Yet she was willing to give him the benefit of the doubt. For now, anyway.

Danny headed to the garage, firing up one of the mowers and heading off for a long day of cutting grass. He'd made his usual morning stop at a local bakery on the way in. He liked Bev's coffee but he also liked his coffee with a donut or two. Once a week, he even brought in a dozen to share with the rest of the staff. On this particular morning, Danny had run

103

into one of his drinking buddies, Ron, a sheriff's deputy who was just coming off duty. Ron knew where Danny worked and had filled him in on last night's incident at the complex involving what had appeared to be an abandoned vehicle. A yellow Honda. He told Danny about Savannah coming out in person and the guy who owned the car suddenly showing up, claiming he had been wandering around looking for his dog for hours. Ron said he wasn't buying the story and suggested Danny keep his eyes open.

As Danny burned away the morning hours going back and forth in monotonous repetition on the mower, he wondered why Savannah hadn't mentioned anything to the staff. Given her friendly wave to Jesse yesterday afternoon from the front porch of the welcome center, together with her giving Danny the brush-off after the morning's meeting, he supposed he really didn't have to guess.

Jesse Whitestone was getting on his nerves.

James pondered again the cryptic text he'd gotten from his twin: *Return as soon as you can. Will explain when you arrive. No questions, just come!*

The time stamp dated the text as having been sent at three-seventeen that morning. James packed his bags.

When Jesse opened his eyes, he didn't need to look at a clock to know he'd slept the morning away. A glance at his phone confirmed it: one-twenty. Not bad considering he hadn't gone to bed until the sun started peeking its head over the tops of trees in the eastern sky. There had been too many thoughts racing through his head to have attempted sleep the moment he returned home. Instead, he'd opted for a mug of herbal tea, chamomile, out on the deck with Kai at his side. The Shepherd knew something was up. Heck, Jesse thought, Kai probably knew a lot more at this stage than he did.

It hadn't taken Jesse long, between sips of hot tea, to conclude it was probably Ellen herself who had painted Kai's dew claw. And not just once but twice. He'd reached down and stroked the dog's head, peering into the chestnut brown of his eyes. It was the first time he had ever wished Kai could talk. What would he say if he could? Jesse wondered.

Would Kai tell him that Ellen had spoken softly to him and stroked him just as lovingly as Jesse, both their hands having touched the same hairs on his strong body within hours of each other? Would Kai be able to tell him if Ellen knew Jesse was coming for her, coming to rescue her from drowning? Coming to erase the terror of that day so they would be able to enjoy countless more anniversaries together, maybe even with the children they had so looked forward to bringing into the world? The thoughts had gone swirling around in his brain like dervishes, filling his mind with dizzying possibilities.

That he would do everything he could to change the events of that fateful day and save Ellen's life he was certain. If Tsor had the power he appeared to have and was willing to teach him how to wield it, Jesse would face whatever risks there might be and snatch his wife back from the death that had swallowed her.

Jesse had sent a text to James asking him to return as soon as he could before stumbling into bed, two hours later, exhausted.

Now, as Kai scampered into the Element and they headed once more to Stillman's Lake, Jesse reviewed his plan for bringing Savannah up to speed on what had happened. He'd fed Kai before showering, dressed, and then hastily made a peanut butter and jelly sandwich to eat on the way to the complex. As he washed down the last bite with a swallow of sweet tea out of his travel mug, he wished he'd made two sandwiches. Depending on how things went, he might not be eating again for a while.

The way Jesse saw it, there was no way Savannah would believe him without seeing the room inside of the boulder for herself. He would tell her all about it first, anyway, to see how it went. But they had known each other for less than a week and, although he sensed she was as much attracted to him as he was to her, his story was too fantastic for their emerging friendship to bear. She'd have to see for herself. He didn't think Tsor would mind. After all, Jesse supposed Tsor was behind the writing on Savannah's car window when she had come to his house earlier in the week for barbecue. It was the only explanation that made sense.

The recollection of having found himself attracted to Savannah hadn't escaped him, either. But that was when he had believed Ellen lost to him forever. Circumstances were different now. A lot different.

Jesse had toyed with the idea of leaving Savannah out of it altogether but didn't see how that was possible. Not only had he and James shared with her about Kai's painted nail and eerie disappearance and reappearance, but there was the matter of the message scrawled on *her* car's window. Not to mention Savannah being concerned enough about him to come out to the lake in the early morning hours to deal with mister flashlight and bail Jesse out of trouble. Besides, all this was happening within the boundary of the complex she was responsible for. No, he couldn't keep her in the dark. He owed her an explanation. For all he knew, the next time he met with Tsor for even fifteen minutes, two months might pass on the outside. He needed to involve someone he could trust. He knew James would be coming, but James had a business to take care of over nine hundred miles away. Jesse needed someone local and Savannah was the obvious choice.

He pulled into the complex at two-thirty, hoping to get to the site ahead of Savannah. He would just as soon avoid going out to the lake together which might raise questions in the minds of curious onlookers. There wasn't much out on the east shore to bring any of the staff out there except for routine maintenance and he'd like to keep it that way.

A few minutes before three, Savannah headed out to the east shore to meet with Jesse, taking one of the ATV's from the garage and choosing to leave Jenny behind at the welcome center with Bev. She didn't know any of the details of Jesse's story but she knew enough to realize he and Kai had gotten separated and she was reluctant to take a chance on Jenny disappearing. She had risked confiding in Bev where she was going and why, just in case she didn't get back by closing time. She had her own key to the garage so putting the ATV away wouldn't be a problem. She was more concerned with Jenny. Bev had told her not to worry. The plumber had called to confirm the pump repair had gone fine and her water system was back to normal. In turn, she'd told Savannah to take her time. If she wasn't back by four-thirty, Bev would take Jenny home with her and Savannah could pick her up later.

On her way out to connect with Jesse, Savannah saw Danny in the distance on one of the mowers. As luck would have it, he saw her, too, and waved. Frustrated, she waved back. She hoped Danny was experiencing a genuine change of heart in the right direction. If not, she'd throw social niceties to the wind and ignore him except for those interactions that were strictly business.

She spotted Jesse's Element and pulled alongside, walking the short distance to the picnic table where he sat waiting for her, Kai lying quietly nearby. "Hey Jesse. Long time, no see," she quipped. "Did you get some sleep?" Savannah smiled in greeting as she slid onto the bench opposite him.

"Enough, I guess. Although it didn't come easily." He gave her a rueful smile. "Sorry to have interrupted yours. You probably didn't get all that much yourself."

"I didn't. But I told Bev to make the morning coffee extra strong and after two cups I at least had enough caffeine in me to stay awake." Savannah grew serious. "So tell me, Jesse. What happened last night? I take it you really weren't out searching for your missing dog." She nodded towards Kai. "He doesn't strike me as the kind that even knows how to get lost."

Jesse spent the better part of an hour telling Savannah what had taken place. He started at the beginning, telling her about seeing the family from Maine and deciding to park a couple of sites farther down so as to not disturb them, then walking the rest of the way with Kai. He didn't say anything about Ellen. He'd have to tell her at some point but he wanted her to be able to first focus on what had happened inside the boulder. Telling Savannah about the drowning would be heart-wrenching for him. Given what he could tell, maybe it would be for Savannah, too. She struck him as a deeply compassionate person.

For the most part, Savannah let Jesse talk without interrupting. His story was beyond fantastic. In fact, in her opinion, it left fantastic in the dust wanting for more excitement. She watched him closely and had no doubt he was convinced of the truth of what he was saying. His eyes were serious and his facial expressions composed. Sure, he seemed wound up, but who wouldn't if they actually believed they had gone through what he claimed?

There were brief moments when she was tempted to almost believe him, he made it sound so *real*. Then he hit her with the yellow brick road and the chair just like the one in his own library at home. The chair, maybe. But a yellow brick road with a gray ball at the center that turned on magic lighting in a room inside a boulder with no ceiling, that you also had to follow to get out? In her estimation, Jesse needed serious help. Somehow, his grief over his wife's drowning had gotten the upper hand in his mind and to cope he'd come up with a way to go back to her. Although Jesse hadn't said a word about Ellen, he had told her about Tsor's offer to help him change the past. It didn't take a degree in psychiatry to connect the dots.

Jesse sat looking at her expectantly, waiting for her reaction. She didn't know what to say.

"I know it sounds crazy, Savannah, but it's the truth, I swear. Every word of it."

"Jesse," she said gently, her face full of sympathy, "I know about what happened to your wife, Ellen."

He was momentarily stunned.

"Bev told me," she went on. "After dinner at my house. We had been talking about the history of Stillman's Lake and I was so excited that nothing but wonderfully positive things had happened here that I think she thought it was important to tell me."

Although Jesse was surprised, it made sense. Bev was a close friend and must have felt torn between their decades old friendship and her obligation to Savannah as her boss. Maybe it was for the best. Now that she knew about Ellen, Savannah would realize how important—no, how *crucial*—it was for him to connect with Tsor again. "Okay," he stammered, "now you know why I come here so often." He looked down and was silent. When he looked up at Savannah again, there were tears in his eyes.

"Help me with this, Savannah." His eyes were pleading with her. "I don't have any idea how long the preparations Tsor talked about are going to take or what's involved. James is coming and he'll help but I need someone here at this end I can trust." His eyes locked on hers, imploring, begging.

She had no choice but to try and reason with him. Maybe she could buy enough time to allow James to get here—if his coming was genuine and not another figment of Jesse's imagination. Sure, Jesse had shown her Kai's painted nail, but he could have painted it himself. She had no sure way of knowing.

"Jesse, Bev also told me how deeply in love you and Ellen were and that her death was devastating to you. By your own admission, you just told me the loss is why you come here so often." She hesitated, but could see no other option than to press on. "Do you think it's possible because of carrying so much grief for so long, you became confused last night and may have imagined what you just told me?"

Jesse was glad he wasn't caught completely off guard by her questioning his sanity. Although he hadn't factored in Savannah's knowing about Ellen's drowning, he still thought the odds of her thinking he had gone nuts for some reason a high potential possibility he had prepared for.

"Look, Savannah, I know how crazy this all sounds. It sounds that way even to me and I was there! You haven't known me for long, either, and here I am telling you some incredible tale! I don't blame you for being skeptical. Frankly, if I were in your shoes I'd be tempted to call the police and tell them to come back. But there may be a way for you to know for sure if what I'm saying is true. And all it will cost you is a few more minutes of your time."

Savannah could guess where Jesse was going. "Are you telling me you want me to go with you, *now?*"

"Yes." It was a gamble and he knew it. He just hoped it paid off.

Savannah's mind raced. She didn't think for a moment the boulder was hollow with a room inside tastefully decorated by some character named Tsor. What she was concerned about was what Jesse's reaction might be when faced with the truth that his imagination had cooked it all up.

She decided to take a chance. It would at least buy more time for James to get here. Savannah prayed he was really on his way.

"Okay, Jesse. Let's go."

Together with Kai, they walked the short distance up the road to the site of the accident three years ago. Maybe if it didn't take too long she'd be able to return to the welcome center and pick up Jenny before Bev left. She'd invite Jesse and Kai to join her for a light dinner somewhere. Someplace public. Someplace safe where they could wait for James.

They entered the site together before Jesse took the lead, making straight for a huge boulder she supposed was *the* rock. As they walked around to the opposite side, she could feel the skin tighten on the back of her neck. *What if everything Jesse told me is real after all?* She ordered herself to get a grip. It was not only improbable, but impossible.

When Jesse stopped, Savannah found herself staring at a fissure, one that perfectly matched Jesse's description.

Jesse reached for her hand. "Ready?"

Savannah nodded.

17

WITH SAVANNAH'S HAND in his, Jesse ducked low and stepped into the fissure, pushing his free arm into the black void, pulse quickening. As before, it was dark inside so he moved slowly, wanting to give Savannah ample opportunity to tune her senses. The shock of what she was about to see would be jolting enough. There was no need to rush.

He could feel her grip tighten and heard her shallow breathing as they entered. She might not have believed him when they were talking in the warm afternoon sunshine, sitting across from one another at a picnic table on the shore of a crystalline lake, but this was different. This was where story morphed from tale to truth.

Surprisingly, they weren't swallowed up in pitch black darkness as he remembered from his earlier visit. In fact, his eyes were adjusting nicely and, in a few moments, presented him with a dim but discernible view of their surroundings.

They were in what appeared to be a cavern about six feet from front to back and the same across, with a ceiling threatening to deal him a nasty blow if he raised himself up to his full height.

"What do you see, Jesse?" Savannah's voice floated softly through the air. "Is this the same room you were telling me about?"

Jesse felt a mixture of frustration and disappointment and, for a moment, was tempted to believe he had imagined everything. What was Tsor up to? Had he guessed wrong? Didn't Tsor intend for Savannah to be included? Worse, had Jesse made an unrecoverable mistake by bringing her and Tsor's offer was now withdrawn? Jesse was horrified by the thought.

"Of course not! I see the same thing you do. We're in a small cavern." He let go of her hand and spun around, facing her. "Look, Savannah, I'm not crazy. And I didn't imagine anything! It all happened exactly as I said." He waved at the walls. "I don't know why it's different now. Maybe I wasn't supposed to tell anyone or bring you with me and Tsor has hidden the room and locked me out. I don't know! I thought because you had a similar experience with Jenny, together with the message written on your window, you had a part in whatever is going on." He was at a loss for words. If she had struggled to believe him before it would be even harder for her now. There was no telling what was going through her mind.

Savannah felt stumped. She'd imagined when Jesse was confronted with the truth he would be embarrassed and confused, depending on her for help as to what was the matter with him. Instead, here he was, defiant and still insisting some Tsor character was behind everything. All she could say to him was, "Let's talk about it outside."

Exiting out the way they came in, they found an anxious Kai waiting for them.

Their exchange was brief, Jesse sticking to his story and Savannah growing increasingly uncomfortable.

"Jesse, I've got to get going. The welcome center is closed by now and the staff will be leaving soon, if they haven't gone home already." She shrugged. "I don't know what to say—or do for that matter. I think it would be best if we both went home and got some rest. Maybe a good night's sleep will help us think more clearly."

"You mean, help *me* think more clearly." He felt deflated.

Savannah gave him a weak smile. "You've got James coming. I assume you're going to fill him in?"

"Yes, he's going to get a replay of the same wild tale you got. Only, if I know my brother, he'll fight the urge to commit me to an asylum and we'll come out here again tomorrow and see what happens."

Savannah could tell from the look in his eyes he was serious.

"Would you like me to come with you?" As soon as the words left her mouth she couldn't believe she'd said them. It was just that there was something about Jesse that was deeply authentic and so totally genuine. She wanted him to know that even if she was hesitant to accept his story at face value she cared about him.

"Sure." Jesse was touched. Maybe tomorrow would be different and Savannah would see for herself he wasn't cracking up.

Savannah promised to be at Jesse's the following morning around ten and watched as the Element drove out the dirt road and was lost to sight. She climbed on the ATV, making for the welcome center, hoping she would arrive in time to pick up Jenny before Bev left.

She returned to find everyone had gone home. Or at least that's what she thought until she saw the overhead door of the garage open. She put the ATV in gear, entering slowly, maneuvering the machine into its usual spot.

"Danny, what are you still doing here?" She tried to keep her voice neutral.

"Oh, hi Savannah." Danny looked as though he had just pulled into the garage himself. Sweat glistened from his sun-browned skin and he looked tired. "I just finished mowing." He wiped his face with the bandana he'd taken off from around his neck. "Sure gets hot out there!"

"Well, the week is nearly over. Tomorrow is Friday and then we'll have two days off before we start all over again." She headed for her car. The last thing she wanted was to get trapped in the garage with Danny.

Danny watched her go. Savannah's leaving was perfect.

He killed some time cleaning the mower, getting it ready for the next round of cutting. He chewed up another fifteen minutes straightening the garage, putting tools away and emptying the trash. He locked the garage and walked to his car, opening the glove compartment, removing a key ring and small box before heading for the welcome center.

If he had guessed right when he copied Savannah's keys, one of them would fit the lock in front of him. He tried the first one. No good. The second, however, slid smoothly into the cylinder. A silent turn to the left and the door opened. He walked inside.

It was funny how a place so familiar, a place where you worked day after day after day, could seem so unfamiliar if you were in it out of the normal context with which you encountered the setting. He had never been the only person inside. Certainly never when the complex was closed and all the staff gone home. Instead of unnerving Danny, it excited him.

He went straight for Savannah's office. Once inside he opened the box he was carrying, removing a small white electrical plug adapter. His eyes roamed the walls, searching for an outlet that suited his purpose. He wanted one that was out of the way but wouldn't be compromised as to the level of sound picked up by the cleverly concealed bug. Grinning, he inserted a SIM card into the device, carefully trimming the edge of the card so it was flush

113

to the surface of the adapter. You couldn't help but appreciate the Internet. It made researching and buying surveillance gear child's play. There were even recommendations comparing performance and price. Yup, it paid to research before you bought.

His choice had been a handy little device you simply plugged into an outlet. A text message sent to the module via his mobile phone would activate or deactivate the bug depending on which of two cryptic, four character messages he sent. Once activated, as soon as the sensor detected a sound in the room, it would call his mobile number and he could listen in. From here on out, what went on in Savannah's office was no longer her private business.

Savannah pulled into Bev's driveway. It seemed more like twin paths running parallel to each other than a road and led across a big field and into the woods beyond. Bev had warned her the place was rather isolated and the dirt road which served as her driveway ran for nearly a mile before exhausting itself at the doorstep of the house. Savannah drove slowly, noting there were more potholes in Bev's private road than what they strategically placed in some of the outlying routes of the complex. And if there were a pattern to Bev's potholes, Savannah hadn't caught on to it by the time she pulled up at the homey, naturally sided two story house that greeted her.

As she stepped out of the car, Jenny came running. Bev waved from the comfort of an Adirondack style rocking chair on the porch. "C'mon up, Savannah! Have a seat and let me pour you a glass of sweet tea."

Savannah took a seat in a matching rocker next to her friend, grateful for a chance to unwind. Bev couldn't help noticing the pensive expression on the pretty blonde's face as she drank her tea, a faraway look in her eyes.

She knew Savannah had been with Jesse out at the lake and that it had something to do with his explaining to her the events of the previous night. Bev marveled at how the lives of these two friends were becoming so quickly intertwined. She prayed for them often, asking God to help them see His great love and care for each of them. It was Bev's deep conviction that if a person could catch a glimpse of Jesus for who He truly is, they couldn't help but be attracted to Him.

"Want to talk about it?" Bev asked gently.

Savannah did want to talk about it. Desperately so. She also didn't want to compromise the trust Jesse had placed in her. But what if it were true his longstanding struggle with grief had gotten to the point where his mental health was in jeopardy? What kind of a friend would she be if she stayed silent? She knew she could trust Bev. After all, she had been Jesse's friend for many years, reaching back all the way to his childhood. Savannah determined to venture to share enough with Bev to perhaps gain insight into what she ought to do.

"When I went out to the lake this afternoon to meet Jesse, he filled me in on what had happened to him last night—at least what he *believed* happened. It was a pretty fantastic story, Bev! The sort of thing you would only see in a movie or read in a book. It involved things so strange I couldn't accept them at face value."

"Why not?"

"Well, for one thing, they would have required suspending the laws of nature." She hesitated before going on. "I'm sorry to be so obscure. It's just that I don't want to break any confidences. What Jesse told me is so crazy I'm worried about him."

"What did you say to him?"

"I told him you had shared with me about Ellen's drowning—not in a gossipy way but out of concern for us both, and that I wondered if perhaps his grief had caused him to imagine what he saw."

Bev closed her eyes and was silent for so long Savannah was afraid she'd done something wrong. "I'm sorry if my telling Jesse you'd told me about his wife's drowning is troubling to you. I just didn't know what else to do."

The eyes of the older woman fluttered open. She turned to her young friend, meeting Savannah's gaze with tender, gentle warmth. "Savannah, you have my complete trust. You can rest assured I'm comfortable with you sharing anything I tell you, with anybody you choose, whenever you believe it's the best thing to do. Don't misunderstand my silence, honey. It's just that there are times when a person needs more wisdom than they possess at the moment. Like right now. And when I find myself in such a place, I've learned it's best to settle myself down and ask God to give me that wisdom."

"And does He?"

Bev's smile was as warm as the look in her eyes. "Always."

She waited a moment before saying more. "Don't misunderstand, Savannah. God isn't some magic genie in a bottle! Like I said when we were talking on your porch yesterday after dinner, God is good. *Perfectly* good. If you ask Him for something you truly need, like the wonderful Father He is, He's going to give it to you. But He's going to do it in a perfect way and at the perfect time. You can count on it.

"So with the slivers of wisdom I think He's given me for now, let me ask you another question. After you suggested to Jesse he might have imagined whatever experience it was he told you he'd had, what happened next?"

"He wanted me to go with him and see for myself what he'd seen."

"And did you?"

"Yes."

Now it was Bev's turn to patiently wait for Savannah to continue. She could see the young woman was troubled.

"I didn't see what Jesse saw. In fact, I didn't see anything out of the ordinary. When I asked Jesse what he saw, he said he was seeing the same thing I was and couldn't understand what had gone wrong. He seemed frustrated but kept sticking to his original story."

Bev leaned forward, cradling Savannah's face in her hands, waiting to talk until she was sure her communication would involve all the sensory pathways that sight, sound and touch could afford. "Then I suggest you believe him, Savannah."

18

SATURDAY MORNING FOUND the brothers having breakfast together, choosing the comfort of the air conditioned kitchen over the drenching humidity outside where a light rain had been falling for some time. Jesse sat staring out the window, the food on the plate in front of him mostly untouched, his mind occupied with a hundred different thoughts but fixated on only one: the possibility of seeing Ellen again. Not only seeing her but saving her and, in the process, infusing new life into them both. It would be nothing short of a rebirth of their marriage.

James ate the last of his scrambled eggs, washing them down with grapefruit juice. He had arrived in the early evening, picking up pizza and wings at Giantelli's on his way through town so they wouldn't have to bother with making dinner. Usually, his brother would devour three-quarters of a large pie by himself but Jesse had only managed a single slice and a couple of wings. James had listened to his twin's incredible story, satisfying his own hunger by devouring the rest of the wings and two slices of pizza.

It had been easier for James to swallow the food than Jesse's account of the events that took place inside the boulder. That Ellen's death had hit Jesse like a sledgehammer blow to the heart, James fully understood. His brother had wrestled with sorrow every day for the past three years and likely had dreamed more than once of seeing Ellen alive again through some far-flung miracle or metaphysical fantasy, but James believed his brother was telling the truth. As crazy as the tale sounded, there wasn't a question James asked that Jesse hadn't answered without having to think about it. James could only conclude it was either a world-class hallucination or what Jesse had experienced was real.

And if it was real, then there had to be someone behind it. Someone with the power to pull it off. Nothing on earth had that kind of power and, in James' mind, the alien angle was ludicrous. Only the supernatural had such awesome capability. For James, the only open question was that of Tsor and whether he was of angelic or demonic origin.

He'd been deliberately vague when Jesse had asked him what he made of it all. His brother hadn't even bothered to ask if he'd believed him. James took it as a compliment. It showed how close the two of them **really** were. James sensed that, for some reason known only to God, his twin brother was caught up in something spectacular. For the moment, it seemed prudent to James to avoid unnecessarily riling his sibling. He'd talk plainly enough when the time came for it. But for now, he thought it best to tread carefully by Jesse's side and see where all this was going.

Savannah showed up a little before ten, Jenny sprinting ahead of her to greet Kai as Savannah joined Jesse and James who were waiting for her on the front porch. Although the skies were still overcast the rain had stopped, and with it, a slight lessening in the humidity.

"How do you feel about cold pizza?"

Savannah laughed as she gave James a hug. "That's a pretty strange question at ten o'clock in the morning! Or maybe that's the way you southern boys greet friends you haven't seen in a few days?" James returned her hug with a gentle squeeze.

She wondered if she should hug Jesse, too. Her hugging James was spontaneous, something that came natural to her when seeing a friend after a period of absence. She and Jesse had never embraced. Their closest contact had been when she had instinctively reached for his hand as they had entered the cavern yesterday.

"How about you, Jesse? Are you up for a morning squeeze of something besides orange juice?" Savannah hoped her light-hearted jest would neutralize the awkwardness she was feeling.

Where hugging James was what she imagined hugging a brother would feel like if she had one, Jesse's was anything but. Without the slightest hint of impropriety, his arms enfolded her with strength and purpose in an embrace that was innocently intimate. Savannah could feel her body temperature go up. "Now what's the story with the pizza, James?" she asked, hoping no one noticed the color rising in her cheeks.

"It's James' idea of always being prepared," Jesse offered. "He was an Eagle Scout in his younger days and I guess it never wore off."

James raised an eyebrow before explaining. "We had pizza and wings last night for dinner and we've got some leftover pizza. Given the unpredictable nature of our planned excursion, I thought I would bring some food along."

An awkward silence descended on the three. Savannah could only suppose Jesse had told his brother the same story he'd shared with her—as well as what had happened when he and Savannah had visited the boulder. Nor could she read James' face well enough to know if he believed his brother or was as concerned about Jesse's state of mind as she had been. Since talking with Bev, she had decided to give Jesse the benefit of the doubt. At least to the extent she was capable.

It was Jesse who spoke first. "Okay, Let's clear the air so we can all be as comfortable as possible given the situation.

"I've told you both what happened to me. I know how bizarre it sounds. It's so far past implausible that *anyone* would find it nearly impossible to believe." He put his arm on his brother's shoulder. "Anyone, that is, except a brother who is a Rams fan and used to believing in the impossible." He turned to Savannah. "I don't have any right to expect you to believe me, Savannah. After all, you've known me for less than a week. I wouldn't be surprised if you were here more out of concern for my safety as anything else." He gave her a lopsided smile but his eyes were serious. "But you're here, and under the circumstances, that counts for a lot."

Savannah reached out, taking hold of each brothers' hand. "You're right, I'm not in the same place as you guys are." She searched Jesse's eyes. "But I don't think you've lost your mind, either, Jesse. I guess I'm stuck somewhere in the middle but I'm trying to be a good friend to someone I care about."

"Fair enough," Jesse replied.

In less than an hour, the three of them stood in front of the boulder staring at the fissure, an anxious Kai pacing back and forth. At Jesse's suggestion they had left Jenny in the Element.

"What's the matter boy? Is Tsor inside?" Jesse felt the apprehension hanging in the air. What would the outcome be this time? Would Tsor open up or would the boulder remain a hulking granite monolith and Jesse would have two people thinking he was crazy. He could feel his pulse quickening.

"I'll take the lead. Savannah, you follow and James will bring up the rear. I know it sounds foolish given what happened the last time out but I think it would be wise if we held hands. If Tsor lets us in and it's anything like it was my first visit we'll be in total darkness and I don't want to lose track of anyone."

119

Not waiting for a response, Jesse grabbed Savannah's hand, bent low, and stepped inside.

Although Savannah didn't expect to encounter anything other than what she'd seen before, a part of her hoped for something different, something that would confirm Jesse's story.

James had all his senses on high alert. Never in his life had his twin told him a lie and he forced himself to accept what Jesse said at face value. But if his brother was right and had had an actual encounter with someone named Tsor, then James would be certain they were dealing with the supernatural and discernment might be crucial to their very survival. He had spent time in prayer long before breakfast in preparation for what they were now doing.

It didn't take long for the three of them to see they had entered the same shallow cavern that had presented itself to Jesse and Savannah the day before. Jesse sank to the ground in frustration. "I don't get it," he said, his voice barely above a whisper. "I'm starting to wonder if you're right, Savannah, and something happened that made me imagine it all."

James tried to lighten the moment. "Almost as bad a shock as the Rams losing Super Bowl thirty-six to the underdog Patriots as time expired, huh?"

"If you're trying to make me feel better, James, you're going about it the wrong way."

"Sorry, bro. Let's head back out and put our heads together. Maybe we're overlooking something."

Jesse took James' offered hand and was pulled to his feet. "Yeah, I guess there's nothing more we can do in here." He looked around, searching the cavern's walls for clues. Maybe there was a hidden lever or something he'd brushed up against on his first entry, something he was overlooking that would transform their surroundings into what he had experienced.

They left the cave in the reverse order they had entered, James leading the way out and Jesse bringing up the rear. As Jesse stepped into the daylight, Kai, who had been waiting for them outside at Jesse's command, darted through the opening.

"Hold on a second," Jesse called out. "I need to grab Kai. I think he's spooked by this place." He ducked his head and went back inside.

120

Although he'd experienced it before, being plunged into pitch blackness again took Jesse by surprise. His first thought was to call out to the others. He didn't know why things had so suddenly changed, but this was a chance for them to see for themselves.

"James! Savannah!" he cried, "Get in here! Hurry!"

As soon as he uttered the words he knew it was no use. Like before, sound was swallowed up by the black void and went nowhere. He searched for the fissure with a similar outcome. There was no exit. He took a few slow breaths to get his heart rate down. Okay, he'd been here before. All he had to do was get to the middle of the room and press the gray disc that turned on the lights. He would go from there.

Dropping down on all fours, Jesse began crawling forward, trying to stay in a straight line, his hands swaying back and forth in front of him as a blind person might use their cane. After what seemed an eternity, he touched what he supposed was the opposite wall. He hoped that, in his excitement, he had simply strayed off course and missed the center of the room. He took a few more deep, slow breaths. *Okay, Jesse, focus! Let's hit the middle this time.*

On his second pass his hand found the mark and when he pressed down, welcome light radiated throughout the room. As his eyes made the adjustment he could make out swirls of yellow brick, the chair like his own and next to it, the stand with the black book. Relief swept over him.

He wondered what Savannah and James would think of his sudden disappearance, picturing them yelling through what he imagined was now a sealed fissure. He had no idea how long he would be inside or, for that matter, how much time would have passed on the outside when he emerged. He was glad he had told them both about the time differential and how Tsor had warned it wasn't linear. They would all have to deal with it the best they could.

He looked around for Kai, guessing if events stayed true to form the animal would be nowhere in sight. No Kai. The only thing left was to take a seat and look in the book. He hoped Tsor had written something for him.

Jesse sat, opened the book, and frowned. There were no new entries. He looked around, perplexed. As a matter of fact, nothing had changed in the room at all. It was as if not so much as a single minute had passed since he was last inside. It was confusing. When he was on the outside, he wondered if what had happened inside the room was real. On the inside, he was tempted to wonder the same in reverse. It were as if he had nodded off in the chair only to have dreamed about spending time with Savannah and his brother and woken again in the same place in the same chair.

He reached into his pants pocket, pulling out his cell phone. He didn't expect to see any bars and wasn't disappointed. After all, he was inside a boulder. But he could still take pictures.

The next few minutes were spent taking shots of his surroundings then double-checking to be sure they were on the smartphone's camera roll. All the photos were accounted for. If Savannah and James couldn't get inside to see for themselves and Jesse couldn't call them and share live video at least he would have pictures to back him up.

He sat back down. It still amazed him how every aspect of the chair perfectly mimicked his chair back home, right down to the amount of wear on the armrests and a missing decorative brass brad.

Now what? I'm inside but no Tsor.

He opened the book again and re-read all the entries. Tsor had said they would be filling in the blank pages together. He had also said Jesse could write down any questions he had.

Finding something to write with was his next challenge. He silently chastised himself for not thinking clearly enough to bring a pen. He looked at the pedestal stand beside the chair. It had a small drawer with a single brass pull. He opened it. To his relief, there was an old-fashioned fountain pen inside. He smiled. Tsor thought of everything. He seemed to know everything, too, as Jesse had a fondness for the classic writing instruments and had a small collection of them at home. He began writing.

Are you here, Tsor?

He turned the page.

I'm always here.

What about Savannah and James? Aren't they allowed to come inside with me?

I have to warn you, Jesse, that you are only allowed three questions per visit. Every visit, you'll get a chance to ask three more questions.

As for why three, I guess I'm captivated by how often the number comes up in the world you live in. For example, parents count to three expecting their disobedient child to do what they ask by the time they get there. In baseball, three strikes and you're out. Three persons, grammatically speaking, express and include all your human relationships. You divide time into the three categories of past, present, and future. Your orators tend to limit the number of points they are trying to get across to three. One of your many religions has a god made up of three persons. Your race has a curious fascination with the number! I just thought we'd catch a ride on the same train. Besides, if you only have three questions per visit, you are likely to use them wisely.

But to answer your questions, the answer is no. Neither Savannah nor your brother, James, is allowed inside. This opportunity is for you alone. You may share with them whatever you like as to what goes on in this room but they cannot enter. I have my reasons.

Having only a single question left, Jesse pondered a while, wanting to make the most of it. There were at least a dozen questions he wanted to ask. He finally settled on what struck him as a practical necessity.

How often may I come?

He turned the page slowly.

I had a suspicion that might be your next question. It's an excellent one, too. It is always best to learn as much as you can about power. And make no mistake, Jesse Whitestone, what I'm offering you is power. Changing history is not to be taken lightly.

We are going to continue with the theme of three in that you may come once every three days.

But I have something to show you, to whet your appetite for our next visit together and to further demonstrate my capability.

Read carefully and do exactly what I say as it is only in your perfect obedience to me that you will acquire the power to change the past. When you have committed the simple instructions that follow to memory, close this book, place it back on the stand, and do not touch it again until you come back in three days.

When you rise from your chair, follow the yellow brick road to the wall. Instead of leading to the way out, it will lead you to a portal.

Think on the desire of your heart. Then look through the portal.

Jesse read the final entry twice more before turning to the first page of the book and reading everything again from the beginning. According to Tsor, he wouldn't be able to return for three days and he wanted to commit the content of the book to memory. He thought about taking a picture of each page but didn't want to chance offending Tsor.

The instructions about the portal were simple enough. He didn't exactly know what Tsor's idea of a portal was or what to expect. He guessed he'd find out soon enough. He made his way to the center of the room and, in accordance with the instructions, followed the yellow bricks to the wall.

The lights dimmed. Whoever Tsor was, he had a knack for the theatrical.

Jesse stood still, patiently waiting for something to happen, staring straight ahead at the unbroken stone wall. If there was a portal in it, he sure couldn't see it. Maybe it didn't show up until... Per the instructions, Jesse began thinking on the desire of his heart. That was a no-brainer. Ellen was the desire of his heart. He thought about her, picturing her in his mind.

Nothing. He was going toe-to-toe with a stone wall and the wall was winning.

He concentrated on Ellen, trying to toss out any other thoughts. It amazed him how challenging it was to focus all of your thoughts on a single object. It seemed as though everything inside and outside of his brain was screaming for at least a fragment of his attention.

He closed his eyes. It helped. At least the world outside his body couldn't distract him now. He decided he needed a context, a setting for Ellen from his memory. Somewhere to place her. He thought about the day she'd drowned and felt an involuntary shudder travel the length of his body. No, he'd save that until he had learned how to use the power Tsor was going to give him. Until he could do something about it, dredging up images of that awful day would only serve to torment him. He let his mind wander among his memories, drawn to the lovely images like a moth to a flame.

Jesse didn't know how long he'd kept his eyes closed, but when he opened them again he found himself looking at the most life-like image he had ever seen. It was super-sized, taking up the entire wall before him, complete with odors and sound, inviting him to take a step forward and move from the room within the boulder to the world before him. The world where Ellen sat on their bedroom floor painting Kai's dew claw Iced Mauve. She was speaking to the Shepherd in soothing tones, telling him how studly it was going to make him appear to all the lady Shepherds. Assuring him that, like Sampson, his polished nail was the source of his strength.

The sight of Ellen was overwhelming and Jesse felt his knees buckle. Without thinking he moved forward, only to find himself unable to enter into the world before his eyes, the desire of his heart.

A moment later and the image was gone. Jesse sank to the floor and wept, his tears falling like rain.

19

THE YOUNG LATINO climbed out of the shower. As he toweled off he caught a glimpse of the now infamous tattoo in the mirror above the sink, the ornate capital letters splashed across his back forever declaring his allegiance as a member of one of the most vicious gangs in America. Originally established in Los Angeles to protect fellow countrymen immigrating to the U.S. from more established Mexican and African-American rivals, his gang had achieved transnational status, earning a well-deserved reputation for excessive cruelty. The reputation had led to their recruitment by one of the more notorious Mexican drug cartels and with it, the increasing interest of the FBI and Immigrations and Customs Enforcement, better known as ICE.

Julio Ramos had a job to do here in Arizona, one that would further establish his reputation with the gang's ruling elite; he would be killing a U.S. Border Patrol agent.

Ramos was good at reconnaissance. It was the key to a successful hit. His three month long observation period had led him to pick a particular man, Derrick Holmes, as his target. His superiors didn't care who he killed, just so it was an agent with the Border Patrol. He'd narrowed down the candidates to three and then turned to his spirit guide, Lavelle, for help as to the preferred victim. He had met Lavelle using a visualization technique he used during periods of meditation. Julio credited her with giving him the edge he needed to stay alive and progress through the ranks. It was Lavelle who had singled out Derrick Holmes. She had also helped him plan the details of the mission, one which would ensure that the objective of instilling fear in the law enforcement community, especially within families, was achieved in dramatic fashion. After all, that was why the cartel had sought the gang out, for their ability to sow fear in the hearts of those who dared trifle with the cartel's commercial activity. As he finished dressing, Julio visualized the hit he was about to make.

It was Saturday, the day Derrick Holmes took his eight year old daughter to Rising Stars Gymnastics where she was enrolled in a tumbling class. It was an hour long morning class running from ten to eleven. Derrick always took his daughter inside and stayed with her until they both came out around eleven fifteen. Derrick would open the passenger side front door for his daughter and help her in, watching her fasten her seatbelt before closing the door, walking around the sedan, and getting inside himself.

It was Julio's plan to drive up as Derrick was opening the door for his daughter and fire his weapon, killing his victim as his back was turned. The gym was a favorite among the Border Patrol community and there were several agents who had kids enrolled in the various gymnastics programs. A bloody murder of an agent in broad daylight in front of his kid couldn't fail to send the signal that, if you wanted to keep your family safe, agents ought to look the other way and let the cartel do their business. Rivalry between cartels was bad enough without the Border Patrol making life more difficult.

Julio walked outside to the SUV that had been rented by a contact he didn't even know. The vehicle would never be returned. Before the end of the day the SUV would no longer even exist. Not in a recognizable form, anyway.

He fastened the barrel to the receiver then checked the operation of the weapon, an automatic assault rifle the cartel had gotten somewhere in northern Ireland. Contrary to popular lore, gang violence rarely involved the use of assault weapons. But for this job, the cartel had decided to equip Ramos with all the firepower he needed in the event something unexpected happened. With this particular weapon, Julio could take on several members of law enforcement if he had to and still come out on top. Placed in automatic mode, the gun could spit out seven hundred and fifty rounds per minute using thirty round magazines, of which he had ten. He didn't intend to use the weapon in automatic mode, however. Not if he didn't have to. His signature kill was always three shots to the chest. Whether the bullets entered his victim from the front or back was irrelevant to him. He flicked the fire selector into position for semi-automatic operation.

Arriving at the gym a few minutes after eleven, Julio pulled into the parking lot, picking out a spot within easy access of his target. There were plenty of cars in the lot and his Hispanic features blended with those of many of the patrons. Dark sunglasses hid eyes constantly raking the area for signs of anything out of the ordinary.

Twelve more minutes passed before Julio caught sight of his quarry. Father and daughter emerged from the building, the man scooping up his little girl and planting her on his shoulders where she spread out her arms, pretending to fly. Her father joined in the fun by weaving his way to their car, dipping and diving, evoking squeals of delight from the colorful young gymnast.

As they neared their car the man gently lifted his daughter from his shoulders, set her down, and opened the passenger door. As he stood holding the door open, three shots rang out, each one ripping through the man's upper torso. In an instant, Border Patrol agent Derrick Holmes' body slumped to the blacktop, his wounds fatal.

As Stanley put the finishing touches on the latest birdhouse he'd made, he couldn't stop thinking about what he'd found early Friday morning while taking a routine inventory of supplies at the recreational complex. For years, part of his job as crew chief involved making sure the complex had adequate stores of the materials needed for maintaining the facility. He'd gotten pretty good at it, too, developing a system for recording what was on hand and matching the results against reorder points established through long experience. Friday's inventory had centered around the garage. It included spare parts for the various pieces of power equipment and vehicles, diesel and gasoline fuel, and even miscellaneous items like key blanks.

That was the problem. The log of keys made didn't match what he had expected to find against the inventory of blanks. As Stanley himself made nearly every replacement key, he had at first wondered if he had made a mistake on the log. Somehow, the inventory showed two blanks unaccounted for. Blanks used in making replacement keys for door locks.

He recalled finding Danny in the garage supposedly making a key for the old Dodge truck, claiming to have broken the original off in the door of the vehicle. Danny had even noted the entry in the log after apologizing to Stanley. But the records didn't jive. The single blank that Danny would have needed to make the replacement key for the Dodge still hung from its hook on the carousel. Stanley planned on talking with Danny about it when he saw him on Monday. The young man had better have a good story or Stanley would be recommending to Savannah they fire him. It hadn't escaped the older man's notice that, during morning meetings, Danny had been eyeing their attractive boss in a less than professional manner. It might be better to let the young bull go now before there were problems.

His musing was interrupted by the phone in his workshop. Stanley sighed, setting the birdhouse down on the bench and reluctantly picking up the receiver on the third ring. "Hello, this is Stanley." His voice had a gruff edge to it. He hated being interrupted while he was working at his hobby.

"Dad, I need you…" Although the woman's voice on the other end was weak and faltering, he would have known it anywhere as belonging to his daughter, Sara.

"Sara, what's the matter, honey?"

It took Stanley a while to sort out the reason for his daughter's call in between sobs of grief that tore him up. In the less than two minutes the call lasted he only knew that Derrick, his son-in-law, had been shot and killed in the presence of his eight year old granddaughter who had now gone totally mute from the trauma. Sara was in shock herself and needed him. She'd begged him to come as quickly as he could.

Within an hour, Stanley was on his way to the Syracuse airport for a flight to Yuma. He hadn't been able to reach Savannah at her house so had called Bev and filled her in with the sketchy details, promising to call with an update before the weekend was over. He didn't know how long he'd be gone and was sorry for the challenges it would pose but it was an emergency. Bev had assured her old friend that Savannah would not only understand but would be waiting to see if she, together with all of them at the complex, could be of help in any way. Bev also prayed with him, asking God to watch over his daughter and granddaughter and give Stanley all the strength he needed for whatever lay ahead.

20

JAMES KNELT BESIDE his weeping sibling, gently placing an arm around his brother's broad shoulders. Kai sat beside his master, his black face flooded with the concern of the wholly devoted.

"Are you okay, Jesse?" James' voice was as tender as his touch. He had never seen his twin so broken.

Jesse kept his eyes shut, not yet ready to leave the world whose image still burned in his mind's eye. He didn't say anything, acknowledging James' presence only by raising his own hand up to where it met and grasped his brother's.

Savannah stood nearby, bewildered, almost frightened. What had happened to Jesse to unleash such raw emotion in a man so strong and self-composed? Only seconds ago, Jesse had gone back inside the cavern to retrieve Kai. The dog had come out as quickly as he'd gone in but Jesse hadn't followed. She and James had waited only a few moments before calling out, thinking the delay prompted by Jesse finding something of interest inside. Getting no answer, they'd slipped back through the fissure only to find Jesse crumpled on the dirt floor, sobbing.

"I suppose you didn't see anything?" Jesse mumbled, his voice barely audible.

"No." James tightened his grip on his brother's hand. "You went inside to get Kai and when he came out without you and you didn't answer us we came back in." He helped his brother to his feet. "What happened, Jesse?"

"I spent some time with Tsor."

"You mean... you were back inside the room?"

"Yes."

The two locked eyes, Jesse's full of unspoken conviction, James' searching until, at length, in the same unspoken manner, answering back with the sort of absolute trust born of unflinching love. Jesse smiled weakly and nodded. The two embraced, allowing their individual hopes, strengths and emotions to pass between them in a bond of brotherhood.

"Somebody want to explain to me what's going on? Preferably outside." Although standing close by, Savannah felt thoroughly alone.

It was James who answered, looking at her sympathetically and calmly replying, "I'm pretty sure Jesse's been with Tsor, Savannah. For how long I don't know. Apparently, you and I aren't invited." He motioned towards the fissure. "But I wholeheartedly agree with you. Let's get out of here and get some air."

The three were soon standing outside. It was early afternoon and the skies were making good on their threat of renewed rain which was once again falling lightly. Savannah would have preferred a cheerful sun instead of the gloom that seemed to seep into her very pores. James, sensing her discomfort, offered a suggestion. "What do you guys say to a change of venue?" He glanced upwards. "It looks like it could rain harder any moment. Is there a microwave in the welcome center, Savannah? Would it be all right if we nuked the cold pizza I brought and had a little picnic inside while we listen to Jesse's story?"

"Sure." The idea suited Savannah just fine. The welcome center had comfortable seating and the familiar setting might calm her nerves. "I'll even supply the beverages."

Danny tinkered with a mower, pretending to be engaged in a repair. He'd been following Savannah since she pulled out of her driveway earlier in the morning and hadn't been too happy to discover she had gone to see Jesse Whitestone. Danny hadn't even known where the guy lived until, watching from a safe distance down the road, he'd seen Jesse's Element come down the same driveway Savannah's Subaru had gone up. He'd followed, guessing Savannah was with Jesse. In fact, it had looked to him like there were three people inside: two men up front and Savannah in the back, together with two dogs. Danny assumed one was Jenny and the other the German Shepherd he had seen sitting in Jesse's sports car. He had been even more surprised when they had driven to the complex. He hadn't dared follow them in. That would have been too obvious. Instead, he had waited several minutes before entering, just in time to see the Element heading off towards the east shore of the lake.

He was beginning to wonder what the attraction was with that part of the complex other than it was the more remote and less visited portion of the lake. Most folks didn't like dodging the potholes and preferred the broader expanse of the beach nearer the welcome center. Besides, wasn't it where the guy's wife had drowned? What kind of weirdo would take his new girlfriend out to where his wife had died?

That Jesse considered Savannah his new girlfriend was a given in Danny's mind. Why else would the man spend so much time with her? For all he knew, maybe the guy had drowned his own wife and was casting around for his next victim. Or maybe Savannah was the type that was fascinated with death and wanted to know more about the so-called accident and where it had taken place. Danny would just have to keep his eyes and ears open so he could sort through the fog and uncover the facts. He was pretty sure that, underneath her façade, Savannah was attracted to him. It might take a while but he'd bag the comely blonde yet.

Danny wasn't concerned about anyone finding him in the garage. He sometimes came in on the weekends, off the clock, to do some of the maintenance and repairs needed to keep the equipment running smoothly. He'd worked out the arrangement with Stanley, who had agreed to let Danny use the garage to work on his car on the weekends in exchange. Savannah knew about it as well so it wouldn't be something out of the ordinary. He'd stick around for a while on the off chance of learning what the three of them were up to.

He didn't have to wait long. Less than an hour after the Element headed out to the lake he heard it pulling up outside. Danny leaned over the mower, pretending to be making an adjustment to the spring tension setup that kept the mower's belt tight. He didn't expect they would come into the garage, but if they did, Danny wanted to appear to be working as usual.

He needn't have worried. Savannah led her two companions straight to the welcome center, followed by the two dogs. Unlocking the door they filed inside, the man he had never seen before carrying a small cooler. Danny wondered if maybe they had been out to have a picnic then changed their mind, deciding to have it inside because of the rain. He didn't blame them. The day had started out with rain but had cleared up as the morning wore on. Now it was pouring out an encore.

Danny grabbed his cell phone, punching in the cryptic message 'GDM1' and sending it as a text to the bug he'd planted in Savannah's office. He didn't suppose they were going to have a picnic in her office but he might get lucky and catch some of what they said.

James shoved the pizza in the microwave while Savannah grabbed sodas out of her office fridge. Jesse plopped himself down in one of the large chairs in the main room, Kai in close proximity continuing his vigil and Jenny curling up on the bed Bev had made for her.

A ding from the microwave proclaimed hot pizza and Savannah joined the brothers, passing out Dr. Peppers before curling up on the sofa. James took a seat on the brick ledge of the fireplace. They ate for a while in silence, James and Savannah wanting to give Jesse all the time he needed to compose his thoughts. At length he began, looking first at James.

"I take it not much time elapsed from the point where I went back into the cavern after Kai and the two of you came back in?"

"That's right. It couldn't have been more than twenty or thirty seconds."

Jesse shook his head. "Even though Tsor told me the time differential between the inside and outside of the boulder wasn't linear, it's hard to get used to. From my perspective, given what went on inside, it felt more like an hour."

"What exactly went on, Jesse?" Savannah supposed her voice reflected the nagging doubts clawing at her.

Jesse sighed. He could read her well enough to spot the telltale signs of internal struggle. He caught himself thinking that even when she frowned she was beautiful. He wondered at having such a thought at this particular moment.

"Don't worry, Savannah. I know how hard it must be for you. But I was a little smarter this time around." He took his phone out of his pocket and held it up. "I took pictures." He tossed the device to James, taking another gulp of soda as James moved to the sofa, sitting down beside Savannah as he accessed the phone's camera roll with Savannah looking on.

Jesse relaxed, confident the pictures would restore Savannah's faith in his mental stability. He'd even thought to double-check them inside the boulder to be sure Tsor hadn't done anything to make the room invisible to photography. He looked at the two of them, expecting to see twin looks of amazement any moment. Instead, he saw Savannah's hand go to her mouth and her eyes close. James' expression never changed. His brother only looked at him, shaking his head in a silent "no".

"You're kidding!" Jesse shot out of the chair, snatching the phone out of his brother's hand. He flicked through the images. The most recent photo was one he had taken of Savannah and Jenny the night of the barbecue. "I don't believe it!" he groaned.

A sudden thought came to James' mind. "Give me the phone," he demanded. A dejected Jesse handed over the phone. James touched the camera icon and took a picture of a fast asleep Jenny in her new bed.

"What in the world are you doing, James?" Savannah was confused.

"You'll see." He checked to be sure the picture appeared on the camera roll. Satisfied, he turned to Savannah.

"You've got a computer in your office, right?"

"Sure."

"Let's just hope it has the software installed I need."

Savannah was beyond confused. "What are you talking about, James?"

Jesse had caught on to what his brother was thinking. As twins, they had had several experiences over the years of near instant recognition of each other's thoughts. "James wants to check the properties assigned to each of the photos. He wants to compare the one I took of you at the barbecue to the one he just took of Jenny and see if there are any gaps." He looked at his twin with admiration. "You are one smart guy, even for a Ram's fan, bro. There's just one problem."

"What's that?"

"The connector cable. I don't have one with me."

"I thought you carried an extra in the Element."

"Nope. That would be too much like you. You're the Eagle Scout. I bailed when I was still a Cubby."

Savannah rolled her eyes, exasperated. "Will one of you please tell me what's going on?"

"It's simple," James replied. "Every time you take a picture the camera assigns a unique name to the image. It may differ from device to device but basically, each camera uses a name which includes a number that is incremented by one with each picture taken. We need to attach Jesse's phone to a computer so we can check the names assigned to each picture."

"So…" Savannah said slowly, her mind catching on to the implications, "are you thinking there might be a gap of more than one digit between the picture of me and the one you just took of Jenny?"

"It's worth a shot."

An irritated Danny watched as the three friends drove towards Highway 8. He doubted they were aware of his presence in the garage. The fragments of conversation he'd managed to pick up weren't much to go on. They seemed to have been excited about some pictures. What the pictures were of and where they had been taken he hadn't a clue.

On a hunch, he decided to take one of the ATV's out to the east shore and look around. He was familiar with the site where the drowning had taken place. That's where he'd look. If anyone on staff happened by he would say he had adjusted the vehicle's brakes and was testing them out to be sure they were operating properly. He grabbed a poncho out of one of the storage lockers on the ATV and took off. The rain would actually help. If they had been out to the site where he was now headed, Danny would know by the footprints left in the damp ground.

Jesse attached his smartphone to the computer in his home office. In moments, they found what they were looking for. James let out a low whistle. "Unbelievable. A gap of seven unaccounted for pictures."

"What do you think happened to them?" Savannah asked. She still wasn't totally convinced but found there was a part of her that was feeling relieved. A good-sized part, too.

Jesse thought he detected an uplift in her voice. "It's hard to say. It might be more a case of *where* they are."

"What do you mean?"

"It's just that where Tsor is concerned, you literally never know where you stand as far as time goes. For all I know, what I took pictures of is in the future and doesn't exist yet.

"The good part is that little brother, here, may have succeeded in keeping me out of the loony bin a little longer." He disconnected his phone from the computer, sticking it back in the pocket of his khakis. "But I still need to tell you the rest of the story."

Jesse spent the next thirty minutes filling James and Savannah in on his latest experience with Tsor, including the theme surrounding the number three and how it played out as far as asking questions and how often he could visit. Savannah and James listened intently.

"Any questions?" Jesse asked when he'd finished.

"Yes. A big one." Savannah's face held a radiant softness and Jesse could see she was hesitant to continue.

"It's okay, Savannah," he said softly. "I can probably guess what it is." He walked over to where a large window offered a broad view of the side yard. Even with the light rain outside, perhaps even because of it, the multitude of wildflowers had raised their delicate heads skyward, unaware of the effect their simple beauty had on the man who couldn't look upon them without remembering how he and Ellen had planted them together.

"Like I said, Tsor opened a portal for me." He spoke without turning away from the view. "What I didn't tell you was what I saw." He stopped abruptly, an idea entering his mind. "Come with me, both of you." Without a word, he walked out of the room leaving Savannah and James hurrying to catch up. Jesse led them up the stairs and into an expansive bedroom.

Savannah's eyes swept the room. Commanding her immediate attention was the bed. She'd never seen one quite like it. It seemed to be made of a living tree with its headboard and footboard fashioned, not from cutting wood into flat surfaces but allowing what had once been a tree to offer itself as a bed. She'd seen the magical artistry of Adirondack woodworkers before and had been fascinated by their skill in working with the natural curves and forms of their materials to create breathtakingly beautiful pieces of furniture of which the bed before her was a prime example.

It was definitely a man's bed, she thought. The comforter, however, was another story. It struck her, as did the window dressings and the soft pastel colors of the walls, that the room was a synthesis of masculine and feminine. A harmonious blend of what it meant to be a man and a woman who had become one flesh.

"The image in the portal filled the entire wall." Jesse continued his story as if there had been no break in its telling. "What I saw was this room. Ellen's and my room." He paused. "Our room." He motioned towards the space between the foot of the bed and a large bay window. "She was right there on the floor with Kai. Painting his dew claw with her nail polish and telling him it was the source of his strength."

Savannah pictured the scene in her mind and instantly understood. The vision would have deeply impacted the sensitive man who slept in the massive bed underneath the comforter he once shared with the love of his life. If her own heart was breaking at the telling, it was no wonder they had found Jesse collapsed in tears on the cavern's earthen floor.

21

THE RESTAURANT WAS one that he and Ellen had enjoyed together on many occasions. In fact, if not their favorite place to dine, it was certainly in the top two or three. Even on the rare occasions when he'd dated after his wife's death he had never brought a woman to Bianchi's. It was an Italian restaurant that, fortunately for Jesse, also served up the most mouth-watering filet mignon he'd ever eaten. Ellen loved pasta. Bianchi's offered them a place where they could each order what they liked best without anyone having to compromise. Not that Jesse disliked traditional Italian dishes. He and Ellen had often dropped in for an early dinner right as Bianchi's was opening for the evening. Instead of sitting in one of the more formal dining rooms they'd grabbed a booth in the cozy space just inside the entrance. They would split a lasagna dinner between them after savoring a simple salad transformed into something wonderful via Bianchi's scrumptious house dressing. Over a glass of wine they would share the day's events, laughing over things that had seemed monumental frustrations earlier in the day which, as they sat side by side, melted into trivialities. Jesse had lost himself in Ellen's chestnut brown eyes.

This evening, as he sat across the table from Savannah, he found himself looking into eyes of a different color. Eyes of the clearest green he had ever seen. And he was marveling that, given the extraordinary events of the day, he was with a woman he was attracted to in a place where only a week ago he couldn't imagine ever bringing a woman to other than Ellen. It was enough to make his head spin.

It was partly James' fault. After Jesse had shared with Savannah and James everything he could remember about his latest visit with Tsor, they had made a pot of coffee and gone out on the deck. Given the overcast day and the intensity of emotions, James had suggested they go out for dinner to unwind. It was only when Jesse and Savannah had agreed that James let them know what *he* meant by 'they' was just Jesse and Savannah, claiming he had something to do and didn't want them around while he was doing it. He didn't want any questions or arguments, either. He just wanted them out of the house for a few hours.

Savannah had gone home to feed Jenny and get ready after first asking Jesse if he had anyplace in particular in mind so she could dress accordingly. She'd expected someplace casual and had been surprised, pleasantly so, by his suggestion of Bianchi's. She hadn't been in town long but, then again, it didn't take long to hear about one of the area's most notable restaurants.

If Savannah had been surprised, Jesse even more so. The suggestion had rolled off his tongue as if it had been sitting there just waiting for him to open his mouth so it could jump out. As the waiter left with their order, Jesse found himself glad James wasn't with them.

The woman across the table was a Savannah he had only seen shadows of up until now. Although he had found her more than a little attractive each time he had seen her, the settings had all been casual. Tonight was different. It was plain they both interpreted the evening as something more than two new friends going out to grab a bite to eat. This was a date, their first, and they both knew it.

Savannah wore a sleeveless dress of some material that struck Jesse as what gold might look like if you spun it into a dress. It shimmered when she walked and showed off her figure in a tasteful, yet undeniably sensual, fashion. Her makeup accented the suggestion of honey in the blonde hair reaching across the top of her forehead on its way to being tucked behind one ear. Gold hoops hung from her earlobes, falling down the line of her slender neck. When they had entered the dining room, male heads turned. They couldn't help it, Savannah was beautiful.

"I bet you didn't figure your first week on the job would have included everything you've been through over the past six days." It wasn't the best opening line Jesse had ever come up with but it was all he could manage. It felt dreamlike being here with Savannah at a place so closely associated with Ellen. He was full of conflicting thoughts and emotions. Savannah sat across the table, her warm smile reminding him of just how great it was to be on the receiving end of a woman's attention. Not just any woman, of course. There had to be some chemistry involved, like what was happening inside of him at that very moment. He wondered if Savannah was experiencing anything similar.

"I don't think I could have dreamed up such an experience," she laughed. "It's been the craziest combination of wonderful and bizarre at the same time. Meeting you and James is part of the wonderful. We've become close friends in such a short time. I guess it's no wonder given the exceptional circumstances.

139

"Which brings me to Tsor and the portals room. That's the part of the week that belongs to the bizarre." She cocked her head, looking at him with an impish grin. "I'm hoping you're not going to hold my struggles with doubts against me?" She didn't wait for an answer. "The gap in the pictures went a long way in helping me to believe you, Jesse. It's just that—"

"It's just that rooms inside of boulders with chairs, a book that writes in itself and a magic wall that shows you another dimension of time, all put together by a character who goes by the strange name of Tsor, isn't the sort of thing a person can glibly swallow." He returned her look with a smile of his own.

"No, Savannah. I don't blame you for having doubts. I have some of my own and I've been inside the room twice now." The waiter returned with two glasses of wine; white for Savannah, red for Jesse. "Maybe this will help." Jesse raised his glass. "To the future unveiling of the truth."

They touched glasses lightly, each enjoying their wine and appreciating its power to ease the tension.

Savannah looked around. Although only six-thirty, the restaurant was already packed. "Popular place."

Jesse nodded. "It is. Some of the best Italian food in the area and definitely the best filet mignon anywhere on the planet."

"On the planet?" Savannah raised an eyebrow. "That's pretty high praise coming from one of the barbecue boys."

"If you beg, I'll share a bite. Then you'll understand."

Savannah was glad to see Jesse starting to relax. She was, too. She was pretty sure, for all of his wrestling with the ghosts of Ellen's memory, he was attracted to her. A guy didn't bring a girl to a place like Bianchi's because he thought of her as his sister. The problem was in knowing how to act. She wanted to allow herself to give Jesse the natural signals a woman sends when she finds herself attracted to a man and wants to encourage his attention and move the relationship along to a deeper level. She sensed, though, the deeper level was already occupied or, at least, hadn't yet been completely vacated.

How different things were from the simplicity of their time together at the barbecue when Ellen was a loving memory the passage of time had almost placed in the appropriate recesses of Jesse's tender heart, leaving the rest of him ready to move on. Tsor and his portals room had changed all that, snatching Ellen back from the dead and presenting her to Jesse alive.

Savannah wasn't jealous. Not really. Just confused. If Ellen were truly alive Savannah would be happy for Jesse and look forward to being counted as one of his and Ellen's friends. But if Ellen was dead, then Savannah wanted a chance to learn more about the man sitting across the table from her. For the moment, it seemed as though Ellen had one foot in the past and another very much in the present. Quite a challenge for them both and Savannah decided she'd simply have to be content to support Jesse as a deeply caring friend as best she could for now and see where things went.

When their food arrived, they found themselves hungrier than they supposed. Savannah had ordered Spinach Carbonara while Jesse hadn't budged from his intention to devour another filet mignon. He caught Savannah looking more than once at the generous portion of beef on his plate, olive oil oozing from a cut cooked to a perfect medium rare. "Looking isn't begging," he stated matter-of-factly. "I think you can do better."

"I was just marveling at how a man could eat his meal in good conscience without offering his date a single bite, especially after I've shared three heaping forkfuls of my pasta with you already!" As soon as the words were out of her mouth, she froze. She hadn't intended to refer to their outing as a date. The word had slipped out before she realized what she was saying. Savannah cast a worried look across the table and was relieved to find Jesse smiling, seemingly unfazed.

"So, we're on a date are we?"

"It just slipped out. I didn't mean anything by it."

"You didn't?"

"No."

"That's too bad."

"Really, why?" If Jesse was trying to arouse her curiosity he was pushing all the right buttons.

"Because it feels like a date to me, too."

Jesse was taking a chance given all the different eddy-currents running amuck inside of him. But it was the truth. It *did* feel like a date. He

141

reached across the table and was rewarded with the answering touch of her hand. "The truth is, Savannah, I'm attracted to you. Very much so." He looked at her through honest eyes. "And I know it's complicated and unsettling to find ourselves in the middle of something as crazy as what this week has been." He grew quiet but never looked away.

"And yes, I still love Ellen and I always will and it's terribly confusing to be in a place where some faceless, voiceless character out of a sci-fi movie tells you he has the power to give you a chance to change the past.

"I'd be lying to you, Savannah, if I didn't tell you that if Tsor can actually give me that kind of power I'll do whatever I can to get Ellen back." He saw Savannah's eyes water but knew he had to confront the truth for both their sakes. He let go of her hand and sat back in his chair.

They were quiet for a time, absorbed in their own thoughts. It was Savannah who broke the silence first. "I can't imagine what you must be feeling, Jesse. And I certainly never expected to meet someone like you so quickly after moving here." She paused as the waiter approached, asking if they would like coffee and dessert. They ordered coffee and decided to share a piece of cheesecake with raspberries.

"I'm sure you know I'm attracted to you, too, Jesse," Savannah continued. "Thank God, the attraction is built on the start of a solid friendship. So I guess we'll just have to play this by ear and see where it takes us. And if, by some fantastic chance it gets you your wife back, I may be a little wistful, maybe even more than a little, but I will truly celebrate your happiness."

James couldn't help smiling at the thought of his brother and Savannah dining together at Bianchi's. When Jesse had told him where they were going, James wondered if he'd heard right, remembering it had been one of Jesse and Ellen's favorite spots. It would be full of memories. If his twin returned with the report they'd had a good time, it would mark a major milestone in Jesse's forward progress. He thought himself pretty clever at having set the two up to go out without him. Then again, they were like two kids at the top of a big slide for the first time, wanting desperately to hurdle down the chute but needing a gentle shove to get them started. It had been his pleasure to supply the nudge.

142

Alone in the big house, James was free to pursue the other part of his plans for the evening. He grabbed his Bible and went into the library, taking a seat in the chair whose likeness his brother claimed inhabited the portals room.

According to Jesse, Tsor had somehow managed to make the counterfeit chair an exact replica of the one James was now sitting in, right down to the minute details of wear and the missing brass brad. James' plan was to make another alteration to the chair. Actually, two. Neither of which he would tell Jesse about until the proper time.

It was plain to James that Tsor wasn't from the right side of the supernatural tracks. He didn't know where Tsor fit into the scheme of things but he was convinced Tsor's intensions weren't good. James would be sharing his concerns with his brother but suspected Jesse would either disagree or dismiss them. For the present, his twin was focused only on the power Tsor was tempting him with. Power that seemed to be for something good. That was the cruelty of it. It was a masking of evil by what appeared to be good.

The first step in James' plans for the chair was simple. He sat down in it, made himself comfortable, opened his Bible to the First Epistle of John and began reading aloud. He didn't stop until he finished reading the epistle's closing verses.

We know that we are of God, and the whole world lies in the power of the evil one. And we know that the Son of God has come, and has given us understanding, in order that we might know Him who is true, and we are in Him who is true, in His Son Jesus Christ. This is the true God and eternal life. Little children, guard yourselves from idols.

Satisfied, James closed the Bible, got to his feet and turned the chair over, revealing a light-colored thin fabric film stretched across the bottom of the frame. He took a bottle out of the pocket of his pants. It was a bottle of Iced Mauve he'd gone out and bought at the drugstore shortly after Jesse had left to pick up Savannah. He grinned as he used the applicator to brush an image of a cross onto the fabric. Underneath the cross he painted the words he had just read: *This is the true God.*

He stepped back, admiring his handiwork. If Tsor was connected to the dark side of the supernatural he wouldn't be too happy about this latest addition to Jesse's chair. Maybe he wouldn't know about it. Maybe it wouldn't even get mirrored in the forgery sitting in the portals room. But it couldn't hurt, either.

James had read the Bible aloud for the express purpose of clearing the room of any supernatural minions that might be spying about the place. He'd never seen a demon but he was going to take God's word for it they existed. If they wanted to stick around while he read Scripture, so be it.

The second alteration he had in mind was a subtle one. It was also something Savannah could control herself. If James was right, and the portals chair mimicked the chair in the library, the second alteration would convince both him and Savannah of the reality of Jesse's incredible story.

22

THE RAIN WAS beginning to taper off and as Danny reached his destination it had all but stopped. He switched off the ATV and walked to the water's edge. Looking out over the lake he saw a lone fishing boat in the distance. It was too far away to make out anyone on board. If he couldn't make them out, they couldn't make him out, either. Anyway, it paid to survey your surroundings before getting down to business. It wouldn't do to get sloppy and find himself surprised while he was preoccupied with other things.

A quick glance around the site revealed nothing out of the ordinary. There wasn't so much as a gum wrapper laying around. The fire pit was empty, too. If it weren't for the faint outlines of footprints scattered about in the rain-soaked ground he wouldn't have known Savannah and her two companions had been here. He was no tracker but the imprints were sufficiently fresh and numerous enough for him to see they had spent time either around, or sitting, at the picnic table. He even came across an occasional dog print.

Eventually, Danny untangled the mass of prints well enough to see that they seemed to have both come from, and gone off in, another direction. His head was down and he was concentrating so intently on the prints leading away from the site he never saw the figure perched atop the boulder until he was only a few feet away. Startled, he stopped dead in his tracks.

He was looking at a young woman, clearly a foreigner. Asian, or maybe Polynesian. Her long black hair was strikingly beautiful and flowed across bare shoulders. She was the most enchanting creature Danny had ever laid eyes on. And she was looking right at him, smiling warmly in greeting.

"You must be Danny." The sound out of her mouth struck him as much like music as words. "I've heard a lot about you."

Danny was speechless.

"Why, Danny. Cat got your tongue?" She tossed him an engaging smile. "I've come a long way to see you. Aren't you going to say hello?"

145

Danny stood transfixed as the magnificent creature slid to the ground, making her way to where he stood. She not only spoke with musical tones, Danny thought, she even walked as though her steps were set to a matching rhythm. She examined him through dark eyes that penetrated into the depths of his skull, making him uneasy.

"Who are you?" His voice sounded thin. He'd better pull himself together. There wasn't a female breathing who had ever worked her charms on him like this one. He'd have to keep his guard up until he knew more about her.

"Ah, you've found your voice. I'm glad." Her eyes held him fast. "My friends call me Lavelle."

"Lavelle?"

"Yes. My real name is much longer and hard to pronounce by tongues unfamiliar with my native land."

"And that would be?"

"Upolu. It is an island in the region of Oceania. I was the first woman on the island." She reached out her hand. "But if you want to learn more about who I am and why I'm here, you'll have to come with me."

"Where are we going?" Danny hadn't seen any boat at the small dock that served the site and a quick glance around didn't reveal any other means of transportation.

"Why, inside the rock, of course." She gestured at the boulder. "Isn't that why you came, to find out what your friends are up to?"

Danny frowned. Whoever Lavelle was, she had her intelligence down pat. "They aren't my friends."

The brown skinned woman laughed. "No. I suppose you're right. Jesse Whitestone is definitely not your friend and I bet if you met his brother, James, you wouldn't like him much, either. But then again," she added, her smile vanishing, "neither do we."

"We?"

"As I said, follow me." She took his hand, leading him around to the opposite side of the boulder. Without pausing she dropped her head, stepping through what looked to Danny like a small entrance to a cave.

146

Before he had time to protest, he'd instinctively ducked, following her inside. It happened so quickly he had no time to form an opinion as to what he would have expected once inside. Even if he had been given a lifetime, it wouldn't have been what lay before his astonished eyes.

It looked like a scene out of a movie, a scene shot somewhere in the Pacific Ocean onboard a billionaire's yacht. Instead of finding himself within the close confines of a shallow cave he was somewhere on an upper deck where two chaise lounges faced seaward, affording a panoramic view of the ocean without a hint of land in sight. There was a bar nearby as well, attended by a dark-complexioned man whose features hinted that he was an Islander as well. Danny was more than taken aback. He could even smell the salt of the ocean and feel the gentle rolling of the ship as the craft plowed effortlessly through the vast expanse of blue water, the muted sound of powerful engines humming in his ears.

Lavelle dropped into one of the lounge chairs, stretching herself the length of it and donning a pair of trendy sunglasses. She patted the chair next to her. "Danny, sit down beside me, won't you?" Her voice was intoxicating. "I know it's a lot to take in. Quite a shock for most people, I suppose. But," she shot him a knowing look, "after all, you're not like *most people*. Are you, Danny?" She didn't wait for his answer. "I can guess some of the questions going through your mind so, while you're acclimating yourself to your new surroundings, let me give you some answers.

"First off, as you can see, the organization I work for is wealthy, big, and very powerful. More powerful than you can imagine. Powerful enough to turn a large rock on the east shore of Stillman's Lake into an entranceway to where you are now."

Danny sank into the chaise next to her. He'd heard about LSD and its hallucinogenic effects. He wasn't against experimenting with drugs, either, but he'd never tried LSD. He wasn't looking so much to expand his mind as he was chasing euphoric sensations. He did his best to focus on what Lavelle was saying.

"As to where we are, suffice it to say it's somewhere out on the ocean. But, don't worry, I'll have you back at the lake within moments of when we met. You see," she smiled knowingly, "we have the power to manipulate time as well. In point of fact," she went on, "there's not much we can't do."

Danny found his voice. "Did you bring Savannah here, too?"

147

"No. Although we're interested in Savannah, we preferred to meet you first. The only one we've made contact with so far is Mr. Whitestone."

"Jesse? You're interested in him?"

"Yes, but not in the same way we are you, Danny."

The man from the bar brought drinks, offering one first to Lavelle and then to Danny. They looked like Bloody Marys. Following Lavelle's lead, Danny set the celery stalk aside and took a sip. He might as well get comfortable. Maybe the alcohol would relax him.

The drink didn't taste like it had vodka in it. "What's the beverage of choice here?" Danny asked, trying to sound like the whole experience was something he'd done a thousand times before.

"We call it Veritas Juice."

"Veritas? Isn't that Latin for 'truth'?"

"It is." She clinked her glass against his. "Truth with a bite to it, wouldn't you say? It's also known as a Bloody J."

He'd tried a lot of different drinks with his buddies but he'd never come across one like this. It tasted wonderful going down, but after you swallowed it left a bitter aftertaste. It was doing the trick, though. He could feel himself mellowing.

Lavelle continued her explanation. "You see, Danny, our interest in Jesse is more of one competitor against another, with Jesse in the middle of the competition. I'll explain to you in greater detail some other time. As for his brother, James, he's on our blackout list and we have no interest in him one way or another."

"What about Savannah?"

"Ah, yes. Savannah." She cast him a sidewise glance. "You rather like her, don't you?" She waited a moment before going on, taking a bite from her stalk of celery, the crisp vegetable yielding with a light cracking sound. "I don't blame you, actually. She's a very pretty girl. But a bit headstrong.

"What we have in mind, Danny," she sat up, leaning close to him, "is arriving at a place where you and Savannah both become part of our organization. Of course, you would have the higher authority with Savannah reporting to you."

148

Danny liked what he was hearing. "What exactly would we be doing?"

"You're getting a little ahead of yourself, Danny. For now, you're on probation until we know you have what it takes." Lavelle tossed him a reassuring smile. "Don't worry. I picked you out myself and I'm a very good judge of character. For now, all we want you to do is continue on with your fact-finding activity.

"Oh, yes," she said, noting the look of surprise on his face. "We know all about the bug you planted in Savannah's office. Very clever work with the keys too—although it cost us some effort to keep you from being found out on that one."

Danny was stunned. How in the world did she know? Worse, what *didn't* she know? And what did she mean about being found out?

As if reading his mind, the dark-haired beauty answered his unspoken question. "Stanley, your crew chief, discovered the missing door lock blanks during his recent inventory and was getting ready to grill you. We thought it best to intervene. You slipped up a bit on that one, but that's where we come in handy. We've arranged for Stanley to go out of town for a while. Believe me, the key blanks are the furthest thing from his mind."

Lavelle adjusted the back of her chaise, allowing herself to settle into a more horizontal position with only her back slightly elevated. With those sunglasses on, Danny couldn't tell if her eyes were open or closed. He was grateful for the break in conversation, though. It gave him a chance to process the onslaught of mental and sensory data bombarding him. He took a big gulp of Veritas Juice and tried to piece together what he knew.

Although he didn't have the name of the organization Lavelle was part of, her claim that it was a powerful one was backed up by both their intelligence capabilities and the sheer fact he'd walked into a boulder on an overcast day of rain and humidity and come out on a yacht in the middle of a sparkling ocean under a blazing sun and cerulean sky! That alone was proof of more power than he could dream of.

Then again, what if he were dreaming? What if he were under some kind of mind control? He told himself not to get carried away. He'd gone out to the site, following footprints leading to the boulder where he'd found Lavelle waiting for him. What he'd found was real. Hadn't Savannah and her companions been talking excitedly about missing pictures? Maybe they had

149

experienced the same thing. Or rather Jesse might have, as Lavelle seemed to indicate they had made contact with the guy. Maybe the organization only needed one man and Danny was in competition against Jesse for the spot with Savannah going to the winner. If that were the case, Danny was determined to come out on top.

He cringed as he imagined himself being confronted by Stanley over the key blanks. That was a close one. He should have seen the inventory coming and bought a couple of blanks to cover his tracks. Okay. Whoever the organization was, he owed them one. He'd play along and see where all this was going. Danny looked over to find Lavelle looking at him, sunglasses now poised atop her lovely Polynesian head.

"There are a couple more things I need to tell you before we head back."

Danny nodded. "Yeah?"

"First, as I said, you'll find that time inside the boulder isn't the same as time anywhere else. So don't be surprised by what you may find when you exit. But don't worry, we'll be sure any difference is to your advantage. We like what we see in you, Danny. You've got potential. We're here to help you realize that potential for our mutual benefit.

"Next on the list is that we have another man on the outside, a young man like you by the name of Julio. In due time, Julio will be getting in touch with you." She laughed. "He's a specialist and not destined for the upper level position we have in mind for you so don't worry about him. He's going to help you. In fact, he already has by getting Stanley out of your hair— although he doesn't know that was the primary goal of his latest mission. When he contacts you he'll be wanting something. Give it to him. Like I said, he'll only be there to help you so give him what he needs.

"Lastly, at least for now, you need to realize how important secrecy is to us. We don't have a lot of rules but strict confidentiality is one of them." She put her face within inches of his, drilling him with her dark, penetrating eyes. "You tell anyone *anything* about what you see or hear when you're with me and you're a dead man. Understand?"

The change in her was terrifying—her features seemed to sharpen into those of a bloodthirsty warrior. An involuntary tremble rippled through Danny's body.

As quickly as it had come, the awful fierceness she displayed vanished, replaced by the soft gentleness of a comely island beauty. "That wasn't meant to be a threat, Danny," she cooed. "But it is true. This is deadly serious business and I wouldn't want anything to happen to someone I had hand-picked for an important role.

"Oh, and one more thing. Don't call us, we'll call you. In other words, don't come anywhere near the boulder without our permission. Understood?"

He nodded again. "When will you be getting in touch with me?"

She patted his hand. "Soon, Danny. Very soon."

Stanley was as good as his word, calling Bev from his daughter Sara's house late Saturday evening around eleven. He hated calling so late but knew she would be anxious to hear from him. He'd called Savannah at her home but had had to leave a voice message when she hadn't answered. Then he called Bev.

Stanley briefly shared with her that his son-in-law had been fatally shot in what police believed to be a murder related to his position with ICE as a border patrol agent. There had been rumors some of the Mexican drug cartels were recruiting gang members to make hits on the border patrol in retaliation for inroads ICE was making in shutting down some of their routes into the states. It looked like the rumor was true and Derrick was the first casualty.

Sara was physically all right but in emotional shock. Their eight-year-old daughter, Olivia, still wasn't speaking. Stanley would call again when he had more he could tell them. He had no idea at this point when he would be returning.

Bev promised to pass along the update to Savannah, explaining that she had called Savannah earlier and had also left a message. Stanley asked if Bev would pray with him and they spent the next few minutes asking God's help with Sara and little Olivia.

23

RETURNING HOME FROM his date with Savannah at Bianchi's, Jesse found his brother waiting for him out on the deck. A bottle of one of Jesse's better wines from his cellar stood open on the table, the glass in James' hand ready for a refill, a smug smile plastered across his face.

"You know something I don't?" Jesse asked.

His brother's pretended innocence didn't fool James. "Bro, you've got the great misfortune to be a Giants fan so you've gotta know that you are fooling nobody with your end-around play. Have you looked at your face in the mirror? I'd say you had a pretty good first date with Savannah."

"It wasn't a date."

"Yeah, right. And I'm not your twin brother."

"That's right. You're adopted. My parents felt sorry for you and thought you'd make a good playmate."

James rolled his eyes. Jesse picked up the empty glass his brother had brought out in anticipation of Jesse's return, pouring himself some wine then adding some to his brother's glass. "Wouldn't want you to run low seeing as how we must be celebrating something."

"Of course we're celebrating! It's been three years since I've seen you this happy! Look, Jesse," James leaned forward, his twinkling eyes reflecting the dancing flame of one of the Tiki torches, "I'm not saying you and Savannah are a sure thing and you'll go on to get married and live happily ever after. For all I know, three months from now she'll catch on to what a lunk-head you are and ditch you. I'm just glad to see you open to the fact life has a lot left in store for you."

Kai was happy to see his master home and had been repeatedly nudging Jesse's hand since he'd returned, looking for attention. Jesse tapped his chest, the signal to let Kai know it was all right for him to dish out his favorite greeting. The dog immediately sprang up, standing on hind legs and placing his great paws on Jesse's shoulders, his canine head nearly even with Jesse's.

"Hey, Kai. How's my best friend?" He placed a hand on each side of the noble face looking up at him, the two exchanging unspoken words of love in that unique bond that exists between some humans and the creatures they have become so intimately attached to.

"And I thought I was your best friend," James feigned injury to his pride.

"Like I said, you were adopted. It didn't work out." Jesse loved to tease his brother. They could both take as good as they gave and he had no fear his twin failed to treasure, as Jesse did himself, how close the two of them had been over the years. It was comforting to have James with him during the present craziness and Jesse wondered how long his twin would be able to stay, suddenly realizing they hadn't yet talked about it. He pointed a finger towards the ground and Kai immediately dropped to all fours. Jesse pulled out a chair and sat down. "So, how long can you stay this time around, James? A couple of weeks? A month maybe?"

James laughed. "As much as I'd like to, I'm afraid my business would go down the tubes if I did." He sipped his wine, savoring the taste. "It's not that I'm indispensible. It's more a case of the state of the economy and the need to personally nurture the relationships I've made over the years. Everybody is competing for a profitable piece of a shrinking market and I need to stay involved to protect my turf."

"Will you be able to stay at least until my next visit with Tsor?" There was no hiding the concern in Jesse's voice.

"Wouldn't miss it. I figure if something happens to you I'll inherit the family heirlooms all for myself. It'll take the sting out of being adopted."

The two sat quietly, enjoying the varied sounds issuing from nocturnal creatures inhabiting the grounds. It was overcast; dark clouds nearly smothering the moon and only a handful of the brightest stars visible in the night sky. Jesse was pleased with James' assurance he would at least be staying through Tuesday. Jesse had only made two visits to the portals room so far but each had made him feel as though he were a blob of dough being kneaded and pressed into a thin, flat wafer. James contributed not only a good mind but a reassuringly calm presence. Jesse was grateful for both.

"Still think aliens are an option?" James probed.

Jesse supposed James was feeling him out, looking to see where he stood as to Tsor's identity. "It's possible. It still makes about as much sense to me as anything else." He shrugged. "To tell you the truth, as strange as it may sound, I haven't really given that part of the mystery a whole lot of thought. The idea of getting Ellen back alive is so fantastic, so overwhelming, it crowds out everything else."

"But not Savannah." James said it without the slightest hint of accusation. "Look, Jesse, I don't pretend to know what it must feel like to be in your shoes. I can't even imagine what it would be like to be tempted by something so powerful as getting back the person you loved the most in the whole world. But I think you still need to consider where the offer is coming from."

"Are we back to your theory of the supernatural?"

"Have you discounted it?"

"Actually, no. I haven't. Aliens, the devil, and God all sound far-fetched to me. But," Jesse confessed, "I suppose, from what I've experienced so far, it has to be one of the three." He caught his brother's eye. "Ever hear of Directed Panspermia?"

"You mean Crick's theory that life here on Earth was seeded by microorganisms sent here by aliens?" James had read about Francis Crick's theory. It didn't get a lot of press in the popular media as the masses still fervently clung to Darwin's theory of evolution. Having been co-recipient of the Nobel Prize for the discovery of DNA, the logical implications forced on the brilliant mind of the man by the knowledge that a single human strand of DNA contains the information needed to direct all the one hundred trillion cells in the human body seemed to had led Crick to embrace intelligent design—albeit by some as yet unidentified, highly advanced life form somewhere else in the universe as opposed to God.

"So you're trading monkeys in as your ancestors in favor of Martians?"

"Look, James. Crick is no dummy. And he's not alone. There are other scientists, like Hoyle and Wickramasinghe."

"I know," James countered. "They believe it's possible the Earth was seeded by complex genes set adrift in space and allowed to drift around like dandelion seeds on a windy day." Clearly, Jesse seemed as resistant to entertain the idea of the existence of the supernatural as the scientists he'd named. James briefly entertained the thought of mentioning other brilliant scientific minds, like Michael Behe and Phillip Johnson, men holding a strong belief in God, as examples for Jesse to consider but thought better of it. This was no time to get tangled up in a pointless argument. He tried to gently steer them back into neutral territory.

"Agreed," James went on, "Those guys are pretty sharp and at least they've come to the conclusion life didn't just pop up out of some primordial soup from a combination of time and chance. I'll give them credit for recognizing that much. I just want to encourage you to keep an open mind as to an alternative explanation." He longed to share the full extent of his suspicions with his twin, urging Jesse to be cautious, but realized it would be to no avail. He was glad that, as much as he was concerned for Jesse's welfare, God was even more so. After all, Jesse might be James' brother but he was God's child. James decided to seek safer ground. "So what do you have in mind for your next date with Savannah?"

"There aren't going to be any more dates." Sadness appeared in Jesse's eyes. "We shared openly about our mutual attraction for one another. It's just that...," he drew in a deep breath, "It's just that I needed to be honest with her and let her know that, as crazy as this whole thing with Tsor is, if it leads to an opportunity to get Ellen back alive, I'll take whatever risks are involved."

Jenny was as pleased to see Savannah as Kai had been to see Jesse, the light golden color of her feathered thighs contrasting beautifully with the darker gold of her back and flanks, as if someone had poured honey over her. The retriever had covered Savannah's face with kisses and now lay contentedly as her owner brushed her. It was their evening ritual. The downside to the Golden Retriever's remarkably good-natured temperament was the continual shedding of her hair. As long as Savannah kept up the grooming, it was at least kept to a minimum.

Savannah found herself a jumble of emotions, wondering if it would be wisest to back off completely and give Jesse all the room he needed to sort through things on his own. She'd thought about it on the way home, the drive after leaving Bianchi's subdued after Jesse's emotional declaration about rescuing his wife. Not that she blamed him. Not a bit. She'd feel the same way if their situations were reversed. She just didn't want to get close to him only to find herself falling in love with a married man whose wife was dead but might come back to life any moment. Under normal circumstances she'd definitely pull back. But these were anything but normal circumstances and she felt Jesse needed her. Savannah shook her head. It was crazy! Maybe things would make more sense after a night's sleep. She headed to the bedroom, Jenny in tow, failing to notice the indicator on her phone showing she had two voice messages waiting for her.

Bev was reading her Bible in bed, the lamp on the nightstand casting a comforting butter-colored glow on the book lying open on her lap. The old book was well worn, one in a long line of Bibles that had given themselves to sharing their precious words of life with this aging child of the ageless Child from Heaven. She had been reading in the gospel of John about some Greeks who had come looking to meet Jesus. In responding to the disciples who had come to let Him know of their interest, Jesus had said:

"Truly, truly, I say to you, unless a grain of wheat falls into the earth and dies, it remains by itself alone; but if it dies, it bears much fruit. He who loves his life loses it; and he who hates his life in this world shall keep it to life eternal. If anyone serves Me, let him follow Me; and where I am, there shall My servant also be; if anyone serves Me, the Father will honor him.

"Now My soul has become troubled; and what shall I say, 'Father, save Me from this hour'? But for this purpose I came to this hour. Father, glorify Thy name." There came therefore a voice out of heaven: "I have both glorified it, and will glorify it again." The multitude therefore, who stood by and heard it, were saying that it had thundered; others were saying, "An angel has spoken to Him."

Jesus answered and said, "This voice has not come for My sake, but for your sakes. Now judgment is upon this world; now the ruler of this world shall be cast out. And I, if I be lifted up from the earth, will draw all men to Myself."

To Bev, the thought that God would draw every man and woman to Himself through His Son, Jesus, was a grand and lovely thought—one that, as she closed her Bible and turned off the light, carried through to her prayers for Stanley's young granddaughter, Olivia. She asked God to give the little girl the patience and strength she would need to carry her through to the day when she would see her father again.

24

JESSE WOKE EARLY Sunday morning. A check of the time showed it to be shortly after five—perfect for what he had in mind. He needed time alone. He missed his old routine of going out to the lake with Kai, sitting at the picnic table out at the site and allowing memories of the happiness he'd known with Ellen to have their way with him. He supposed it was a form of self-torture, a comfort that also hurt like crazy, even after three years. But he didn't know how to give it up.

Meeting Savannah had struck him as a way out of the fierce grip the past had on him. He realized she was special and still thought their meeting was more than coincidental. Jesse found long dormant thoughts and feelings coming alive again, as if he were an extinct volcano showing renewed signs of life with detectable stirrings and rumblings.

That was before he'd encountered Tsor and the portals room. Jesse couldn't tell if the timing was lousy or perfect. He supposed it all depended on the outcome. If, incredible as it still sounded to him, he was able to get Ellen back, Tsor would be his hero and Jesse would howl at the moon on Tsor's behalf. On the other hand, if he lost both Ellen and Savannah in some half-baked scheme cooked up by the father of Directed Panspermia or whatever else was out there in the universe... well, there was no telling what it would do to him. He might just hit the road with Kai and never be seen again.

With Kai in tow, Jesse grabbed the thermos of coffee he'd made and headed for the garage. If he timed things right, James might even have breakfast waiting for him when he returned.

He was in autopilot on the drive to the lake, the route so familiar Jesse had to remind himself not to let his mind wander so far he forgot he was driving. He figured he'd get to the site just before dawn, before the sun began to work its magic on the lake's surface, transforming the placid morning water into a landscape of a gazillion sparkling diamonds, each one tossing the sun's brilliance back into the sky from whence it came.

Most people focused their attention on the sun itself as it rose from its nocturnal slumber. Jesse preferred to watch its impact, pointing himself in the opposite direction, poised to trace the yellow fireball's effect on the

157

landscape, as if watching an artist's canvas as his painting took form instead of the artist himself.

Actually, as long as he chose to be on the eastern side of the lake, he had no choice. If it was the sun you wanted to see you'd better get yourself over to the more popular western side. The eastern shore was for sun*sets*, something he and Ellen had taken in on countless occasions, with each dipping of the sun etching in their memory an unforgettable moment.

As usual, Jesse parked down the road, walking the remaining distance to the site with Kai beside him, the two forms enveloped in the last fleeting shrouds of lingering darkness. The sun, not yet visible, was giving preliminary warning of its pending emergence, replacing the deep darkness of night with the misty glow of pre-dawn's light.

The creatures of the day were already stirring and Jesse could hear the sounds of songbirds mixing with the cooing of doves and the raucous caws of crows greeting one another higher up in the hills. Chipmunks and red squirrels were competing for the occasional crumbs left either by careless picnickers or intentionally contributed by those who sought to give God a hand in feeding His creatures.

God? What made me think of Him? Maybe it's the residual effect of a long tradition of Sunday mornings going to church when I was a kid. Better eat while you can, guys. If you're depending on God, you may be in for a surprise!

He drew near his destination in silence, his steps carefully taken so as to avoid disrupting the natural sounds of awakening life all around. Suddenly, he froze, a form at the picnic table having suggested itself to his mind as someone sitting looking out over the lake with their back to him. He strained to bring the image into sharper focus. Yes, it was a person. A man. From what he could make out, a black man.

Jesse didn't have a prejudiced bone in his body but he couldn't help feeling a rush of irritation. He didn't care if the guy was black, white, or purple! What in the world was he doing here at *his* site at this of all mornings?

For several moments, Jesse just stood there. He didn't know if he should barge in and introduce himself, hoping the guy wasn't planning on staying for long, or retrace his steps and head back home, counting the morning an unfortunate disaster. Kai saved him the trouble of having to decide. Without warning, the dog moved forward.

158

Kai's approaching the stranger took Jesse by surprise. It was way outside of Kai's normal behavior, not to mention the hours of training he'd received. Jesse thought about commanding Kai to stay but didn't want to startle the guy. He looked so peaceful, sitting and looking out over the water just as Jessie had planned on doing. Before he could say anything, Kai reached the table, standing quietly alongside where the man sat. Jesse watched, fascinated, as the man showed no sign of surprise, simply reaching out a hand to stroke the animal.

"Good morning." Jesse spoke the words softly. "I'm sorry to disturb you. It's just that my dog decided to make your acquaintance before I could stop him."

The man answered without turning, as if such things happened to him all the time. "It's all right. He knows I'm fond of dogs." He waved a hand over the space on the bench beside him. "Now that you're here, why don't you have a seat and join me. Sun's coming up and you wouldn't want to miss the show."

Feeling awkward but not knowing what else to do, Jesse took the offered seat, Kai coming over to take up his usual position beside his master, looking proud of himself for having connected the two men. Jesse was about to introduce himself when the man spoke again, still gazing out over the lake.

"Never get tired of seeing the sun come up, watching how light spreads itself out over the earth, slowly but surely attending to the work God gave it to do."

The man looked to Jesse like he might be somewhere in his late fifties or early sixties. Must have been a handsome man in his younger days, Jesse thought. Even now, although most of his hair was tinged with white, his appearance remained one that would attract attention. His skin was a dark ebony and he had a physique suggesting he had been no stranger to either athletics, hard work, or both. His massive hands rested comfortably on the table's surface. Jesse caught the hint of a tantalizing scent coming from the man—a delightful odor that reminded him of the wildflowers in his gardens at home. Jesse felt his frustration at what he had considered the unwelcome finding of a stranger at the site melting away. It were as if the calmness of the big man next to him was oozing out into the atmosphere, affecting anyone breathing it in.

The two of them sat in silence as dawn broke over Stillman's Lake, rewarded for their willingness to come at such an early hour by the "dance of the diamonds" as Ellen used to call the transformation of the water's surface at the first strike of the sun's rays.

"Name's Michael," the man said as daybreak took a firm grip on their surroundings. Jesse's hand was dwarfed by the one Michael offered.

"I'm Jesse." He nodded towards Kai, "And that rascal is Kai. He really does know better and I'm sorry we barged in on you."

The two shook hands. Even through touch, Jesse sensed the unhurried pace of the big man. If people considered Jesse laid back, this guy was human valium.

"Actually, I didn't take your being here as an intrusion. For me, it was more like icing on the cake." A warm smile spread across Michael's face. "After all, the best things in life are the things we share. Wouldn't you agree?"

Jesse was quiet, a lump growing in his throat. How many times had he sat here alone, wishing for even five more minutes he could share with Ellen? He managed to nod his agreement. "I used to come here with my wife."

Michael didn't say a word.

"We came here a lot. It was our favorite place to be in the whole world outside of our home."

"Sounds like the two of you have something special," Michael said.

"Had. My wife died three years ago. She drowned right out there." Jesse pointed. "We were having a picnic in celebration of our sixth anniversary. I was manning the grill and Ellen had gone out on the lake in an inflatable raft to sunbathe. The food was about ready so I'd motioned for her to come in. She knocked an oar overboard as she got ready to row. When she reached for it she lost her balance and fell into the lake."

Jesse's eyes remained fixed at the point where he'd last seen Ellen in the bright yellow inflatable. The scene of her tumbling overboard and him chuckling at the sight had played itself out in his mind countless times. If he'd known she would never come to the surface again he would have reacted instantly, perhaps in time to have saved her. "She was a great swimmer," he went on. "I wasn't concerned even when I didn't see her come

160

up for a while. She was also a great tease," he explained. "She would have loved goading me into the water just so she could have ambushed me as I swam by.

"Anyway, when she still didn't appear, I panicked and dove into the water trying to find her. I never did." He inhaled deeply. "It took divers twenty minutes to recover her body." Jesse closed his eyes. The memory of seeing her being brought up out of the lake still wracked his insides. *What am I doing spilling my guts out to a guy I've just met, a total stranger?*

As if sensing his discomfort, Michael laid a hand on Jesse's shoulder. "Thank you for telling me, Jesse," he said softly.

They sat quietly for a time until Jesse remembered his thermos. "I've got some coffee. Let me pour you a cup. I hope you like it black."

Michael grinned. "Is there any other way?"

They sat drinking the steaming liquid, listening to a loon in the distance, her crazed calls echoing over the water. Jesse's fascination with the loons never ceased. He could listen to them forever. He remembered that, when they were boys, he and James would go out on the lake in their father's canoe trying to get close to a loon. Every time they drew near, the loon would dive, coming up after what seemed several minutes at some distant point far from where they had guessed it might. Mostly, the creatures poured out their haunting cries as the sun came up and then again when it went down on the far side of the day.

"I don't know what it feels like to lose a wife," Michael remarked, "but I lost a lot of close friends, including my best friend. Oh, they didn't die," he went on to explain. "It was more a case of abandonment. We were serving together in the same outfit. I'd say any way you look at it, it hurts when a meaningful relationship is suddenly cut off." He drank more coffee then raised the cup. "Good stuff, Jessie. Thank you.

"I suppose, when your wife died, you looked around for someone to blame. I bet you even put yourself at the top of that list." His brown eyes never wavered. "From the sound of it, the only other person available to put on the list would have been God, given the two of you were the only ones around at the time besides Kai here. Am I right?"

Michael's observation took Jesse by surprise. It was true. Ellen shouldn't have died. Jesse should have gone into the lake the moment she'd fallen out of the raft. But he was only human. How could he have known the innocent mishap would lead to such a tragedy? God, on the other hand, supposedly knew everything and had unlimited power. If that were true, it made Him a guilty bystander. In Jesse's eyes, God was in the same league as a lifeguard who, hearing a drowning swimmer call out for help, sits back in his white chair high above the fray swigging Coke while the poor guy in the water flails around until he sinks below the waves. He had expected more from God.

"Yeah, you're right," Jesse confessed.

"I thought maybe it might be so."

"What do you think, Michael?" Jesse asked. "Doesn't it make sense given God's supposed ability of knowing everything and having the power to do something about it if someone's going to get hurt, or even die?"

"Things are happening all the time in this world around us, Jesse, where folks are getting hurt and dying. Do you think God should step in and stop all of it from happening?"

"Sounds like a good idea to me."

"And where would you have Him draw the line for intervening?" Michael shook his head. "If you think it through, you end up with God making the world into some kind of padded nursery room inhabited by stillborn children incapable of both harm and love. Poor creatures with no opportunity to grow up into the likeness of their Father." Michael stood. "I need to stretch these legs of mine. Want to walk down the road a ways?"

Jesse brought the thermos to his lips, draining the last of the coffee before screwing the top back on and joining his new acquaintance. As the two walked along the dirt road, Michael stopped and knelt down. "Look at these guys, will you?"

Jesse peered over his shoulder. Along the edge of the road a swarm of ants were scurrying in and out of what he supposed was their nest, somewhere below.

"Fascinating and industrious creatures, aren't they?" The big man chuckled. "What do you think they'd say if I were to sit down right here on the road next to them and explain that, sometime over the next ten years, this dirt road is going to be paved and they need to move their colony to a safer place?"

"I'd say you're so big you'd likely scare the daylights out of them. Not to mention they would have no idea what you're talking about—setting aside the fact I'm not aware of any plans to blacktop this road." Jesse was amused at the thought of Michael talking to ants. It would be like a mountain talking to a grain of sand.

"Agreed! They wouldn't understand a word I was saying. I could talk all I wanted but they'd never understand. If I really cared about them and wanted to help them, I'd just have to go ahead and dig up their colony and move them to a safe place."

Jesse raised an eyebrow. "I take it you've got a point you're trying to make?"

Michael laughed. "I do. But let me continue for a minute before I get to it." He placed a tiny stick directly over one of the openings in the ground. In moments, several ants swarmed over it. "They don't much like their little world disrupted." The two of them watched as a small army of the creatures managed to shove the stick away from the hole. Michael picked up where he left off. "As I was saying, if I wanted to rescue these little guys from being entombed in blacktop, I'd have to dig them up and move them. In the process, they'd likely be confused and angry in their own ant-like way, even though I was actually helping them. They simply wouldn't understand."

He rose, looking at Jesse. "It's the same with us, my young friend. God knows what's coming and He cares enough about us to be always doing whatever needs to be done for our welfare. He can't always stop and explain because of our inability to understand the One who created the universe speaking a language a lot higher than ours." He pointed to the ground. "I'd say the knowledge gap between us and those ants is a lot smaller than what exists between us and God! The good news is we've got a leg up on the ants. They can't even begin to comprehend us whereas you've been made in God's own image and have at least some inkling of what He's like," he tapped Jesse's chest, "because He put some of Himself right in there."

It was somewhere around ten in the morning when Savannah noticed she had two voice messages waiting for her. She accessed the system, smiling as Bev's familiar voice floated into her ear. Her smile quickly faded as Bev's brief message told her that a serious family matter had arisen for Stanley and he'd had to catch a flight to Yuma on Saturday to be with his daughter, Sara.

Bev would explain more when Savannah returned her call. Bev's voice was calm but Savannah sensed the matter was serious.

Her concern heightened when Stanley's voice came on next. He hadn't known if she had had a chance to talk with Bev so he wouldn't go into any details other than saying he was sorry for his abrupt departure but it couldn't be helped. He didn't know how long he would be away, either. He'd call her again at the welcome center sometime late Monday afternoon with an update. He hadn't left a number where he could be reached, saying only that Bev would know. Savannah sensed that, whatever the problem was, Stanley wanted Bev to be the one to break the news to her.

She placed the phone back on its cradle. Was the news so awful that Stanley and Bev were concerned with how she would handle it? She snatched the phone back up and punched in Bev's number.

"Hello? This is Bev." Savannah breathed a sigh of relief. Her friend's voice sounded steady.

"It's me, Savannah."

"Good morning, Savannah. I suppose you're calling about the message I left?"

"Yes. Stanley left one, too, but didn't give any details. What happened? What's wrong with Sara?"

The line went silent for a moment before Bev spoke again, her voice calm but laden with concern. "Sara's husband was killed, yesterday."

"Killed? You mean in an accident?"

"No, it wasn't an accident. He was murdered."

Savannah put a hand to her face as tears began welling up in her eyes. "Oh my God! Poor Sara! What happened?"

"It might be better to talk about it in person, Savannah. Do you mind coming over? I'll put on a fresh pot of coffee."

25

THE MONDAY MORNING meeting at the complex went as well as could be expected, Savannah thought, considering the sobering news she'd shared with the staff. She had been as tactful as possible, telling them only that Stanley had gone to his daughter's in Arizona due to an emergency involving the death of his son-in-law. At this point, the date of his return was unknown as Olivia, Stanley's granddaughter, had been deeply impacted by her father's death. Stanley wanted to be there for his daughter and granddaughter until both weathered the terrible emotional storm.

Bev had listened, silently applauding Savannah's handling of the matter and let the others know they were accepting donations for flowers to be sent on behalf of them all for the upcoming funeral. Danny was the first to contribute, handing Bev a twenty dollar bill when the meeting broke up, remarking on how sad the whole thing was and that he was confident Stanley's presence would prove a source of strength to his daughter and comfort to Olivia.

Danny was deeply impressed. He didn't have the details but he assumed Lavelle and her organization were behind whatever had happened in Arizona and that it had been engineered for his benefit as part of their scheme to lure Stanley away. Admittedly, it was too bad someone had to die but he supposed it had been necessary to assure Stanley's departure. At least it hadn't been Stanley's daughter or granddaughter. Just his son-in-law. Not even a blood relative. They'd be fine. There was probably a chunk of money coming their way from the dead guy's life insurance.

Although Savannah had chosen someone else to temporarily serve as crew chief, Danny had volunteered to pick up a couple of Stanley's responsibilities while he was out—including handling all the inventories. He hadn't heard from Lavelle again but he wasn't worried. Little more than a day had passed since he'd spent time with her on the yacht. The incident had been mind-boggling and Danny was amazed how quickly a person could get comfortable with something so freaky. He was pumped and ready for action. He just hoped they didn't leave him hanging too long. Idling was his worst gear. Danny was built for action.

Savannah retreated to her office, trying to keep her mind on her work, her brain churning through the weekend's events. At the moment, she couldn't decide if she had landed her dream job or a nightmare! Whichever it was, it wasn't what she had expected.

She'd had less than ten minutes contact with Jesse since their dinner together at Bianchi's, calling him Sunday afternoon after returning from Bev's where she had learned the grim details surrounding the murder of Derrick Holmes. She was glad Jesse hadn't suggested getting together. Maybe he sensed she needed time to process everything going on, both between the two of them and this new crisis at work. She had agreed, however, to join him and James for dinner tonight. Tomorrow would be the third day since Jesse's last trip to the portals room and James had asked her help with an alteration to Jesse's library chair he claimed might provide definitive proof of his brother's experience with Tsor. James said the alteration was something Savannah would have complete control of so as to assure the validity of the outcome in her mind. He'd also asked her to swing by a hardware store and pick up a replacement keyset for a door. He'd given her the details she needed to choose one that would fit the door he had in mind. He couldn't pick it up himself as it would defeat the goal of her controlling the experiment but assured Savannah she would understand perfectly before the evening was over.

The rest of the day passed without incident, the mood of the staff somber but everyone attending to the extra workload resulting from Stanley's absence without complaint. Although she was usually the last one out the door, Savannah wanted to leave early so she could stop at a hardware store on the way home. She arranged with Bev to cover for her. She had hoped Stanley would have called by now but supposed events on his end were such that flexibility was needed. She'd given Bev instructions to pass along her mobile number to Stanley in the event he called in the half-hour remaining before the staff went home. Savannah hadn't yet talked with Stanley directly and she longed to do what she could to let him know how sorry she was and ask what she could do to be of help. She wanted to set his mind at ease by telling him to take all the time he needed without worrying about things at the complex. Stanley had been a devoted employee for years and, as long as she was in charge, the complex would return the favor by supporting him.

Danny finished making the changes to the inventory count covering the items in the garage. He'd picked up the two key blanks he needed and hung them on their proper hooks on the carousel. Only Stanley knew the truth and it didn't look like he'd be back anytime soon. If Danny was lucky, by the time he did, Stanley would have forgotten all about key blanks and the next time the old guy took inventory everything would be in order.

He'd listened in on Savannah's office throughout the day, the information gleaned pretty lean. Not much going on—at least concerning anything Savannah had going with Jesse Whitestone and the site out on the east shore. Danny had spent as much time in the garage as he dared throughout the day, ear-buds connecting him through his cell phone to the transmitter in Savannah's office. Now, as he heard the sound of someone coming out of the welcome center and saw Savannah heading for her car, he supposed he might as well shut the bug down for the day. He was just about to send the text message deactivating the device when he heard a phone ring in his earpiece and Bev's voice calling Stanley's name. He opted to keep listening.

By the time Bev hung up, Danny was glad he had stayed on the line. The gods were on his side. It was clear to him, even from the single side of the conversation he could hear, Stanley had not only updated Bev on how Sara and Olivia were doing, but had mentioned his concern with Danny as a result of his latest inventory of key blanks. From what Danny overheard, Bev had likely been filled in on the details. So much for Lavelle's claim the keys were the furthest thing from Stanley's mind!

Before hanging up, Bev had told Stanley that Savannah was eager to talk with him and had passed along her cell phone number, an unexpectedly juicy piece of information Danny had hurriedly jotted down for future reference. Much to his relief, Bev had urged Stanley not to say anything to Savannah about the inventory discrepancy, telling him Savannah had a lot on her plate at the moment and assuring him she would fill Savannah in herself in the morning. If it was a question of needing to replace Danny, giving Savannah an evening free of any additional challenging news might help her to get a good night's rest so she could deal with this latest development with a clear head.

Danny could feel beads of perspiration building up on his forehead. The old coot! Stanley just didn't know when to quit. Danny would have to think fast. Something needed to be done before morning to either change Bev's mind or keep her from ratting him out.

Savannah arrived at Jesse's house to find the brothers throwing a Frisbee around in the front yard. She let Jenny out the Subaru's hatch, retrieving the newly purchased keyset from the back seat. "Don't tell me," she admonished. "I'm sure this isn't just an innocent tossing of a plastic disc? I bet it's some sort of war between the Giants and the Rams waged vicariously through the symbolism of a Frisbee! My guess is whoever wins, somehow transfers their good fortune to their team and it comes out next season in the form of a Super Bowl victory. Am I right?"

Jesse nodded to his brother. "The woman is on to us. I told you she was smart."

Savannah took a seat on the porch steps. "So, what are the rules? You've got footwear on so you can't be using your toes to catch the thing."

"We tried," Jesse grinned. "It was a little too messy what with all the bleeding."

Savannah wrinkled her nose. "Yuck! How gross!"

"I wouldn't have mentioned it if you hadn't brought it up first." Jesse sent the orange disc hurtling toward James in a wide arc. "But as for the rules, they're pretty simple. It's the Frisbee version of the game PIG.

"Each player's throw has to be catchable, although you can throw the Frisbee as fast, high, or curvy as you want. You can even make the other guy run for it just as long as it's possible for him to conceivably catch it—in one hand, of course. And as we're both righties, it has to be with our left hand.

"If you miss a catch you get a letter. Same for a bad toss. Throw something uncatchable and you get yourself a letter for that, too. First one to get three letters is a PIG and loses the game."

Savannah laughed. "You guys are nuts! And who decides, by the way, if a throw is uncatchable?"

"That's easy," James offered. "The only one of the two of us with the mathematical brains to calculate the possibilities correctly and render an unbiased opinion."

"Let me guess." Savannah was cracking up. "That would be you, James. Am I right?"

"Bingo!" James yelled, racing across the lawn, just barely managing to snag the Frisbee inches before it hit the ground.

"So, what's the score?" she asked, as Jesse, using every bit of his six-two frame, leaped to his right, just missing the hurtling disc as James sent it rocketing by.

"G!" James screamed, instantly going into his version of an end zone celebration. "You're a PIG Jesse Whitestone and the next Super Bowl belongs to the Rams!"

"No way!" Jesse protested. "Michael Jordan couldn't have caught that thing. The final letter belongs to you!" He turned to Savannah. "I appeal to the beautiful, impartial judge sitting in the umpire's chair to decide the call."

Savannah laughed, raising both hands. "No way! Don't get me mixed up in the Whitestone clan's shenanigans! Besides, I'm a Chiefs fan, being from Topeka and all."

The two brothers moaned in unison as they joined Savannah on the porch. "I guess we'll just have to chalk it up as a draw," James lamented.

"Yeah. What does that make now?" Jesse asked. "Our five hundred and twenty first game of Frisbee PIG in a row ending in a draw?"

"You guys are idiots," Savannah declared. The brothers thought the remark hysterically funny, slapping each other on the back, pointing at one another shouting, "Idiot!"

Savannah was amazed at what a little testosterone could do.

The three went inside and after a light dinner of grilled cheese and tomato sandwiches with fruit salad and chips on the side, gathered in the library where James explained his idea. "Jesse, you said the chair in the portals room is identical to this one, right?" He motioned to the chair beside him.

"That's right."

"You also claimed it was even missing the same brad. This one right here." He pointed to the vacant spot once occupied by the missing brass brad.

"Right again."

James held up a screwdriver and pliers. "Any objections to Savannah extracting another brad of her own choosing?"

Jesse knew exactly where his brother was going. "Not in the least."

Turning to Savannah, James handed her the tools. "While you're figuring out which brad you want to pull, Jesse and I will be installing the new key set in the library door. Be sure to note the exact location of the brad you pull but don't share it with either of us." He opened the box Savannah had given him, withdrew the keys, and handed them to her. "You are now the mistress of the library, the sole possessor of the way in." He turned to his twin. "Come on, Junior. We've got a lock to change. We'll see you outside in the hallway when you're ready, Savannah," he called over his shoulder.

Working as quietly as possible, Danny wrapped the wire twice around the trunk of the slender tree just off Bev's porch. The tree grew close to the porch steps, leading up from the ground to the porch floor, a distance of six feet. He would have preferred there to have been a sidewalk instead of dirt at the base of the steps. The impact of hitting concrete would cause greater injury but, given Bev's age, he figured the fall down the eight steps would be bad enough to seriously injure, if not kill her. He'd bought a kitten at a local pet shop, telling the salesperson it was a birthday gift for his niece. When he was ready, he'd tether the creature out in the yard a ways and shoot it in the butt with his pellet gun. That should get the thing screeching loudly enough to make Bev come out and see what was going on.

Danny finished running the wire across the top of the second step and over to a large pine tree where he planned on positioning himself. He had even thought to paint the wire black making it nearly invisible should Bev turn on the porch lights as he imagined she might. The wire was just thick enough to serve as a good trip-wire without cutting into the skin. At least that was what Danny hoped. He didn't want to arouse suspicion.

He'd learned Bev's address from her personnel file in Savannah's office. He already had a key to the building and had snuck inside after everyone left for the day. Although the filing cabinet was locked it was of the economy variety and hadn't taken Danny more than ten minutes to jimmy open without so much as a scratch to the painted surface.

A glance at his cell phone showed it to be a little after ten. Earlier than he liked but he didn't want to take a chance on waiting. The last light inside the house had gone off earlier in what Danny supposed was the old woman's bedroom. He wanted to get her outside before she slipped into the coma-like sleep he ascribed to all elderly people. If she did, she might not wake up even if he ran a train through her front yard.

The kitten squirmed and meowed as he tethered it to a stake he'd hammered into the ground with a rubber mallet. It didn't matter. He didn't think the sound anywhere near loud enough to be noticed inside by someone Bev's age.

The porch lights snapped on. A surprised Danny turned to see the front door open, Bev standing in the doorway, calling *his* name. "Is that you, Danny? What in the world are you doing?"

Danny's mind cycled through his limited options at breakneck speed. Using his body to shield Bev's eyes from what he was doing, he slipped the loop of the tether off the kitten's leg, cuddling her to his chest and rising to face the woman he had supposed deaf to his activity. No problem. He'd improvise. It would make a good impression on Lavelle.

"Hey, Bev! Look what I have!" He held the kitten out. "I bought him for my niece for her birthday today but it turns out she's allergic to cats. I can't have pets in my apartment so I thought I'd check with you and see if you'd help me out and keep her for the night until I can make other arrangements." He walked towards the porch. "He got away from me for a moment and you must have heard me trying to catch him."

Bev's gaze went from the young man in front of her to a quick scan of her driveway. "Where's your car?"

Danny silently cursed every gray hair on the woman's head. "Back down your drive a ways. My exhaust hangs pretty low and I was afraid of catching it on something. Your driveway is a mile long and has more potholes than the worst road at the complex!" He flashed her his most innocent-looking smile.

"Well, come on up then and I'll take a look. As long as it's for just one night I might be able to help you out."

As he neared the top step, Danny held the kitten out to her. Bev took the furry bundle and began talking to the creature in soothing tones, Danny positioning himself close and pretending to look over her shoulder. The next instant, he slammed his body against her, sending the elderly woman

171

careening down the porch steps, the kitten flying out of her arms. She lay in a heap on the ground, gurgling sounds escaping from her lips, eyes closed and one of her legs sticking out from under her robe at a grotesque angle.

For a moment, Danny's initial reaction to the sight of the elderly woman in such a helpless state caught him by surprise. It quickly passed. Compassion was a currency he couldn't afford. He went to work retrieving the wire he'd positioned and the stake with the tether line attached, jamming them into the rucksack he'd brought. He tossed the mallet in with them then headed down the driveway to where he'd parked, a good two hundred yards from the house. The sound of the kitten's plaintive cries came wafting through the night air. In response, Danny muttered the same words spoken to him when he was only seventeen, the last words his alcoholic stepfather had said to him before shoving him out the door. "You're on your own, kid."

Lavelle read the latest intelligence report with satisfaction. Danny was showing initiative. According to the report, there was a moment where it looked as though it might have gone either way, but the moment had passed and the woman, although not yet dead, was heading in that direction. Tsor would be pleased with her. Just as he had been pleased with her work with Julio Ramos. Lavelle was making a good impression on the leader. Her star was rising.

She had found Danny when he was six, the only son of a third generation Italian who drank heavily and beat his wife, Danny's mother. Eventually, his mom filed for divorce. After two years of trying to make it on her own she'd remarried out of sheer financial desperation. By then, Danny was twelve.

At first, the young boy was hopeful, longing to find himself part of a family who loved each other. Unfortunately for Danny, his mother's choice for husband number two wasn't any better than her first. In fact, his stepfather made his dad look like a saint by comparison and the two males waged a non-stop battle. Danny's weapons were psychological and subtle, targeted at making his stepfather's life as miserable as possible. The older man went straight for the physical stuff, smacking Danny around as much as he could without leaving too many tell-tale marks. Danny's mother knew what was happening but, out of either self-preservation or sheer apathy, kept her mouth shut.

Through it all, Lavelle had secretly nurtured Danny's growing lust for revenge to the extent Danny vowed that one day, when his stepfather was old and gray, he'd pay him back. Everything Danny had done since was preparation for that great and glorious day. In Danny's mind, love was a myth. The cosmic joke of the ages. Nonexistent except in books and movies. A dream that would break you if you were foolish enough to buy into it.

Lavelle chortled, thinking how frustrating it must be for the opposition. Sure, they had plenty of power. More power than even Tsor. But for reasons that had always struck her as ludicrous, they often refused to use it, opting to let earth's inhabitants struggle in pursuit of what the opposition called truth. For all his strength, that moron Michael had confined himself to telling Jesse a story about ants. Idiots! He and the others of his kind were fools!

The two camps had once been united until Tsor had seen his chance to grab the reins and take the lead. In Lavelle's opinion it might have worked, too, if Michael and the others had abandoned their first estate and joined with them in the attempted coup. Now they were sworn enemies.

Truth? Lavelle's side didn't have much use for truth. Power was so much better.

26

IT WAS FIVE minutes before the morning meeting was to start and still no Bev. Savannah had called her at home, twice, only to connect with the old-fashioned cassette tape answering machine Savannah had seen during her recent visit on Sunday. Bev had noticed her staring at it and remarked that when something had served you well it deserved to be kept around instead of being replaced by the latest electronic gadget. Savannah marveled they still made tapes for the thing. Bev's punctuality and ritual of making the morning coffee at the complex was legendary, accenting her absence. Savannah ended up confining the meeting to only the most pressing issues so as to keep its duration brief. She couldn't shake the uneasy feeling that something was very wrong. There was no way Bev wouldn't call if she were going to be late and Savannah's mind flooded with all kinds of possibilities as to what the reason might be for her absence, none of them good.

Although they were already shorthanded with Stanley being out, the others had insisted one of them go with her to Bev's place. The whole thing was so out of character for the senior member of their staff they were fearful as to what Savannah might find. Maybe Bev had had a heart attack or stroke. Heaven forbid, she might even be dead. There was no way they were going to let Savannah go on her own.

Looking over the list of the day's maintenance tasks, the only one that wasn't time sensitive and could slide without causing problems was mowing. That meant Danny, as mowing was his responsibility. Savannah groaned inwardly. She would have preferred one of the others. Spending more time in Danny's company wasn't what she had planned on. But then again, neither was Bev's absence and, if there were some kind of serious problem, time was of the essence and Danny's youthful strength might come in handy.

Before joining Savannah in her Subaru, Danny grabbed a toolbox from the garage saying that it wouldn't hurt to have it along just in case. Savannah had already placed one of the complex's first-aid kits on the back seat. She decided to leave Jenny inside the welcome center before locking the building and placing a note on the door explaining that, due to a staffing emergency, the welcome center was closed for the day.

Although nervous, Danny found himself excited, too. He didn't know if they would find Bev alive or dead. His preference would be the latter but he was prepared for the worst. That's where the toolbox came in. In the event Bev was alive and able to talk, and in doing so possibly implicate Danny as the cause of her accident, he'd have to take drastic measures. If it came to it, he'd find a way to finish the old woman off. Knowing of Lavelle's interest in Savannah—not to mention his own—he would have to do it when Savannah wasn't looking and in a way that wasn't obvious. He'd think of something. If he was lucky, they would get there too late and Bev would be gone. The thought almost made Danny smile but he forced himself to keep his mask of concern firmly in place. It wasn't easy, though. The idea of a distraught Savannah throwing her arms around his neck and clinging to him for comfort in her distress sent shivers of pleasure racing through him. This might turn out better than he'd expected.

Jesse read the text message Savannah had sent and frowned. There wasn't much to it. Some emergency had come up at work and she wouldn't be there when he and James arrived and headed out to the east shore for Jesse's scheduled rendezvous with Tsor. She would get in touch with them when she could. Jesse was sure, whatever it was, it must be important if it was able to deflect Savannah from her meeting them as planned. He supposed it couldn't be helped. He and James would have to go ahead without her and count on the three of them connecting later.

As she neared the house, Savannah spotted Bev's crumpled form on the ground, still clothed in her robe. She slammed the car into park, yelling at Danny to call 911 as she sprinted to where her friend lay.

There was no sign of blood but Bev's body looked lifeless, all color gone, her left leg sticking out at a sickening angle. Savannah called her name, repeatedly asking Bev if she could hear her, cringing at the sight of the older woman's frail body lying broken on the ground. She didn't dare move her, not yet knowing if Bev were still alive and fearing she might cause even more damage if she was.

Savannah placed her ear close to Bev's mouth and thought she detected shallow breathing. Gently grasping a frail wrist and horrified to find it cold to the touch, she frantically searched for the pulse that would confirm Bev to be still alive.

"The ambulance is on its way." Danny was kneeling beside her now. "Is she…is she dead?"

"Her breathing is shallow and I can barely get a pulse but she's alive. I don't think we should move her. There's no telling what internal injuries she may have suffered." Savannah looked up at the porch. "My guess is she fell down those stairs. There's no telling how long she may have been lying here." Savannah got to her feet. "I've got a blanket in the car. Jenny uses it to lie on but it will have to do. We've got to keep her as warm as possible. Keep an eye on her Danny. I'll be right back."

If he were going to do something to ensure Bev's death, he would have to do it quickly, Danny thought. It wouldn't take Savannah long to grab a blanket. He thought about suffocating her, simply placing his hands over her mouth and nose. Given Bev's condition it probably wouldn't take long and he doubted she would even struggle. She was already unconscious. Then again, why should he take the chance? She looked pretty bad. He decided to wait and let things play out.

Savannah returned with the blanket, tenderly placing it over the elderly woman's body. The day promised to be a hot one, the sun already making its presence known, the cool of the morning fading. Savannah found herself mouthing a silent prayer for her dear friend, pleading with God to let Bev live. She could hear the welcome sound of a siren in the distance. *Hold on, Bev! Help is on the way. Just hold on!*

James had watched Jesse stoop and enter the portals room through the fissure. At least he assumed that's where his brother was. He called Jesse's name out loud for the second time and got the same answer: silence. All he could do now was wait. And for how long? Jesse's last visit with Tsor took only moments. However, Tsor had warned Jesse it could go either way on the outside—longer or shorter—and by any duration of time. James walked back to the site, wandering down to the water's edge, Kai keeping him company but constantly looking towards the boulder. Without James being with him, Kai would never have taken so much as a step away from the rock.

Using Jesse's description as a guide, James tried to imagine what it was like inside the portals room. It was of limited help. It was simply too fantastic to visualize. There was no point of reference with the reality of his own catalog of life experiences.

Reality... Was the portals room reality? What was that quote of Einstein's Tsor had referred to? Something about reality being a persistent illusion. Put a man and a dog out in a field together and their realities differed according to the sensory and mental abilities of each. The dog smells deer droppings two hundred feet away. On the other end of the spectrum, looking up, the man catches sight of a hot air balloon floating overhead with four people inside the gondola, waving at him. His eyes give him the ability to discern the balloon's bright colors. His reality has people in a sky full of color. The dog's reality is shades of gray but bursting with scent. The realities for each are markedly different. Throw in quantum physics and you learn that whatever reality is, it's beyond human perception and intuition. Add to the mix a mind like Einstein's and you spend years chasing after a 'unified field theory', the elusive theory of everything. Einstein's famous formula had only one constant, the speed of light. James couldn't help but be reminded of God being described in the Bible as "light". Well, if there were only one constant in the universe, God was it.

Funny how you could get somewhat used to the fantastic, Jesse thought, as once again the darkness inside the boulder gave way to the now familiar sight of the portals room with its fanciful yellow brick road. He'd found the disc in the center of the floor on his first try this time and wondered why Tsor hadn't made it easier to turn the lights on. There was no sure way to find the gray disc other than crawling on his hands and knees. He would have preferred a light switch just inside the fissure. Preferably a backlit one.

He'd been a bit concerned about James' plan to modify the chair in the library, wondering if Tsor would take offense. But Tsor had assured him it was okay to share whatever he liked with James. Savannah, too, for that matter. As long as he didn't disobey any specific instruction he supposed it was safe enough. Even so, Jesse decided beforehand he would try to make his inspection of the chair as innocent looking as possible and had deliberately worn sneakers, untying the laces of one prior to passing through the fissure. As he walked towards the chair he stopped short of it, bending over to tie the flopping lace and, in so doing, quickly scanning the decorative brads. Sure enough, there was another one missing. Leave it to Savannah to choose the brad immediately below the already vacant hole. It made his task easier as he didn't have to count positions. Mission accomplished, he finished tying his lace and took a seat, reaching for the black portals book on the stand.

Unlike his last visit when he had found the contents of the book to be exactly the same as when he had left it on his first visit, Tsor had made an entry.

Pretty amazing last time, wasn't it Jesse? A foretaste of the power I am making available to you. Today, you'll come one step closer to correcting the unfairness of the past.

I'm sure you have questions.

Yes, he did. Lots of them. Knowing he had only three available per visit Jesse had given his selection considerable thought.

How many more visits before I'm ready to change the past?

Impatience seems to run strong among you humans. Always in a hurry. But I have an answer for you: on your sixth visit. Today is your third. Three visits from now and you will have the power to — how do the clever ones of your kind put it? — Oh yes, you will have the power to rock your world.

More threes… Three more visits. Nine more days and he might once again hold Ellen in his arms! He could feel his heart thumping in his chest at the thought. *Nine days.* It seemed like such a short amount of time and yet he knew it would feel like an eternity in passing. He forced himself to calm down.

You said time here isn't the same as in the outside world. When I rescue Ellen, where will the two of us be in time?

Excellent question. I can tell you have been giving our time together the thoughtful attention it deserves.

You will pick up right where you left off. That very day and the very place where you are now and were then, Stillman's Lake.

Jesse had wondered if that might be the case. It made for a lot of questions. A bunch more than the final one remaining to him now.

He wondered what would happen to all the events that had taken place over the past three years since Ellen's death. Would they be as though

178

they never happened? Would he and James have even so much as a single memory of this whole fantastic episode? And what about Savannah? Jesse assumed she would be back somewhere in Kansas or wherever she was three years ago. Maybe he wouldn't meet or see her ever again. Then again, what would it matter if he didn't recall meeting her in the first place?

But what if he did remember? What if all his memories remained intact? After all, if he was to save Ellen from drowning, didn't that require retaining at least some memories of the present? The flood of apprehension caused by not knowing forced his final question.

If I pick up right where I left off, on the same day and in the same place, what will happen to all the memories I've accumulated since?

You will remember everything.

At the moment, Jesse didn't know if that was good or bad. In the end, it didn't matter. A good chunk of those memories were filled with the pain of his grief. The joy of being with Ellen again would wipe the grief slate clean.

Patching up their differences and being close again with James was a good thing and it was wonderful to have their relationship restored. He felt closer to his twin than ever. Yet apart from the tragedy of Ellen's drowning they wouldn't have drifted apart to begin with. So what if when he saw James after saving Ellen he remembered their period of estrangement.

Finding Savannah was the best thing that had happened to him since Ellen's death. Could he live with the sadness he knew he'd feel if he never saw her again? He'd have to. Their relationship was only beginning. It was nowhere near the depth of his and Ellen's. Sure it would hurt, but it couldn't be anything like the loss he felt with Ellen gone.

That brought up the matter of what James and Savannah would or would not remember—not to mention everyone else in the world! What would happen to all their collective memories of the past three years? It was frustrating to be limited to only three questions. He had no choice but to save finding out until his next visit. He turned his attention back to the book, finding a new entry on the following page.

And now for today's lesson.

When we were last together you learned how to focus on the desire of your heart, visualizing it, transforming what you created in your mind's eye into something real, not unlike the mythical Christian god some in your world worship who, supposedly, made the universe and everything in it merely by speaking. Believe me, it isn't that easy.

I want you to take it a step further by not only visualizing your wife, Ellen, but the very setting. This is crucial to your gaining the ability to control the exact point in time in which to exercise your chance to change the past.

You need to keep in mind that I am the one who controls that opportunity. It would be disastrous for you to imagine you could accomplish any of this without me.

This time, I want you to visualize your fifth anniversary together. Right down to the exact time and place of the celebratory event.

As before, humor me and follow the yellow brick road.

Jesse sat, allowing his mind to drift back four years to the fifth anniversary of his and Ellen's marriage. He swallowed as the event's location clicked into place. It was Bianchi's.

A feeling swept over him not unlike what he imagined it might be like to be caught shoplifting; an awful feeling of guilt and discomfort mixed with regret. Although he had known the place was a favorite of his and Ellen's, and they had gone there together many times, he hadn't thought about it when he'd taken Savannah, overlooking the fact it was the site of their fifth anniversary celebration. Whether it was coincidental or intentional on Tsor's part, Jesse had no idea. He rose slowly, and obediently followed the brick pathway to the wall, once again feeling foolish as he traced the swirls but fearing to do otherwise might spell catastrophe.

Upon reaching the wall, as before, the lights dimmed. Jesse closed his eyes and thought of Ellen, thinking back to when they had celebrated their anniversary at Bianchi's.

Ellen had worn a green dress, one of Jesse's favorites. Her long brown hair fell cascading across her shoulders, delicate diamond earrings pointing towards a larger diamond hanging from a thin gold chain around her neck, his gift to her on this memorable occasion. For her part, Ellen had given him exactly what he wanted: a picture of her. It was a tradition, faithfully kept for five years now, each portrait a reminder to him of the woman he so desperately loved.

180

Jesse opened his eyes to find the incomplete image in his mind come alive in front of him with all the missing details filled in, complements of the portal through which he viewed the past.

The ambulance was on its way to MercyQuest Hospital with Savannah inside and Danny following in her Subaru. According to the two EMT's who had attended to Bev, her injuries were not life threatening now that she had been found. Her greatest threat had been shock and exposure. Her leg was badly broken and she likely had some cracked ribs and maybe even a fractured hip; a CT scan would tell the story. Apparently, she'd taken a fall down the porch steps. They'd found a kitten hanging around. Perhaps the elderly woman had tripped over the creature. Savannah hadn't noticed a kitten when she'd met with Bev on Sunday to learn the details about the incident involving Stanley's son-in-law but that didn't mean the kitten wasn't hers. It might have been napping somewhere.

Bev was still unconscious and that worried Savannah, but the EMT adjusting the fluid drip going into Bev's arm assured her that, under the circumstances, it wasn't unusual. Older folks got dehydrated quickly and Bev being outside for who knew how many hours had taken a toll above and beyond her obvious injuries. The woman was lucky Savannah and Danny had found her. He doubted she would have lasted much longer if they hadn't.

27

IT WAS AFTER two by the time Savannah left the hospital. She had sent Danny back to the complex in a cab shortly after they had arrived. She had no idea how long she was going to be there, Savannah had told him. They could leave the welcome center closed until tomorrow if they had to. She wasn't about to leave Bev until she knew their beloved co-worker was going to be okay.

After the examinations and CT scan were complete the news had been better than expected. Savannah involuntary shuddered every time the image of Bev's body lying in a heap at the foot of the stairs floated across her mind. The broken leg was no surprise. Nor the assortment of bruises splattered over Bev's body. Two of her ribs were cracked. Slight hairline fractures according to the attending physician, a red-haired woman maybe fifteen years her senior who smelled like formaldehyde and never seemed to look directly at her, making Savannah feel as though there were someone over her shoulder the doctor was really talking to. Bev had a sprained wrist, too, but that was the extent of her injuries. Nothing really major but enough to cause someone her age plenty of pain. They expected her stay in the hospital to last five to seven days. Given her age, once released, Bev would need to go into a skilled nursing facility for follow-up care. They would begin physical therapy on her wrist, then when her ribs and leg had healed enough, expand the exercises with the ultimate goal of seeing Bev regain enough strength and movement to safely take care of herself at home. All told, it might take a few months.

Savannah couldn't picture Bev as a helpless invalid for three weeks let alone three months. She suspected the medical establishment was in for a surprise. For the moment, as she headed back to the complex to update the others, Savannah had time to let her mind consider the fact that earlier in the day, Jesse had entered the portals room for the third time. She wondered if he would return knowing the location of the missing brad she'd pulled from his library chair. She didn't know how she would feel if he did. Right now, Savannah felt as though her emotions were a plate of spaghetti—lots of strands all woven together into one big tangled heap where you couldn't sort out where one strand began or another ended.

The waiting was difficult. Whereas the last time had taken less than a minute, Jesse had now been gone for more than six hours and James didn't know what to think. Sure, Tsor had warned about the time differential but it was so open-ended it left you dangling in mid-air. James was glad to have Kai's company. Even so, the hours dragged by with monotonous slowness.

His biggest concern centered around the modifications they had made to the chair. He had no idea how Tsor would react to the image of the cross with the accompanying proclamation he had inscribed below it. He doubted Tsor would be troubled by the sight of another missing brad. That could have been the natural result of wear and tear. His artwork, done in Iced Mauve, was another matter entirely. He hadn't done it to mock Tsor. Not if he were who James suspected him to be. That would be foolish. According to the Bible, even God's most powerful archangel hadn't engaged in mockery, choosing instead to leave retribution in the Lord's hands. James' intention was to insert into the portals room something more powerful than Tsor's deceit—the truth. A few words of absolute truth could stand up to a lot of evil and, in James' opinion, the portals room was full of evil.

James remembered when it was Jesse whose faith in God seemed the stronger of the two. In high school, Jesse had proven a standout athlete in three different sports: football, baseball, and wrestling and had used his notoriety to help others. On more than one occasion, he had hauled some teenage social outcast out of a compromising situation involving alcohol or drugs. He seemed to have a sixth sense, knowing when someone was being set up for a fall by the 'in crowd' who loved luring those on society's fringes with promises of inclusion and friendship if only they could pass their dangerous initiation rites. Of course, the bullies never had any such intention, even if the kid they were setting up managed to jump through all the hurdles placed before them. If you were no one else's friend, you knew you were at least Jesse Whitestone's.

It wasn't until he'd met Ellen, back when he was working on his MBA at Cornell, that Jesse's faith had begun to show its earliest signs of fray. Not that it had anything to do with Ellen, personally. It was more a subtle shift in focus. Between his dogged pursuit of excellence in his education with the vision of creating his own consulting firm and the dream of a life with Ellen according to the script he'd written for them in his mind, Jesse simply fell into a spiritual starvation diet. He existed for a while burning the stored calories his heart had banked in previous years. By the time of their parents' accident his faith had grown so lean he couldn't weather the disappointment of losing them. Ellen's death was the final blow. A gale, actually. A wind so strong the tattered remnants of Jesse's long-neglected relationship with the living God simply collapsed altogether.

James believed God wanted to build something stronger and better between Himself and Jesse. Something so solid that nothing in heaven or on earth could shake its foundations. Somehow, the craziness taking place inside the boulder played a part. Only God had the wisdom and the power to perfectly transcend even Tsor's deceit into something good. Something that would speak to Jesse's soul of the love and majesty of his Heavenly Father and nudge the prodigal homeward. Jesse was a complicated man with a big and tender heart who had gotten off track while he was hard at work chasing the American Dream. God had bigger dreams for His child. Ones Jesse couldn't even imagine.

Kai heard the approaching vehicle well before the sound became audible to James. He looked up, aligning his gaze with the direction suggested by the dog's keen ears. Presently, Savannah's white Subaru pulled into the site. Moments later, a haggard-looking Savannah was making her way towards him.

"If you don't mind me saying, you don't look so good," James said as she drew near. "Jesse told me there was some sort of emergency here at the complex. Everything okay?" Savannah's troubled face suggested otherwise.

"No," she said, sitting down next to James at the picnic table. "But at least the floodwaters have crested and appear to be receding." She noted James' quizzical look. "I'll tell you the whole story right after you fill me in on what's happening with Jesse." She patted Kai's head. "If Kai's here and Jesse isn't, that must mean he's still inside the boulder, right?"

James nodded his affirmation. "That's right. It's been over six hours and there's been no sign of him. I stuck my head inside a couple of times but all I see is the same old cavern." He smiled wryly. "I guess I'm not on the guest list."

"How long are you planning on waiting?"

"Jesse and I talked about it last night. We figured it would be wise to have a contingency plan in place. He suggested that if he wasn't back by closing time, if possible, I should leave the Element where we parked and see if I could bum a ride home from you." James smiled. "Of course, I told him I couldn't do that without feeding you so, if you're open to it, I suggest we

184

stop somewhere along the way so I can buy you dinner and you can fill me in on your emergency."

Savannah *was* hungry. She had missed lunch completely and the bagel and juice she'd had for breakfast was a distant memory.

No amount of coaxing by James could convince Kai to come with them. Jesse had thought about the possibility and had told James to let the dog stay. At least for the night if Jesse hadn't shown up. If he still didn't appear sometime Wednesday, James would have to improvise as he thought best. He hoped it didn't come to that.

They stopped off for pizza at Giantelli's, James explaining how pizza was a critical part of his diet and he'd started to suffer withdrawals because he hadn't had any since their impromptu picnic inside the welcome center. After grabbing a booth where you could catch a glimpse of the pizza chefs hand-tossing dough they decided on a medium pizza, half ham and pineapple for James and vegetarian for Savannah. Over sodas and a salad, Savannah filled James in on Bev's accident.

James' initial reaction of dismay was followed by a barrage of questions as to the outlook for Bev's full recovery. Savannah passed along the doctors' assurances that, in time, the twins' old friend would be back to her usual active self. James then wanted to know how the complex was going to manage with both Stanley and Bev out for an unknown duration.

Savannah shared with him how the complex was part of an association of state parks with access to a pool of trained staff available for temporary assignments lasting up to six months. She would be calling them in the morning and arranging coverage for both a grounds person as well as general office help at the welcome center.

Savannah looked weary and James thought it might be helpful to get her mind off Bev's accident. "So, what else are you passionate about besides managing large tracts of public land?"

"You mean there are other things in life besides parks?" she teased. "It's certainly true the great outdoors captured my heart at a young age and has held it tightly in its grasp ever since. Along the way, my love of nature went from a passionate hobby to a lifelong vocation." She looked wistful. "I used to spend more time participating in outdoor activities than I do now and I'm looking forward to getting back to my roots, so to speak."

"In what way?"

"Take kayaking, for example. I used to travel as far away as Idaho to taste the thrill of whitewater kayaking."

James noticed Savannah beginning to perk up as past memories of doing something she loved gained traction. "Jesse used to kayak, too. And loved it! He's got three kayaks stored somewhere at the house. Whenever I'd come to visit, he'd load them up and he, Ellen and I would bring them either to Stillman's Lake or hit Lake Placid during the spring run-off when the mountain snows swell the rivers. Some of the runs include class three, four, and five rapids. It's a hoot! We've kayaked Blue Ledges, Mile Long, and Big Nasty together." He prodded her. "Maybe if you hinted to Jesse you'd love to go kayaking, the two of you could get back into the sport. Might do you both some good."

Savannah shook her head. "I don't know, James. The future looks awfully murky. I had my heart broken once a few years back when I was in my twenties. I've learned from the pain of that experience to take things a lot more slowly. Besides," she added, "aren't you forgetting something? Like the possibility Jesse might actually be able to kayak with Ellen again?" It sounded crazy even saying it. But wasn't that what Tsor claimed possible?

James considered sharing his suspicions about Tsor with Savannah but decided to hold off until Jesse's return. Jesse's prolonged absence, together with the potential of his identifying the position of the brad Savannah had pulled from the chair, might convince her of the authenticity of Jesse's experiences. Once convinced, James would see if she'd given the question as to Tsor's identity any thought.

Kai lay near the boulder waiting for the reappearance of his master, the passing of time having little impact upon him. All the dog knew was that Jesse was somewhere beyond his sight, hearing, or smell. Yet somewhere in his repertoire of senses there was a non-physical one. An indefinable sense telling him this was where he should wait. That waiting for his master's return here by the boulder was his duty. And whatever Kai understood as his duty, he did.

Michael sat on the ground beside him, resting a massive black hand on Kai's back, drawn to the spot by a similar call of duty. His unseen presence had been here since Jesse's first encounter with Tsor and every encounter since. In fact, Michael had often accompanied Jesse at various times in Jesse's life, on each occasion without detection. Only this past Sunday had Michael shown himself to Jesse when they watched the sunrise together and he had shared the analogy of the ants with the young man of Adam's race.

Whereas Kai could only vaguely sense something involving Jesse was happening inside the monolith before them, Michael could clearly see every detail. He was well aware of Tsor's intentions and the playing out of his scheme. In fact, Michael possessed the power to bring it to an immediate end. But that wasn't always the way Michael's own Master went about the business of rescuing His children from evil. God often chose to use frail vessels of clay; in Jesse's case, James and Bev. These two played important roles in God's plan for His own glory and Jesse's good. There was no conflict between the two. Jesse's good *was* God's glory.

Michael had often had to fight against the rage inside of him at what had often struck him as the triumph of evil. Seeing God's Son crucified on a Roman cross had been one such time. He longed to fight the enemy of God directly, to bind him in chains and cast him into darkness for a thousand years. The God Michael served had stayed his hand at Jesus' crucifixion— together with countless other celestial warriors at Michael's command. Michael hadn't seen clearly the extraordinary significance of that day with its unbelievable sacrifice where the spilling of God's own blood through the wounds of His Son would serve to rescue Adam's race, together with the entire universe, from Tsor's treachery.

He sighed, his body swelling with emotion. Tsor had once been Michael's closest friend. He had looked up to him. But Tsor's own power and beauty had turned the mighty spirit's gaze inward upon himself instead of continuing to honor the God who had created him. It had led to a rebellion in heaven that had spilled over to earth. Down to the creatures God had created in His own image. Frail creatures God loved so much that He had written Himself into their world through the incarnation of his Son, Jesus, their Deliverer. Both their and Michael's Lord.

All that his eyes beheld going on inside the portals room, while absent of the approval of God, nevertheless took place by God's leave. In time, Tsor's present effort, like every diabolical scheme Tsor had attempted down through the ages, would be turned against him and, as the very resurrection of Jesus had so gloriously demonstrated, be transformed from

187

darkness to light. If there was one thing Michael had come to realize it was the power of love. Love *never* fails.

28

DANNY SNAPPED HIS cell phone shut. The call had been from his friend, Ron, at the Sheriff's department. They'd gotten a call from Danny's boss, Savannah Garret. She wanted them to know she had given Jesse Whitestone permission to be at the complex after hours on an indefinite basis and if, on any of their patrols a deputy happened to come across Mr. Whitestone's Honda Element parked out on the east shore of the lake, it was okay. Mr. Whitestone was involved in a research project. It had sounded suspicious to Ron so he had passed it along to Danny.

Yeah, you bet there's more to it, Ron. More than you could ever imagine!

Danny didn't know what Jesse was up to but he didn't like the sound of it. He wondered if he were being double-crossed by Lavelle. She said her organization had an interest in Jesse but, supposedly, not in the same way they were interested in Danny. How had she put it? Something about Jesse being the object of a competition, whatever that meant.

Danny toyed with the idea of heading to the complex to see if he could find out what Jesse was up to. Maybe he would later in the week, but right now he needed to figure out what he was going to do in the event Bev remembered Danny was the one who had shoved her down the stairs. If she did and told Savannah, he could not only kiss his job good-bye he would be facing serious legal charges leading to who knew how much prison time. He wasn't about to let that happen.

When he fell asleep that night, Danny dreamed he was back on the yacht with Lavelle drinking more Veritas Juice and basking in bright sunshine out on the open sea. The dark-haired beauty was more tantalizing than ever, her brown body scantily clad in a bright orange string bikini. She was complimenting him on his initiative with Bev and was apologetic the organization hadn't seen trouble coming, believing Stanley far too preoccupied with family matters to have remembered the glitch in the inventory. Just went to show you how older folks could be stubborn. Aging made them unreasonable and unpredictable. The best thing that could happen for society as a whole would be some kind of international law where, when a person reached a certain age, they had to undergo an annual examination. Pass and you get to contribute to society for another year. Fail and... well, your ticket gets punched. All quite painless, of course. After all,

189

the cost of keeping people alive after a certain age was draining a substantial portion of the world's resources that could be put to better use elsewhere, didn't Danny agree?

Of course he did. Who didn't agree with a voluptuous island beauty wearing a bikini and leaning so close he could smell the earthy fragrance her body gave off. She could tell him it was going to rain chocolate cats and he'd agree.

But until the world wised up, Lavelle said, Danny would have to deal with Bev himself. She'd help him, of course. She was good at coming up with ways for dealing with these kinds of problems and would be in touch.

Jesse emerged from the portals room to find Kai waiting for him. "Hey there, big guy!" He looked around but didn't see James. Maybe he was over at the picnic table. Jesse looked at the sky and, from the position of the sun, calculated it couldn't be much later than when he had entered the boulder.

"Glad you could make it, bro. Are you hungry or is there room service inside that rock?" James had heard his brother greeting Kai and hastened to join them. He had already been at the site for two hours after an uneasy night's sleep spent wondering what was happening to his twin.

Jesse checked the time. "Why would I be hungry? It's only a few minutes past nine."

"It may be only a few minutes after nine but it's not the same nine. You've been in the belly of the whale for twenty-four hours."

Jesse pulled his phone back out and looked again. Sure enough. He'd gone in at nine in the morning on Tuesday but his phone confirmed it was now Wednesday. He scratched his head. This was going to take some getting used to. It was an odd sensation knowing the world had burned through twenty-four hours while he had been... had been what? He searched for the right word to describe what people did while whatever dimension of time they existed in flowed by. Was it called *living* simply because they were alive? He looked around. "Have you heard from Savannah?" Jesse remembered her having sent him a text about an emergency at work and wondered what had happened.

"She said if you showed up before the complex closed we should meet her at the welcome center if you were up to it," James answered.

"No problem. I'm fine. We can swap news while we're all in the same time zone."

Jesse needed a few minutes to think through what he felt comfortable sharing. Tsor's revelation that Jesse would find himself permanently back at the point in time of the fateful day of Ellen's drowning had implications. If the past three years of his life since that day were blotted out for him as if they had never been, would it be the same for everyone else in the world? Jesse was already making a mental list of follow-up questions to ask Tsor that might bring more clarity. He didn't want to raise anyone's anxiety level unnecessarily.

Bev had never been hit by a Mack truck but supposed it couldn't feel much worse than she was feeling now. The young doctor with the trendy stubble on his jaw who had come in earlier in the morning had given her the rundown on the varied parts of her body that were sending out pain signals and why. He had also filled her in on what she could expect along the road to recovery. At least his version. For her part, Bev had no intention of spending the next several weeks, let alone months, anywhere other than in her own home. If she needed physical therapy they'd know where to find her. In fact, if they would stop jabbing her with needles and waking her up to check her vitals and take pills, she might get some much needed rest and get out of their hair so they could fill the bed with someone who wanted to be there.

She pushed back the tray holding her lunch. It consisted of a soup she supposed was meant to be vegetable but contained nothing more than a watery broth and dull-colored pieces of mush. It was accompanied by a slice of dry toast and some applesauce in a small plastic container with a tear-off foil lid she'd finally opened by jabbing a hole in it with her fork until she could get a good enough grip to tug it off. She hated most packaging nowadays. It not only kept the bad guys out it kept you out as well. Bev had eaten everything on her tray. Not because of any culinary appeal but because lying in the dirt outside your house at the bottom of the porch stairs all night had a way of making even hospital food palatable.

They had asked her if she knew what had happened. She remembered everything perfectly. That's why she had told them she

191

supposed she'd fallen down the porch steps. It wouldn't do to get Danny in trouble before she had a chance to talk with him and find out why he had pushed her. After all, she was his grandmother's sister.

Adjusting the tilt of the bed through the control unit in her hand, Bev closed her eyes, resting her head on what passed for a pillow. In her opinion, it was too thin to qualify. She'd asked the nurse for another two hours ago. But she could be patient. Her Lord had seen far greater pain and suffering on her behalf and was in full control of what happened to her. She trusted Him and believed even her accident would achieve a good purpose in the end. It might not be visible to her on this side of eternity but, one day, she'd see how it fit into His plan. God never wasted pain.

Danny had no idea the two of them were related. Her sister's son had wrought enough havoc in the young man's life. Actually, when it came right down to it, they probably weren't legally related. Bev's sister was the mother of the wretched creature who was Danny's stepfather. Bev had gone to the wedding between Alvin and Danny's mother, Becky. The marriage was doomed from the start. Alvin was a drunk and a bully. An ugly combination. Danny was just a boy then and Bev had seen the hopeful longing in his young eyes and knew he was a child desperate to be loved. Bev's sister died of cancer within a year after the wedding, not having had much contact with her son, Alvin, whose sole objective in life seemed to be the consumption of alcohol. Bev never saw Alvin and Becky again although she tried several times to make contact, inviting them over on holidays but never receiving a reply.

She'd often thought about little Danny and wondered how he had fared growing up in that unhappy family. The next time Bev saw him was a chance encounter when he was fifteen. By then, the hopeful look she had seen in his eyes as a boy had been replaced by a stone-cold stare. He had no idea who Bev was as she stood behind him in the checkout line at a convenience store.

Knowledge of Danny's whereabouts had vanished again two years later when she learned that at seventeen, Alvin had thrown the boy out of the house to fend for himself. It was then Bev became convinced God wanted her to find Danny and do what she could to help him. Not in a financial way but in the way Danny needed most; by showing him the love of God. He needed to be set free from bitterness and anger, forgiving those who let him down and hurt him in life.

Through the sort of divine choreography only God can engineer, Danny came to live in upstate New York. Bev had sent him an the anonymous newspaper clipping of the advertisement for a groundskeeper at the Stillman's Lake recreational complex where she worked and encouraged Stanley to give the young man a chance. Since Danny's hiring, she had worked hard to try and build a relationship with him. Now that he was older, Danny had traded his angry scowl for what he considered an irresistible smile no member of the opposite sex could resist but had rebuffed her every attempt at friendship. And now, for some reason unknown to Bev, Danny had tried to kill her. At least that's what it appeared. The boy who had yearned for love had attempted to silence the very vessel bearing him that love because he no longer recognized or believed love existed.

As she had done countless times before, Bev began praying for Danny, asking God for the wisdom to know how to handle this latest turn of events and the strength she needed to do whatever God asked of her.

As Savannah stood on the welcome center's porch with Jenny beside her, watching the two brothers drive out of the complex, her thoughts drifted back to the first time she'd stood on this same porch waving good-bye to Jesse. He'd been driving his other car then—a yellow sports car with Kai sitting in the passenger seat looking as though Jesse was his chauffeur. A lot of water had flowed under the bridge since that innocent day. Jesse had just shared his latest episode in the portals room with her and James. He'd covered a lot of ground but Savannah's intuition told her he was holding something back. He had also identified the location of the brad she had pulled from his chair, prompting her to dig around in her purse and toss him the keys to his library door as a reward. No doubts lingered in her mind. As fantastic as Jesse's stories sounded, Savannah was convinced strange and incredible things were taking place inside the big rock not so very far from where she stood. And according to the timetable Tsor had outlined, in three more visits Jesse would either be holding Ellen in his arms or have his heart crushed into human jelly. Either way, Savannah struggled to see where she fit into Jesse's future. For the first time since arriving, she wished she had never come.

Julio Ramos was packing for a long trip. He had been meditating earlier, looking to link up with his spirit guide, Lavelle. She hadn't let him down. She had asked him to go to a small town in New York and wait for further instructions. It had nothing to do with either his gang or the cartel. This was something off the books, something Lavelle said she wanted him to do for her. She reminded him of her faithfulness over the years and how she had kept him safe in the dangerous and violent world he moved in. She needn't have bothered Julio thought to himself as he shoved a modified 8mm pistol into a pack. He knew he owed her. If she had something personal on the side that needed taking care of he was glad to return the favor. Besides, the cross-country drive would give him time to do some career planning. His latest hit on Derrick Holmes had significantly added to his reputation. He might as well think about the kind of position he would suggest to his superiors as a suitable reward.

29

IT FELT STRANGE to Jesse, sitting in the chair in his library, one whose counterpart he had sat in on Tuesday in the portals room as he met with Tsor. When it came down to it, he mused, he didn't really meet with Tsor. He'd never seen his likeness or heard Tsor's voice. The only knowledge of the guy he had was the writing in the black leather book. For all he knew, Tsor could turn out to be the name of a female alien.

Jesse reconciled himself to believing that, whoever Tsor was, he wasn't some spiritual phantasm. James could stay on that track if he liked but Jesse wasn't buying it. You didn't have to go around spiritualizing everything you didn't understand. There were always rational reasons if you looked hard enough. If a smart guy like Francis Crick could discover DNA, win the Nobel prize, then go on to develop a theory as to how that DNA came about which included aliens, that was good enough for Jesse. It was practical and something he could wrap his mind around. Angels and demons kept you chasing your tail.

Jesse wondered what Savannah thought, now that she seemed convinced of the reality of his experiences. He leaned forward, running his hand down the line of brass brads until he felt the two-brad gap. It was crazy how the portals chair mirrored the one he was sitting in now. He wondered what would happen if he stuffed a few thousand dollars in cash under the cushion. Might be an easy way to double his money. The light-hearted thought was chased out of his head by a far more sobering one, that of his old friend Bev Foster now lying in a hospital bed at MercyQuest. Pretty tough piece of bad luck falling down your own porch steps. He'd cook up some barbecue and take it to her down at the hospital. She'd like that. James could go with him. Bev would like that even more. She hadn't seen the two of them together in what—over two years?

Jesse saw Bev often. Especially during the winter months when he would go over early in the morning and plow out her driveway with the old Ford pickup she left parked out near the road. The thing didn't even have plates but it was good enough to shove snow out of the way so Bev could get in and out of her mile-long driveway. The plow never came off the truck. She just let it set out near the road in a little clearing Jesse had made for it. The plowing would usually take him less than half an hour and Bev would have hot coffee together with scrambled eggs and pancakes with real maple syrup waiting for him inside. Like James, she was religious. Well, so had Jesse until the pile of bad things had gotten so high his faith couldn't bear the weight of it anymore. Shoot enough holes into a believer and you could sit back and watch the faith drain out of them. Not that he wished tragedy on anyone, especially Bev.

"Somehow, I don't think you're sitting there dreaming about your beloved Giants." James entered the library, taking a seat opposite his brother, a look of concern in his blue eyes. "You okay?"

"I'm fine—that is for someone who has a date with a rock every three days." Jesse offered his sibling a weak smile. "Actually, I was just thinking about Bev and how maybe you and I could cook her some barbecue and take it to her at the hospital tomorrow."

"But tomorrow is Friday."

"Yeah, I know. I'm counting on Tsor giving me a break and letting me out of class early." Jesse hoped that would be the case, anyway. He was still trying to get over having missed out on a day. He couldn't explain it but it felt funny, like having a tiny hole in his personal history, a cavity that wanted filling.

"Speaking of Tsor…" James walked over to one of the many bookshelves lining the opposite wall, returning with a Bible, setting it carefully in Jesse's lap. "You might want to open it up to the book of Ezekiel."

The Bible was Jesse's own, one Ellen had given him on their first anniversary. He hadn't opened it in three years, refusing to touch it after her death. There were times when he had been in the library looking for something to read where he had stared at the Bible sitting on the shelf, wondering why he even kept it. Now it was sitting in his lap, staring at him. For several moments Jesse didn't touch the Book, as if they were two participants in a contest of wills. Finally, he opened it and began turning pages until he came to the Old Testament book of Ezekiel, the feel of the Bible stirring memories, and with them feelings he had assumed long dead. He looked up at James. "What chapter? And what does the Bible have to do with Tsor?" Jesse grew suspicious. "Is this in any way connected with your spiritual conspiracy theory?"

"Humor me a minute, Junior." James hoped his attempt at levity would gain him his brother's indulgence. "Read chapter twenty-eight, verses eleven through eighteen."

Jesse read to himself the words on the page.

Again the word of the LORD came to me saying, "Son of man, take up a lamentation over the king of Tyre, and say to him, 'Thus says the Lord God, "You had the seal of perfection, full of wisdom and perfect in beauty. You were in Eden, the garden of God; every precious stone was your covering: the ruby, the topaz, and the diamond; the beryl, the onyx, and the jasper; the lapis lazuli, the turquoise, and the emerald; and the gold, the workmanship of your settings and sockets, was in you. On the day that you were created they were prepared. You were the anointed cherub who covers, and I placed you there. You were on the holy mountain of God; you walked in the midst of the stones of fire. You were blameless in your ways from the day you were created, until unrighteousness was found in you. By the abundance of your trade you were internally filled with violence, and you sinned; therefore I have cast you as profane from the mountain of God. And I have destroyed you, O covering cherub, from the midst of the stones of fire. Your heart was lifted up because of your beauty; you corrupted your wisdom by reason of your splendor. I cast you to the ground; I put you before kings, that they may see you. By the multitude of your iniquities, in the unrighteousness of your trade, you profaned your sanctuaries. Therefore I have brought fire from the midst of you; it has consumed you, and I have turned you to ashes on the earth in the eyes of all who see you."

When Jesse finished reading, he looked up at James. "And your point?"

"Do you know what the Hebrew word is for Tyre, as in the "king of Tyre" referred to in verse twelve?"

"No, I don't. But I bet you're going to tell me."

"It's *Tsor*." All pretense of humor had vanished from James' face. He leaned forward as if to underscore the importance of what he was about to say. "I believe the Tsor of the portals room is this same Tsor."

The color drained out of Jesse's face. He was familiar with the passage in Ezekiel, having read it more than once back during the years when the Bible in his hands was as familiar to him as the touch of Ellen's skin. Neither was there any need to challenge James to prove his claim. Although no Hebrew scholar, James' competence with reference tools was pretty solid.

197

The revelation didn't necessarily prove the Tsor of the portals room was the Tsor referred to in the Bible. Tsor had shown himself to have a sense of humor, albeit an odd one what with the yellow brick road and all. Wasn't it possible for an alien to adopt a name out of the religious book of a foreign planet just for kicks? Look at all the crazy names people took for themselves on social network platforms not to mention the few million blogs out there in cyberspace. Jesse shared as much. "I think you're grasping at straws trying to hold on to the alien angle."

James was frustrated but trying to keep his emotions under control. "You need to at least consider the possibility the two Tsors are one and the same."

Stanley watched as the casket bearing the body of his son-in-law was lowered into the ground, his heart aching for those on either side of him whose hands he held tightly in his own. Olivia hadn't yet cried or said a word and Sara, her mother, although verbal was still in shock.

The police hadn't caught the gunman and Stanley wondered if they ever would. He had been told by one of Derrick's fellow agents the slaying had all the marks of a professional hit by one of the Mexican cartels: three shots in the back, one of them punching a hole in Derrick's right ventricle on its way through his chest.

The funeral was packed with members of various branches of federal, state and local law enforcement. ICE had even set up a secure perimeter around the cemetery just in case the cartels decided to underscore their point with a dramatic graveside hit. They were vicious enough to have given the matter consideration.

As Stanley guided his daughter and granddaughter to the waiting black limousine they were approached by a well-dressed African-American whose eyes seemed to enfold them in an atmosphere of warmth. "I knew your husband, Mrs. Holmes," the tall, graying man said. "I had occasion to be with him at times. Derrick is a fine man and he spoke often of his love for you." The big man knelt so that his face was level with Olivia's. "Your daddy loves you very much, Olivia," he said, his brown eyes holding the young girl's gaze with steadfast tenderness. He cradled the child's face in his palms. "I know you miss him a lot." He paused for a moment, searching the young girl's face. "God wants you to know He loves you." He was quiet for a moment before continuing on. "No matter what happens, Olivia, Jesus is always with you. He will never leave you alone."

He stood, offering Stanley his hand. "My name is Michael. I'm glad you're here, Stanley." He smiled, then turned and walked away.

Sara cast her father a puzzled look. "That man called you by name, Dad. I take it you know him?"

"I've never seen him before in my life," Stanley murmured, running a hand through his thinning hair.

"He's the man in my dream." Olivia's small voice was barely audible. "The one who told me it wasn't my fault Daddy got shot at my gym class." Her delicate chin was quivering and the tears that had been building up in her heart, waiting for a chance to comfort her, began streaming from her eyes as her mother pressed her tightly to her breast while Stanley wrapped his arms around them both.

30

IT WOULD BE his fourth visit to the portals room and as Jesse approached the stand of hemlocks surrounding the boulder, accompanied by James and Kai, he found himself riddled with conflicting emotions.

On the one hand, he was only six days away from the unfathomable possibility of seeing Ellen alive and holding her in his arms. The very thought made him giddy with a joy which contrasted sharply with the mounting apprehension that, try as he might, he couldn't silence the thought in the back of his mind his brother might be on to something. That Tsor, instead of the alien intelligence Jesse had clung to, might actually be a supernatural being described in the Bible. The fact he still held out a sliver of hope for Crick's alien theory was probably the only thing steadying his nerves and keeping him moving forward.

Then there was Savannah. Jesse had called her before heading off to bed the night before to see if she would meet him and James in the morning. He had been surprised when she declined telling him that, with Bev and Stanley both out, she had her hands full even though the two replacements she had arranged for had arrived. Jesse thought Savannah's voice carried in it a vein of sadness, her usual vibrancy subdued to the point of nearly undetectable. Although he was sure Bev's accident, together with the awful incident in Arizona, had an impact on her, Jesse wasn't so clueless as to be unaware of the struggle Savannah must be going through regarding their relationship. They were attracted to one another. Maybe even to the point of falling in love. It was as if, during their falling, the world had tilted at an odd angle, arresting their fall and propping them back upright. He wondered if it were possible to love two women at the same time then shook off the thought. He needed to clear his mind. It wouldn't do to enter the boulder without his wits firmly about him.

James insisted on praying before Jesse entered the boulder. "Father, watch over my brother for good as he meets with Tsor this morning. I don't know all the reasons why this meeting between them has to be but I trust You and believe it has to do with helping Jesse find his way through the grief he's carried for so long. As your Son showed us, the way out lies through the thorns." James wrapped his arms around his twin, his embrace strong and full of warmth. "God bless you, Jesse," James whispered as his brother's body slipped through the fissure.

Savannah was guilty of clock-watching all morning. She had given Jesse a thin excuse for not meeting him and James but didn't know what else to do. It was past nine and Jesse should have entered the boulder by now. She wondered what Tsor had in store for him. She wondered, too, if Jesse thought of her as she was thinking of him.

The morning staff meeting had been routine. The replacements were professionals and hit the ground running. Even Danny was on a streak of good behavior. Ever since Bev's accident he had been the epitome of helpfulness, taking on whatever jobs needed tending to. He had even suggested the staff all go to the hospital that evening to visit Bev, saying it would cheer her up to see them. Savannah had checked with the hospital right after the morning meeting to get an update on Bev's status and see if a group visit would be okay. According to the nurse on duty, Bev was making remarkably good progress given what she had gone through and would likely enjoy their coming.

It was nearly instinctive now for Jesse to drop down on his hands and knees as soon as his head cleared the fissure. He didn't have to grope about much, either, on his way to the gray orb in the center of the portals room, the curious disc that served as a light-switch. As his eyes began adjusting to the light he thought he saw the outline of a man sitting in the chair. When he could see clearly, he saw it was the same man he had met at the lake Sunday morning when the two had watched the sunrise together.

"Hello, Jesse." Michael rose, and in two strides covered the distance between them, his hand outstretched in greeting, a light smile on his handsome ebony face. "I bet you're surprised to see me here."

It took a moment for Jesse to recover. "Yeah, I am, although I guess I shouldn't be. After all," he waved a hand in the air, "this isn't exactly your normal boulder, is it?"

The big man's face grew solemn. "No, Jesse. It sure isn't. In fact," he went on, "you could say I'm as much a guest here as you are." Noting the puzzled look on Jesse's face he hastened to explain. "I'm here mostly as an observer. I wish I could say more but there is a limit as to what I can share. For now, suffice it to say my presence is of benefit to you." He motioned to the chair. "Please, have a seat. I've been sitting so long I welcome the opportunity to stand."

Jesse slowly lowered himself into the chair. "Are you Tsor?"

The handsome dark face of the big man grew even darker. Michael shook his head. "No. We were close friends once but no longer."

"Then why are you here? Did Tsor invite you?"

"I can only say that the one I serve has a competing interest in you, Jesse, and under a previous agreement Tsor is compelled to honor, Tsor has no choice but to accept my presence here—although, as I said, there is a limit to what I can say or do. For the moment," Michael said apologetically, "this is really all I can say." He pointed to the black leather book with the *Portals* inscription. "I must not keep you."

Jesse reached for the now familiar book. It was an odd twist having a physical audience and he wondered why Tsor kept himself hidden. But maybe Tsor would make his own appearance later.

In a way, Michael's being here was comforting. Jesse had taken to the big man when they sat side by side at the picnic table, drinking coffee and watching the effect of the sun's rising on the lake. Like children, the two had delighted in the "dance of the diamonds" on the water's surface as the sun showed off its transforming power. Perhaps, Jesse wondered, given James' theory of Tsor and Michael mentioning something about being part of a competing organization, the big man was Tsor's counterweight in the supernatural realm. Either that or Jesse was further along the path to total lunacy than he realized.

Opening the portals book, Jesse began writing his first question, the one he had wanted to ask during his last visit but couldn't.

What about James, Savannah, and the rest of the world. Will they remember everything that has happened to them over the past three years, too, if I change the past?

He flipped the page.

No. Only you will remember.

That was a relief. Altering the course of history was crazy enough without having the added burden of the world's population feeling as though it were Ground Hog Day. He supposed everyone would make the same choices all over again, allowing history, so to speak, to repeat itself. Except for Jesse and Ellen. The two of them would walk out of the past together, creating a new history different from the one that had dropped on them like a bomb.

Why are you helping me?

He had often wondered what motivated Tsor. Why he had singled Jesse out.

It's simple. You were wronged. I have the power to help you set things right again. I help people. It's something I enjoy doing. Sort of a hobby of mine.

Given Tsor's reply, Jesse almost decided against asking the third question he'd prepared in advance of his coming. One prompted by the passage in Ezekiel James had shown Jesse.

Is your name known here on earth as Satan?

He held his breath. What if Tsor really was the devil? Would he explode with anger at being found out, incinerating Jesse in his own chair, filling the room with the stench of Jesse's burned flesh? Maybe that was why Michael was here, to keep a lid on things if supernatural tempers began to flare.

Jesse slowly turned the page.

Really, Jesse. I'm surprised at you. I didn't think your brother's wild speculations would find much traction inside that rational head of yours. But I suppose James needs to cling to his beliefs, as archaic and misguided as they may be.

I'm actually quite familiar with your religious legends, including Christianity and its claims. Rather narrow-minded as religions go with its insistence on being the only truth and all. But even if it were taken at face value I would think the devil to have gotten a raw deal. After all, he strikes me as one of the only free-thinkers in the tale. Of course, as the story goes on to reveal, God can't handle the competition and blows his stack, insisting that everyone choose sides and then punishing all those lining up with the opposition. Even if I were him, the devil I mean, I'd say I have behaved better towards you than God ever has. In fact, today's lesson should underscore my point.

Today is show-and-tell day. Today, when you look through the portal, you'll see a vivid reminder of just how unfair your brother's supposedly loving God really is.

I believe you know the way. Follow it, and you'll know the truth as well. It will help you get your life back.

This was different. There didn't seem to be anything for Jesse to do, no exercise to hone his developing skill at manipulating the past so as to focus the portal on a particular moment in time. Oh well, he might as well continue to trust Tsor. He'd shown good faith up to this point, even refusing to take offense at Jesse's insinuating he might be the universe's ultimate bad guy.

Jesse glanced up at Michael who had stood behind him, looking over his shoulder at what transpired between Jesse and Tsor through the portals book, never uttering so much as a single word. If Tsor had been a dangerous enemy wouldn't Michael have sprung into action, or at least sounded an alarm? Even now, the man's face was a portrait of impassivity showing no trace of concern. Jesse took it as a positive sign. Careful to follow the yellow bricks as they wound their way in circles to the wall, Jesse made his way to the portal.

As the lights dimmed and the portal opened, he saw in the expanse before him a wintry scene. Snow was falling; swirling through the air and whipping around, flung about by capricious blasts of an icy north wind. Jesse could feel the cold and hear the roar of wind rushing along its unseen course. A road lay before him, vaguely familiar but one he couldn't immediately place. Then he heard the sound of an approaching vehicle although he couldn't yet see it. Then the outline of a silver Buick came into view.

Jesse froze, the blood in his veins turning as cold as the icy scene in front of him. As much as he wanted to tear his eyes away from the vision he knew he couldn't. He knew he was looking at his parents' Buick the night of their fatal accident. He could see the bridge in the distance drawing nearer as the car motored on, his father oblivious to the ice underneath the tires. A deer suddenly appeared on the shoulder of the road, the doe's ghostly face illuminated by the Buick's headlights.

The Buick swerved. Nothing severe. No violent jerk of the wheel. His father was too good a driver for that. It was the sort of maneuver you could do a thousand times without incident—as long as you weren't doing it on black ice. With sick fascination, Jesse watched his father fight a losing battle to bring the skidding Buick back under control. The silver car his father loved to drive refused correction, slamming head-on into a bridge abutment, the air bags never deploying.

Jesse thought he would retch as he watched the car settle into an eerie stillness, his parents, having been tossed about inside the vehicle like rag dolls, now as bent and lifeless as the twisted metal surrounding them.

A man was approaching the car, his deliberate steps firm in the face of the howling weather swirling around him. A tall, black man.

Jesse whirled, screaming at Michael, hurling all the pent-up fury that had boiled inside of him for so long at the big man. "You were there! You were there and you didn't do a thing! You just stood there and let my parents die!"

31

JESSE WAS GLAD to find that only a few hours had passed in the world outside when he emerged from the boulder to a waiting James and Kai.

"How'd it go?" James wanted to know.

Jesse shrugged. "It was different."

"How so?"

Jesse didn't answer and James decided not to press. His brother's drawn face and silence were proof enough something significant had taken place in the portals room. James just couldn't tell if it was good or bad.

The two brothers spent the afternoon tending the smoker where Jesse's barbecue was cooking for Bev's dinner, a coin toss having awarded his chicken the honor. Every so often they would jump into the pool to cool off. James' suggestion of a rematch of swimming pool golf fell on deaf ears. Clearly, Jesse was in another world, the struggle taking place inside of him leaking to the surface through a combination of distracted looks and muttered responses to any questions James asked.

Jesse and James arrived at the hospital shortly before five. They didn't want the barbecue waylaid by Bev having already eaten whatever fare MercyQuest's kitchen might dream up. They needn't have worried. Although the supper tray had been delivered earlier, Bev had taken one look, pushing the food away after the nurse left the room. The main dish was puréed meat of the mystery variety and she wasn't about to ingest anything she couldn't identify.

Jesse knocked lightly on Bev's door.

"As long as you're not wanting to stab me, shove pills in my mouth, check my pulse or feed me something puréed past the point of recognition, you can come in!" Bev's bruised face beamed as she recognized her visitors as none other than the Whitestone twins. "Well, imagine that!" she exclaimed. "Almost makes my getting busted up worth it just to see you two together!" She caught sight of the package Jesse was carrying at the same time her nose smelled the aroma of barbecue. "And you even brought me some real food!"

"I don't know how much you're going to like it," James quipped. "We flipped a coin and Jesse won so it's his recipe I'm sorry to say."

Bev started to chuckle but the pain from her ribs changed the sound from a joyful one to a gasp. "You boys are going to have to promise to lay off the joking," she scolded. "I've got a couple of cracked ribs that don't appreciate being jostled—although I have to admit it feels good to have something to laugh about for a change."

James swapped out the hospital food for the barbecued chicken and for the next several minutes, between mouthfuls, the brothers got an update from their old friend on her condition and what had happened to her. For her part, Bev was careful to stay consistent with her previous explanation that she must have lost her balance and fallen down the porch steps.

Their conversation was interrupted by the appearance of several newcomers and, in short order, the room was filled with Bev's co-workers from the complex, Danny leading the parade of bodies, peeking around a large bouquet of flowers he was carrying and a surprised Savannah bringing up the rear.

"Oh, I'm sorry," she apologized, catching sight of Jesse and James, "we didn't know you had company, Bev." She began moving towards the door. "We'll just wait outside."

"Nonsense!" Bev exclaimed. "The more the merrier! It does me good to see everybody. That is," she grinned, "just as long as I don't have to share my bounty." She held up a piece of barbecue. "I'm usually good-natured. But when it comes to Whitestone barbecue, I draw the line."

Savannah introduced Bev to the two replacements who had come to help out at the complex and for the next several minutes the room buzzed with conversation, Bev continuing to enjoy mouthfuls of barbecue in between answering questions about how she felt and asking questions of her own about how things were going at the complex. Sean, one of the replacements, assured her he was doing his best but was certain folks visiting the welcome center would be much happier when she returned adding that practically everyone who came in asked for her by name.

Danny watched Bev with keen interest looking for any telltale signs she was uncomfortable with his presence. Although he didn't detect the slightest hint of fear in her, she did look at him with what he thought a curious sadness, as if Danny were the one who had fallen instead of her.

207

The fact Bev had so many visitors hadn't escaped those on duty at the nurses' station down the hall, many of whom had known Bev for years either from church, some community event, or having visited Stillman's Lake. They were willing to bend the rules but after thirty minutes sent Emily down to shoo them out. Nobody messed with Emily. As Jesse filed out behind the others, Bev motioned for him to stay and, after thanking everyone for their thoughtfulness and promising to get better soon, patted the bed beside her.

"Thanks for sticking around, Jesse. And thanks for the delicious barbecue." She licked her lips. "Darn near tempts me to proclaim you the winner over James after all these years." She touched a finger to the tip of her nose, adopting a thoughtful pose. "No," she said solemnly, "that would never do. Might dry up the golden barbecue goose if I did that." She grinned, "I've got a good thing going with you two and I'd hate to derail it!"

Bev's smile faded and Jesse saw she was tiring. He hated to see her lying in a hospital bed. It was so out of character. She never ceased to amaze him with her vitality for life.

"Would you mind reading me a verse out of my Bible before you go, Jesse?" She motioned towards the stand beside her bed.

Jesse wasn't in the mood to read anything God had written but didn't have the heart to disappoint her.

As if she sensed his reluctance, Bev gave him an reassuring pat on the hand. "Only one verse, my dear. But a very important one. A verse that keeps coming into my head almost every time I pray for you."

Jesse was touched. The fact that Bev was praying for him hit a tender spot in his otherwise hardened heart.

"John chapter fourteen, verse twenty-seven."

Jesse opened the Bible, turning to the gospel of John. Over the years, Bev had thoroughly marked the pages with all sorts of notes and underlining. Finding the verse she wanted him to read he saw where she had written his name beside it in the margin. He could feel a lump forming in his throat and found it growing as he read aloud words Jesus had spoken two thousand years ago.

"Peace I leave with you; My peace I give to you; not as the world gives, do I give to you. Let not your heart be troubled, nor let it be fearful."

Jesse's heart was both troubled and fearful. Peace seemed a distant memory. Jesus had spoken these words to His own disciples knowing that, in only a matter of hours, He would be betrayed and handed over to the Romans for crucifixion. It seemed a strange time for the Lord to be talking about peace and an untroubled heart. Jesse bent over and kissed Bev on the cheek, returning the Bible to its place on the bed stand. "Thanks, Bev. You're a dear friend." He gave her hand a squeeze then left the room.

Although she was tired, Bev had some important work to do. Work she believed with all her heart was part of God's plan for good to those she loved so much and knew God loved even more. It was nearly ten by the time she finished writing and laid her head down on the pillow allowing her weary eyes to close.

32

THE THREE DAYS until he could revisit the portals room passed with unrivaled monotony and it had taken all the self-control Jesse could muster to keep a lid on his emotions. He spent part of the time connecting with his mildly bewildered staff, reviewing project status and doing his best to deflect their questions as to when he would be resuming his customary role in the daily operations of Orange Risings. They were a highly capable crew and could operate indefinitely without him but they missed his creativity and energy. Jesse's style was personal and caring. They seemed satisfied with his explanation that he hadn't seen his brother in two years and needed some catching up time. He wouldn't stay this detached for much longer, he promised.

James had tried again to pry out of him what had taken place in the portals room during Jesse's last visit but to no avail. His twin stubbornly held to his position that, at this stage, he needed to sort things out on his own. True, it cut him off from what counsel he might have gained from James but it also freed Jesse to focus on dealing with Tsor in his own way.

Jesse half suspected James was right about Tsor's identity. Thinking back on Tsor's response to his question about his being the devil, Jesse found it absent of any flat denial and chock full of innuendo. If Tsor was Satan, Jesse was playing a dangerous game. Yet withdrawal was out of the question. If he had to deal with the devil to save Ellen, he would. However, it begged the question as to what Tsor might want in return. Up until now, Jesse hadn't given it much thought.

There was also the matter of Michael. It had been over a week ago that Jesse had met the big man. If Tsor was the devil, who was Michael? It seemed a gigantic stretch to think of him as the mighty archangel of biblical renown. But then again, why not? The very existence of the portals room was already beyond fantastic. Why shouldn't the supernatural occupants be two angels, one fallen and one yet loyal to God?

But if Michael were an angel, why hadn't he done something to save Jesse's parents? Why show up only after they were already dead? Weren't angels supposed to help people? Maybe he would ask Tsor about Michael. If Tsor was a super-intelligent life form from somewhere else in the universe maybe Michael was, too. Maybe they represented two alien cultures in competition with one another. Kind of like Google and Microsoft on steroids. Jesse still preferred the alien theory over the supernatural. It made things easier.

He checked the time. He and James would be heading to the lake soon. Jesse knelt and wrapped his arms around Kai's neck. The Shepherd was keeping close, his canine intuition sensing his master's need for support.

Thoughts of Savannah drifted across Jesse's mind. Part of him wished she were going to meet them at the site. Although he'd always come back from the portals room okay, he felt as though anything could happen. If he never made it back out, it would be nice to have a fresh image of Savannah among his last.

Danny snapped the phone shut. The conversation had been brief. That the voice on the other end belonged to a dangerous man he hadn't the slightest doubt. It was heavy, menacing, as if its owner were a ticking bomb ready to go off at any moment. Lavelle had said Julio would be getting in touch with Danny and now he had. How Julio had gotten his cell phone number was another matter but, given the intelligence capabilities the organization had already demonstrated, Danny supposed he shouldn't be surprised. Julio would be coming over to the apartment Tuesday after Danny got out of work. Over the phone, Julio had asked for Savannah's address. It was the key to her house Danny had made that Julio wanted to pick up.

Savannah climbed into her car, driving out of the hospital's parking lot marveling how Bev had managed to convince her doctors that unless she took an unexpected turn for the worse she could go, not to a skilled nursing facility but to her own home, on Wednesday. Bev assured the doctors she had plenty of friends to help her with meals and any cleaning or yard work needing to be done. That was true enough, Savannah mused. People would likely be queued up a hundred yards deep waiting for a chance to help the much-loved woman. And the health insurance company would be delighted to reduce their expenses by having a physical therapist visit Bev three times a week at her house. Much cheaper than a stay in a skilled nursing facility.

What baffled Savannah, as she headed to the coffee shop where she planned to meet James, was Bev's insistence on accepting Danny's offer over Savannah's to pick her up and drive her home from the hospital. Ever since her fall Bev seemed to gravitate to the young man with an interest that went beyond Savannah's comprehension. When she asked Bev about it, the older woman had simply smiled and said it was nice to have the attention of such a handsome young man and that she saw something in Danny needing only a bit of watering to make it bloom.

It was lunchtime at the coffee shop when Savannah arrived, the place packed, James waving from a corner table. "Are you hungry?" he asked as she took a seat. "My treat." He smiled and, as if reading her thoughts, handed her a menu saying, "I tell you what. Clear your mind of everything except food for the next five minutes. Then we'll order and I'll give you an update on Jesse."

After a short wait, a harried-looking young man with blue-streaked hair arrived to take their order after first reciting the day's special. Savannah ordered a tuna melt while James went for the special, an open-faced hot turkey sandwich with fries. He grinned when Savannah raised an eyebrow as he asked the server to be sure to put gravy on the fries, too.

"I take it you aren't concerned with your cholesterol count?" she chided.

"Nope. I've got it scientifically calculated so by the time I reach my eighty-first birthday my arteries will fully close and I'll be heading home at last. No stents, open-heart surgeries or any of that stuff for me. I'm more the massive heart attack type."

Savannah wrinkled her nose. "Now I know why you aren't married. Having someone who watches over you and cares about your health would put a definite damper on your lifestyle."

James asked about Bev and Savannah brought him up to date, including the welcome news about Bev going home on Wednesday. Savannah said she was planning on taking over some meals Bev could just pop in the microwave and reheat. James offered to fire up the smoker again and cook up some barbecue pork so Bev could get the taste of Jesse's inferior fare out of her mouth and give her taste buds a break.

Their conversation was briefly interrupted by the reappearance of the server. He set their orders down, depositing the check in the middle of the table. James slid it over to his side. "Like I said, my treat."

James allowed himself a few mouthfuls of hot turkey sandwich before switching subjects to the one he knew was uppermost on Savannah's mind. "Jesse and I went out to the site this morning at the usual time. He disappeared into the rock at nine, same as always. Kai and I stuck around until it was time to come here." He dipped a forkful of fries into a puddle of gravy.

"I know it's been hard on you," James acknowledged, seeing the troubled look in Savannah's green eyes. "You and Jesse meet each other and there's some obvious chemistry between the two of you. Then Tsor comes along with his portals room, tempting Jesse with the possibility of changing the most painful day in his past. Suddenly, the world gets turned upside down and the two of you get your emotions tossed around until you don't know what to think or do." His eyes softened and Savannah knew he sympathized with what she was going through.

"I don't blame you for distancing yourself," he confessed. "I think I'd do the same if I were in your shoes." The fries moved from the plate to his mouth. "But don't write Jesse off just yet. He's a guy so it takes him a while to figure things out. But he is also God's child. None of what is happening is taking God by surprise. Everything that can be done to show Jesse what is true, God is doing. I'm sure of it. What Jesse does with the truth is up to him."

Jesse sat in the chair inside the rock-walled room, the black leather book lying unopened in his lap. He had expected to find Michael waiting for him, his massive form sitting comfortably in Jesse's chair before rising and inviting Jesse to take his place. Jesse thought it strange that, as angry as he had been at Michael at the conclusion of the previous session, for some reason he missed him. Perhaps his outburst had convinced Michael he wasn't welcome. If that were the case, Jesse couldn't blame him for not showing up. Although he still had no answer as to who Michael was or why he hadn't intervened to save his parents he couldn't help liking him. There was something about Michael that conveyed a sense of peace in a language beyond words.

Jesse opened the portals book and began writing his first question. Although there were always more than three questions in his mind, each begging to be answered, he had settled on which ones were of the most immediate interest.

Who is Michael?

Turning the page, he read Tsor's terse reply.

As Michael himself told you during your last visit, he is a former friend.

The answer was frustrating. Jesse already knew that much. He had expected Tsor's reply to be more definitive and hated feeling as though he'd just wasted a question. Maybe his second try would shed light on both Michael's identity and the reason for his being at the scene of his parents' accident.

Why was Michael with my parents when they died?

I can tell from your facial expression you were dissatisfied with my previous answer about Michael's identity. Good for you! Dissatisfaction leads to clever thinking and aggressive action - two attributes I deeply admire. As a reward, let me expand on my earlier response.

Michael is a field agent for what I call the opposition, a collection of misfits unable to think for themselves who are into self-denial and believe there is only one reality in the universe. I, myself, was once one of them and under the same misconception. However, I found by looking within that reality is whatever you choose to create for yourself.

As for what Michael was doing at the scene of your parents' accident, you could see for yourself. Nothing. Although he had the power to change the outcome in any number of ways, he did nothing. Not that he didn't want to, mind you, but because he was obeying orders from the top. From the one who leads the opposition. You see, Michael is under the delusion loyalty supersedes the wisdom of one's intellect. Left free to act on his own, I don't doubt Michael would have kept your parents safe. However, he wasn't free to act on his own.

That's where you have an advantage, my friend. Three days from now you will have the freedom to act on your own initiative, in direct opposition to the decisions made by the leader of the opposition the day your wife drowned. In fact, Jesse Whitestone, you will have a chance to be like god.

Jesse's brain was working hard sorting through the veiled meaning of the words Tsor had written. It was maddening how the guy seldom provided a straight answer. Before he closed the portals book, Jesse determined to read Tsor's entries several more times, committing them to memory so he could reflect on them later. He had a growing sense there was a lot more to Tsor's offer to change the past than what appeared on the surface.

Before entering the boulder, Jesse had been undecided about his third question. No more. His jaw set, Jesse began writing.

What do you want in return for giving me the power to change the past?

He felt his body tense.

Your worship.

Jesse was stunned. Of all the responses he might have expected, this was the least anticipated. It hadn't even been on Jesse's radar.

His brother's suspicions regarding Tsor's identity rose anew in his mind, gaining added traction by the revelation of the payment that would come due by accepting Tsor's help. If James was right, it amounted to nothing less than brokering a deal with the devil, something you might hear in the lyrics of a heavy metal tune or in some dark movie with a twisted plot but nothing you expected to encounter in real life.

Until now.

What if he played along, rescued Ellen, then double-crossed Tsor? He tried to assess the risk and concluded it would be pure suicide. If the Bible was right and if Tsor were truly Satan, he was arguably the most powerful creature ever created. Jesse wouldn't stand a chance. But what if, after saving Ellen, he asked God to protect him? Jesse didn't know the answer to that one. It might work. But then again, it might not. After all, his motives would be less than pure and based, not on wanting God for who He is but for what He could do for him. There was a difference. He'd hesitated long enough. Whoever Tsor was, Jesse didn't want him changing his mind. At least not until he had sifted through his options and come up with a plan. He turned the page to get his instructions for the day's portal exercise, apprehensive as to what it might be after his last outing.

As I'm sure you realize, Jesse, this is your last visit before you are faced with the opportunity to change the past and save your wife. Consider this a deadly serious dry run. As

215

you'll need to know exactly where Ellen is in order to rescue her from drowning, I'm giving you a chance to pinpoint her location. This is absolutely critical as, on your next visit when you walk through the portal and enter the past, it will be at the exact moment when your wife falls out of the raft and into the lake. Every second will count.

Like you've done four times before, follow the yellow brick road. And remember, what you are about to see is courtesy of the opposition. Apart from them, Ellen would still be alive. Remember this.

Jesse felt an adrenalin kick tear through his body. If he understood Tsor right, he was about to witness his wife's death. The thought sickened him. Yet, what other choice did he have? If he was going to save Ellen he would have to man up and get through it, keeping his mind focused on getting an accurate read on her location. He wound his way to the wall following the yellow bricks in the floor, his stomach a churning mass, while the lights dimmed and the portal sprang to life.

A three-year-younger version of himself stood cooking burgers over a portable grill at the familiar site on Stillman's Lake. Jesse could smell the aroma given off by the cooking meat and hear the fat sizzling on hot coals. Kai sat nearby, attentive, knowing one of the burgers cooking on the grill was for him. Jesse saw himself looking up, turning his head so as to catch a glimpse of Ellen out on the lake in the yellow raft. Mesmerized, he followed his own gaze.

There she was, looking intoxicatingly beautiful as she bobbed up and down in time with the lazy swells of the lake. How had he described their love? Pretzel love. Yes, that was it. The intertwining of things physical, mental, and spiritual.

Jesse watched as he saw himself turning back to the grill to flip the burgers. Time was running out. He would be waving Ellen in soon, letting her know it was time to eat. Time to celebrate the sixth year of their being joined together as husband and wife. Time to send her the loving wave of his hand that would signal her death.

Right on cue, the Jesse in the portal waved to the brown-haired woman in the raft who smiled and waved back, rubbing her stomach in a show of faith in his culinary abilities. The body he loved to hold reached for the oars, knocking one into the water. Jesse heard her laugh as she reached for it then, losing her balance, fall into the lake.

The image in the portal went instantly subsurface, as if he were in a glass submarine capable of a three hundred and sixty degree view of the watery underside of the lake.

Jesse saw the telltale smile on Ellen's face as she swam, her strong arms and legs propelling her effortlessly through the water. He had been right. She had planned to lure him into the water, bent on ambushing him when he dove in to rescue her. He could see it in her mischievous brown eyes.

Ellen was making her way through a field of rocks and boulders. He knew the location, having snorkeled there on several occasions with James when he and his brother were teenagers. A few small bubbles leaked from Ellen's lips. She was swimming towards a gap between two rocks, one larger than the other. But as her body passed through, Jesse saw her left leg dip at the end of a kick, low enough to drop through a notch, becoming wedged between the two rocks.

The sudden jerk to a stop sent more air bubbles escaping from her mouth. Ellen reached behind her, tracing her leg back to the point where her ankle lay in the vice-grip of granite rock. More bubbles escaped and Jesse watched the concern in her face giving way to panic and then raw, unbridled fear. She was writhing, kicking as hard as she could, breaking bones in her own ankle in a final effort to wrench herself free.

Horrified and sick to his stomach, Jesse wept as Ellen's battle began to subside. Her lips parted and the final exhale was followed by an intake of lake water spelling her death. With tortured slowness, the lovely body went as limp as the plants in the lakebed, waving thin tendrils in time with the gentle currents of their underwater world.

33

DANNY HAD BEEN on edge most of the day but done his best to keep it hidden and go about his work as usual. Everything about the day was typical for a Tuesday. What wasn't typical was handing over the key to Savannah's house to the possessor of the voice he heard over the phone but had never met, Julio Ramos. They hadn't set a specific time to connect, either. They had left it that Julio would be by after Danny got out of work. Danny just hoped the guy didn't keep him waiting.

He'd met with Lavelle again, too. Over two rounds of Bloody J's, the Polynesian beauty laid out a plan for dealing with Bev. The organization was keeping her under surveillance and had come to the conclusion it would be best for everyone if Danny finished what he'd started. The fall down the porch should have caused her death but she proved tougher than her age would suggest. Lavelle also said there was a field agent for the competition, a guy named Michael, who helped Bev during the long night she lay outside on the ground. If Michael hadn't interfered, Lavelle fumed, Bev would already be dead. Lavelle was now opting for a more traditional approach. Shooting the old woman would not only shut her up but do the world a favor by diminishing the elderly population by one. If everybody did their part like Danny was about to, they would help free up increasingly scarce resources old people were hogging.

Lavelle had instructed Julio to give Danny a gun when he picked up the key to Savannah's house. She had also asked if Danny knew how to handle a pistol. Not that it would matter. The hit would be at close range. Place the barrel of a gun directly against the skull and pull the trigger. There wasn't much that could go wrong. Nevertheless, Lavelle was pleased to learn of Danny's having been to the shooting range several times with his deputy friend, Ron, and was familiar with firearms. There would be no problems.

Danny rented a small house on the outskirts of town. It wasn't much to look at but it suited him. The only people he entertained were a handful of his buddies that showed up for the weekly poker game and the occasional female either foolish enough, or drunk enough, to fall for one of his lines. He grabbed the mail while unlocking the side door and stepped into the kitchen, tossing his keys on the counter as he shuffled through the varied envelopes and flyers wishing that just once he'd get something other than bills and advertisements addressed to 'current resident'. It was depressing. He didn't know who would write though. His mother had stopped writing a year after he'd left home, probably at the insistence of the scum she'd married. It would be just like his stepfather to enforce a total communication blackout. He tossed the junk mail in the trash, grabbed a beer out of the refrigerator, and headed into the living room to see what ESPN had to offer, coming face-to-face with a grinning Julio Ramos sprawled lengthwise on the sofa, a pistol on the coffee table within easy reach.

Julio being Hispanic was something Danny had expected given his name. His facial markings, however, were ominous. Teardrop tattoos could mean a lot of things since theme variations were common. But one look into Julio's eyes signaled to Danny that the original meaning—the wearer had killed someone—was the intended message. In fact, if it were a gang rule you had to have a teardrop for *every* person you had murdered, Danny guessed the guy's face would be plastered with them. The gang member wore death like a garment.

"I take it you're Julio." Danny let the words fall out of his mouth as nonchalantly as he could muster. After all, it was *his* house. How Ramos had gotten in he hadn't a clue but supposed it was easy enough if it was something you did for a living.

"And you're Lavelle's new pet." Julio spat the words, his welcoming grin morphed into a snarl. Danny felt his temperature rise but knew he would be no match for this killer in any kind of physical altercation he could imagine. Besides, they were supposedly on the same team. Lavelle had called Julio a "specialist". He could see why. The guy was probably a human machine good for only one thing: killing. While killing might be something Danny might have to do on rare occasions, he didn't see himself in a hit-man role. Lavelle had hinted of things at a higher level. Danny let the comment fall unanswered and instead reached into his pocket, setting the key to Savannah's house on the table next to the weapon.

"I'll trade you."

The grin reappeared on the tattooed face. Julio swung his muscular body upright, pocketing the key before walking out the door.

Jesse didn't even hear the big rig until it was almost on top of him. He and Kai were walking on their favorite dirt road, the one they had always traveled when they took the back way to Stillman's Lake, the one Luther and his buddies drove on hauling their drilling gear. Jesse needed to think and couldn't imagine a better place to do it than on this road with Kai, a road they had walked together so many times he could let his mind wander where it would without concern.

He had emerged from his time with Tsor in the boulder, some five hours after entering, to find James and Kai waiting for him; James at the picnic table and Kai at his usual post outside the fissure. Jesse hadn't needed to say anything for James to know that conversation was out of the question. If there was any advantage to being a twin, the evolution of a non-verbal language between the two was one.

Considering everything that had taken place inside the portals room, Jesse could only conclude James had been right all along. It wasn't some other-worldly intelligence from another galaxy making him an offer. It was the prince of darkness. The deceiver. The being who had, if you believed the Bible, corrupted the whole of creation by tempting the earth's first inhabitants to trade away their special relationship with God for a life of independence littered with fear and folly.

Tsor's astonishing revelation, that in exchange for giving Jesse the opportunity to change the past he expected Jesse to worship him in return, had led Jesse to take his long-neglected Bible off the shelf. Turning to the book of Isaiah, he recalled reading years ago in college a passage in chapter fourteen about Satan's fall from his once lofty position.

I'm being tempted by the devil to forsake any remaining remnants of faith and plot my own course instead of trusting God with my past, present, and future.

The thought hit him like a sledgehammer! It was the perfect temptation to use against him, too. After all, he hadn't been on speaking terms with God for over three years. And what *wouldn't* he give to have Ellen back? Hadn't he told James he was willing to do whatever it took, even if Tsor were the devil himself? Of course, at the time he'd said it he hadn't believed for a moment Tsor was the devil. Now he didn't believe otherwise.

He thought about what Tsor had said in an earlier session. "Even if I were him, the devil I mean, I'd say I have behaved better towards you than God ever has."

Wasn't it a valid point? Tsor had done nothing whatsoever to threaten him in any way. On the contrary, he had done only one thing: offer Jesse the

220

chance to get his wife back to right a wrong. And in exchange, all Tsor wanted was for Jesse to acknowledge his gift with a token of gratitude. From Jesse's vantage point it was hard to see a down side, especially after the indescribable anguish he'd witnessed Ellen suffering. The image of her writhing was impossible to shake. He hated the thought of it being the picture of her he would carry around in his head for the rest of his life. How could he go on living with the knowledge he could have saved her if he refused Tsor's offer?

Julio appreciated the cover of darkness. Normally, he preferred to work in the day. Correction. What he preferred was shooting his victims when there was enough daylight to illuminate both the target and confirm the results. Working with bombs made him uneasy, a sensation he rarely felt. But Lavelle had insisted. She wanted a backup plan in place in the event Danny failed her. From what Julio could see, Danny was a born loser, the kind of human target his gang would tell a new recruit to blow away just to see if the kid could shoot straight.

He didn't know who lived in the house connected to the porch he was crawling around underneath and he didn't care. The driveway was a mile long dirt road full of potholes, the house in the middle of nowhere. It was supposedly empty and he hadn't detected any signs of life other than a stray kitten wandering around.

Working with the cartels provided him with the connections he'd needed to acquire the IED he was carefully positioning—no sense in letting the Arabs have all the fun and call it simply a bomb. It was actually pretty sophisticated. A call to the device would set it off and... well, suffice it to say there would be no more porch or anything connected to it. If the back wall of the house was still standing he'd be surprised.

Julio had his cell phone programmed with the IED's phone number listed as ICE: In Case of Emergency. He liked the double irony.

34

THE DAY WAS a mix of clouds and sun. Danny was glad the only thing on his to-do list at the complex had been mowing. He'd been anxious all day. If killing Bev was something he had to do in order to move into the official ranks of the organization then so be it, he wasn't opposed to shedding blood. But he hated the waiting part. Whereas Bev's falling down her porch steps would likely have been called accidental had she died, a bullet through the head was another matter. And being the one to pick her up from the hospital would place him high on the list of potential suspects. He had said as much to Lavelle who had assured him the organization would provide him with a cover. She hadn't bothered to share any details.

After Danny got Bev into her house and made her comfortable he was to tape a note on the door saying she was resting and didn't want to be disturbed. The note would stop any visitors from barging in. Danny was to go to work the following morning as usual and at noon, make his way to the boulder where he had first met Lavelle. She would meet him there.

Just before Danny left for the day, Savannah reminded him she would be bringing some meals over to stick in Bev's refrigerator. A quiche for breakfast, a chef salad for lunch and lasagna for dinner. Danny suggested she come by as early in the evening as possible as he wouldn't be surprised if Bev found herself tired after her stay in the hospital. It was the way things generally went. You had to get out of the hospital and go home before you could get a good chunk of uninterrupted sleep. As he headed home to shower before going to MercyQuest, Danny rehearsed his options given there was no way of knowing when Savannah would be showing up. It was inconvenient but he'd handle it.

He was sweaty and grimy from the day's mowing. It felt good to take his time lathering up under the warm water streaming from the shower head. It helped him relax, taking the edge off the anxiety that had clung to him all day like a lead vest. Danny toweled off, taking his time shaving and styling his hair, pleased with the image looking back at him in the mirror. He'd spotted a cute nurse on Bev's floor. Might as well look his best. No sense in leaving any stone unturned.

Danny loaded the gun Julio had given him. He liked the way it felt in his hand. It was a perfect fit. He was pleased to find himself relaxing more as time passed and the actual moment of killing crept closer. Excitement was addicting. And the more dangerous the assignment, the more powerful the sensation. He almost envied Julio. The guy probably felt pumped all the time.

He set the weapon inside his toolbox figuring he would explain to Bev he had brought his tools just in case there was something loose on the porch that had caused her to trip and fall. If there was, he'd fix it for her.

Bev's popularity at the hospital made her departure a lengthy affair but Danny didn't mind. He was trying some new lines out on the nurse he had been hoping to see and they were getting results. Without hesitation, she had produced her phone number and was now in the process of scribbling her address on the back of a sheet torn from a prescription pad. It was too bad she was working a double. Danny couldn't think of anything better than spending the night with a pretty nurse after ridding the world of an ugly old woman. Out with the old, in with the new.

After Bev dispensed her last hug, Danny and his nurse friend helped her into a wheelchair then brought her down an elevator and out to the patient discharge area. The physical therapy Bev had had during her stay was enough to enable her to get around on crutches as long as she didn't have far to go. But they opted to wheel her the short distance to Danny's car, anyway. As he was shutting the door after getting Bev settled, Danny let his hand linger around the waist of the nurse. Flashing one of his trademark smiles, he thanked her for taking such good care of his dear old friend. He would call her to set up a date before the weekend. A moment later, he and Bev were heading out of the city.

"How's it feel to get out of prison?" Danny kidded.

"Oh, it's not that bad once you get used to the fact there really isn't any routine to get used to," Bev said good-naturedly. "They always tell me on their way out after poking, prodding or pricking, to get some rest. If they really meant it they'd leave me alone long enough to take them up on it!"

Bev looked at Danny, trying to read with her eyes what lay beneath the surface of the young man. She had no illusions about what the evening may hold. After all, that Danny had apparently tried to kill her was the only conclusion she could come to considering his actions on her porch. She assumed he supposed the trauma of her injuries had wiped her memory clean of what had precipitated her fall. As long as he was convinced she

223

didn't remember anything she might be safe. But she doubted it. Anyway, her plans called for a different course of action, one that might put her personal safety in jeopardy. Well, if it did, so be it. Her life wasn't her own anyway, it belonged to God and He could do with it as He knew best. She was running out of time to make the difference in Danny's life she longed to make. The opportunity was now. She could sense it.

The trip home was littered with the usual chatter covering everything from the weather expected over the next few days to how things were going at the complex. Bev seemed genuinely interested in learning how Danny felt about his job and especially if he could see himself staying on into the future. Bev said she hoped so and that the lawns had never looked nicer nor the equipment kept running in better condition. If he kept it up and was willing to learn new things and take on more responsibility she believed he would be the natural choice for taking Stanley's position as crew chief when he retired.

In light of what Lavelle's organization could offer him, the thought of working at the complex until he was as old as Bev and Stanley seemed ludicrous. Danny's world was about to take a dramatic upturn. Too bad Bev wouldn't be around to see it.

By the time they got inside and Danny had her resting comfortably in bed it was nearing seven. Bev had already taken her supper at the hospital. Not wanting to disappoint anyone, she had eaten every bite of the turkey dinner the kitchen had sent up especially for her. She had to admit it was better than their usual fare. Not much, but at least it was identifiable. Danny excused himself for a moment and went outside. When he returned, he was carrying a toolbox.

"What's that for?" Bev wanted to know.

Danny shrugged. "My toolbox. I thought I'd check the porch while I was here and see if there was anything that needed tightening up. I wouldn't want you tripping on a loose board and falling down the steps again!"

"But I didn't trip the first time."

Her words hung in the air, bringing everything in the room to a sudden standstill. Even Danny's heart seemed to stop beating.

"Excuse me?"

"I remember everything. I may be old but I'm not senile." She was looking directly at him, her watery blue eyes holding him captive. "I don't know why you pushed me down the steps, Danny, but I want you to know I forgive you." She offered him a frail smile.

Her words caught Danny off guard. Okay, so she knew he'd shoved her. Fine. All the more reason to finish what he'd started. As for forgiveness... if she had so much forgiveness in her maybe she could spare some more. She'd need it for what was coming next.

Danny's thoughts were interrupted by a knock at the door. A moment later they heard Savannah's voice calling out from the kitchen.

"It's just me, Savannah. I thought I'd let myself in so I could put some meals for tomorrow in the fridge for you, Bev. I'll be in to say goodnight in just a minute."

Danny flipped open the toolbox, waving the pistol in the direction of the kitchen. "One wrong word and the next thing you'll see is Savannah lying in a pool of blood," he hissed.

Bev nodded. "There's no need for that," she said, her voice soft but steady. "I won't say a word. Just don't hurt Savannah."

Danny returned the gun to the toolbox. A moment later, Savannah peeked her head through the doorway. She hurried to the bed, wrapping her arms around the gray-haired woman she had grown to love. "I'm so glad you're home, Bev! It must feel wonderful to be in your own bed for a change!"

Danny watched them closely, his piercing eyes straining to detect the slightest hint of betrayal. It struck him as odd how Bev remained so calm. It was almost as if she was expecting everything to unfold as it had.

"It's wonderful to see you, too, honey," Bev murmured. "And yes, it is nice to be in my own house and my own bed." She released the younger woman, holding her gaze lovingly in her own. "But you know," she added, "this house isn't my home. As I've often said, my real home is in heaven and I'm looking forward to going there one of these days."

"Well, just so you don't make it too soon," Savannah chided. "I don't think I could bear it here without you."

The conversation was making Danny nervous. He didn't want Bev sending some sort of coded religious signal hinting she was in danger. The sooner Savannah left, the better off they would all be. He'd kill them both if he had to but he would much prefer to let Savannah live. After all, if Lavelle had her way, Savannah would be working for him at some point.

As if reading his mind, Bev's next words were right on cue. "You'll have to excuse me, Savannah, for taking a rain check on visiting more with you this evening. As you can imagine, I'm pretty tired. I've got a few more things to discuss with Danny then he's going, too, so I can get some sleep."

Savannah's eyes fell on the toolbox. "What's your toolbox doing here?" She gave Danny a questioning look.

Before he could get a word out, Bev answered for him. "I've asked Danny to check the porch for loose boards. I wouldn't want to give an encore performance, you know!"

Danny was amazed at the old woman's poise. He had to hand it to her. She was dishing out an Academy Award-winning performance.

Satisfied, Savannah bent down and kissed her friend goodnight on the forehead.

Danny waited until he heard the crunch of car tires before opening the toolbox and pulling out the gun, chambering a round as he approached the bed. Bev's eyes tracked his every move. She was alert but showed no sign of fear. "There are other ways, Danny," she said softly. "Other ways to deal with the pain and disappointment in a person's life."

"I don't know what you're talking about."

"I think you do."

For a moment, the thought of an alternative to what he was about to do sounded wonderful and Danny found himself hesitating. Then the image of his stepfather, Alvin, pummeling him with his fists after an all-night binge stirred up the molten rage inside. No! He had made his choice a long time ago when he had walked out the door of his mother's house for the last time. It was too late to change now.

Danny placed the pistol's barrel against wisps of gray hair surrounding Bev's temple and pulled the trigger. He stood motionless, staring at Bev's lifeless body. He put the gun back in the toolbox and walked away, his exhilaration giving way to numbness. If the act of killing was supposed to produce a climactic high, something had gone very wrong.

On his way out of the house, he taped a note to the door asking visitors to respect Bev's need for sleep.

35

THE KILLING left Danny's body flooded with too much adrenalin to make sleep a possibility. Besides, it wasn't yet nine when he arrived back at his house. If it weren't for Lavelle's demand Danny return to work in the morning he would have tried to connect with the nurse from the hospital when she came off duty.

As usual, he had snatched the mail out of the box near the side door earlier in the day when he had come home to shower before heading out to MercyQuest. Too excited at the time to pay it any attention, he had tossed the mail on the kitchen counter. Now, having nothing better to do, he shuffled through the meager pile. Expecting to find nothing but the usual assortment of bills and junk mail, Danny was surprised to see a hand-addressed letter. He was even more surprised to find the return address to be none other than Bev's.

He tore open the envelope. It contained a letter written to him in Bev's flowing script. Danny couldn't imagine why she would have written to him, let alone what she might have to say. Then he remembered Bev telling him she could recall every detail of the misadventure with the porch steps. Maybe it had something to do with that. dHe grabbed a beer out of the refrigerator before wandering into the living room to sprawl out on the sofa. He read slowly, taking large swallows of beer early on that grew less frequent as he progressed.

Dear Danny,

I have no idea when you will be reading this but I want you to know I forgive you. As to what I forgive you for, let me say that it includes every unkind act you have already done or may yet do to me. Every one.

Before you think that my doing so is the foolishness of a senile old woman, let me assure you my motive is grounded in God's love for us both. You see, Danny, despite the experiences you had when you were young, God loves you. He did then and He does now - no matter what you have done. If you don't believe me, you can read it for yourself in the Gospel of John I've enclosed. I do hope you'll read it.

As for how I know what you went through when you were young, I was waiting for the right time to tell you that we're sort of related; I am the sister of your stepfather, Alvin's, mother. We met for the first time at Alvin and Becky's wedding when you were just a boy.

You might be tempted to think God cruel for your having a stepfather like Alvin when what you really wanted was a father you could love and who would love you, too. But I've come to realize the truth about God's ways being so much more wonderful than our own! If God is real, then the most important decision we make in all of life has to do with what we believe about Him. That's why God sent His Son, Jesus, into the world. To explain God to us. Of this I'm certain: God found ways of making Alvin's coming into your life work for your eventual good. I believe my loving you is a small part of those ways.

As long as you draw breath, Danny, it is never too late to do the right thing and follow after God. Jesus will show you the way. Trust Him in everything!

In the unfailing love of God,

Bev

36

WITH JENNY CURLED up at her feet, Savannah sat out on her porch reading the letter that had come in the day's mail. It was just like Bev to hand write a letter in a day when emails and computer-generated correspondence was the norm. Clearly, Bev wanted to communicate what she had to say with as much personal warmth as possible and had sent her words in a form where they could be read as often as Savannah cared to read them.

Dear Savannah,

I had no idea how wonderful it was going to be to have you, not only as my boss but even more, as a dear friend. I am so grateful to God for this blessing of you in my life I could burst! Yet the blessings of God are so varied, and so often well-disguised, we sometimes mistake them for the very opposite of what they are. If I'm not mistaken, your meeting Jesse falls into this category.

Honey, it may seem to you like a cruel twist of fate the two of you met, were attracted to each other, and then found the road of romance as full of potholes as my driveway! Oh, don't be so surprised that I know more than I've let on! (And nobody has been gossiping, either.) If you live as long as I have, you become adept at reading between the lines. I can tell you've been troubled lately and suppose it may have something to do with your relationship with Jesse and his having to work through some final strands of the past having to do with his wife, Ellen. No surprise there. When God ties up the loose ends it can get messy along the way! But don't fret, God does all things perfectly. Wait on the Lord, Savannah. Jesus can be thoroughly trusted in every affair of life.

In the unfailing love of God,

Bev

Well, if knowing God resulted in becoming anything like Bev, so full of life and love for everyone around her, Savannah would have to give God more thought than she had. Everything about the woman attracted her. She nudged Jenny with her foot. "How about I let you out in the yard for a bit while I go inside and clean up the dishes?" Savannah stretched, yawning. "You might not get another chance! I think we could both use turning in early for a change." She opened the screen door and Jenny ambled off into the rapidly darkening twilight.

Savannah felt encouraged by Bev's letter. Distancing herself from Jesse had been hard but, in her opinion, necessary given the circumstances. She hoped Bev was right and the future would show the two of them had met for good reason. She went into the kitchen and began washing the few dishes she'd set in the sink, trying to pick out Jenny in the back yard through the window but it was too dark. As she strained to catch sight of the Golden, Savannah caught the reflection of a man standing behind her.

With a gasp and stabs of fear, she spun around and was confronted by a young man with teardrop tattoos at the corner of his eyes. Eyes that were drilling her with an icy stare.

37

TODAY WAS, AS far as James was concerned, his brother's 'ground zero' and James had spent the entire night in prayer, asking God to give Jesse the wisdom he would need for his final confrontation with Tsor. He hadn't a hint of what his twin's decision might be but, from the haggard look on Jesse's face, James wasn't the only one who had spent a sleepless night. Only Kai appeared calm. Although Jesse was the focus of the dog's attention, the Shepherd's dark face showed no sign of anxiety, only watchfulness.

The two brothers embraced, Jesse whispering his thanks into his twin's ear, his strong arms pressing James fast to his own chest. They had gone over all the possibilities they could think of last night over glasses of Jesse's best wine. If Jesse chose to go through the portal and rescue Ellen, he alone would remember all they had been through together. He assumed James would find himself wherever he had actually been on that fateful day three years ago, never imagining he was about to repeat the last three years of his life all over again. There were a lot of unanswered questions as to the impact of Jesse returning to the past and the ripple effect doing so might have on not only his own future but the lives of others—the famous butterfly effect half a world away. All were questions Jesse had no answers to. On the other hand if, for some reason, Jesse were to reject Tsor's offer, then… well, who knew what would happen?

"God is with you," James reminded him.

Jesse released his brother, smiling. "You know, James? With the great good fortune of having you for my brother, I almost believe you."

At Jesse's insistence, James reluctantly agreed to stay behind. Jesse had made it clear the night before that this was something he had to do alone. James would take Bev over some of his pork barbecue, enough for at least two or three meals. Visiting Bev would help pass the time.

Jesse pulled into the usual spot, two sites before his destination, and parked. He and Kai walked the rest of the way in silence, Jesse absorbed in his thoughts and Kai instinctively reflecting his master's quietness. They reached the monolith housing the portals room a few minutes before nine.

With a farewell to Kai and a dip of his head, Jesse went through the fissure and disappeared.

On hands and knees, Jesse groped his way to the gray disc in the center of the room. As he traveled over the inlaid bricks in the floor he noted how much of their individual detail his mind had stored. There was the one his left hand would touch after three shuffles that seemed slightly higher than the others. Later, his right hand would find one whose corner was chipped. In fact, although every brick looked the same to his eyes once the lights were on except for their color, his hands provided him more intimate knowledge, conveying the subtle distinctions making each unique. The reality of each brick expanded when additional senses were brought to bear. It made him wonder if they might even smell different from one another and he was sorry he hadn't thought of it sooner. There was no time today for such casual experiments. His hand found the orb and pressed, sending a flood of welcome light through the room.

Rising to his feet Jesse saw the familiar chair, the twin to the one in his library, in its usual spot and beside it the small round stand holding the black leather portals book, his means of communicating with Tsor. Jesse had half hoped Michael might be here. He wasn't. Jesse was alone. It would be only he and Tsor.

Jesse walked over and picked up the portals book. It was odd Tsor chose to reveal himself to Jesse through a book. Why didn't he show himself or at least speak audibly? Why a book? He sat, opening the book, turning pages until he came to a blank one. He was down to his last three questions. He took the pen out of the drawer and began to write.

Who is the mightiest being in the universe?

Admittedly, it seemed like a silly question to be asking given his reason for being here. But there was a definite purpose to it.

Me.

Tsor's answer didn't surprise him. In fact, it was along the lines of what Jesse expected. He decided to continue the line of questioning that had come into his head during his long, sleepless night.

What is your real name?

Tsor is my name. At least one of them, anyway. There are others. Perhaps the one by which I am most widely known is Heylel.

Jesse froze. James may have been right all along. Heylel was a Hebrew word found only in a single verse of Scripture in the fourteenth chapter of the book of Isaiah. In most modern versions of the Bible the word was translated "morning star" or "star of the morning". In the older King James version the word was rendered "Lucifer". On a hunch, Jesse had spent part of the previous night researching the various words in the Bible used to describe the devil.

He was down to his final question. If he pressed on, what might the consequences be? Would Tsor take back his offer? Was Jesse willing to ask knowing it might so anger Tsor that Ellen would be lost to him forever? He had to know for sure if it was Satan he was dealing with.

What would you say to those who claim that Jesus, the living Christ, is the Lord of lords and King of kings and all power belongs to Him?

Jesse turned the page, surprised to find it blank. Maybe Tsor was going to ignore the question.

Within the space of a single heartbeat, the stillness of the room was shattered by a hideous roar. A stench filled his nostrils. It were as if a thousand wild beasts were being burned alive, their screams hammering at him, the odor of their charred flesh nauseating. He found himself thrown to his feet, the chair literally ejecting him as it went hurtling across the room, smashing into pieces as it struck the portals wall before bursting into flames.

And then he saw it. A cross on the underside of the chair. A cross painted in Iced Mauve with the inscription, *This is the true God.* As if to underscore the chaos swirling around him, a single word thundered throughout the portals room: CHOOSE!!

The image flashing across the portals wall was all too familiar. A yellow raft bobbing innocently on the gentle swells of Stillman's Lake. A yellow raft with Ellen inside. She was waving at him, rubbing her stomach in anticipation of the meal they were about to enjoy once she rowed in to shore. Again, the wayward paddle fell into the lake followed by Ellen's laughter. She stretched herself to her full length, fingers straining to close the gap. In another moment, she would tumble into the water, never to reappear unless Jesse stepped through time and rescued her.

Jesse would later say that it was amazing how much time God could pack into a single moment. For in that moment the grace and love of God struck Jesse anew. *This is the true God.*

Yes, the cross and what it represented was true, not Tsor's façade. Bev was right, God's peace was different from what the world had to give or anything Tsor might tempt him with. Jesse turned away. He wasn't going to watch Ellen's death again. Neither was he going to usurp God's place and attempt to change the past. He still didn't know why Ellen had to die. But if God could bear the death of his Son for Jesse's sake, Jesse would trust Him for the strength he needed to bear Ellen's.

He heard a splash and knew Ellen had fallen out of the raft into the lake. Then there was silence, only the lapping sound of water as it met the shoreline. An agony of silence. Jesse closed his eyes, remembering Ellen's fighting in vain for the breath of air that would never come. At long last, he surrendered her into the care of the God who had made her and given her to him for a time.

Tears flowed freely down Jesse's cheeks, splattering on the red and yellow bricks of the cavern floor. Tears of sorrow and pain. But also, after so long a time, tears of farewell to the wife of his youth. He turned and began walking toward the fissure. He was done with Tsor.

A woman's scream erupted behind him. A woman screaming his name, calling out to him in a fear-filled voice.

Savannah!

He spun around. The image on the portals wall was no longer that of Stillman's Lake but of Savannah's house. She was looking directly at him, eyes wide with terror, a knife at her throat held by a young, brown-skinned man with tattoos. The man glared at him out of eyes devoid of feeling. The knife-wielder was shouting. "Your life or hers! Thirty minutes. You have thirty minutes!"

Jesse flew down Highway 8, straining the Element's handling to the limit. It took nearly twenty minutes to get from the welcome center to Savannah's house. It had taken him another five or so just to get out of the boulder and reach the gates of the complex. Although he might be done with Tsor, Tsor obviously wasn't done with him. Clearly, taking Savannah hostage had been planned well in advance.

Jesse had no plan of his own other than to give the man with the knife whatever he wanted in exchange for Savannah's life. If it cost him his own, fine. He'd accept that. At least he would be saving one of the women he loved.

That he was in love with Savannah was plain to him. And although Tsor hadn't intended it, his scheme had backfired. Not only had Jesse's faith been revived but he had found the courage and strength to trust God's wisdom and let Ellen go, confident that a time would come when, beyond the world in which he now existed, he would see her again. His duty now was to Savannah and he would forfeit his life for her if he had to.

Jesse briefly entertained the thought of calling the police. But he was pretty sure if he did, the SWAT team would arrive only to find a dead corpse. There was no way he would let that happen.

He pulled into Savannah's driveway and jumped out, commanding Kai to stay put. He wasn't going to take any chances that the sight of the dog would prompt the tattooed man to react. He had tried to make Kai stay back at the site the moment he had emerged from the boulder but the Shepherd had ignored him. Sensing danger, he had run alongside his master, leaping into the Element the moment Jesse opened the door.

From the outside, Savannah's house was a picture of tranquility save for Jenny's frantic barking coming from somewhere out back. Jesse sprinted to the door. Without hesitating, he pressed the latch and went in.

He was standing in an entranceway, a dining area off to his left. The only sound he heard was the rhythmic beat of a pendulum clock on a wall in the living room straight ahead. The image he'd seen in the portals wall had showed Savannah captive in her kitchen which would take him across the living room and then through a doorway to his left. He moved slowly yet deliberately. "Okay, I'm here," he called out. "Don't hurt her."

"Come and get her, hero." The voice was taunting, spitting out the order as if he were slapping Jesse's face.

Jesse could hear his own breathing. His heart banged in his chest. Yet his mind was clear and focused on only one thing: saving Savannah. *No matter what it takes, Lord, protect her. My life for hers is fine by me.* He turned the corner and faced the tattooed man he'd seen in the portal.

Julio had traded the knife for a gun. Knives were okay for effect and had served to generate the electrifying fear in Savannah's voice he sought in luring Jesse to his death. But a gun was his weapon of choice. It gave him a sense of power and security like nothing else. And at the moment, he had his gun pressed against Savannah's head.

"You said if I came you'd let her go," Jesse challenged. "I'm here." He could see the fear in Savannah's eyes. Jesse didn't know how long she'd been held captive but he could see that her terror was mixed with fatigue.

"So I did. And I'm a man of my word." Julio swung the pistol, aiming directly at Jesse's chest. "I'll let her go. Then I'll kill you. And then," he said mockingly, I'll kill her, too."

The moment Julio shoved Savannah away, Jesse lunged. Surviving the impact of being shot long enough to get a grip on Julio, and in so doing giving Savannah time to escape, was all he wanted.

The first shot ripped through his shoulder, the bullet tearing through everything in its way before exiting his body. Despite efforts to keep his balance, Jesse stumbled and fell to the floor. Three more shots followed.

Jesse couldn't help thinking that, if this was what it felt like to be dead, it wasn't so bad. His shoulder hurt, and that seemed strange to him if he were dead, but maybe it took a while for the sensation of pain to fade away. He thought he heard someone calling his name, too. A woman's voice. A voice he recognized.

It took a while before his head cleared enough to realize he wasn't dead but still in Savannah's kitchen lying on the floor next to another man. The man with the teardrop tattoos. The man with the gun who had just shot him. Jesse struggled to make sense out of it.

He could hear the scream of sirens drawing steadily closer. Moments later, a small army of deputy sheriffs burst in, weapons drawn, the officer in charge bawling orders. An EMT came into the room, stooped, and began tending to him, cutting away his shirt and stemming the flow of blood pouring from the bullet hole in his shoulder. Savannah was holding his hand, wiping tears from her face, a look of relief taking the place of the fear he'd seen in her eyes. "Thank you, Jesse," she murmured, pressing his head against her bosom. "Thank you for coming for me. Thank God, you're alive."

"What happened?" Jesse whispered. He looked over at Julio. He counted three bullet wounds in his back. It was then he noticed the window over the kitchen sink with its shattered glass.

"Here he is."

Jesse had heard the voice before. It was mister flashlight, the same deputy he'd run into out at the complex the night of his first encounter with Tsor. There was a young guy with him in handcuffs.

"Danny! What are you doing here?" Savannah turned to the deputy. "Why is he in handcuffs?" She pointed to Julio's body. "This is the man who took me hostage, Danny didn't have anything to do with it!"

"Look, Ms. Garret, my name is Ron. Remember me? We met out at Stillman's Lake the night Mr. Whitestone," he pointed at Jesse, "was out wandering around looking for his lost dog." He rolled his eyes as if to underscore he still wasn't buying Jesse's story. "Danny is a friend of mine. But he's also told me he's the one that shot and killed the guy lying on the floor over there." He motioned towards the lifeless body. "And until we get things sorted out, we're taking Danny into custody."

Against Jesse's objections, the police insisted he be taken by ambulance to the hospital where he could be more thoroughly examined and his wound properly dressed. A deputy would accompany him. When he was released he would be brought to the sheriff's department to give a statement. Savannah, too.

As the others were herded out the door, Ron stayed behind, bending over Julio's body, pulling a cell phone from the dead man's pocket. He flipped it open, scanning through the list of contacts. The entries might as well have been coded. In a way they were. Nothing but a list of aliases. Gang member names. Well, if they were lucky enough to figure out where the guy was from maybe the cops on that end could benefit from the intel.

A thought came to his mind and he checked the entries again. Yeah, there it was. ICE: In Case of Emergency. Ron punched the Send button. Might as well have a little fun and let the guy's homies know they could pick up their buddy's body.

James stood on Bev's porch reading the note taped to the door and wondering what he should do with all the barbecue he'd brought. He tried the knob. If the door was unlocked he'd put the food in the refrigerator. Maybe poke his head in just to check on Bev, too. The knob refused to turn. He guessed he'd just have to come back. Maybe Jesse would be around to come with him. He hoped so. He had been praying for Jesse nonstop since they'd parted. He wished he knew what was happening.

James was on the top step when the bomb under the porch went off, detonated by Ron's capricious call to the emergency contact number he'd found on Julio's phone.

38

SUNDAY FOUND JESSE rising well before sunup and, together with Kai, heading to Stillman's Lake to catch the sunrise. Only this time, they would have company. Pulling into the driveway, Jesse smiled broadly as the Element's headlights captured Savannah and Jenny waiting for them. This was going to be a good day.

Nearly two months had passed since Bev's funeral, a bittersweet event, a time of both tears and laughter. Bev had touched the lives of so many people the church was filled to overflowing with those who either wanted or needed to pay their respects and say their last goodbyes to the spirit of the woman that had meant so much to them. Her absence generated an ache that could only be borne with the help of tears. Yet, as one after the other of them went to the podium to share personal stories of how God had used Bev to touch their lives, there was also, mixed in with the sorrow, laughter and tears of joy that their beloved friend was now home with the Savior she loved and had served so well.

A day or so after Bev's funeral, Jesse had finally gotten around to catching up on the mountain of mail that had accumulated. In working through the pile he had come across a letter from Bev.

Dear Jesse,

It goes without saying I think of you and James more like sons than mere friends. The two of you have blessed my life with your friendship. Especially you, Jesse, with your constant care for me over the years. You'll have to forgive me in that I have often prayed for a good snow during the winter months just so I could fix you breakfast when you came by to plow me out!

I realize how great a blow Ellen's death was to you, my dear friend. I saw how it knocked you off plumb as far as your faith in God is concerned. It reminded me of Peter and so, like Peter's Lord, I have prayed for you over the years that your faith wouldn't fail and that once it had revived – which I have no doubt it will! – you will be used by God to strengthen the faith of others.

It is a hard thing to lose someone you love, Jesse. But I think God has been faithful to fill the void in the heart inside of you that He has enlarged

240

through this trial. In my opinion, one of the forms His faithfulness has taken is Savannah. Take your time and enjoy loving her…

In the unfailing love of God,

Bev

Now, as Jenny scrambled into the back of the Element to greet Kai and a beaming Savannah buckled her seatbelt before leaning over to give him a hug, Jesse reflected on the advice Bev had given him. *Yes, I will definitely take my time and enjoy loving Savannah!*

For the first time since Ellen's death, Jesse drove to the site on the eastern shore of the lake without parking two sites away. Both he and Savannah knew that Jesse was coming one final time to bring closure to his experience with Tsor and how it tied in with the past, present, and future.

As Jesse and Savannah walked to the picnic table, they made out, in the fading gloom of the pre-dawn morning, two forms sitting side-by-side at the table, waiting for them. As they approached, a smiling Michael rose in greeting, embracing first Savannah then Jesse, who then turned to Michael's companion. "Glad you could make it, little man. Long drive from South Carolina. You should have come up a day earlier and stayed with me instead of pulling an all-nighter." He laughed. "But then again, I suppose that would be out of character for you." He bent down and gave his twin a hug.

"Easy there, Junior, these ribs of mine haven't healed to the point where they can endure the primitive pawing you Giants fans seem to enjoy lavishing on one another!"

"Sorry, I forgot what sissies you Rammies are."

"Do you two ever let up?" Savannah laughed, bending down, giving James a kiss on the cheek. "It's wonderful to see you, James." She noticed something moving on his lap. "What's that?"

"That's my new kitten," James replied, stroking the furry creature purring contentedly on his lap. "I found him wandering around at Bev's after the blast. I didn't have the heart to leave him there. He didn't seem to have a home so I adopted him."

"What's his name?"

James grinned. "Well, given he's black and has pretty big paws, I decided to name him Mikey in honor of our mutual friend here, who saved my life."

The rising sun found the four of them looking out over the lake, marveling at the "dance of the diamonds" wrought by the sun's powerful rays and choreographed by God, Himself. For nearly an hour they sat quietly, each absorbed in their own thoughts but now and then with one or another of them opening the Bible Jesse had brought, softly reading a passage aloud as led by the Spirit.

After the sun had fully risen, Savannah and James set about arranging the breakfast Savannah had prepared while Michael and Jesse walked over to the boulder. At Michael's invitation, Jesse dropped low and stepped through the fissure. He was surprised to find that, instead of the familiar portals room, the inside of the cavern was as it had been when he had brought Savannah and James inside. The walls and ceiling could be clearly seen as the natural rock of the boulder and the floor, earthen. The only thing different about it Jesse could detect was the size. It was as large as the portals room had been.

"God made this cavern out of rock," Michael explained, noting the look of surprise on Jesse's face. "Tsor sought to change it from what God had made into something different."

"Tell me," Jesse ventured. "If I had chosen to go back in time to save Ellen by walking through the portal, would it have been possible?" He looked up expectantly into Michael's dark face.

"No." God's angel shook his head. "Tsor's temptation was based on a lie. Tsor is the father of lies and lying is his natural language. He could only show you images of the past. Even if Tsor had the power, it would not have been allowed. The love of God is perfect, Jesse, even if difficult at times to see and understand with mortal eyes."

Jesse was thoughtful. Yes, there was a lot he didn't understand. As the Bible said, for the present, we can only see as in a dim mirror. Trusting in the character of God, while not always easy, was possible because God had come into human history in the form of his Son. Where words wouldn't suffice, Jesus became the living answer.

"Is Ellen with God now?" Jesse could only manage to whisper the question.

"Yes." Michael looked at him with compassion. "No one comes to the Father but through the Son. So you can be sure that her being with God has everything to do with a genuine faith on her part in Jesus, who died on a cross to save her."

"And what about Julio?" Jesse had often thought of the gang member who seemed to have so thoroughly embraced evil and appeared far removed from anything good.

Michael shook his head. "That is not for you to know. But I can assure you of this: there is no event throughout the course of the young man's life unknown to the God who made Julio in His own image.

"There are mysteries beyond our comprehension as to the thoughts and doings of the Almighty, Jesse. Of this you can be sure; God is love. If it were possible to change an evil heart by the torments of hell into one loving the righteousness of God and longing to be reconciled with Him through Christ, then hell may play a part. When you are home with God at last you will learn if such a thing is possible. As I said, great are the mysteries surrounding God's ways. There was once a time when I did not believe any of your race would come to be with us in His kingdom and now the number is beyond counting!"

Michael motioned towards the fissure and, dipping his head, Jesse exited, doubting he would ever return. Once outside, he found Kai faithfully waiting for him, Michael nowhere in sight.

Jesse threw his arms around Kai's neck, burying his face in the dark fur of the animal's chest. "Thank you for always being here, big guy." Kai licked Jesse's face, covering his master with canine kisses.

"C'mon, Kai. Let's join the others and get some breakfast."

Epilogue

(Three years later)

Danny pleaded guilty to the charge of murder in the first degree for the death of Bev Foster, for which he received a life sentence and was sent to a correctional facility in upstate New York. Although the judge had given consideration to the fact that Danny's shooting of Julio Ramos had likely saved the lives of both Savannah and Jesse, the law required the harsh penalty for Bev's premeditated murder.

In Danny's opinion, the sentence was just and he held no bitterness towards the jury or judge. In fact, he was fond of telling others how he was more content and free inside prison than he had ever been on the outside. God had used Bev's letter to soften his heart. Then Jesus broke it open wide. Wide enough to come in when, staying up all night after reading Bev's letter, Danny had read the gospel of John she had enclosed and with tears and regret, begged God to forgive him for killing Bev, surrendering his life to Jesus Christ. With his betrayal, Lavelle had sought him out only to be foiled by a large black man whose power, according to Danny, was far superior to hers. In her anger, Lavelle had let slip Julio's abduction of Savannah. The rest was history.

Today, the Bible study Danny co-led with Stanley was hosting a barbecue and the two of them were busy with preparations. Stanley had received one of Bev's letters during his year-long stay in Arizona with his daughter, Sara, and granddaughter, Olivia, who were now much better and moving forward in life. Olivia had made first team in gymnastics and trained with the same determination others had seen in her father. In her letter, Bev explained her relationship to Danny and implored Stanley to consider joining with her in loving the young man for Christ's sake. Stanley had and the Bible study was one of the fruits of their blossoming relationship.

Ironically, Danny's stepfather, Alvin, was an inmate in the same facility. He was as mean as ever and spit in Danny's face when Danny invited him to their Bible study. For a moment, all the old feelings of anger and hatred rekindled and Danny had wanted to flatten his old nemesis. But then he remembered Bev and how Jesus had used the woman Danny had killed to teach him of God's love. If God wouldn't give up on Danny, Danny wouldn't give up on Alvin.

Jesse, Savannah, and James had come to the barbecue, too. They had to. After all, Jesse and James had a reputation to uphold as Danny bragged about their chicken and pork barbecue to everyone who would listen. Even the warden was looking forward to a plate.

After only forty-seven days of getting to know one another, Jesse and Savannah had married, convinced that a loving God had brought them together for just such a purpose. The ceremony was a simple one, taking place in the welcome center at Stillman's Lake. Jesse and Savannah each sold their houses and built a new home of their own. As far as anyone could tell, Kai and Jenny seemed delighted with the arrangement.

Today, the two brothers were each working their own smoker so they could produce barbecue according to their respective, well-guarded, recipes. Each carried in his pocket a letter from Bev, precious beyond the words she'd lovingly penned. That they were in blissful ignorance of the postscript Bev had appended to the other's was a good thing Savannah thought, as she watched the two hard at work. When the brothers had each shown her the letter Bev had written, Savannah had had to stifle her giggling when at the bottom of each she found in Bev's flowing hand, "P.S. I'm especially fond of your barbecue!"

Acknowledgements

It has been a great pleasure and blessing to me during the writing of this, my first novel, to have enjoyed the support and help of many friends and family members. Some have given me permission to name them here while others wish to remain anonymous. (They know who they are and, again, I thank you 'publicly' here!)

To the Efthimious, Marc and Sue, whose Corning home sheltered and surrounded me with their love and warm friendship in the writing of *Portals*. Your constant encouragement, Marc, was such a benefit along the way, fueling me with hope this day would come. Thank you for struggling with me to stay on course, as true to God's word as possible given the dim mirror into which we peer. Your friendship along the road to our celestial home is ever my delight!

To the Cornfields, Doug and Jackie. The friendship of your presence, Doug, so constant and tangible, helped me to keep my sanity during lonely times when I needed a friend I could see and touch. The times you and your family nourished my body with home cooked meals and my spirit with your kindness and attention will never be forgotten. Jackie, thank you for helping me to stay 'real' within the context of a work of fiction.

To my father, Dyrel, I thank you for your gracious generosity through long periods of travail.

To my beloved brothers, Mark and Blaine, not ones to read much fiction but who read *Portals* along the way, adding to the long list of means by which they carry the love of Christ to me. And to my sister, Vicki, who has always believed in my writing.

To those who believed and desired through faith and friendship to send *Portals* on its way, my heartfelt thanks. The fruit of your financial support is now something you can hold in your hands.

Joseph St. Angelo
Doug & Jackie Cornfield
Tina Howe
Derrick & Nicole Jeror

Blaine, Dyrel, Mark, and Vicki (Davis) Kimball
Steve Mathews
Jonathan & Melissa Maxim
Jeff & Rachel Perry
Alex Rawleigh

Lastly, to my wife, Sheila, my "Savannah" come to life. Who would ever have imagined such a marvelous grace and gift of God as you! May this novel be the first of many as we join our lives in pursuit and service of our Lord Jesus Christ, the greatest love of our hearts.

About the Author

Michael Kimball offers as his introductory novel a story filled with unforgettable characters, face-offs between good and evil, and unpredictable twists of plot.

Michael has lived in various parts of upstate New York, mostly in the region known as The Finger Lakes, with the Hudson Valley being his present home.

To stay connected with Michael visit MichaelKimball.me.

Printed in Great Britain
by Amazon

29497657R00146